SHED SO MANY TEARS

A Novel By

Roderick 'Rudy' Bankston

Copyright© 2011 by R.V. Bankston

ISBN13:978-1523394234

Printed in the United States of America

This is a work of fiction. Names, characters, places, and incidents either are the product of the author's imagination or are used fictitiously. Any resemblance to actual events or locales or persons living or dead, is entirely coincidental.

Dedication

To the Warrior Women who love me
My loving Mama
Mrs. Pamela J. Shead

My amazing comrade, Donna

My good friend, Pat

To my wonderful children
Shakeris Z. Bankston
Diamond U. Bankston
DeVondrick V. Bankston
And my Grandyoungin Dior "Assata" Bankston

For all of you I live, for all of you I wouldn't hesitate to die.

Preface and Acknowledgements

This project has been a long time comin'. I started writing it in G.B.C.I., a max prison in Northeast Wisconsin. The first draft followed me to the state's supermax in Boscobel where I revised it in the crucible of psychic brutality, sensory deprivation and auditory over-stimulation. During that time I met a wonderful woman by the name of Pat. She became my writing teacher and a crucial source of support and inspiration and later a very dear friend. Without her assistance (typing, editorial wisdom, etc.), without her altruism, I don't know how this story would have managed to reach publication. Pat, thank you in multiples. You've not only made vital contributions to my growth as a writer but also as a human being.

There's also the indefatigable Donna. I can't thank you enough for who you are and the precious role you're playing in numerous aspects of my life. Our friendship feels like destiny unfolding into freedom. i am We. Let's Get It.

And to Pamela Shead, that grand ol' sista who I have the biological fortune of calling my mama, and to my son, De'Von, and daughters, Diamond and Shakeris. It was the four of you who I had in mind as I wrote the first words to this book and pressed on towards the final draft. I feel as though I owe y'all so much. Please take this as a very humble deposit.

Shout-outs also go to Boo, Lynda, Nita, Sharilyn, Queen and the Whighams family, Karen Emily and the 4Struggle Mag comrades, Mr. Milwaukee Marcus 'Moxiano' Austin (what's up, bloodline), Ceven, Tee, Cal and London a.k.a Booman, Corky, Chaos Talibandx John Hardaway, Phillip 'Cloud' Green, Trone, Vision, Fat Mack, My Kemet Brother Askari a.k.a Sean 'Milk' Wilson, Rodney O, Silk, Marcel, Slick Pulla off Hamp, Story, Chico D a.k.a Berto, Icylyrics, Lil Joe a.k.a Johnnie Green, Slim, Gator, Poppa Love, Boobie, Big Tone (O'Quin), Rocco, Lil D, June, Vedo a.k.a Zahir, T-Rex, Big Tone (Hoover), K.C., G-Ball, S.T., Moses, Damali, C-Ride, Lonnie Davis aka Troub, Leonard 'L' Parker, Kyle Cornelius, Jevon, B-Real, Gage (R.I.P.), Byron L., Jimmy, Luck, L.A., Congo, Grand Pop (R.I.P.), Caliph El,

The Snipe Boys and Breaking Barriers, John Spicer, Water Bottle, Gigolo Jackson, Teigo The Boss, Lil James, 1 Pac, Marvin Beauchamp and Chris, (My homeboys and barbers), Misty, Denisha, Dave a.k.a Crocket, Brianna, Brit, the Twins, Trell, Le-Le, Victoria, China, Liz, and the rest of the family, Guerrilla Hec, Sammy Hustle, Blunt, Bimp, John Furgeson, Heru (SOULS NEED REST!), Dyzae and Krisis Kemet (R.I.P.), Larry Love (R.I.P.),YAE (R.I.P.), Milwaukee and the hoods throughout, all the brothers and sisters locked down around the country, around the world (Get Free or Die tryin'!), my Muslim and Christian comrades, whoever I've not mentioned by name but hold in my heart, and last but certainly first in importance The Almighty God who has made possible all that's good in my life.

In Struggle & Solidarity,

Rudy

Roderick V. Bankston
rbiamwe@aol.com
www.iamweclassics.com

"In our liberation pedagogy, we must teach young Black folks to understand that the struggle is a process that one moves from circumstances of difficulty and pain to an awareness, joy, fulfillment."   bell hooks

CHAPTER 1

Liz reached up from under the quilt and hit snooze on her old, faithful alarm clock. A doze-inducing silence descended on her bedroom, tempting her to return to the land of Nod. She turned the radio on her nightstand to V100 and heard the hyper voice of the host. He was introducing a song by a local hip hop artist. Liz listened as the beat came on. But once the gangsta lyrics hit her ears, she switched the dial to a jazz station.

The zero hour of another week had arrived, finding Liz's body quite resistant. She lay there under the covers as the voices in her head started up with the same ol' early morning spiel. The voices often talked their slick jive, kicking up all sorts of irrational—sometimes rational—racket inside Liz's noggin. Like right now. They grew noisier, more dogmatic by the moment. She listened and kept her position in bed. The voices cooked up a buffet of excuses for her to take the whole week off; juicy excuses that sizzled inside her psyche like ring bologna in a skillet full of hot grease.

Trick no good!

Liz hated pork products, so she blocked out the swinish yackety-yak and yanked back the blanket. "Come on, body," she uttered, dragging herself out of bed. "Rise and shine. It's time to get on the grind." She wrapped on her robe and headed for the bathroom.

She turned on the shower and adjusted the temperature. A new chapter in her life was less than a year away, and she'd be damned if the pages stopped turning now. Keepin' her eyes on the prize wasn't enough at this point. She understood that she had to keep reaching for it, clawing at it if need be.

Liz disrobed and stripped out of her tee shirt and panties. She faced the full length mirror on the door. Her nude image stared back. She cupped her breasts, perked them up, and let them dive back into place. *Not really saggy, just well-endowed. Still some bounce, too,* she mused, grateful that time and gravity hadn't betrayed her just yet. And thank God no lumps! She slid an

1

open palm down her tummy until she felt the lawn of her secret garden. Lately, she kept close watch on her stomach region. Growing a gut was something she wanted to seriously avoid. She felt her body going through the changes and this tended to make her feel self-conscious, at times. Being three years shy of forty, Liz had to be careful. *Need to start a workout routine,* she acknowledged.

Now the last part of the physical exam, she sighed, slowly turning to survey her badunkadunk. She couldn't refute it… her ass was determined to outgrow the rest of her figure. The reflection in the mirror affirmed this expanding fact, as did the lustful glances she got from the young men at night school. The older guys paid attention too, but they were usually more subtle or discreet with it. Whenever any of the overzealous fellas got beside themselves and stepped to Liz wrong, she checked them with the quickness, although right below the surface, some of the attention flattered her. What woman, with her degree of loneliness, wouldn't be a little buttered up? *My prerogative anyway,* she asserted to herself, stepping into the steamy shower.

The hot water fondled her neck, her back, her butt, and as she turned around, it slid down her cleavage, her breasts and nipples. She snapped out of it and added her soapy touch. "Focus, girl."

She stepped out of the shower, fully galvanized, and with a self-promise to start a workout regimen on the weekends.

She debated what to cook for breakfast as she shook her shower cap and hung it up. Malik's favorite would be on the menu this morning, since she planned to wake him up a little early. For the last several months, their schedules conflicted, making it difficult for them to really sit down together and talk. They used to get decent time in while Liz drove Malik to school, but then her work hours changed and he began catching a ride with his best friend, Andre.

She harbored a fear of alienation settling in between her and Malik. She'd witnessed it happen too many times before: parents too caught up in their own doings, with too little time to sit with their kids and discuss things. Once the communication collapsed, so did the bond. This left the child searching for advice, answers and guidance, in all the wrong places, and they were bound to find some fool eager to feed them flimflam that'll leave them stuck in a jam. The blind leading the blind. Ain't no way, Liz decided long ago. It won't go down with her child if she could help it.

"Malik," Liz called through his bedroom door as she battered pancake mix in a bowl. She knocked when he didn't answer. "Lik?"

"Yeah, Ma, what's up?" Irritation and fatigue laced his words.

"You know what's up," she shot back. "School time. Out that bed and get ready."

"I'll be up in a min…"

"Oh, no you won't," she cut him off, voice raising. "Right now."

She rested the ladle in the bowl and waited. She leaned closer and heard no movement on the other side of the door. No rustling. She knocked with aggression this time. "Lik, get out that bed," she commanded. "I done warned your butt about stayin' up all night talkin' on that phone with those little fast girls. That's on you, but you're getting out that bed right now." She headed back to the kitchen, quite sure that he'd heard her loud and clear.

Malik definitely heard her. Too loud and crystal clear. He begrudgingly snatched the pillow from over his head and flung it to the foot of the bed. *All that yellin' ain't even called for this early in the morning.* He rose up on an elbow and squinted his eyes open. It wasn't even light outside yet! He still had time to sleep. *Mom's trippin' fo' real,* he thought groggily, collapsing right back into a sleeping position.

"Malik, you up in there?" Liz asked, her question snatching him back before he could surrender to slumber again. "I don't hear any movement. It's Monday so you know the routine. Get in motion."

Malik had no wins. He sat up, yelling, "Yeah, I'm up," then mumbling, "hell, a nigga would swear it was Sunday with all the preaching."

"I heard your ass," she piped. "I'm not gone tell you 'bout using that N-word under my roof again."

He waited… more alert now. "Nigga, nigga, nigga," he muttered way under his breath, and pulled up out of bed. He slid on his house shoes and

3

loosened his doo-rag. Seeing his stereo already on, he forwarded his Makaveli disc to track nine, and tapped the volume button. No sound came out the speakers. He held down the button until the digital bar hit its limit. Nothing. The lit up screen showed it was on, but still no music. "Pac, ya hauntin' my system from thug mansion or something?" he asked, then figured out the problem and hit the pause button.

"WHAT'S WRONG WITH YOU BUMPIN' YOUR HEAD AGAINST THAT WALL" came blasting from the speakers. Malik damn near knocked his CD player over, trying to turn it down before... too late! Stomping feet approached rapidly.

"I'ma be the one bumpin' heads against something if your ass don't keep that mess down," his mother snapped. "Did you forget it's early in the morning, boy?"

"My fault," he frowned towards the door.

"You hurry up and stop meddlin' with that radio," she said, adding, "don't need that mess this early anyway." The stomps retreated.

Your mess or the music's. Malik turned it back up a few notches and headed to his closet.

The fresh aroma of breakfast cooking drifted into his room. *Smells like sausage and eggs.* Malik took it for granted that the grub was for him. He picked out his school gear for the day: a crispy pair of Akademik blue jeans with faded baby blue spots, the baby blue Akademik polo style shirt, and toppin' it all off with the white dookies (aka Air Force Ones) with the embedded baby blue checks. He loved gettin' fitted and fresh. As he dressed, his mind piggybacked on the 2Pac lyrics whispering from the speakers:

> Where my daddy at
>
> Mama, why we live so poor
>
> why ya cryin'
>
> heard you last night
>
> through my bedroom door

4

White Man's World was in Malik's top ten favorite rap classics. Malik might've never lived poor, but he could relate to the lyrics. They made him think about his own incarcerated father. As he looped his belt, his mind flashed back on the night the police snatched up his pops.

The decade-old memory remained vivid. Malik was six years old on the dreadful night when the crack-crashing booms terrorized him out of a sound sleep. First he laid there stunned, seized by confusion, and frozen from fright. The yells and loud commotion sounded outside his bedroom door. He leapt out of bed, heart slamming into his chest plate. "Get the fuck down!" someone demanded. Malik heard his mama scream. Sporting tighty-whiteys and socks, he broke toward the door. And stepped out into the hallway. A barrage of infrared beams sprung from both directions, dotting his bare chest and face. He froze up in his tracks.

"Hold! Hold!" a man called out. "Just a kid." He marched toward Malik.

Malik took one look at the husky white man and yelled. "Mama! Daddy!" then ducked around him and broke left. Two muscled arms scooped Malik clean off his feet. "It's okay. Calm down."

Malik went wild, yelling and desperately trying to pry himself loose. "Let me go, shithead!"

"That's my son!" Malik recognized his dad's voice but couldn't see him, so he kept fighting, cussing, finally drilling his teeth into his captor's forearm.

"Little bastard!" the cop roared out, prying Malik's mouth off his assaulted skin. Malik stared around at the intruders, their hardened looks, dark attire, and heavy artillery. "Please don't hurt my baby," he heard his mama pleading. She sounded afraid. Kevy, Malik's dad, sounded pissed. Malik scanned around and couldn't catch sight of either one. Another cop hoisted Malik up into his arms, saying, "It's alright, lil man."

Malik tried hard to wiggle loose. The cop tightened his grip and toughened his tone. "Calm down, son," he ordered.

"I'm not your son," Malik replied, unable to move his limbs. He couldn't muzzle Malik's mouth, though. His throat flared as he yelled for his parents. His screams poured throughout the house. The cop carried him to the living room and dropped him down on the sofa next to Liz. Malik crawled onto her lap, and she held him in her arms tighter than the cop had. Her forceful kiss subdued his panic.

"I wanna see a damn warrant," Liz demanded of the raid team.

"Me too," Malik also demanded.

"This shit don't make a bit of sense," Liz fussed. "Y'all bargin' in my damn house like this. I want all names and badge numbers."

"Shut your mouth, miss," a rude cop snarled, towering over them.

"You shut up," Malik blurted. "Can't talk to my ma—"

Liz pulled his face to her chest before he could finish checking the white officer. "Hush, baby," she urged as tears trickled from her eyes. Her hair was a total mess.

Kevy was escorted into the living room and seated on the couch. Two cops had huge weapons trained in his direction like he was still a threat with his hands cuffed behind his back. Malik would never forget this image of his father. Kevy's eyes glistened with utter contempt. The task force came deep. They roamed through the house, searching every nook and cranny. The front door dangled almost off the hinges. Then all the weaponry. Malik only saw those types of guns on TV.

While Liz fussed in Malik's ear at the cops, Malik fixed his gaze on Kevy. He wondered why the police invaded the house, why they had Kevy in handcuffs, why they read Kevy his rights. The whole scene perplexed Malik. He made eye contact with his dad, and the ice thawed in Kevy's eyes. His look became painful. Mortifying. He told Liz to call his lawyer. She read over the warrant and fussed on.

Anger soon toppled Malik's fear. It all registered in his mind: his dad was going to jail. He leapt from Liz's lap and dove onto Kevy's, locking his small arms around Kevy's neck.

"Daddy, don't let 'em take you!" He felt Kevy's beard against his ear. Malik held on tighter after a cop tried to grab him.

"Wait," Kevy sneered. "This is my son. I'll talk to him. You don't need to touch him." The grabby cop was ordered to "step back" by his superior. The other two officers lowered their guns.

Tears blurred Malik's vision. "Dad, stay with me and mama." He held on to Kevy's neck with all his might.

Kevy promised to "straighten all this out and return home real soon." Malik relaxed his iron grip, leaned back, and stared into his eyes. He searched for some assurance. Liz came over and said something to Malik that he wasn't trying to hear. He wanted to hear his dad.

"I want you to look after your mom 'til I get back," Kevy said. "Alright?" Malik slowly nodded. He didn't want to let Kevy down.

"I'll look after my mama 'til you get back," he vowed.

Kevy forced a smile. "That's my lil' souljah." The strain on his face gave Malik little comfort. Liz took Malik into her arms as the police stood Kevy on his feet.

"And you better practice on Mortal Kombat," he warned Malik, "'cause I gotta have my get-back. Last game you got lucky."

Malik forced a grin. "I'ma beat ya again soon as you get home." But his heart brimmed with a rising dread of his father returning no time soon.

"Time to go, Mr. Freeman," a cop said.

"Come on, Malik," Liz said in a quivery tone. She pulled him away as the police escorted Kevy out the door and out of their life.

And over a decade later, Kevy was yet to make it back home. Still no rematch on Mortal Kombat. After countless court dates, two trials—the first one ending in a mistrial—an all-white jury found Kevy guilty of first degree intentional homicide and attempted murder. The judge later sentenced him to life plus. Malik didn't care what the police, D.A., or the lying witnesses said. His daddy "ain't kill nobody." He never even asked Kevy or Liz if the allegations were true.

7

Once Kevy got shipped up north, Liz and Malik hit the highway on a regular. Malik looked forward to every trip and visit. He cherished every fifteen-minute phone call. He treasured each letter Kevy sent and kept every last one of them in the small chest at the foot of his bed. Soon another blow of bad news struck eight years into Kevy's bid: the State of Wisconsin began shipping inmates to private prisons in the south. Kevy ended up on the transfer list.

Malik received the news one rainy afternoon when he came home from school. At first, he took it in stride, under the impression that the transfer was to another joint in Wisconsin. It didn't sink in until Liz elaborated.

"Baby, it's in Oklahoma."

Malik posted up next to the refrigerator gulping down Kool-Aid straight from the pitcher. "What's in Oklahoma?" he asked.

"The prison he's-"

"What?" he snapped, the sweet fruit punch taste instantly turning sour. "They can't just ship someone out of state like that." It felt like Kevy was being snatched out of his life all over again.

"He's fightin' it but the D.O.C. is talkin' some mess about easing prison overcrowding," she said. "He's appealing the transfer. I'm also writing a state senator in protest."

"Appeal?" Malik bellowed in bitter disbelief. "Screw an appeal. We're still waitin' on the other dang appeal."

"Lower your voice," she told him. "I'm upset too, boy."

He shoved the pitcher back on the shelf and slammed the fridge door. "I swear I hate those people." He leaned against the counter, "Straight up bogus." His insides churned.

Liz put on a sympathetic face. "It's real bogus," she agreed. "It gets you pissed, and that's a normal emotion. But hate can't become your normal reaction. Whenever someone moves you to hate, they can push you to self-destruct. They can control you and manipulate you and distort your

8

perspective. That's too much power for anyone to wield in your life." She went on to tell him to keep the faith.

Malik went on to hate the system. He had no love for it until this day. And anyone who did its crooked bidding could get it too. As long as his pops languished in prison, *they all can get it. In the worst way! Makin'a killin' offa niggas' misery,* Malik grumbled inside, coming out of his early morning reverie.

"'Lik, you 'bout ready in there?" Liz asked. "Come on so you can eat breakfast. I whipped up my delicious blueberry pancakes."

"On my way." His gaze fell on the framed 8x10 photo of Kevy that sat on the dresser. Malik missed him. Wanted him free. Back home. More now than ever. He grabbed his wave brush, killed the music, and bounced to the bathroom. The appetizing aroma of breakfast permeated. Malik brushed his grille. Washed his mug, ears, neck. Then rubbed on the cocoa butter cream. He sized up his presentation in the door mirror, admired it, and bounced to the kitchen. He tore off into the fluffy pancakes before his butt could hit the chair good. He attacked the honeyed sausages and scrambled eggs in the process. He got his grown man grub on, careful not to spill anything on his gear.

"Slow ya butt down, boy," Liz smirked, stepping into the kitchen. She was dressed for work, in jeans and dark blue blouse.

"This off da skillet," he complimented her culinary skills. He bit into a sausage. "Need to do this more often. I prefer breakfast in bed next time though." He grinned with syrup-stained lips.

"I got your breakfast in bed," she assured him as she poured a glass of orange juice. "I'll drop you off at school today." She took a seat across from him. "I have time."

Malik grabbed the glass of juice. "Drizzle already scoopin' me." He took a swig. "Good lookin' though." He downed another swallow and got a glimpse of her frown over the tilted glass. "What?" he said. "This wasn't for me?" referring to the juice.

Liz evil-eyed him and got up to pour another glass. "Did Andre get back in school yet?" she asked, referring to Drizzle by his government name.

9

The name 'Andre' sounded too square to Malik. *Could at least call my nigga 'Dre.* He knew better than to voice this preference. "Not yet," he replied. "Family issues and his music consume most of his time."

"I feel it strange that Andre finds time to take you to school, pick you up from school, but can't find time to attend school," she said. "What's so important in between time?" She sat back down.

Here we go. Malik knew where this was going. "I guess he's doin' what he gotta to make it." He tipped the glass to his lips and swallowed... too hard this time. Clearing his throat, he added, "He's doing what he needs to do to survive."

Her stare sharpened. "An essential part of surviving is making the right decisions. For instance, earning an education." Her words lingered with authority. "A quality education is the foundation."

"Drizzle's talent will carry him," he said. "Keepin' it real, he rawer than a lot of these nig—" he caught himself, "I mean, a lot of these wack rappers all over the radio and TV. His foundation is solid. All he needs is the right plug."

Liz's face tightened as her glass hit the table. "That's not keepin' it real," she breathed on him. "That's keepin' it wrong. Talent without knowledge will get him exploited. What is he gone do when he starts dealing with college educated corporate crooks?" She waited a moment. Malik didn't have a comeback to that. "Better yet," she continued, "what happens if the music thing doesn't pan out? What's Dre's plan B?" Another moment. "You think about that and make sure he considers it also." She rose from the table.

At least you called him 'Dre. Malik forked up the last of the eggs and chased them down with juice. Liz was quick to slam truth on the wood. *Usually as she saw it,* he thought, although under his stubborn demeanor, he felt her. Malik couldn't do anything but respect the real. And he knew his mother was up on game and real life thangs. She experienced too much not to know the business.

Liz rinsed out her glass. Malik got up and rubbed his stuffed stomach, feeling well fed. "I can't convince no one to do something one way when

10

they're set on doin' it their way. All I can do is suggest." He handed her his empty plate and glass.

"And as his friend, it's for you to suggest the right things. Including those things that he might not want to hear but needs to know. Real friends challenge each other to protect each other."

Their conversation was disrupted by the faint vibrations that quickly deepened and shifted through the kitchen walls and floorboards. Someone's ride was pounding outside. Subbin' hard!

"Who in the hell--" Liz's words followed Malik out the kitchen.

He looked out the front door window and spotted Drizzle's money jungle green '85 Caprice Brougham at the curb. The 26 inch Davins elevated his ride so high off the ground to the point it resembled a hovercraft. Malik had to admit that his fam did that. And the European front clip and horizontal grille were only complementary accessories to a project already well put together. Drizzle sat behind the wheel, bobbin' his noggin to the beats.

"I know that ain't Andre out there with that loud ass music," Liz fussed.

Malik split towards his bedroom to grab his things. His mother fussed up a storm from the kitchen. Or dining room. Or living room. From one of the rooms. "You tell that boy to cut that mess down when he comes over here this early in the morning... shouldn't be..."

Malik gathered his schoolbooks, Pelle Varsity jacket and wave brush. Almost forgot the New Era Fitted cap. He backtracked and grabbed it off the speaker. *Good to go.*

"You hear me, Malik?" his mother was asking.

"Yeah, Ma. I got ya." He heard the gist of her rant.

"Don't get mixed up in what that boy has no business doin'." She dug in her purse.

Malik came with his hand out. "My pocket's hurtin'," he grinned. "Can I get a loan?"

11

"How about you get a job," she shot back. But still broke him off a crispy twenty dollar bill.

"Good lookin' out." He kissed her on the cheek and pocketed the loot.

"Be your own man," she said. "You hear me?"

"No doubt." He zipped his jacket and headed for the door. "Love ya."

"Love you too."

CHAPTER 2

"Dawg, you gotta turn down the sounds when you push through this early," Malik said as he settled into the front seat.

Drizzle killed the music. "Since when you don't want me comin' through beatin', nigga?"

"Since momz almost went into cardiac arrest after her walls started shakin'," he laughed.

"Damn, my fault." Drizzle looked worried. "I thought she hit it to work already." He stared toward the house. "She salty at me?"

"She won't hold it against you. Just keep it down when she's at the crib," he advised. "Or we're both bound to get stood on."

Drizzle dipped out into traffic. "No doubt."

Malik picked up the joystick and powered up the Sony Playstation. "Ya kinda early. What's the b.i."

Drizzle got geeked. "I wrapped my first demo last night, and I'm tellin' you, fam. I'm lyrically diggin' in niggas' chests," he jacked. "Six cuts of uncut product."

"Straight P?" Malik asked.

"Straight P, no mix," he confirmed. "And ya know I'm obligated to give you the young exclusive." He aimed the remote at the Pioneer DVD Flipout. "The beats are so-so but ya boy spit it ridic'. Check it." He subbed the sounds. The four 12 inch Kicker Solo Barics started breathing thru the back seats. All the mirrors vibrated along with Malik's whole being. They bobbed their heads and exchanged nods of approval. Drizzle rapped along with his recorded vocals, gripping the steering wheel with one hand, gesticulating with the other to add emphasis to what he was spittin':

"...Cut me in or cut it out, don't give me

the cold shoulda/ ya either roll wit' us

or you get rolled over/ livin' everyday

like it's my last day/ I only know how to

get dough inna fast way/ ..."

From the chorus he went into the verses. Drizzle twisted up his mouth like a man intent on convincing the world that he's the undisputed truth. Both boys swayed in perfect unison. Each track got them more geeked. By the time the last one ended, they were riding high on the waves of adrenaline rushes.

"Fam, you zoned out," Malik complimented. They pounded fists.

"We 'bout to bizzle, my nizzle," Drizzle said, "Now all I need is that right industry plug and it's curtains for cats' careers. Cut us in or cut it out." They drove up and parked in front of Rufus King High School. All eyes fell on Drizzle's Chevy. The routine admiration didn't give Malik much of a thrill this morning. He focused on the future. "When you comin' back to the classroom?" he asked, shutting down the video game. "You know our minds need to weigh a ton for what's to come. Feel me?"

"I do need to pick back up those books," he acknowledged thoughtfully. "Been so caught up on this paper chase, try'na--" the soft tap on the driver's window stopped him in mid-sentence. There stood a bevy of smiling girls. Drizzle relaxed, shifted into playa-mode, and lowered the window. "What's up, pretty young tenders?" he greeted with debonair flare.

One of the girls eased closer, her smile expanding. "What's up, 'Dre and Malik?" said Kila. She shared 4th hour lunch with Malik. He'd scoped her and her buddies out on a couple occasions, but never tried to holler. It wasn't no secret that Kila's crew were certified dime pieces and they all stayed fitted in the slickest fashions, year round. And Kila stood the baddest P.Y.T. of them all, hands down. Rumor had it that she only messed with ballin' cats, years older than Malik. "I wanted to invite y'all to my birthday party on Friday," Kila told them. "I'm throwing it down at Kemet Quarters."

Kemet Quarters? thought Malik. This was the hottest, most jumpin' club in the Miltown. A ghetto tycoon named Prophet Kemet owned it. Malik and Drizzle had wanted to make their presence felt ever since it first opened its doors last summer. But the 21-and-older policy got religiously enforced. The

14

closest Malik and his underage peers got was the parking lot. All of the grown ballers, hustlers, stunnas, fly chicks, and other patrons rode up in their fly whips, hopped out, and strutted and strolled up to the club, getting in with no problem. Drizzle would've been cool with getting in just on Fridays, during the Flow Session. On these nights, the owner booked known acts or allowed locals to perform. Drizzle even planned to hit the highway to Illinois for a fake I.D.

So Kila's invitation piqued their curiosity. Drizzle was on it. "I'd love to shoot through and party," he assured Kila, "but K.Q. card at the door every whop. So unless you can pull a rabbit outta hat, we're burnt up."

Kila didn't conceal her pride. "No need for tricks," she said. "My uncle P owns K.Q. He said I can have my party there, but it's going to be more like a teen night."

Malik was with that!

Drizzle's game face was on. "Can we get V.I.P. status?"

Kila leaned closer. "Baby, you can have it all if you put your mind to it."

Drizzle leaned closer too. "In that case, it's a wrap. Me and my nigga will have our face inna place."

Kila dug in her purse. "Here's my number." She handed it through the window. "Call me if you have any last minute questions… about the party or whatever else," she smiled flirtatiously, like she was inviting him to more than one kind of party. "My name is on there too."

Drizzle scanned over the info. "Killa, huh?" he smiled. "Drop dead gorgeous Killa?"

Corny, thought Malik as he suppressed a chuckle. Kila smiled from earring to earring. "It's Kila," she corrected him. "You emphasize the 'i' sound." The girls giggled. Malik wondered if he mispronounced her name on purpose.

"Malik, why you so quiet?" one of Kila's buddies asked.

15

He didn't know her name but recognized her face and dug what he saw. "I'm just coolin', layin' in the cut," he replied.

"Nana, ask the boy for his number," Kila fronted her off.

Nana? The name was familiar. Malik eyed her as she rolled her eyes at Kila. *Nana*? Where did he know that name from? He scanned his memory... then it hit him. "Nana Taylor?" he blurted out.

Drizzle shot him a quizzical look. The recognition brought a smirk to Nana's face. "'Bout time you stopped actin' all stuck up," she said, "like you ain't know me."

Malik sat up to get a better view. "Never that," he said, "I didn't recognize you, girl." And he spoke the truth. How could he have known that was her? Damn! did she grow up in the rightest of places. Was this really the same Nana who stayed next door to him years back? Who gave him his first girlfriend-boyfriend kiss? Who used to sneak in the basement and engage in humpfests with him? "You coulda spoke a long time ago," he told her. "We've crossed paths in school too many times. A 'what's up' woulda been nice."

"I spoke to your ass when I first saw you," she claimed. "You ignored me. Kept right on goin' so I was like--" the school bell sounded, cutting her off for a few seconds. "Shit, we're late." Her buddies took off. "I'll get up with you later, 'Lik. Can't be tardy again." She split.

They watched the girls hightail it up to the school. "She thick as all outdoors now," Malik admired Nana's jiggling gluteus maximus. *The firm-fitting Apple Bottoms shaped that ass to perfection.*

"Goodness gracious!" Drizzle piped, "You keepin' secrets from ya boy," he accused Malik. He stored Kila's number into his cell. "Make a nigga wanna return to school."

Malik slung one foot out the door, "I'll put you up on her later." They exchanged double pounds. "Luv."

"Luv, fam."

16

Malik jogged up to the school and ducked off inside. *Now I might have to hear this crank ass dude's mouth,* he thought, slamming his locker. He dashed to homeroom and slipped into the first empty desk he saw. He opened his geography book and pretended to read.

"Malik Freeman?" Mr. Ashcroft called out.

Malik turned a page in the text book. *Like this lame don't see me sitting back here.* He stalled for several seconds, then slowly raised his hand. "I'm here," he answered with inflated indifference. *Right back here, dick head.*

Mr. Ashcroft shot him an intolerant glance and scribbled a mark on the attendance sheet. Malik didn't enjoy him as a teacher, and he was sure the teacher didn't exactly cherish him as a student. Their mutual enmity took root one day in civics class during a discussion on American democracy and the 2000 presidential election. Malik had no plans on clashing political heads with Mr. Ashcroft. When the discussion had first begun, he really wasn't paying it any mind. He was more interested in the XXL magazine in front of him. He decided to let the other students debate over the debacle that was Al Gore and George Bush's 2000 race. Malik did catch bits and pieces of the class discussion and noticed how Mr. Ashcroft threw subtle jabs at Al Gore's camp.

As the debate intensified, it became clear to Malik that the class was basically divided along racial lines: mostly Blacks and Latinos for the Democrats, and whites for the Republicans. Malik glanced up from his magazine every once in a while when a student said the right, or wrong, thing. But he remained silent. That's until he looked up and peeped Mr. Ashcroft scoping him out. When the teacher's decrepit face hinted at a sly smirk, Malik pretty much predicted what came next.

"Mr. Freeman, what do you have to add to the discussion?" Mr. Ashcroft asked. "Who would've been your candidate, Bush or Gore?"

The question quieted the class. All eyes fell on Malik. He took his sweet time in replying, still flipping through the hip hop mag. "Why does it have to only be those two candidates? What's up with the Green Party?" Malik asked. "Why not add Ralph Nader to the equation?"

This only touched off the frustration of several students.

17

"Ralph Nader only stole votes from Gore," a pony-tailed girl complained. "If it wasn't for him, Gore would've won easily."

"Al Gore did win but got robbed by Jeb Bush and his political saboteurs in Florida," Shakeris added her two cents. Then the class erupted into discord. The teacher asserted authority, bringing order back to the debate. He wasn't done with Malik just yet, though. "So, Mr. Freeman. The Green Party would've received your support?" The teacher wanted to know.

Nor was Malik done with him. "I'm not exactly feelin' dude either," he shrugged, "but I would've probably considered Nader's vision if democracy was real in America."

"My gosh..." Mr. Ashcroft's face lit up with incredulity, "I mean, we do live in a democracy. The very best that the world has ever witnessed." He beamed with enough patriotic pride to blind the entire classroom.

Couldn't blind Malik. "Yea, it sound good in theory, but the practice is bogus, corrupt and straight up racist." He paused for effect, sensing some of the other students' discomfort at the mention of the R-word. "If anything, we live in a plutocracy," he continued, "Money runs this country. Those without it, go without."

"This isn't a discussion on race or racism, Mr. Freeman," Mr. Ashcroft stated. "Stay on the subject."

"We're on the subject," Malik said. "Politics or so-called democracy or the election process is built on race." He felt himself getting heated. He checked his emotions and continued, "It's romantic to think otherwise. Al Gore and Bush are two slightly different sides of the same counterfeit coin."

"And what coin is that?" The teacher's face scrunched up into curious contempt.

"The coin of white supremacy," he replied.

Mr. Ashcroft self-tanned. "Come on! Save the conspiracy theories."

"Naw," Malik smirked. "I've never seen a UFO." Laughter around the class. The teacher glared it into silence. "I have seen what anyone else can see who has a brain unpolluted by U.S. propaganda."

"Sounds like what you're claiming is propaganda at its finest," a fellow white student accused Malik. The tension was thick enough to smother someone.

"The media blinds you to think that," Malik told his classmate. "I know it's no real difference between Bush and Whore—I mean Gore."

"You don't believe that," Mr. Ashcroft tried to convince Malik. "There's a vast contrast. In their visions and ideological convictions." He stood in a challenging pose.

Malik sat up farther in his seat like he was steadying himself to push something heavy. "Right, right," he said. "Say we're compelled to believe that myth. That it's some difference. I share an apt metaphor that my pops once shared with me. Bush is like crack and Gore is powder cocaine." He waited for the murmurs, giggles, and chuckles to subside. "Most of us know that crack rock is more detrimental and addictive than plain powder cocaine. So if forced to choose the lesser of the two evils, most people would opt for the powder. Now I'm not saying the blow isn't toxic and potentially fatal too. Crack rock just destroys a people or community quicker and more is lost in less time. Bush is crack. Gore is powder. Blacks cast their bid with the latter, but still got ready rockin' George."

Laughter and chatter tailed his words and battled for recognition. Malik caught a couple of Caucasian Gore-ites and Bush backers shoot unfriendly looks. He aimed to boost their animosity by adding, "And white supremacy is like the coca leaves of both candidates."

"What about Bill Clinton?" a Latina peer, Dawn, asked. "They say he was like the first Black president."

This made Malik chuckle. "If he was, he was a straight up uncle Tom."

More laughter, more chatter, more hostile stares.

"What about Ralph Nader, Malik Freeman?" one of the white Democrats asked in utter disgust. Mr. Ashcroft inched toward her like he had her back.

"He's that green sticky-icky-icky," he retorted as the bell sounded.

19

Malik bounced from class that day feeling like the most hated and admired pupil in the school house. And since then, Mr. Ashcroft sweated him for any real or imagined infraction. The rumor about Malik being a racist flared up and fizzled out before he got the chance to really give a fuck about it. He refused to take an apologetic stance on his views. He didn't make the world the way it was; he just saw it for what it was and lived life accordingly. He also lived hip hop. Not the commercialized thug-murk-a-nigga-pimp-a-ho-mack-a-bitch hip hop. He understood certain aspects of it, but never lived that life. But it was all a part of the cultural spectrum: the grimy and the gutter, the rebellious and the reactionary and revolutionary, the simple and the soulful, the so fresh and the so clean. And what was conscious music? Malik didn't buy into the popular definition. If an artist spit about real life situations, Malik considered it conscious music. Scarface. Outkast. Dead Prez. Kanye. They all had valid claims on the conscious rap title. Cut out the embellishments about the 'hood life and spit about the raw truth, and it was all good, although it wasn't. Being conscious ran hand-in-hand with the music. Malik felt one fed the other. He loved reading about reality, observing reality, and listening to music that exposed reality. In his mind, culture was the best curriculum to learn from. Second came books and music, which basically consist of word-play. Reading dealt with understanding the meaning of words, and words were employed to describe reality. Quite often, reality in the ghetto, in the 'hood, in the world, was hard, hectic, at times downright horrible. So all hip hop music did was reflect all of this, including many of America's ills. The flaws in hip hop mirrored the flaws in the U.S. of A.

Malik believed that the rap critics like Bill O'Reilly didn't want to acknowledge this. Instead they preferred to smooth self-righteous gloss over the red, white and blue bullshit spoon-fed the public. Malik couldn't stand the taste of it. Their shouts of 'life' and 'liberty' and 'this great country of ours' sounded Greek. All smoke and mirrors. A smoke screen blew by the have-gots to camouflage the oppression of the have-nots, the voiceless of good ol' America.

Hip hop emerged and equipped the voiceless with a voicebox. It became their bullhorn to shout out their ignored reality; it allowed them to musically wrestle with their demons, vent their rage, express their resiliency, and make known that the so-called American Dream was all too often their

20

nightmare. It vexed Malik when the people who were born on, or already ascended, the Crystal Stairs attacked the folks stuck at the bottom.

This increased Malik's appreciation for the street poets. His favorite was Tupac. Kevy put him up on the slain rapper years ago, but Malik didn't really start listening to his music until recently. Really listening. Tupac voiced a lot of Malik's pain and frustration and articulated many of the conflicted sentiments beefing inside Blacks growing up on the block. Tupac wasn't some distant observer; he was a product of the ghetto, who grew up fatherless. His music painted a vivid picture of the good, the bad, and the ugly. Malik also gave Tupac, and hip hop, some credit for his interests in politics, history, and words. Malik devoured a gang of books and articles on 2pac, which led him into reading about the Black Panthers, J. Edgar Hoover's COINTELPRO, and other subjects related to the Black Struggle. When he mentioned this positive influence to certain critics of so-called 'gangsta rap', they usually looked at him sideways. "Is this the same Tupac whose music is infused with misogynistic lyrics, and busin' caps in some whore ass nigger's ass?" was their sarcastic comeback. Malik advised them to listen to the whole albums instead of snippets, then maybe they could start to better understand his generation. His advice usually fell on deaf ears.

Kevy was more open minded. He listened and often reached out to Malik and put him up on a lot of different things about life, the streets, the system, the world. Some of Kevy's letters read like essays, challenging Malik to think deeper on the simplest matters. Malik and his father also perused some of the same books and discussed them over the phone and through letters.

Malik never knew just how much all this would shape his perspective on things, nor could he ever predict how future events and personal situations would alter this perspective.

"Mr. Freeman, I want to see you." It was his nemesis, Mr. Ashcroft.

He would wait for the bell to ring. Crank. Malik waited for the students to file past his desk.

"What's up?" he asked Hitler's descendent.

The teacher adjusted his thick spectacles. "This is your last warning about your tardiness," he said. "You need to be punctual to all classes, including homeroom." His eyes dared Malik to say something slick.

"Yessuh," he replied in a slavish tone. "Now I betta run on befo' I end up late for first hour too." He turned and left.

CHAPTER 3

Liz walked on aching feet out of night school. Her entire body craved the comfort of bed, and she knew sleep planned to kidnap her the moment she got home. Answering Kevy's letter tonight seemed a distant possibility. "I know he's gon' call me trippin'," she sighed, easing behind the wheel of her black Ford Focus. She clicked on the news radio, then started the journey home.

The news topped off with the habitual themes: budget cuts, tax debates, and school voucher proposals. As a side note, two homicides were reported. Liz paid close attention for the victims' names and ages: One black male killed on the north side; one Latino male killed on the south side, both by gun violence—names and ages unreleased.

She drove past Sinai Samaritan Hospital. Seventeen years ago, she'd given birth to Malik there. And each time she passed the hospital she thought of better days. She worried about Kevy being shot or killed back around that time. Now the concern was shifting toward Malik.

Several more blocks down the road sat Highland housing projects and the beginning of the Milwaukee ghetto. The sudden contrast between the two areas appeared an optical illusion. The peace and order of downtown mocked the slums a stone's throw away. Gloom engulfed Liz whenever she entered this part of town at night. The rundown houses and dilapidated buildings cast a shadow of bleak brokenness. Some of the inhabitants' looks and stares spoke volumes about their despair. Marvin once told Liz it all reflected a 'breathing nihilism'; no meaning to life, no hope.

Even police cruisers looked more menacing on this side of town. Liz slowly halted at a red light on 27th and Lisbon Ave. and instinctively hit the door locks. A sleazily dressed woman standing on the corner rolled her eyes and tossed Liz a 'bitch-please-don't-nobody-want-shit-from-you' look. She walked up the street. Liz watched the offended lady flag down a white pickup truck.

23

The walking dead went to and fro, back and forth across the streets. Human shadows peeked out of gangways.

A group of kids hung out in the lot of an Amoco gas station. Liz recognized one of the young boys. Earlier that day, he'd boldly approached her car when she stopped at the gas station. He'd offered to pump her gas for any spare change. She gave him a few bucks and made him promise to be careful and in the house by nightfall.

Now here his little lying ass is still outside hustling strangers. They need to have their asses home in bed, she thought. The light turned green.

She pulled away, shaking off the frustration. *No telling where the parents were.* Change seemed like a pipe dream. The crack culture continued to wreak havoc on the city. Liz lost count of her friends, past associates, and relatives who got caught up in the storm. Some were dead, some walking dead, many in prison. Only a few were able to bounce back.

Liz's survivor's guilt stemmed from the fact that she'd reaped benefits out of the destruction. The house she lived in and portions of her material possessions were purchased with Kevy's drug money. Up to this day, some of the illegal tender still supplemented her work checks. The voices constantly reminded her of all this, more now since she strived to rebuild her life.

She pulled up at home and parked in front. Relief eased through her after she saw the porch light glowing. Malik was home safe and sound, and most likely stubborn as ever. Soon she'd have to cut the umbilical cord and grant him freedom. She feared if she didn't he'd rip off the cord himself. This fear competed with an evolving fear of the streets enticing her baby into darkness.

Liz stuck the key in the door lock and felt the vibrations. *This boy and this loud ass music,* she frowned, stepping into the house. A rap tune's bass boomed from Malik's room. *Got my whole damn floor shaking,* Liz hissed. She tossed her keys on the couch and went and banged on his bedroom door. "Malik!"

Malik snatched it open. "What's up?"

24

"Turn that mess down," she demanded. School books lay scattered across his bed. "How the hell are you studying with that damn music busting your ear drums? Turn it down or turn it off."

He chose the first option, and followed her into the kitchen. "My fault. I forgot you're getting old and irritable," he teased. She glared at him, not seeing any humor in his comment. She grabbed the Sunny Delight out of the refrigerator. "What did I tell you about leaving empty cartons in the fridge?" She tossed it in the trash bin and poured a glass of water.

"My daddy called," he said. "He told me to stand on you if you hadn't answered his letter yet." In a playful manner he stepped up to her as if to carry out Kevy's order. "Did you write my pops back?" he asked. Liz wasn't in any mood to be played with. She finished off the water and pushed the empty glass into his hand. "Rinse this out and get out my face, silly boy."

He blocked her attempted exit out of the kitchen, determined to tax her patience tonight. "Did you hear me?" he smiled crookedly.

"You better go somewhere before your daddy get you and him hurt." She pushed past him and headed for her bedroom.

"You better get at my pops befo' I do some hurt—"

Liz shut the door to block out his idle threats. No time was wasted. She undressed, pulled back the covers, and sank down on the soft bed. *I'll write him tomorrow,* she told herself. The aches in her feet subsided as soon as she slid them down the sheets. *Sweet comfort.* She pulled the quilt up to her chest and relaxed her head on the pillow.

Suddenly, a sexy feeling crept over her. She reached over to the night stand, clicked off the lamp, and closed her eyes. Horny sensations took hold of her. She tried ignoring them. One minute dragged into ten. Then twenty minutes passed at a snail's pace. Liz tossed and turned, lowered the quilt, glanced at her clock radio, sighed, and tried to shake the unwanted images out of her mind. She mentally searched for Kevy's face. She reached for Kevy's face. She reached for Kevy's touch. But too much time had elapsed since Kevy held her—or since she held him. Too much damn time! Now another's image kept fighting for Liz's full attention—and winning. Marvin's image.

For the first several years of Kevy's incarceration, Liz remained sexually loyal to him. Then time made the fidelity falter. She and celibacy bickered; masturbation failed at reconciling their differences and quelling Liz's craving. Eventually she cracked under pressure and started dating. Soon afterwards, she broke her twelve years of devotion to strictly Kevy. This break in protocol led her to a short list of other male lovers. She kept the liaisons on the deep downlow and shunned any semblance of a relationship.

It was only temporary intimacy and/or sex. No attachments formed, no feelings allowed to surface. She controlled the temperature each and every time. Kevy would remain sole proprietor of her heart and no man stood a chance of trespassing that threshold, Liz determined. Kevy did ask her about other men, and she told him nothing. Prison was stressful enough on him, so there wasn't a need to add to the strain. At least this was the excuse she told herself for the deception. *No! Deception is a misnomer. R*eally, she just withheld certain information from Kevy.

Liz clicked on the radio. Mary J. Blige's happy love lyrics whispered out the small speaker. The song made Marvin's image stronger, more vivid in her head. Thoughts of her most recent lover pushed forward.

They'd met four months back down at M.A.T.C. where Liz attended night school. Liz had accidentally bumped into him as she came down a corridor. The impact sent her books crashing to the floor. When she bent down, a pair of caramel hands offered assistance. She stood, thanking the hands' owner, and got momentarily dazed. The brother was fine with a capital F. He was about 5'11"—three inches taller than she—and perfectly groomed with a small afro, beard, and goatee. His caramel complexion had a radiance that caught her attention and held it captive. And the way he smelled was an aphrodisiac in itself.

"Thank you," Liz had repeated after regaining focus. His smile was instantly inviting. He handed over one of the retrieved books.

"I should be the one extending gratitude," he replied. "I love to see my sistahs so intent on getting where they're trying to go. I bet that reflects your focus in life too." He flirted, but came across sincere. Liz smiled faintly and made her escape. Having been seven months abstinent, she took no chances.

26

She knew the slightest wind would nudge her right into a man's embrace; definitely a man as fine and as debonair as he.

She avoided him the following weeks. It was kind of childish on her part, but she knew they shared a mutual attraction. Then a month from their first encounter, fate betrayed Liz's wishes one night at a downtown Dunkin' Donuts. Liz was sitting at a table, eating a vanilla long john, and reading Ebony Magazine. Who would stroll through the door? None other than 'mister-caramel-hand-handsome-well-groomed-inviting-smile-flirtatious-but-sincere' himself. Right away, Liz pretended not to see him. She focused on the magazine until Marvin gracefully invited himself over to speak.

They ended up talking for hours that fateful night in Dunkin' Donuts. She enjoyed his conversation. Marvin told her all about himself. His status: single, never married, and no kids. She smiled inside at that revelation. He was born and raised in Milwaukee, taught business management at M.A.T.C., and was active in the community. His love for Black folks showed in his gestures and speech, Liz took notice as they discussed a variety of issues. She kept the focus on him. She didn't want to go too deep into her personal life. And he fascinated her. He seemed so down to earth and well balanced. The brotha was sharp; Liz couldn't deny it. Apparently a little too sharp, because weeks later they ended up in a suite at the Hyatt Hotel.

Once the sexual bliss wore off, Liz decided, *no more Marvin. Too dangerous 'cause he felt too good.* Liz never gave men her personal information. This left night school Marvin's only hope of contact. She doubted they'd bump into each other outside of M.A.T.C. No more visits to the downtown Dunkin' Donuts—or no time soon. The more she tried to avoid him, the more he pursued. Recently, he'd left a bouquet of red roses attached to her windshield wipers. He wrote a short apology inside the card for any 'unknown offense' he might have committed. *Such a considerate man.*

Liz reflected on all this as she finally found herself dozing off. After clicking off the radio, the voices spoke up. They told her that Marvin was the real reason she hadn't written Kevy.

****

27

The next morning, Malik surprised Liz with breakfast in bed. Wendy's did the cooking, but she appreciated his *beau geste*. It didn't take long for her to figure out his ulterior motives. She waited until she showered and dressed for work to give him an answer.

"If you feel an iota of tension, you get the hell out of there." Liz instructed Malik. "I mean that."

He stared at her like he wanted to protest.

"I want you leaving a good 30 minutes to an hour before the party lets out for the night," she continued. Well experienced with the club scene herself, Liz didn't like the idea of Malik attending a so-called teen night or friend's party or whatever it was supposed to be.

Malik got up from the couch. "I got you, Ma. And don't worry, I can handle myself," he said.

Liz shot him a dead serious look, suddenly having second thoughts. "You can't handle a bullet if some nut starts shooting. You leave an hour early or you don't go."

"It's cool—30 minutes to an hour early. I got you," he said.

"An hour. The 30 minutes is off the table. Matter fact, have your ass back in this house by 11 p.m. No later."

Malik sighed. "Alright."

She watched him slump toward his bedroom. "I want to speak with Dre before Friday also."

Malik turned back toward her. "For what?"

"Don't question me," she said in a lighter tone. "You just tell that knuckle headed boy I want to speak with him by Friday."

He eyed her, trying to read her face for motives. "His head doesn't look nothing like a knuckle, either" he mumbled.

He entered his bedroom and closed the door. As bad as Liz wanted to handcuff him to the radiator, she knew that wouldn't be wise. She planned to give him a little space at a time. Allowing him to go to a club was quite a

28

leap—more for her than for him. A long sigh. More doubts as she grabbed her purse off the dinette table and left for work.

CHAPTER 4

"She's too damn overprotective," Malik complained, staring out the car window as Drizzle drove down Center St. "Like a nigga sleep to what's poppin' in these streets." Malik couldn't stand how his mother still interrogated all his friends.

Drizzle swerved over into a side lane. "Shidd, at least you got someone carin' 'bout you. Some cats don't have that." He stopped at a red light on 35th St. "She didn't really trip. Just told me to have you back at the crib by 11 o'clock," he continued.

That didn't sit well with Malik. "See what I'm sayin'?" he frowned. "Like I'm your prom date or something."

Drizzle burst out laughing. "Dawg, you silly as hell."

"Straight up," Malik said, then laughed himself. "Have me home by eleven. Momz be on some weirdo shit sometimes, fo' real."

"She got at me 'bout school too." Drizzle made a right on 23rd St. A clique of boys hung on the corner like they owned it. Drizzle threw up the deuces to them and they returned his salute.

"She's sweated me about it, but I let her know you're try'na get your musical plans in motion."

Drizzle parked in front of his house. His little sister stepped off the porch and headed over to the Chevy.

Drizzle checked his phone messages. "Keepin' it real, it was all good that she thought of me enough to want me to go back." He lowered the window as She-She walked up. "Did you wash my gear?" he asked his little sis'.

She ignored him, smiling through the window at Malik. "Hey, 'Lik, what's up?"

"What's up?" he replied.

"Girl, you hear what I just asked yo' lil fast ass?" Drizzle asked, irritated.

She took a step back and frowned. "Didn't I say I was?" her attitude an obvious exaggeration. "Where's my dough for puttin' inna work?" She extended her hand and popped the gum in her mouth.

"Did you iron my shirt?" Drizzle leaned back and dug in his front pocket.

"Nope." She blew a bubble.

"Why not?"

She didn't reply. An awkward silence passed between the two siblings.

"Why you ain't iron my shit?" Drizzle asked again.

"'Cause somebody stole the dang iron," she blurted, eyes rolling. "That's why!"

Malik knew who the prime suspect was in the iron heist. He shut down the Sony PlayStation.

"What you mean somebody stole it?" Drizzle said.

"Ask Jesse," She-She advised.

"I'll be back in a minute, 'Lik," Drizzle said and got out the car. Malik overheard him interrogating She-She as they trekked toward the house. A confrontation between Drizzle and his mother's boyfriend was imminent, Malik figured. He removed the keys from the ignition and climbed out. Drizzle had griped a couple times within the last month about Jesse. Drizzle said the nigga smoked dope and freeloaded. Apparently he was also the iron thief.

Malik leaned against the Chevy. Across the street, an elderly Black woman swept off her porch steps. Malik didn't obey the urge to go offer her help; only because Drizzle might need his aid and assistance any minute. He stayed on point for the SOS.

Meanwhile, Malik checked out the battered neighborhood. Houses with grass-starved lawns and shabby exteriors decorated the block. The clique

31

of boys on the corner abruptly took flight. Malik watched them scurry away in any escapable direction. He wondered why they were ass and elbows all of a sudden... until an unmarked cop car bent the corner at full throttle, tires skidding. Malik jumped out the way as it barreled past him, bent another corner and disappeared. The presence of the elderly sister kept Malik from yelling out obscenities at the police over their reckless driving. He bridled his tongue out of respect for her. She approached the curb, broom in hand, and tossed Malik a wary look. He smiled at her and repositioned himself next to the Chevy, then looked away. But the accusatory stares and quick judgment irked Malik.

At the same time, he somewhat understood why she convicted him without evidence. Constant drama plagued the Metcalf Park area. The local media recently stigmatized it the worst 'hood in the city. Crimes ran the gamut: gang shootings to dope selling in plain view. Plus some.

One recent incident involved the fatal beating of a thirty-eight year old man by a mob of youngsters—their ages ranging from as young as ten, to no older than eighteen. The local news people ate it up and catapulted the case into a cause célèbre. According to the media reports, the situation kicked off when a neighborhood boy hit the man in the back of the head with an egg. The man caught the culprit seconds later and shoved him to the ground. Another boy jumped in between them and got slugged in the mouth. The blow left him a tooth short. Bleeding from the gums, the toothless boy and his egg-throwing crony ran away, and soon returned with kith and kin. The angry assembly captured the man and proceeded to maul him. The news reports repeatedly pointed out that the victim was punched, kicked, struck with slabs of wood, broken brooms, a bike frame, and whatever else his attackers could get their hands on.

Malik noticed how the media primarily focused on the age of the youngest alleged assailant. The ten-year-old helped sensationalize the story. Besides, as Drizzle pointed out to Malik, weeks prior to the fatal beating, the inner-city was hit by a string of murders. Ten killings in a twelve-day period; one of the victims only thirteen years old. But absolutely no radio or television coverage outside of Milwaukee. No hoopla over the violent deaths of so many young Blacks, period. The Green Bay Packers victory over the Seattle Seahawks received more coverage that week.

Malik ruminated on all this as he stood in that very Metcalf Park 'hood. Some of the boys that fled the cops were starting to reappear on the other end of the block. The elderly sister mumbled something in their direction. Malik couldn't exactly process what she said, but knew it wasn't kind words.

"Lik!" She-She ran out the house in tears.

"Yeah!" Malik took off toward her.

"Jesse hit my brother—they inna house fightin'!"

Malik heard the tussle when he rushed through the front door. "Come on, fam," he urged, grabbing Drizzle and stepping in between them. Before Malik knew it, he felt a hard blow to his jaw. Jesse's sucker punch dazed him. It took Malik a moment to realize he got hit.

Drizzle leapt past Malik. "Push on this, chump," he snarled, tearing back off into Jesse. Malik spun around and administered quick fanatical jabs to Jesse's head, neck, and back. As they socked away with all their might, She-She's screams resonated throughout the house. "Kick his bitch ass, y'all!"

Janice, Drizzle's mother, stumbled out of the back as if she was in a half-conscious state. "What you boys doin' to my man?" she asked, words dragging. She looked strung-out on something. Malik paused long enough for Jesse to break loose. Jesse shoved She-She out of the way as he made his escape. Drizzle was right on his trail, clocking him in the back of the dome. The impact sent Jesse staggering out the door onto the porch. Malik filed out behind Drizzle. Drizzle raged as he scooped up an old milk crate and smashed Jesse in the face with it. Malik jumped in before Drizzle could hit Jesse a second time with the crate. Malik kicked Jesse down the stairs and spat at him. Drizzle made one last desperate attempt at inflicting more pain by slinging the crate. But Jesse was in the wind.

"Don't bring your hype ass back over here no mo', you thieving ass punk," Drizzle yelled after him. Jesse was halfway down the block by then.

"What the hell was that all about?" Malik rubbed his throbbing jaw.

33

Drizzle stomped back in the crib. Malik heard him fussing at his mother. Stepping off the porch, Malik noticed the elderly sister across the street. She stared in obvious contempt.

Damn. Malik forgot about her presence. Now the earlier judgment of him appeared accurate. The evidence was now there. Malik avoided eye contact as he walked up to the Chevy. She stood at the curb, glaring his way, broom still in hand.

"You young men show no shame," she got at Malik. He leaned against the car and looked away.

"Gone beat me too?" she continued. "It's sad that we're not safe in our own community because you young people run around here like hoodlums and heathens. No respect for anything, anyone. Justa goin' 'round terrorizing your own people." Her anger and defiance mounted as she assaulted Malik's conscience. "I'm not worried though. Not one bit. I've lived in this neighborhood for over thirty years and never seen so much betrayal and disregard for human life. No common decency."

Her emotions poured out into the street and submerged Malik in shame. All he could do is listen. "You Black brothers suppose to be the warriors protecting the village, making the women and children feel safe and secure." She slapped the curb with the broomstick. Malik looked up, thinking she was about to attack him. Physically.

She went on with her castigation. "Instead of blessed warriors y'all make us want to curse the womb for birthing so much misery, hate, self-destruction," she vented. "Y'all are the new slave drivers!"

Drizzle stormed out of the house with two large overflowing plastic bags in hand. "Pop the trunk, fam," he told Malik. "This dope fiend ass nigga ain't 'bout to tear me off."

Malik got to it, relieved to get out of the line of the woman's fire. Drizzle loaded his things in the back, then they got in the car. Malik stole a glance of the elderly sister. She tossed him another indignant look and retreated towards her house. The ancient pain in her eyes came from a deep and sincere place. Malik wished that she knew him better. If only she knew that he took no pleasure in the chaos that plagued the community. Only if she

34

knew about his dreams of unity, peace, and Black empowerment. Although he lived in more of a neighborhood than a 'hood, his heart was still drawn toward the pain and tragedy that gripped the ghetto. If only she knew, he lamented as Drizzle hit the gas and smashed out.

Malik couldn't push her words out of his thoughts, nor could he delete her pained expression from his mind. Maybe one day he would show that his mother's womb birthed a blessing: a blessed warrior who contributed to the cause and community. Something positive...

Malik reached over and hit play on the CD player. He hoped the music would free his mind. He just wanted to escape for awhile.

CHAPTER 5

Liz sat watching 'Love and Basketball,' munching on caramel corn and sipping on lemonade iced tea. Why did she torture herself like this? The movie had an insidious way of reminding her of a man's love and affection. Things she wanted but didn't really need at this point in her life. The drama in the story line made her nostalgic. The only conflict she'd been dealing with was internal. Loneliness and temptation teamed up against her will power, trying to break her down and...

Kevy screened across her mind. *Maybe tomorrow*, she thought. The Hallmark cards to him did all the talking. Or none of it. The cards were a convenient way to let Kevy know that he was in her thoughts without telling him that another man was on her mind at times. Kevy sensed something afoot, she could tell, because his recent letters were peppered with innuendoes about her infidelity. But did he understand how vulnerable the heart got in such a lonely state? The state that gripped her right now? She doubted it. And the burden of holding back from him weighed on her, more heavily now since temptation was bullying her into calling Marvin.

Liz checked her watch. *Still kinda early.* Most likely, Malik would push his curfew to the very limits. She debated herself... *One call can't hurt nothing...* She grabbed the phone. She hesitated dialing his number. Malik might pop up earlier than expected. *His sneaky butt.* She hung it up. *Must cover all ends.* She went to his room to see if he left her cellular on the charger. *Of course not,* she found out. *That boy really thinks that cell belongs to him. Ain't paid any bill.* She scribbled him a note and went to get spiffed up a bit. So what the new jeans hugged her ass tightly and the blouse told on her breast size. She sprinkled on perfume, got her keys and was out the door.

Liz got in the car and put on some R. Kelly. His soulful, sexy, sweet nothings were right on time. As sick as the allegations were against the singer, his music still put Liz in the mood for luv. Lord knows if that had been her daughter though.

Pulling into Gas N' Go, she parked next to a pay phone. *If I can't catch him on the first try, I'll take it as a sign and take my ass back home,* she reasoned with herself. *Talk to me, Most High, or let me talk to this man.* She reached out the window and paid for the call, hoping she wouldn't later have to *pay* for the call.

Marvin answered with smooth urgency in his voice. Liz wondered if he was expecting a call. Maybe hers. A volt of sensual energy shot through her.

Hang up, said the voices.

Hush up dammit, she countered before speaking into the phone. "Can you talk?" she asked him.

"Only if this is the sistah I was hoping to hear from," he worked it.

"Who might that lucky sistah be?" Liz relaxed. What if it wasn't her? She tensed up. This shit had her trippin' fo' real.

"Next time I catch some z's, I'll snatch her dreamy image, then push her beautiful description your way," he worked it harder. Waited, then added, "Although you know her like you know yourself."

You just don't know. "You sure she'll pop up there?" Liz felt like a fast teenybopper on the phone with her adolescent boo. It felt sneaky, sexy.

"Believe you me, I know," he ran it. "She'll either pop up in my nocturnal dream, or my next daydream. She'll definitely come." A titillating moment of silence. "Of course, I much prefer her here in the flesh. Just to talk. Laugh. Maybe dance." His beautiful baritone, his suave words, were just too damn enticing. Liz knew she should have hung up right then and there. And flown back home! But Marvin's romantic witticism lured her away from better judgment. She hung up the phone and drove off, traveling down a road that would be hard to get off of. A collision was almost inevitable. Yet she pushed on through the doubts, driving forward toward it.

****

37

Hitting up the same suite, at the same hotel, they went at it like newlyweds. He stoked her fire. The passion ran wild between them. Untamed. And how qualified his tongue! Liz celebrated. He licked her there, kissed her here, sucked on the most sensitive spots on her body. The foreplay was inspiring, so she climbed on top. He palmed her ass cheeks as she swayed, grinding his stiff manhood inside her. They were eagerly engaged in it. The feeling controlled, consoled, inflamed them. Then a soft smack to her ass. Another and another one. This increased her drive. Their moans got louder as they mounted their peaks... Liz felt it bubble up like the hottest sensation. She froze up, screamed unintelligibly—she didn't even understand it—and let it go. What a delicious feelin'! Marvin stroked upward... way, way up inside of her. They floated together 'til every wave of ecstasy poured free.

Liz descended into his arms and let him hold her. Once he got up to go to the bathroom, she sat up and considered what this meant. Something felt kinda different this time. Liz wasn't sure what it was. The feeling had her mind hazy. What feeling? Then it hit her. Guilt. Weak guilt. Comfortable guilt massaged her conscience. She reached for something else. Something punishing. She only felt Kevy fading further away into the shadows of her mind.

Marvin emerged from the bathroom. He, still naked. She, still naked. He strolled over, lifted her into his sculpted arms and carried her to the bubbling hot tub. His arms felt safe. *Got me luvin' it when I know I shouldn't be,* she thought and waited for the voices to rub it in. They stayed mute.

"Is this your attempt at romance?" she smiled at him.

His head went sideways. "Attempt?" He lowered her into the pleasant water. His nudity caressed hers. "I thought I was doin' my thang."

"I'll let you know when ya doin' ya thang," she kissed his lips. He kissed her lips and inserted his tongue. His piece hardened between her legs... finding its way up to her... She pulled back and gave him the look. He knew what time it was and reached over the side of the hot tub. He came back with a condom. A Magnum.

The nerve! "Oh, you just knew you was gettin' some mo', huh?" Like she would've denied him. Denied herself.

"Just in case, baby," he grinned. And kissed her on the ear. The neck. Then the...

Liz wrapped his waist in her legs as he eased inside. They moved in a slow, fluent motion. She wanted this moment to last forever. And eva! She relished the way he touched her body, the way he whispered her name, the way he did his thang. She relished the whole freakin' fantasy. She was in no rush to awaken from it.

CHAPTER 6

"Fam, you did da damn thang tonight," Malik propped Drizzle as they kicked it in KQ's VIP. The club was straight jumpin'.

"I see these lil jumpdowns givin' a nigga thirsty looks already," Drizzle nodded in the direction of a thick-boned chick who stood outside the VIP's entrance. She and two other girls repeatedly cut glances at Malik and Drizzle. The girls chatted it up and giggled in a manner that begged for attention.

Malik considered calling home to give his mother some lame excuse for running late. It was already thirty minutes past his curfew, and he didn't plan on leaving any time soon. The club atmosphere sucked him in. Held him hostage. Moments earlier, Drizzle took the stage and spit it hard. All thanks to Kila's gift of persuasion, Prophet Kemet gave the green light for Drizzle to perform. Drizzle called Malik around two in the morning the night before to give him the news. He also asked Malik to choose which songs he should make his debut with. Half awake, Malik picked his favorite ones and rolled back over to sleep. It all worked out because the audience yelled for more once Drizzle's set ended.

"Who is ol' girl with Kila?" P-nut asked, joining them in VIP. "That hoe bad."

Malik gazed toward the bar and spotted Kila and Nana. They laughed and waved.

"That's Nana," Drizzle told P-nut, and grinned at Malik. "'Lik's future wifey."

P-Nut shot Malik a disbelieving look, then stared back toward the girls. "This nigga don't know what to do with that bitch," he said. "Let me handle her fo' ya, playa," he addressed Malik.

So disrespectful, Malik thought. He felt the "hoe" and "bitch" epithets weren't really called for. "Probably can't handle her." Malik expressed no sign of frustration.

"Nigga, we don't kick it like that," Drizzle breathed on his cousin. "Fuck you talkin' bout?" The smile vanished off P-Nut's face. "Out of all these flippers in here, you wanna focus on the one fam fuckin' with," he kept scolding P-Nut.

"I'm not trippin'," Malik said. He wanted to defuse the tension. "She's a free agent. Nothing between us is official."

Drizzle was relentless. "It's the principle and potential for bullshit. If we family, we're family and respect boundaries. Ex-girls and current ones are off limits."

P-Nut got up to leave. "Well, I'm 'bout to find some slut to run up in tonight," he jacked, and headed out. Drizzle glared his way.

The thick-boned girl invited herself into VIP. Her two buddies followed her lead. Malik stared past them and watched P-Nut approach the bar.

"I was feelin' ya flow tonight," Thick Bones complimented Drizzle. "When ya droppin'?" She moved within inches of his face, the smile on her juicy lips sayin' it all. "Gotta cop and support that." Her buddies acted kinda shy. Or timid. One of them kept eyeballing the dance floor. Almost like she was on the lookout for danger or something. Malik checked her out. Next thing he knew, the other girl tensed up and said, "Tab, heads up," to Thick Bones. Uneasy looks came over the girls' faces as two dudes mean-mugged their way over and right into VIP.

"Bring your ass here, Tab," one of the dudes ordered Thick Bones. His baby face belied the aggressive display.

Tab swung around and gave Baby Face a boatload of attitude. "Boy, don't come in here trippin'. I was just asking Drizzle when his CD was droppin'."

Baby Face and his partner stared Drizzle and Malik up and down. "This cat ain't signed," Baby Face chuckled in scorn. "The streets ain't even askin' for him." His snide comment got Malik and Drizzle to their feet. "Square ass nigga, you in ya feelings over this tramp?" Drizzle got in Baby Face's face.

41

"I'm not no tramp," Tab said, and eased away. "Let's go, Rob," she told Baby Face.

"Yeah, go 'cause your multiple dick breath is bogus," Drizzle told her. "All up in my face like I wanna smell that shit." She rolled her eyes and stomped out.

People gathered near VIP, some individuals entering to see what was unfolding. Malik wasn't feelin' the forming crowd. *Should've left like I was suppose to*, he started regretting.

Kila, Nut, and Nana rushed in to see what was going on.

"My nigga Al-Coca Leaves is the truth on the rap tip," Rob bragged about his partner.

Kila stepped in between Drizzle and Rob. "What's up? It's not about to be no mess in my uncle's club tonight."

"Y'all battle rap then," someone instigated.

"I gotta stack on my nigga Al," Rob challenged Drizzle. "He'll shit on you and whoever you come with."

"Jacked on 'em," said another as other agitators egged on the battle.

Drizzle finally relaxed. "I tell ya what," he addressed Rob, "Yo' guy Al-Corny," laughter around the room, "can spit a verse. Then I'll spit one, and the people present shall be the judges. If Al wins, I'll autograph that dusty ass Chicago Bulls hat you're wearing," laughter sprouted again, "and when I win, I'll let you keep your imaginary G-stack."

Al stepped forward. The anticipation pulsed throughout VIP. P-Nut solicited bets until Kila and Nana hushed everyone. The battle was on. Al lunged into his verse:

"I'm Chi-town's finest, the city where the win blow/

The land where real nigs hold major figs and lay low/

where most Milwaukee cats dread to go/

'cause they know da city's rep/

42

come outside and find fiends dead on ya do' step/

overdosed wit' a needle prickin' his veins/

The sky cloudy, but fuck Drizzle, it po' black rain/-"

The spectators' uproar flooded out Al's voice. Rob smiled like victory was a done deal for his homie. Malik swallowed all doubt. Drizzle maintained his nonchalance. Prophet stepped in the room and observed without uttering a word.

"Be quiet so Drizzle can go," Kila yelled.

Malik and Drizzle exchanged super cool, unworried looks.

"Yeah, you're semi-slick," Drizzle gave it up to Al-Coca Leaves.

"Family, wrap this on up," P-Nut told Drizzle. "Hold the applause until after the slaughter, please," he told everyone else.

Drizzle shot Malik a cocky stare and went in:

"I'ma hitman, fuck Rob, I got ties wit' the Haitians/

actually I done more jobs than Jamaicans/

ice Al like Jacob, he won't wake up/

for a small fee I waste cats/

smack niggas inna mouth/

they still try'na get they taste back/

I knock the black off a nigga/

he still try'na get his race back/

for that same small fee I'll lace tracks/

'cause we all know that rap is like a juggling act/

If I start struggling, go back to smugglin' crack/

It take a lot fo' me to back stab and get shice/

Al tested but I pass every time like trick dice/

We can fight or we can go right into gun fire/

Rob tried to slide but I'm callin' ya out like umpires/

I don't know why he even assigned Al, dude's lame/

and oh yeah, most ya Chi-towners sound the same/

I'll spit a verse/--"

The brouhaha drowned out Drizzle. "Chill y'all," Kila silenced the rabble rousers. "Let him finish." Drizzle waited for them to calm down before going back into his zone:

"I'll spit a verse and fuck 'round and drown ya man/

pay me to write yo' shit 'cuz I'm ya last hope/

yo' flow been stepped on too many times like bad dope/

I'm taking over now and if you try 'n stop me/

I'll hide in the bushes and click cannons like the

paparazzi/

murkin' ya whole city's rep/

killin' it like the dead fiend on ya door step/"

Cheerful pandemonium broke out amongst the gathering. Malik saw a faint smile form on Prophet's grille. Al wanted to spit another verse to save face.

"Alright, y'all clear on out before I get cited for fire violations," Prophet said to the hangers-on. They cleared out without grumble or gripe. Prophet came over and took a seat; Malik and Drizzle parked it too. Kila was full of cheers as she cuddled up to Drizzle.

"Your mama said call her," Prophet told his niece. Then he turned his attention on Drizzle. "I see you pulled if off tonight. On and off the stage."

"I'm grateful for the opportunity, big homie," Drizzle replied.

Malik sized up Prophet on the sly. Word on the streets was that Prophet was straight gangsta. But Malik didn't really see it from his

44

appearance. His 5'9" frame, clean cut, and smooth disposition made him seem more a lady's man.

Prophet observed the energetic adolescents through the large VIP window. "Y'all party harder than my regular crowd," he acknowledged. "Might have to make this a permanent thing."

Please do, Malik secretly encouraged.

Prophet turned and addressed Drizzle. "They felt you out there. Bet you could smash a lot of the established acts that come through here."

Drizzle nodded.

"You try'na bust some moves on the business end?" Prophet asked.

"No doubt," he replied. "Just laid some tracks last weekend. My next step is creating a local buzz and meeting the right people. The Miltown been locked in underdog status for too long. Coo Coo. Baby Drew. Both went for it but they barred the gate. If we was in ATL. somewhere, they wouldn't deny us."

"Can't let 'em deny you."

"Can't stop, won't stop. I'ma get the city poppin' or lose my voice tryin'," Drizzle vowed.

"I feel that," Prophet said. "I think you can pull it off if you stay focused. Get out of the city, on the road, going to other places. Then bring it back home. Get you some computer nerds to set you up on the internet and all. Lose yourself in it 'til you find what you're tryin' to get out of it."

Malik took in the conversation. Prophet's prosperity and reputation already had the town respecting him. Now hearing him speak, Malik saw that the man had some substance to him, some meat on his head. Kinda reminded Malik of Kevy.

"You get down with the music?" he asked Malik.

"I get down with my nigga so you can say I do."

"'Lik my one man brain trust. He's more on the business end of it all," Drizzle said.

45

"Definitely need those thinkers in your circle," Prophet said. "One weak link is all it takes to break the chain. Each one must be solid."

Malik saw P-Nut and Nana talking and laughing it up near the bar. Out of his periphery, he peeped Prophet watching him. Malik turned and made eye contact with the club owner. It looked like Prophet was trying to remember something.

"You remind me of some —" Prophet began, but Kila's re-entry stole his thought. Or distracted him away from it.

"Uncle P, I told my mama I'm living with you until tomorrow night," Kila said.

Prophet stood to his feet. "That's cool," he said. "And don't think you're staying out all night. Using me as a pawn."

Kila tossed him a defiant look and plopped down next to Drizzle.

"You brothers keep it solid. And strive for an a-to-z understanding of that rap industry. Talent without it is worthless to you. People will try to pimp your gifted ignorance." He placed a hand on Kila's shoulder. "Take it easy on my niece too. I recall my teen years."

Drizzle shifted a little.

"Stop it, Uncle P," Kila said. "You know I handle mines. You're better off asking me to take it easy on them."

"So you say," Prophet chuckled. "Y'all stay smooth." He left the room.

Kila snuggled up to Drizzle. "Unc be on one," she smiled. "knowin' I'ma maintain my me regardless."

Drizzle got up. "Ready to roll out, 'Lik?"

"Yep." He could hear his mother's voice in his head. *Probably worrying to death.*

"Why you stiff-arm Nana all night?" Kila asked Malik. "What's up?" She hugged Drizzle.

Nana just so happened to be standing by the dance floor kickin' it with a group of male admirers. "She was too busy collecting dudes' numbers for me to stiff-arm her," he replied.

"Like a scientific calculator," Drizzle added.

"You don't seem the jealous type," Kila teased Malik.

"Never that. Just discreet about the company I keep."

Drizzle checked his phone. "It's wise to be discreet, fam," he told Malik. "We can't afford to court trouble out here. And if a chick is diggin' a dude, she won't try to introduce any unnecessary drama into his life."

"Y'all way too philosophical for me tonight," Kila said. "Drizzle, call me later so I can learn more about your metaphysics on females." She nodded to Malik. "I'll see you in school, 'Lik."

On the way out the club, Drizzle was approached by Al. "Call me, G," Al said, handing him a number. "My folks gotta studio in Chicago. We need to collab on a track." Drizzle pocketed the piece of paper and kept it movin'.

Malik and Drizzle climbed in the Chevy and smashed out. P-Nut caught a ride with some girls who he bragged wanted to rape him. Malik doubted his claim. He wasn't feelin' P-Nut or his faulty vibe.

Drizzle cut down the sounds. "Ya momz gone kill us." He sped down Sherman Boulevard, swervin' and dippin' past traffic.

"Dawg, slow down," Malik said. "Mess 'round don't make it to the crib alive to get killed."

"Fuck dat," Drizzle chuckled. "Ya momz a killa."

"She's a creampuff."

Drizzle hit a left down North Ave. He pumped the brake after spotting a squad car parked in Amoco.

"Betta slow ya roll, 'cause I know it's a warrant out for ya arrest," Malik said.

Drizzle cut a curious glance. "A warrant?"

"Yeah," Malik smirked, "You murk'd dude Al in that battle," he said. "Got at 'em something viciously after he tried to dooky on our town."

"Them dudes always try'na down da Mil like it's some sorta hick town. Ran into a couple of those cats when I was in Juvenile Detention last time. Always jackin' 'bout Chicago. Know they probably got ran out of there."

"Ya think he really got a studio plug?" Malik asked.

"Probably not, but we're gonna take a look anyway." He turned down Malik's block. "Need to make something happen soon, so I can get my lil sister in a better living situation." His demeanor changed. "It's all on me."

"No doubt."

"Alright, I'll holla," Drizzle rushed him out of the car. "Hurry up befo' ya mama run out airing at the Chevy."

Malik opened the door to get out. "You leaving me to get shot by myself."

"I got love fo' ya, but ya momz ain't no joke." They knocked fists. "One love."

"Love," Malik laughed and got out. He expected the third degree the moment he stepped in the house. He found his mother gone. Relieved, he went to his bedroom. The note she attached to his stereo player let him know that she left before his curfew. She'll never know that he was quite late. The P.S. at the bottom threatened stern discipline if he came home past the designated time. He tossed the note in the trash, turned on some music, and went to fix some grub. *Momz don't wanna see me like that,* he thought bravely, knowing he was frontin' with himself.

CHAPTER 7

Liz rushed in the house and answered the phone. "Hello," she breathed hard.

"I'm not interrupting anything, am I?" It was Kevy.

"Kevy?" Liz was surprised to hear his voice. He rarely called on Saturdays.

"What's up, Ms. Hard-to-catch?"

She ignored his sarcasm. "You finally called, I see."

"I've been calling for the last several months. Writing too. You're a busy woman nowadays."

"Working and going to school will consume a person's time like that." Liz sat her bags down on the kitchen table and took a seat. "Saturdays and Sundays are my only days off to do other things."

"You're not too busy now, are you?" His sarcasm continued.

"Nope. I just got back from the spa and doing a little shopping." She regretted mentioning the spa. Especially since Marvin gave her a gift certificate to enjoy the few hours of pampering.

"The spa? Since when did you start treating yourself to such top notch comforts?" Kevy asked.

"I do deserve a little pampering after such a hectic schedule," she said defensively.

"You deserve to be pampered and a lot more, Liz."

She couldn't tell if he was being sincere or not. "Have you spoken with your lawyer?"

"I'm coming to the county jail next month for a hearing. Hopefully something positive will come out of that, but I'm not overly optimistic."

"A hearing?" Liz said.

"Yeah."

"Something should come out of it. I would think they wouldn't come all the way to Oklahoma to get you for nothing—since they're always yelling this D.O.C. high budget shit."

"They love to tease a person's hopes. We'll have to wait and see."

"Will I get to visit you while you're in Milwaukee county?" Liz asked, digging in her shopping bags.

"If you want to."

"If I want to?" She got irritated. "What's that all about?" She knew what it was all about.

"You tell me."

"Don't start, Kevy. I've been doing my best trying to put my life back together and raise your son."

"Where's 'Lik at?" he suddenly changed the subject.

Liz sighed. "He left earlier this morning with his friend. They said something about going to a music studio."

"Let him know I'll write soon. Is he staying focused?"

"He's stubborn as ever, but he's taking care of business with school. He went to a club a couple weeks ago and his friend Andre performed. Now he wants to go out every Friday, it seems." She went to look out the window. "This might be them pulling up now with this loud ass music shaking my damn house." She saw Dre's Chevy parking behind her car. "Yeah, this is them. Hold on a sec." She sat the phone down.

"Lik!" she yelled out the front door. The boys bobbed their heads, not even noticing her. *How the hell can they stand this racket in their ears,* Liz wondered, approaching the car. She tapped on the window. They both reached to turn the music down.

Malik put on a weak smile and lowered the glass.

50

"I told y'all about coming around here disturbing the peace," Liz scolded them.

"My fault," Drizzle said.

"Your daddy is on the phone," she told Malik.

Malik hopped out the car and rushed off. Liz took a seat in his place. She sensed Drizzle's discomfort, although he tried to camouflage it by fumbling with his cell.

She checked out his car. "You look like you're doing pretty good for yourself. Can you get 'Lik a job where you're working at?" she asked.

"I'm not working right now. Been putting my all into this music," Drizzle spoke in a subdued tone.

"Do your parents help you out?" Liz knew the answer. Malik had already told her that Drizzle's father was killed years ago and his mother had some kind of drug addiction.

He slumped a little in his seat. "I take care of myself for the most part."

She noticed his further discomfort and regretted bringing up his folks. But something pushed her to keep going. "I want to meet your parents. Why don't you bring them over next weekend or have one of them give me a call."

Drizzle exhaled. "My pops passed away when I was 'round ten years old," he said without much feeling. "And my mama got her own issues she's dealing with." He sat up and stared in the side mirror. "I'll let her know you wanna talk with her though."

Liz sensed the masked pain underneath his cool veneer. A part of her wanted to hug and squeeze out all of his hidden affliction. "We all have issues. Some people's are deeper than others," she told him. She felt tempted to ask about school again. "We also have to make our own decisions in life. Hard decisions that will either make us or break us. Luckily for you, you're still at an age where you're able to overcome what's in front of you and learn from what's in back of you. It's all about decisions."

51

Malik appeared on the front porch and yelled for Liz to come to the phone.

"I'll be there in a second," she told him, before turning back to Drizzle. "Always remember two things. Just because a person isn't loving you the way you like, doesn't mean they're not loving you with all they have."

Drizzle nodded.

Liz continued. "And what doesn't crush us only strengthens our shoulders." She stepped out of the car, closed the door, then leaned down and said, "Stay focused on what you're trying to accomplish. If you need a helping hand or someone to talk to, don't hesitate to come to me, okay?"

"Alright," Drizzle said, a little warmth in his voice now.

Liz went back inside the house and grabbed the phone.

"I hope you wasn't interrogating my guy," Malik eyed her suspiciously.

"You just keep that mess down," she said.

"Pops, stand on her," Malik yelled.

She frowned. "I keep telling you that you're gonna get you and your daddy hurt," she warned.

Malik left out the door.

"You better stop getting jazzy with my son," Kevy joked.

"If I don't?" Liz lay down on the couch and carried on their conversation, the tension from before no longer evident. As much as Marvin breathed romance back into her life, hearing Kevy's voice reminded her of her true love. She missed Kevy so much and wanted him home so bad. Talking to him only intensified the yearning.

By the end of their phone call, Liz was sure that her flings with Marvin were in their twilight. She studied her freshly manicured fingernails. He'd just treated her. Damn. The least she could do was show some gratitude. She would break it off with Marvin completely once she finished school. Sooner than that if Kevy's court date bore any fruit. Maybe bring it down a notch or two and maintain a platonic friendship with Marvin from here on out.

****

Later that night, Liz found herself in Jazzman's night spot. She was sitting at a corner table, taking stock of the scenery. A live band performed on stage while the small crowd socialized and vibed to the music. Liz was out of her element. These were upper middle class Black folk: Marvin's ilk. She still enjoyed the ambiance.

"This tune is pretty nice, isn't it?" a man's voice spoke up from behind. Liz turned, startled. Marvin stood there grinning. He pulled a chair up next to hers and sat down.

"You can't be creeping up on a sistah like that, man." Liz smiled, then added, "I almost cut you."

He chuckled. The smell of his cologne instantly turned her on. He leaned closer, his lips inches from her ear. "Would you like a drink?" he asked.

Liz remembered what happened the last time they shared a couple of drinks. "I'll just have a wine cooler for now," she said.

He waved over a slim waitress. "Two coolers. Pina colada." The waitress wrote down the order, asked if that was it, then left. Liz wondered if he mirrored her request to win points. He wrapped his arm around the back of her chair. She relaxed. The pleasant energy inspired her to have second thoughts. A platonic relationship might be a little premature right now. They sat quietly and took in the atmosphere. Liz focused on the band. She felt Marvin watching her closely. The waitress returned with their drinks and sauntered back off. Liz sipped from her glass; he ignored his and kept staring. All the special attention made her a bit self-conscious. She finally asked, "What is it?"

"Just trying to figure out an enigma—the enigma of Liz," he replied. "The mystery called Liz."

53

"Mystery?" Liz knew where he was going. The last time they got together, he alluded to coming to her house and meeting Malik. She quickly diverted the conversation then, and was ready to do the same now. "There's no mystery. Your mind is just over-analyzing things." She took another sip of her drink.

"If not a mystery, then how about a deeper you," he said. She detected some impatience in his voice. "Can I experience the Liz inside of Liz? I'd like to erase the distance between that deeper woman in you and the deeper man in me."

Liz pushed the glass away and leaned back. "I told you it is what it is. Me and simple are companions with an unbreakable bond. Maybe this imagined distance is what keeps us in harmony."

"I just want to get to know--," Marvin began, then changed his approach. "Well, tell me why haven't you given me a phone number to contact you. It's like I'm involved in an illicit love affair because of the secretive nature of our relationship."

A middle-aged man came over and greeted them. Liz said hello and let them talk small talk. She was a little frustrated over Marvin's comment about their relationship. This was the first time he mentioned something about a relationship. She wished he would stop trying to pry open a door that needed to remain shut. She thought about excusing herself to the bathroom, then slipping out the back door. Too rude on her part, she figured. Eventually they would run into each other again. The timing wasn't right to make her escape just yet.

The old school brotha said his goodbyes and walked off. Marvin wasted no time getting back to the subject at hand. "How's Malik doing?" he asked, a little too pointedly.

"He's doing okay." Maybe a cold move was needed to freeze things over after all? Marvin must have picked up on her reluctance to dive deeper. "Are you feeling this band?" he asked Liz.

"Yeah. I'm going to get more into jazz one of these days. It has a nice groove to it." She did want to tell him the reason she hadn't introduced him to

54

Malik. But did she really need to divulge that much information? Naw. Better to stay a mystery instead. An enigma.

CHAPTER 8

Malik pulled on his fitted cap and exited the school building. The nippy nibble of fall was feeling more like the harsh bite of winter outside. Zipping up his coat, he looked around for the Chevy. To his mild disappointment, it wasn't parked in the usual spot. *Where is fam?* Drizzle always made it up to the school to scoop him on time.

Malik strolled down the concrete walkway toward the curb. The student body was deep on the premises, hanging out, making their way to their transportation, and doing whatever high school students did. Malik expected Drizzle to roll up any moment. He posted up near the flagpole and stared back and forth. The Chevy was nowhere in sight.

Across the street, Kila, Nana, and several buddies stood next to a brand new BMW. *Dude is gettin' major dust,* Malik admired upon spotting Prophet Kemet sitting in the driver's seat. Usually all eyes would be on the Chevy. Not today though. Prophet's ride killed the scene and had everyone in the vicinity stalking and wishing they were ballers. Malik's presence barely got acknowledged. Kila and her clique gained instant celebrity off of her uncle's wheels.

Malik looked away. People were so fickle. One day, it was all love; the next, their shoulders were shrugging you off. Once the objects of esteem were gone, so went all of the attention. The person with more loot, flyer gear, flashier bling, a slicker whip, became the next 'hood idol. It was all too transitory. Thanks to Malik's generously giving mother, he stayed fitted up in new kicks and dapper fits. All the jewelry didn't really appeal to him. He wasn't the stuntin' type. But he did want something nice to cruise through the city in. Borrowing his mama's car was getting old. Riding shotgun with Drizzle sometimes made Malik feel like a scrub.

Why was he having this conversation with himself? *Trippin'.* He didn't want to live fast. No headlong rush to grow up. Malik set his clock of success for more than 15 minutes. The street fame wouldn't last long enough. He was convinced that destiny called him to be much more than another sad statistic. Malik aimed to give the beast a bellyache and heartburn. Better yet, a heart attack. A Black man manifesting into his inherent greatness always dealt the white supreme machine a staggering blow. Malik's pops told him that a long time ago. So the straight and narrow would continue to be his path, and the struggle his calling.

Malik was too stubborn to let peer pressure get the best of him. He wanted to become something. Somebody. He desired longevity. And if death did claim him at a young age, the reason had to prove meaningful. He wanted to matter. Wanted to steer clear of the 'early grave or prison' two-way street and pave his own unique path. *That's what's up.*

Nana and Kila got inside the Beemer. Malik watched it pull off and head in his direction. He diverted his stare, but out of his peripheral vision, he peeped it slow up.

"Hey, 'Lik," Nana piped out the car window. "Ain't Drizzle picking you up?" she yelled loud enough for the world to hear.

Malik maintained a cool front. "Yeah," he nodded, feeling mildly embarrassed. "He'll be here in a minute." If only he felt as confident as he tried to sound.

Prophet offered him a lift.

"Good lookin' but I'ma wait on my nigga," he declined. Pride.

Traffic piled up behind Prophet. Two or three impatient drivers honked their horns. Prophet disregarded them. "You and Drizzle come see me down at KQ. I got something y'all may be interested in," he addressed Malik.

"Right away," he replied.

"Alright. Stay smooth on your pivot," Prophet said.

"Call me later, 'Lik," Nana yelled as Prophet drove on down the street.

What did Prophet want with him and Drizzle? Malik was super curious. *Interested in what?* he wondered, looking up and down the street. No Chevy rolling up; no Drizzle showing up. What the heck! Malik wasn't feeling this MIA stuff. He walked over to the steps and sat on top of his books. Waiting. Wondering. Thinking of all the rumors he'd heard about Prophet Kemet.

57

After Kila's birthday shindig at Kemet Quarters, Prophet converted all Fridays into Teen Night. Seven o'clock to 11 o'clock p.m. The time frame ran neck and neck with Malik's curfew. He hadn't missed a Friday yet. And Drizzle rocked the mic each time. Malik was glad for his homie. Now Drizzle had a venue to regularly perform and showcase his music. The local buzz was starting to spark up already.

This could have something to do with Prophet's request to see them. Malik was optimistic but wary. Prophet did have a gangsta rep in the streets. This Malik heard. Prophet also ran what appeared a legitimate night club. This Malik saw. He was taught to believe half of what he saw and none of what he heard, so what he saw held fifty percent credibility.

Maybe Prophet found Drizzle a plug with some industry cats? Malik hoped so. It had to be that. All Drizzle needed was that right connection. The world of hip hop wouldn't know what hit it.

Twenty-five minutes passed by. Most of the students had cleared off of school grounds. Teachers were now exiting the building to go home. Malik rose to his feet. Drizzle seemed like a no-show. Malik could only hope that his homie was alright. He reached inside his pants pocket and fingered the loose change. He went back into the school to use the pay phone. He called Drizzle's cell multiple times. No answer besides the voice mail. He left one message. "Fam, I'm at school waitin' on ya. Something must've come up. It's 3:15. In another five minutes I'ma bounce to the bus stop. The Capitol to Sherman and the 30 to Locust. Holla at ya boy."

Three different teachers greeted Malik as he walked down the hall and back outside. He was waiting for one of them to offer a ride. He planned to accept with the quickness. But none of them did. Why didn't he just let Prophet drop him off? Pride. Fuck pride now. He considered his travel route. Four blocks to the bus stop. A thirty or forty minute wait for the bus. Then due to overcrowding, he would probably be forced to stand during the entire bus ride. Sometimes life just sucked! School books in hand, Malik began his journey. As he walked up the block toward Capitol Drive, the idea of saving up some money to cop a car crossed his mind. Working a menial gig looked quite unattractive. He just couldn't see himself slaving for minimum wage. *Uncle Sam would want his cut too. It'll take forever to buy a ride.* Unless

Malik found a good job that paid 21st century wages? He had to think of something. His mother was already sweating him about going to college. Wasn't no need for her to because his mind was already made up to go. For what and to which one was another story.

Two blocks down. Two more to go. Halfway into the third one Malik saw Prophet's BMW bend the corner and speed in his direction.

"The police got Drizzle pulled over on 55th Street," Kila said out the car window. "Come on."

Nana swung open the back door and Prophet motioned him over. Malik got in.

Prophet asked if Drizzle had a driver's license.

"No doubt," Malik assured. "We both got ours at the same time last summer." He could only guess what the police were on.

Prophet parked on the opposite side of the street. Malik got out and jaywalked over to where the cops had Drizzle. He was anxious to see what was up. Drizzle sat in the back of a squad car. One officer stood by writing something on a notepad. His partner searched the Chevy.

Malik posted up near the entrance of a furniture store. He tried to decide what to do: approach the pigs and ask what was going on, or wait to see if they'd let Drizzle go?

The cop with the notepad spoke with Drizzle through the squad car window, then turned and asked Malik, "Do you know Mr. Cross?"

Malik stared at the short fat man. The question was asked in a really friendly manner—a little too friendly. Malik was about to walk off, until Drizzle nodded for him to come over.

Reluctantly, Malik strolled toward the officer. "What's up?" he asked.

"Mr. Cross is coming with us," the cop replied. "He wants you to take his car. If you don't, we tow it."

"What is he being arrested for?" Malik asked. Kila walked up and stood next to him.

"On a warrant for battery and assault with a dangerous weapon," he told Malik. "Are you taking his vehicle or not?" His rude attitude sprung out of nowhere.

A haunting feeling came over Malik. The other cop finished searching the Chevy and moseyed over.

"Where are the keys?" Malik asked the policeman. Anger and helplessness welled up inside him. He wanted to drill the pigs for more information. He wanted to snatch open the police car door, hoist Drizzle on his shoulders and spirit him away. He assumed the warrant had something to do with Jesse and the beat down they put on his crack head ass. Malik held his tongue. The cop might have his description too. He was handed the car keys. Malik stared at Drizzle through the car window. They exchanged brave nods.

Kila stepped up to the police car and told Drizzle to call her asap. One of the officers admonished her to stay back. She smacked her lips, rolled her eyes and walked off toward the Chevy.

"Where y'all takin' him?" Malik asked the police.

The short fat cop got inside the squad car. His partner said that Drizzle was on his way to the 7th district for booking, and afterwards out to the Juvenile Detention Center on Waterplank Road. Malik knew the location of the latter destination. His twin cousins were locked up there on numerous occasions in the past.

The police drove away. Malik stood at the curb staring at the back of Drizzle's head through the rear windshield. He started for the Chevy once the squad car disappeared in traffic.

Kila exuded angry Black girl attitude. "Battery?" she said.

Malik peered into the Chevy; stuff was in disarray. "They didn't have to tear his shit up like this." He picked up the CDs left gratuitously sprawled all over the seat and floor. The police was the holice.

"Straight up out of order," Kila complained.

Prophet rode up. "What they snatch him up for?" he asked out the window.

60

Malik said, "Something about a battery."

"Call and let me know what's up," Kila said, getting into the BMW.

"Holla at me if he need money for bail or anything," Prophet said.

"Alright," replied Malik. Nana again told him to call her later.

Malik slid in behind the wheel, started the Chevy and maneuvered into traffic. *What the fuck did Jesse's snitching ass tell the police? It's no way a milk crate constituted a dangerous weapon.* Malik was salty as hell.

CHAPTER 9

"Lizzy, please say you brought my penis pills and nudie books," Bobcat said as Liz entered the room. The old man was a resident at the nursing home she worked at, and his penis pills were Viagra that he wanted her to smuggle in to him.

Liz gave him a look of censure. "What I tell you about making those offensive requests?" she said, stuffing his bed linen into a laundry bag.

Bobcat sat there in the chair beside his bed with a devilish grin on his wrinkled face. "What's offensive about that?" He ran his lusting eyes over her and licked his chapped lips.

Liz spread clean sheets over his mattress. "Now do you want a write up for inappropriate behavior?" She finished making up the bed on the opposite side.

"I apologize, Lizzy." He sounded less than contrite. "I've been naughty and deserve correction." The grin came back. "Even worthy of a nice 'ol spanking."

"Keep it up!" Liz held back her giggle. She knew that Bobcat was just being Bobcat. He never meant any harm and her threats of a write-up were totally idle. She learned to appreciate him during the tedious work hours. His quirky behavior offered needed humor on certain days.

"I'm truly sorry," Bobcat said in a sincere tone. He crawled onto the bed, resting his back against the headboard. "I just get so lonely," he sighed deeply.

"Socialize with some of the other residents," Liz advised. "Stop being so anti-social."

His face flooded with color. "I don't have anything in common with these old hags around this dump!" he snapped. "Get out of my room, wicked lady," he demanded. Liz granted the old fella his wish. She double-checked the nametag on the bag, then tossed it in the laundry cart in the hallway.

Next stop: Tessa's room.

Liz found Tessa sitting in her wheelchair reading the Bible.

"Hello and God bless, young lady," she greeted Liz. The always sweet Tessa.

"Thank you," Liz smiled. "How are you today?" She began the same routine of gathering used linen and making up the bed with fresh sheets.

"I'm blessed," Tessa oozed with conviction. "The Lord is my sustainer, a very present help in trouble." That was just like Tessa. Always giving God the glory.

Liz checked the time. "It's a couple minutes til," she said and clicked on the television. She tuned into TBN. It was almost time for Tessa to watch T D Jakes program on the Christian station. Just a few days before, Tessa got so fired up in the spirit that she ended up falling clean out of her wheelchair. Liz had rushed in and found her laid out on the floor, dancing with the holy ghost and praising Jesus.

"Ms. Tessa, please be careful today," Liz said, wheeling her up to the TV. "We don't want you to have another accident. Gave me a scare last time."

Tessa smiled. "Why don't you watch with me," she suggested. "Can never get enough of the Word." She patted the worn Bible on her lap. "We need as much as we can get to get closer to God and ward off the wiles of ol' Satan."

"Not today," Liz replied. "I'll be heading home shortly, but maybe some other time."

Tessa reached out and grabbed Liz's right hand. A solemn expression came over the elderly Black woman's face. "Time can run out in an instant," she warned Liz. "You must be ready because He comes like a thief in the

63

night." There was pity in her brown eyes. "A thief in the night, chile, and all the old things that consumed our time will pass away."

Tessa turned her hand loose. Liz got the hell out of there. Tessa was trippin', she thought, dropping the laundry bag in the cart. She headed to her locker. The first half of her day was done. *Thank God!* Liz didn't have time to figure out what caused Tessa's weird behavior. *There's that word 'time' again,* the voices spoke up.

Liz grabbed her things and was out the door. "Gotta hurry up and get me another job soon as I graduate," she mumbled to herself.

CHAPTER 10

Malik found a parking spot a block over from the Milwaukee County Jail. Getting out of the Chevy, he fed coins into the meter and headed off. It had been years since he last saw his father in the flesh. He felt a feather of apprehension drop into his gut.

Approaching the corner of 9th and State, he jogged across the street, hoping not to encounter any obstacles. The so-called justice system continued to incite Malik's animosity. The last few weeks really left him plotting revolution. He'd taken three different trips out to the juvie detention center to visit Drizzle, and each time he was denied visitation. "Only immediate family are permitted and visitors under eighteen must be accompanied by an adult," was the stupid rule quoted. Malik couldn't convince the guy at the desk to let him slide. He left in frustration, then waited a couple of days before returning to give it another shot. Once again he was given the same drag, this time by a sistah who acted sympathetic but absolutely refused to bend the rule for him. Three days later, he went back and the guy was working again. This round, Malik knew the business, so he did a quick 180 and bounced.

Malik was salty. Drizzle hadn't called or contacted anyone yet. She-She was worried too. Malik checked on her daily, making sure she was all right and didn't need anything. He tried to get Janice, Drizzle's mother, to accompany him out to D.T., but this proved futile. Every single time Malik stopped by, Janice was either too high or deep in a coma-like sleep. Making herself presentable to visit her son seemed the last thing on her mind. Five days ago, Janice asked Malik for a loan, and he turned her down, knowing she wanted it to buy dope. She responded by offering him a sexual favor in exchange for the cash. Her proposition sickened Malik. Disgusted him! He'd felt like snapping on her, and quickly left the house before he did. A sad pity, he thought. Janice's addiction robbed her of all dignity.

"I need to see a valid state I.D.," a lady deputy told Malik at the reception desk. He handed her his driver's license.

"Here to see Kevy Freeman," Malik said. After she ran a check in the computer, she buzzed him in and handed back his I.D.

The whole process brought back memories of when he and Liz used to come see Kevy there. That seemed eons ago.

Malik walked through the metal detector unmolested. The waiting area told a familiar tale. Young women and their kids waited to see their relatives. Malik recalled this part well. He took a seat next to a Hershey-hued sistah. She had short neat dreadlocks and big brown eyes. Malik sensed a come up. He estimated her age range at early 20's. *A challenge*, he smiled inside. Her sweet perfume lingered. She smelt lovely. Malik leaned back in the plastic chair to get a less obvious gander at his future girlfriend. She sported a burgundy and white jogging suit and matching kicks. Underneath her gear, he imagined her to be well endowed. She had an unintentional beauty about her. She caught him checking her out and said, "You finally made it in, I see." her pretty lips adopting a partial smile.

"No doubt," he said, "that line can be Hades."

His reply made her smile complete. "Gotta get here early to beat the devil, I guess," she said.

This is action, Malik thought. "Maybe we can ride together next time or something," he suggested.

She laughed at him. "Slow down, brotherman, before you catch a speeding ticket."

"Tell me a good pace for you," Malik chuckled.

She took a hold of his hand, shook it, and introduced herself. "Hello, my name is Brianna. What might yours be?"

They both shared a light laugh. The vibe felt genuine.

"My fault," Malik said. "I guess I was smashing hard on the gas. I'm Malik. 'Lik for short."

66

"Thanks for sharing that bit of info," she said, with another heart-stopping smile.

"No doubt," Malik said. "Your man won't get salty over you shaking my hand, will he?" *Damn, I'm being too obvious,* he thought.

"I'm going to give you the benefit of the doubt," she said, giving him a knowing look, "and assume that question wasn't posed for nosy reasons."

He struggled to keep a straight face. "What ya mean?" he acted confused. "I was just—"

"Try'na be all up in my business," she finished for him. Malik's guilt-ridden grin acknowledged her accurate observation. What he really wanted to know and hear came next. "I'm single," she said. "Happily single."

With that information put out there, they fell right into more dialogue. Brianna spoke candidly which inspired Malik to do the same. She was there to see her mother, whose constant trips to jail stemmed from a decade-old drug addiction. Not a speck of shame came into her expression when she mentioned this. Brianna's love for her mom obviously ran deep. *Pain is love,* thought Malik, allowing the conversation to float into a less personal stream. Malik's curiosity created a free flow between them. She gave straightforward answers to his questions. She said that she currently attended Alverno College for cosmetology and business management. One of her ambitions was to run a chain of beauty salon/spas. Malik admired a sistah with vision. At age 19, Brianna was walking in hers, trying to work it to reality one step at a time. He started to lie when she asked his age. But he had to keep it real. He admitted he was 17 and went to Rufus King High School. This didn't disrupt their flow. He also confessed his uneasiness over seeing Kevy after so many years.

"Just relax and be yourself," she advised. "Your daddy will be happy to see you." They kicked it like old buddies for almost an hour. "Brianna Higgins," a deputy called out. "Visit."

Malik poised himself. He was just about to ask for her number before she beat him to the punch.

"I like your energy," she said. "I want you to call me." She got up to get something to write with. Malik met her halfway as she returned and handed him the digits. "Hit me up," she encouraged him.

"No doubt," he said. *You think I ain't, babygirl?* he gushed inside. His eyes were all over her as she entered the elevator. She threw up a peace sign and smiled his way before the doors closed.

Malik's nose was wide open already. Sucka fo' luv! He wanted to flip a cartwheel, hop up in the air, and click his heels. Brianna was fine as hell, smart and two years older; plus, she was feeling him.

A deputy's voice interrupted his internal celebration. Malik got up to go see his pops.

"What's up, lil souljah?" Kevy saluted once Malik put the phone to his ear. Concrete and a thick glass window separated father and son.

Malik was glad to see him. "Pops, you must be hittin' those weights hard," he said, admiring his bulky build. "You look swoll under that shirt." Kevy wore a bright orange county jail jumpsuit.

He pulled back a shirt sleeve and revealed a lumpy, chiseled bicep. He flexed muscle. "I need to stay fit and ready, ya dig?" he ghetto smiled. Then added "damn, boy, you've grown up on me." He studied Malik, proudly.

Malik grinned. "Mama said she'll visit you tonight after class." His uneasiness gave way to relaxation. They reconnected and discussed what was going on in each of their lives. Malik talked about his boredom with school, besides when he clashed with Mr. Ashcroft, and his undying vow to graduate and go on to college. He told Kevy about Drizzle, their fight with Jesse and about his new friend Brianna and how they'd just met. Kevy didn't judge or preach. He just listened and asked questions and made a couple suggestions. They kicked it.

After a while, Malik felt like he was monopolizing the conversation; his dad had barely gotten a paragraph in. Malik asked "what exactly is this court date for?" He wanted to give Kevy the floor.

"It's an evidentiary hearing," he said. "We don't expect much here, but it's part of the process."

"You alright, pop?" Malik asked. He thought he detected a hint of sadness in his father's disposition.

Kevy leaned sideways. The whole time he eyed Malik. "You do know that I never wanted to be in this position?"

The question sort of discombobulated Malik. The tone of it did. "What ya mean?"

"This position." He sat up and rested his elbows on the concrete slab in front of him. "My imprisonment. My absence from your life all these years. You needed me and I was cooped up in the joint."

Malik was at a loss for words. They'd never really touched on this subject before.

Kevy continued. "You're sitting there damn near a grown man, and I'm proud of that, seeing how well you've developed, but I'm also burdened from knowing that I wasn't there to watch you grow. Help you grow and become a man."

Malik shrugged. "Keeping it real," he said. "You been there for me more than some cats' fathers who aren't in prison. A lot of my guys don't have fathers at the crib. It's just a reality. I know in my heart you'd be there for me if you was free," and he spoke this from the heart.

"You know, it's cool to be upset with me," he said. "We can talk about it—deal with it now so it won't creep up later and get in the way of your future success."

"I'm more pissed at this system than anything," Malik said, "not with you at all."

"This system isn't all to blame," Kevy said. "I am too. I say this because I don't want you to fall victim to it like I did. We know that this beast don't care about us or our unification or elevation. They aim to keep us asleep. And kill us in our sleep. But, it's our responsibility to overcome. Doesn't matter who's to blame in the enemy's camp. If you fall in their trap, they're going to try to keep you there." Kevy tapped his temple with an index finger. "Use your mind and outthink them. Build your mind strong and cultivate consciousness, ya dig? Instead of getting bitter, get better."

69

"No doubt."

A deputy appeared behind Kevy. "Time to wrap it up," he said coldly.

Malik mugged him as he walked off. Kevy smiled at Malik's reaction. "Chill, souljah. It's all good."

He relaxed his mug. "Call me tonight."

"I will," he said. "And no matter what, I'm going to keep fightin' to get free. You stay focused out there. You're at that age where you'll start to see and experience a lot of new things. Some of it won't be good. May even test your entire belief system. It's up to you to maintain your balance and avoid the pitfalls. Prison isn't your fate, 'Lik. Remember that. Life is too full of possibilities to get wasted in a jail cell. Feel me?"

"Absolutely."

"You keep the lead and let the rest follow," he advised. "Drizzle sounds like a good comrade. Y'all maintain loyalty and help each other navigate those murky waters." Kevy stood. "I love you, son."

The phone went dead. They nodded their goodbyes, their eyes communicating the love. Kevy stepped out of the visiting booth, head high, confident stride, and complete composure. Even in chains, he sustained the posture of a king.

Malik left wishing his father was leaving with him.

CHAPTER 11

"Your glow gives you clean away, girl! Some man is touching you in all the right spots," Wanda blurted to Liz while they shopped. "That's why your fast tail been so hard to catch lately."

Liz glanced up the aisle. "Hush, girl." She hoped no one else heard her girlfriend's big mouth. "You don't know what you're talking 'bout." A guilty smirk landed across her face.

Wanda looked determined. "Who is he?"

Liz stopped her shopping cart next to a clothes rack. She picked up a burnt orange and turquoise blouse and looked it over.

Wanda snatched it from her. "You know damn well you're not interested in this hideous thing. Looks like something my nutty aunt Bettymae would wear." Back on the rack it went. "Good try though. Now who is he, what's his status, and how long have y'all been knockin' boots?"

Liz couldn't contain it. "Be quiet," she laughed, "before somebody hear you and think I'ma freak." A young white couple shopped nearby. They couldn't help but hear, although they acted like they didn't.

"Please," Wanda yapped. "Ain't a thang wrong with getting ya freak on. I bet whoevah's ear hustlin' right now get down and dirty themselves." She shot the couple a brazen look. They moved on.

Liz shook her head. "I betta go grab this hosiery before you get us kicked out of here." She steered her cart away.

Wanda was right on her heels "This conversation will continue in the car. I'll meet you up front in ten minutes. Gotta go get some cleaning supplies." She busted a U-turn and guided her cart away.

That woman is crazy sometimes, thought Liz. But she loved Wanda to death. Their friendship spanned almost three decades back, and while time and drama weakened most bonds, theirs only grew stronger. Wanda always stayed on the front lines with Liz. Kevy's imprisonment had sent her through all sorts of emotional changes. So-called family and friends turned their backs, acted funny. They were the same ones who'd kept their hands out begging for loans. The same folks who later gossiped about Liz and secretly celebrated when Kevy got popped off and convicted. Then acted 'holier than thou,' criticizing Liz behind her back. All of a sudden Kevy's hustle became so abominable. They sure seemed to have forgotten to pay back the dope money they saw fit to borrow. Liz didn't waste time trying to collect on the debts. Once upon a time she did expect some gratitude. A little sympathy would've been nice too. But naïve, foolish her. What she got were shrugs and cold shoulders. And abandoned like it wasn't nothing. And talked about like she wasn't nothing. An emptiness hollowed out her heart.

Wanda refused to take much pity on her either. Girlfriend wasn't havin' it at all. Her love toughened once Liz's depression became almost clinical. She snapped on Liz and kept snapping until Liz finally decided to snap out of her funk.

Fortunately, money never added to the burdens. Kevy had left Liz a hefty stash and fully-paid-for house. The depression had run deeper. Liz needed to achieve something for herself. So the first thing she did was get a part-time gig. Two employed months later, she still felt empty. Unfulfilled. She yearned for something more meaningful. A career. But a high school diploma was her only real credential. Wanda encouraged her to take a couple college courses. Liz said she would think about it. Wanda didn't see what there was to 'think' about. "Time to be about it," she told Liz upon showing up one morning. She kidnapped Liz and took her right down to M.A.T.C. to sign up. Liz enrolled and hadn't turned back since. Wanda's support never wavered. During all this, Liz realized what true sisterhood was all about and cherished the one they shared.

This was why it was nearly impossible to hide certain things from Wanda, especially when it came to men. So, soon after they left Wal-Mart, Liz cracked under pressure and confessed. She confided everything on the ride back to Wanda's house. She gave up the 411 on Marvin, their chemistry, the way he stimulated all her senses, the borderline addiction she sometimes felt for him, and her schizophrenic determination to kick the habit. Liz also mentioned the recent visit with Kevy and how it resurrected the guilt. And how that guilt vanished and lust took over that same night when she made a 'booty call' to Marvin.

"I'm feelin' him," Liz said, parking in Wanda's driveway. "But Malik is my main concern at the moment."

Wanda grabbed her shopping bags out the back seat.

"Now Marvin is interested in meeting Malik," Liz continued. " That's never going to happen."

"Why not?" Wanda wanted to know.

"'Cause that boy loves his daddy too much to let another man slide into position. I do not need the drama," she explained.

Wanda reveled in the confession up until now. Her expression shifted from contentment to discontent. Liz knew that look. A lecture was coming.

"I feel your concerns for 'Lik," Wanda said. "Just keep in mind your right to live your life…" A pause. "Look at you, Liz. You've gained momentum and the progress looks good on you. You wear it well. Kevy can't trip. You stuck it out with him longer than anyone I know would've had the patience to. Myself included." Another pause. Then, "You better treat yourself to what you deserve. Hell, you got it goin' on. 'Bout to finish college, got a brotha injecting some serious romantic intimacy back into your life… even got you glowin'." She sized Liz up with a smile. "You betta seize the opportunity. Ain't like we're young girls. An available, stable Black man is hard to find these days." A giggle. "He is a brothah, right?"

"You got jokes," Liz giggled.

"Not really," Wanda said. "No tellin'. I might end up…" she shook off the thought. "Nothing. We're on you. I'm not saying run off and marry Marvin. Just stay aware of fate and fortune, girlfriend." She opened the car door. "You never know. Malik might embrace the man, or at least tolerate his presence. If not, so be it. You're the mother, he's your child." She gathered her things and stepped out. "Call me later."

"Okay," Liz said. She waited for Wanda to get in the house before pulling off.

Heading home, Liz thought long and hard. Wanda kept it real. Liz couldn't refute that. Nor could she fully heed girlfriend's advice. There were too many unknowns. Too many questions that only time could answer. During the county jail visit with Kevy, he basically suggested she move on with her life. It was like he sensed her deception. Maybe noticed the glow? Liz glanced up into the rearview mirror... no glow that she could see. Wanda was crazy.

Then the issue with Malik and Marvin. Ain't no way in the world Malik was going to accept another man's presence in their lives. Liz held no doubt about that. And jeopardizing the bond with her son wasn't even an option. HELL to the NAW! The field of uncertainty was too risky to do battle on right now. Maybe the coast would be clear in a few years when Malik hit adulthood. Until then, things would stay on the low low with Marvin, she decided.

Liz rushed through the front door, not even bothering to lock it. Nature called, loudly. Bathroom door wide open, she planted her derriere on the toilet, released, and heard the phone ring. *Shit! As soon as I get on the damn toilet,* she complained, tempted to let it ring. Malik wasn't home yet, so she hurried up and finished her business. She answered the phone too late; the caller had already hung up. Liz star six-nined to no avail. "It figures." She took her shopping bags to the kitchen and started unloading the contents onto the table. Then she thought she heard a noise in the next room. "Malik?" There was no answer. "Malik?" she repeated. Still no answer. Only an eerie silence. Liz eased slowly out the kitchen.

"Boo!" Malik hopped out, almost giving her a heart attack.

"Boy!" Liz snapped, planting stiff blows to his arm and head. "Why yo' ass playin'!" she breathed. "Scared the hell outta me!"

He cracked up with laughter. "You're the one who left the door unlocked. Teach you a les—" he dodged a haymaker.

"I'm gon' hurt yo' ass," Liz threatened before returning to the kitchen. He followed her at a cautious distance.

74

Malik spotted the shopping bags and forgot all about the danger to his person. "What you buy me?" he rummaged through them. Liz reached in one and pulled out a job application.

"I brought you this." She handed it to him. "Fill it out and let me know if you need any help."

Malik's forehead wrinkled up. He glared at the paper like it was an arrest warrant. "No thank you," he said and tossed it on the table. "The kid don't work for a couple dollars."

"Better to work for dollars in freedom than for pennies in some prison," she pointed out.

The phone rang again.

"Get that phone," she ordered. "It's been ringing off the hook.

Malik casually answered, but hearing Drizzle's voice gave him a jolt.

"Nigga, what's up? Why haven't you called or flew a kite?" Malik blurted.

"Hey! Watch your mouth with that N-word," Liz yelled from the kitchen.

Drizzle told Malik about the allegations against him: battery and assault with a dangerous weapon, courtesy of Jesse's lies. "That nigga told the police I pistol whipped him and threatened to kill him," Drizzle said. "They had me in that detention center sick as hell. Fam', they only allowed calls to immediate family."

"I know. I've been sweating the hell out of them people," Malik said.

"Now I'm in this punk ass group home until I go back to court." He continued to clue Malik in. "That's in like two months. I'm not allowed weekend passes 'til they meet momz or a legal guardian. You know that's burnt up with my momz."

Malik listened, already devising plans in his head. Liz could pose as the legal guardian, he figured. Drizzle asked about She-She, school, Kila, his

75

car, and other things.   Malik let him know how deeply She-She and Kila missed him.

"They've both been bugging me to death about you," Malik said. "She-She is all good. I've checked on her daily." He didn't mention that Jesse was asleep on the couch the last time he went by there.

"I need you to bring me some clothes up here," Drizzle said. "Go by the crib and have She-She give you my gear and stuff."

After the call ended, Malik told Liz the situation. She was sympathetic, agreed to pose as Drizzle's mother, and said she'd give Malik some money for Drizzle in the morning. "I won't be able to go up there until next Saturday. I'll call before then.   Y'all work things out and let me know," she said.

Malik rushed out the door. He wanted to go tell She-She to get Drizzle's things together for tomorrow's visit. Malik couldn't wait to tell him about Brianna. *With her sexy chocolate self,* he thought as he drove down Center Street. She was sending him mixed signals, but he respected the chase. Brianna did have him by two years. They'd talk on the phone for hours, with Malik flirting here and there, even suggesting that they were soulmates, destined to be more than just friends. Brianna basically ignored answering him on this subject every time, which only strengthened his attraction to her. Over the last three weeks, since their first encounter, he'd upgraded his understanding of what kind of woman he wanted. Brianna had all the right qualities.

Nana Taylor seemed the polar opposite of Brianna. Within a week of Malik's reunion with Nana, she was more than willing to have sex. And during the act, Malik had no complaints. But he also noticed undesirable traits in her. She tried to be too slick and often bragged about other dudes who wanted her. She also befriended the guys she thought she could gain celebrity off of. Every time Malik tried to engage her in a deeper conversation, she reverted to silly shit like when they were kids sneaking in the basement. She gossiped too much, too. Always talking about people, who they were fucking, what kind of car rims some nigga had on his ride. Then her boasting about older men wanting to trick on her.   This left Malik wondering what she said

76

about him when he wasn't around. *Ain't no telling,* he thought, turning down Drizzle's block.

He pulled up and parked out front. A couple of shabbily dressed women had just stepped off the front porch. He stared as they hurried off down the street. "Who the heck they come to see?" he whispered and got out of the Chevy. *Must've had the wrong house.* He walked up and knocked on the door.

"Yeah, what 'ya spendin'?" someone asked from the other side.

Confused, Malik checked to make sure he had the right house. The voice couldn't have belonged to Jesse; it sounded too young. "Who is that? Is She-She or Janice home?" Malik asked tentatively.

Silence. Then muffled whispers. Malik leaned forward trying to hear until someone began unlocking the door. An unfamiliar face appeared in the doorway. He looked a few years older than Malik.

"Yeah. Come on in, my guy. I'm Jesse's nephew," he introduced himself.

Malik felt a bad vibe as he stepped inside the house. The smell of weed hit his nose. Three guys sat on the living room floor, playing Sony Play Station, talking shit, sharing a blunt, and laughing. She-She walked out the back with a frown on her face. "'Lik, can you take me to get something to eat?" she asked with attitude.

"Derrick, I'm smashing this nigga," one of the video game players bragged to Jesse's nephew, never taking his concentration off the TV screen.

Derrick ignored the braggart and stared at She-She.

"You need some money, She-She?" he said before adding, "I would've took you to get something to eat." He pulled out a thin bankroll. She-She rolled her eyes and marched out of the house. A black firearm lay on the floor next to the video game console. Malik put two and two together, and instantly felt a disdain for all four dudes. He tried to mask his anger. Derrick must have picked up on it, because he went to explaining. "Jesse and Janice are in the back, probably asleep. I'm helping out 'round here with the bills and shit," he said. Malik was speechless.

77

A man appeared on the front porch. His skin was ashy and he had a vacant look in his glassy, bloodshot eyes. Malik stepped to the side as Derrick invited the man in. "What's up?" Derrick asked him.

"Can I get six for fifty dollars?" asked the addict.

Derrick nodded, whipped out a sandwich bag, and selected six crack rocks from it. The dope fiend handed him the money, Derrick handed him the dope and told him to spread the word. The fiend nodded and hid the six dime bags under his tongue, then left.

Malik wanted to snatch the pistol off the floor and clear out the house. He couldn't believe this. "Where is Janice?" The indignation in Malik's voice got Derrick and his boys' attention. They stared at Malik with a mixture of suspicion and hostility. Derrick said something but Malik was already heading for the back room. Janice's bedroom door was shut. Malik didn't bother knocking. He pushed it open and couldn't believe his eyes. Jesse had a crack pipe in his mouth, and Janice was on her knees giving him a blowjob. Malik held his breath, afraid he'd inhale the putrid crack fumes. Janice continued her oral activities, not even noticing Malik's presence. Jesse snatched up his pants. "You don't know how to knock, young muthafucka?"

All this was too much for Malik. He tore out of the house, angry and annoyed. She-She stood by the Chevy with her head down. Malik chirped the alarm, and they got inside. "How long this bullshit been going on?" he asked her, cranking up the engine. She hunched her shoulders.

"You're not staying here," Malik resolved. "Go get you and Drizzle's stuff!"

"I'm not going back in there," she said defiantly, and teared up. "Jesse stole my brother's stuff anyway!"

Malik got out and marched back up to the house.

This time Jesse answered the door, sneering at Malik as he pushed past and stomped to She-She's room. Malik tossed as many of her things on the bed as possible, wrapped the bed sheet around them, and swung it over his shoulder. Janice stumbled every inch of her pitiful self into the room and asked, "What ya doin', Malik?" She floated high as a kite.

"She-She's staying with me. She don't need to be around all this garbage!" Malik yelled. Janice started to fade out. Malik caught her by the arm and walked her to the bed. She sluggishly opened her eyes. Malik gave her a look that could've shamed Satan. "Do you even care that your son is locked up because of that nigga out there?" he asked her. She remained withdrawn. A spacey look played on her face. With slurred speech, she said, "I'ma go see my baby. I need some money for cab fare. Can you give me a few dollars?" A sparkle of life flashed in her eyes.

"That lil nigga in jail 'cause of his damn self," Jesse stood in the doorway saying, "not cause of me." His words poured gasoline on Malik's outrage. Derrick stood right behind his uncle. Malik didn't conceal his disgust as he stormed back out of the house.

In the Chevy, about to pull off, Malik was stopped by a knock on the driver window. Derrick stood there gesturing for him to lower the glass. Malik got out the car instead and closed the door. They stepped to the rear of the car.

"What's up?" Malik glared.

Derrick scanned the vicinity and swiftly upped a gun. He pointed it at Malik's midsection. Threats leapt off his tongue.

"Check this out, stud," he sneered. "If the po-po just so happen to come through here, ain't no secret who tipped 'em off, so you can believe I'll be to see yo' bitch ass if they do."

Malik's anger averted his fear. He didn't budge. He stared Derrick down hard.

A wicked smirk formed on Derrick's lips. He tucked the gun in his waistline and strutted back toward the house.

Malik got in the Chevy and smashed out.

CHAPTER 12

"Malik, I still need to speak with her mother," Liz told her son. He retreated to his bedroom, closing the door behind him. Liz sensed that something had happened. And whatever it was, it left her son deeply troubled. She heard it in his voice and read it on his face as soon as he burst in the house with the young girl. He'd introduced her, saying, "This is 'Dre's little sister, She-She," and that she needed to stay with them for the night, maybe longer. Liz didn't mind the girl spending the night—or nights—at all. But she did want to know what was going on.

Liz went and stood by Malik's bedroom door. Vaguely hearing him talking, she assumed that he was on the phone.

She-She sat on the sofa. She looked uncomfortable, almost embarrassed, and had a hard time looking Liz in the eyes.

"Have you eaten dinner yet?" Liz asked, her motherly instincts kicking in. "You hungry?" she smiled to help the girl relax and hopefully cheer up.

"Yes, Ma'am, I'm a little hungry." She spoke in a low, respectful tone.

"Come on, let's whip something up," Liz said. "And you can call me Liz, Auntie—anything but ma'am. That ma'am stuff gives us too much distance and makes me feel old."

She-She smiled and followed Liz into the kitchen. The hospitality disarmed her some.

"Cut on the radio," Liz gestured toward the counter. She-She turned it on. An Al Green oldie played out of the small speakers. She-She took a seat at the table, while Liz rummaged through the freezer. "We got chicken nuggets, pizza, and—" she thought for a second, then went to the pantry, searching for other options.

She-She chose the pizza.

"That's what I was thinking myself," Liz said. She got out a pan and turned on the oven. She-She, a noticeable tremor in her voice, told her "Thank you."

80

Malik came into the kitchen. "Ma, I'll be back in a minute. I need to make a quick run." He looked less upset but more focused. He turned and addressed She-She.

"Make sure you put together an outfit," he said. "I want to get an early start in the morning to see your brother." He zipped up his jacket, then adjusted the skully on his head.

Her face lit up with a blissful smile. "Okay." She sat up higher in the chair. She-She's whole demeanor betrayed the crush she had on Malik.

"Eleven o'clock," Liz reminded him of his curfew. "And make sure She-She's mom has my number."

"I'll go over there tonight," Malik said, then recanted, saying, "or, I mean, tomorrow. I'll stop over there tomorrow. Right after I visit Dre."

Liz's sensors went off. Something was definitely up. "Lik, is everything alright?" she asked.

"Yeah," he said, looking away, heading out the kitchen. Liz watched him walk out of the house. Malik didn't look back.

CHAPTER 13

"License and registration?" the portly cop said, standing outside the Chevy in M.P.D. uniform. Malik had just turned off his block when police lights flashed behind him. He assumed the music had gotten their attention. "What's the problem, officer?" he asked, handing his license out the window.

He shined a flashlight on Malik, then on his I.D. "Sit tight," he said, and walked off.

The fight with Jesse flashed across Malik's mind. Jesse could have lied on him, too; maybe even reported the description and plates on the Chevy. Malik stared into the side mirror. What would the squad computer say? He tapped on the steering wheel with both hands, glanced in the rearview and side mirrors repeatedly, and mentally assessed the possibilities. What if Derrick and Jesse worked up a scheme that quick? Malik took a couple of deep breaths and leaned back. He didn't have anything to fret over, he told himself. Perhaps the traffic stop was an omen.

Before Malik had left the house, he'd called up his twin cousins, Brandon and Brian, and put them up on what had transpired at Drizzle's house. Malik knew that the twins wouldn't appreciate Derrick's threats, especially the part about the pistol. Brian had urged Malik to come over right away. The malice in his voice calmed Malik's anger but it also indicated Brian's intention. Malik comprehended the consequences of involving his cousins. They were both 'bout that life.

Liz prohibited Malik from hanging around the twins. She'd heard all about their lifestyle and street shenanigans. She also knew their tragic history. When the twins were a mere six years old, their parents were brutally murdered. This forced Kevy's mother to try to raise Brandon, Brian and their baby sister. The younger girl was only a toddler at the time of the home invasion/robbery. But the twins were old enough to understand what had happened after waking up to the sounds of their mother's screams and multiple gun shots. Brandon, the older twin, was the one who made it to the bedroom first. He discovered his mother and father soaked in a pool of blood, in bed, their lifeless bodies twisted on top of one another. In the years that followed, the family watched as the twins grew into little hell-raisers. By the time the boys hit their teens, they were both full blown gangstas. Malik remembered the many nights Liz woke him out of his sleep because something crazy had happened at his granny's house. It was constant drama that had direct links to the twins. Police and enemies alike showed up, the latter shooting bullets in the house on two different occasions. Things eventually became so hectic that the twins decided to move out on their own. Peace had prevailed at their grandmother's house ever since, and the family had breathed a collective sigh of relief.

Now at age 20, the twins lived together on the lower east side of town. They lived ghetto fabulous and their names rang heavily throughout the city. The family knew that their main source of income came through drug dealing, and they had basically accepted it. No one wasted their breath trying to preach to the boys. They were who they were. And in the streets they were respected. The twins' ruthless reputations followed them from the bricks to jail, from jail back to the bricks. The official word was *Don't fuck with those wild ass Freeman twins 'cuz the niggas will sweat something.*

Malik never witnessed his cousins demonstrate in the game, but he was well aware of their philosophy on life. Malik also knew the inevitable drama they'd bring to Derrick and anyone with him. All this really began dawning on him as he sat waiting for the policeman to return. Second thoughts crystallized in his mind.

The cop reappeared. "You can go," he told Malik, handing over his driver's license. He sounded disappointed.

"Why did you pull me over?" Malik asked

He walked off, saying, "I racially profiled you. Write the NAACP, buddy," and got back in his squad car.

"Bitch ass," Malik mumbled as the pig rode past and down the street.

Shifting from 'park' back into 'drive,' Malik pushed out. The traffic stop might've been a blessing in disguise. *Or a forewarning*, he considered.

As he approached the eastside, his mind went into deliberation. He thought about Kevy and what prison must be like. He thought about Liz and how hurt she'd be if he ever got arrested. He thought about Drizzle, She-She and Brianna—all his friends, his family, his future, his freedom. He imagined himself locked up in some little bathroom-sized jail cell. Kevy often mentioned the courts' eagerness toward convicting teenagers as adults and shipping them to prisons. Malik's stomach constricted, chills slithering down his spine at the prospect of being incarcerated. "Fuck that," he spoke out loud, turning onto the twins' block. He kept right on driving past their house. The traffic stop, the doubts that surfaced, the potential for prison… it was all enough to change his mind. He'd wait and talk with Drizzle about the Derrick issue. Drizzle had a gangsta edge to him too, but Malik saw it more as a defensive gangsta. The twins were straight gangsta—offensively, defensively, and spitefully. Malik didn't see himself as a gangsta nor did he want to be.

Halfway back home, Malik felt the urge for feminine company. Brianna's was preferable, but Nana's house was a lot closer. He wondered if Nana's mind was functional tonight. He doubted it. His hormones sent him horny signals though. He dipped the car over into a gas station and parked next to the pay phone. He leaned out the window, grabbed the receiver, dropped coins in the slot and dialed. It rang. He fell back in the seat and leaned sideways. Drizzle's demo grinded in the CD player.

A beat-up black Monte Carlo slowed to a stop at a red light next to the gas station. The two occupants inside stared at the Chevy. Malik eyed them, then the huge dent in their passenger door, then them again. *Guess they're lovin' the young Chevy on spinners*, he figured, as Nana picked up.

"State ya business," she said.

The light turned green, and the Monte Carlo drove off, its cranky exhaust groaning loudly.

"You tell me the business," Malik replied.

"'Lik?" She sounded hopeful.

"A.K.A. ya sucka fo' luv," he smiled.

Nana's voice grew cheerfully soft. "Baby, I was just laying here fantasizing about your fine ass." An Alicia Keys slow jam played in the background. Malik's hormones yelled: *We told you so!*

Nana and Malik flirted back and forth for the next five minutes. Then Malik thought he saw a shadow outside the driver window. The side mirror reflected someone creeping up on the side of the Chevy! Malik's heart tightened inside his chest when he saw the chrome gun barrel.

"You move you die young," the carjacker sneered, sticking his weapon through the window. He yanked open the door. "Out!"

"Wait brotha!" Malik dropped the phone. "Don't kill me. You can have—"

He snatched Malik out of the car. "Fuck that, get the fuck flat," he snarled, shoving Malik to the pavement. Malik laid and obeyed him.

The carjacker hopped inside the Chevy and burnt rubber out of the lot and down the street.

Malik felt helpless. It took a moment for him to gather himself. He couldn't believe it; he got poked! Rising to his feet, he stared around. An old white man pumped gas into a Blazer a few feet away. Judging by the look on the man's face, Malik knew he had no idea what had just happened. His gaze zoomed in on Malik. Suspicion sprang into his eyes as he replaced the nozzle and quickly got in his Blazer. Malik understood. He didn't approach him for help. He turned toward the pay phone; the receiver dangled on its metal cord. Malik snatched it up.

"Nana?" he said.

"Damn, nigga, what the hell?" she bitched.

He yelled into the phone, "I just got robbed." He was on the verge of tears.

"For Drizzle's Chevy?" she asked. Her stupidly insensitive question further pissed him off. She didn't bother asking if he was alright. *Just like a car worshippin' broad*, he thought.

Click.

After hanging up in her face, he dropped some change in the phone and dialed home. It rang once, and he hung up. His mother had just warned him last week about driving around with the expensive rims and loud music,

85

courting so much attention. He didn't want to hear her "I-told-your-ass" lecture.

Malik slowly dialed Brianna's number. She answered on the second ring. Set at ease to hear her voice, he briefed her on the robbery.

"Oh my God," she gushed with concern. "Are you okay, 'Lik?"

"I'm cool," he said, feeling better already. "Just a little shook up and stranded at Gas 'n Go."

"Call my cell," she urged, "so I can talk to you while I come pick you up."

Malik ran in the gas station to get change for a dollar. He came back out and called her cell and constantly surveyed the area for any more signs of danger.

By the time Brianna pulled up, she had Malik smiling. She got right out of her Nissan Maxima and hugged him. Her affection was right on time. They got in the car and left.

Malik reclined in the passenger seat and recapped his crazy day for her. She drove and listened. He told her about the call from Drizzle, the encounter with Derrick, and the traffic stop. She shook her head sympathetically, repeatedly glancing over at him. Details about the carjacking made her sigh deeply. She had this knack for getting him to relax and open up. Usually, he'd safeguard all knowledge about Drizzle's home situation. Liz was told only the bare minimums. Everyone else never got an iota of info out of him. But here he was confiding so much in a woman he'd met not too long ago.

Brianna parked in front of her apartment building. "Come on," she said. They got out of the car. Malik followed her inside, wondering how he would get out to visit Drizzle the next morning. The prospect of dropping more bad news on his homie disheartened Malik. He took a deep breath, thinking, *when it rains, it pours too heavy.* Brianna led him inside her pad. This was the first time she invited him in, and Malik was quite impressed. Brianna's place was decked out with a creamy leather pit set, big flat screen TV, plants, little African knick-knacks, polished end tables, and accentuating throw rugs on beautiful hardwood floors; DVDs and CDs lay neatly stacked on top of the sound system. "Make yourself at home," she said, picking up a remote. She aimed it at the stereo.

Malik cloaked his surprise and curiosity. Jill Scott's 'Beautifully Human' CD began to play. Malik scanned the living room walls decorated with portraits of famous Black people. He admired the afrocentric motif. He also felt conflicted, thinking about the black males who had victimized him earlier.

"You hungry?" Brianna asked from the kitchen.

"Depends," he said, stepping into the kitchen. "Do you know any voodoo?" he joked.

"Voodoo?" she said. "Please. I know you don't believe in all that?" She opened the fridge.

Malik's gaze fell on her little plump rear end. She bent down and got a pan out of a counter drawer. Malik saw a panty line print in her jeans. He sat down at the table after feeling a rise between his legs. "I'm not paranoid or nothing," he replied after she caught him stalking. "I just remember when my auntie got mad at my uncle one day, and the next thing he knew, he had erectile dysfunction. Word is she put a hex on ol' Unc's stroker. So you tell me."

Brianna opened a box of frozen fish sticks. "I can't tell you much about that," she said. She spread the fish sticks out on the pan. "But you needn't worry about me. I have no beef with you or your little dude."

"Why it gotta be little?" he grinned.

She slid the pan in the oven. "Be back in a minute," she said and left the kitchen. She disregarded his question like she hadn't heard a word he'd said. He didn't trip though. He was making progress. He got the invite inside the apartment and already had her cooking a little something-something for him. That had to mean something. He got up and strolled back into the living room. Brianna lived in a nice neighborhood, in a nice apartment, drove a nice car, and clearly could afford nice things. *But how?* He wanted to know. Her part-time job at the telecommunications company must pay real handsomely. Malik knew better. A woman going to college, working part-time with no man

87

and independently living on her own? There had to be something Malik was missing. It seemed too tacky and nosey of him to ask her straight out. He cut on the TV and surfed the channels.

"Malik, keep an eye on those fish sticks for me," Brianna called from a back room. He went to the kitchen and opened the oven. The smell rushed his nose and provoked his hunger. The fish sticks still had some time to cook. Malik walked out the kitchen and turned left down a hallway. He came upon a bedroom with the door ajar and lights on. He stepped inside. It resembled an office. A computer sat on a small desk beneath a bookshelf that spanned the wall. Malik sat in the comfortable desk chair and studied the book titles.

"What you doin', dude?" Brianna snuck up behind him. He almost fell out of his seat. She'd scared him on purpose.

"Girl!" he said, gathering himself. "You spooked the heck out of me." She laughed at his fright, leaning into his chest. He liked her touching him. He really dug the shorts and night shirt she'd slipped into. He sure needed condoms—just in case. They were in the Chevy, unfortunately.

"You're going to report that car stolen?" Brianna handed him the phone.

"So this is how you look in your nightwear," he smiled slyly.

She walked out the room, basically brushing him off once again. Malik wasn't deterred. Sooner or later her feet would get tired of running… from him. He called the police to report the car stolen.

CHAPTER 14

Liz tapped her pen against the notepad. It was hard to focus on the letter to Kevy. Her mind was elsewhere. Malik hadn't made his curfew or called, and she was concerned. The time on her little clock radio read 1:20 a.m. This wasn't like Malik at all. The girl Nana called earlier and said that someone stole Andre's car. Liz figured Malik told Nana that to cover his tracks. He would have called home first if anything like that really happened. Liz's concern deepened into worry as she sat up in bed considering the possibilities.

Something else bothered her. Kevy's nephew, Brian, had called about an hour after Nana. He wanted to know if Malik had left yet. Liz wondered why Malik planned to visit the twin's house. And why hadn't Malik mentioned this before he'd left? Her curiosity was fast turning into suspicion, adding on to her worries. The question echoed in her head. *Why was Malik going to see the twins?* She didn't like him hanging around them whatsoever. Brandon and Brian were double trouble, prone to violence and dealing in the dope game. All things she wanted Malik far away from.

Liz started calculating in her head. When Malik came in the house with She-She, he'd said little and shot right to his room and closed the door. *And got his ass on the phone. And apparently called the twins.* Now that she thought about it, Malik was acting really secretive earlier before he left. Liz's heart rate increased, as something else dawned on her. After Malik left, Liz and She-She had eaten their food and talked. She-She opened up and told Liz about her and Andre's home situation, about how bad their mother was on drugs, and about the fight Malik and Andre had with Jesse, her mother's boyfriend. Malik never bothered to let Liz know about the fight. She-She also went on to tell Liz about Malik's angry reaction to finding Jesse's nephew, Derrick, selling drugs out of the house. It upset Liz that Malik said nothing to her about any of this. The fight with Jesse—a grown ass man—happened over a month ago. Malik had had ample time to tell her, and didn't. Liz tossed aside the pen and notepad, the tension thickening inside her.

Why the hell did he contact the twins? Liz got up... thinking, suspicions mounting. Brandon and Brian were gunslingers... thugs. Liz shuddered to think of her baby getting turned out. *Something isn't right*, she thought, springing into action. She snatched up the phone and found the twins' number in the caller ID. She dialed earnestly and paced the bedroom floor.

"What the fuck?" Brian answered on the seventh ring, frustrated by the disturbance to his sleep.

Liz cut to the chase. "Where's my baby?" she said. "Where is Malik? What happened to him?" Her barrage of questions sounded accusatory, anxious—almost desperate.

"Auntie?" Brian asked.

"Yes," she said. "Malik isn't home yet and the last you told me he was supposed to come over y'all house. Where is he?" She braced herself for bad news. Her emotional state was in a frenzy.

"He never made it," Brian claimed. "Brandon and me waited damn near two hours for him. That's why I called you, remember?"

She disregarded the irritation in his tone. "Why did my son call?" she asked. "Why was he coming over there?"

"Calm down, auntie," Brian sounded hesitant. "He was just stoppin' over, I guess."

He wasn't being truthful. "Don't lie to me, Brian," she said. "I know he called about that boy upsetting him earlier." Liz's lie was justified. "So why did he want y'all to know and what exactly did he say?"

Brian stalled.

"What's goin' on?" Liz pressed.

He exhaled and told her. It was just what she'd suspected... except of course the part about Derrick having a gun. Liz felt a deep penetrating ache when she learned that Malik was threatened. Her brain reeled; she got dizzy. *What if they hurt my baby!* The room spun. Liz paced the floor, then fell back on the bed, feeling slightly faint. *Oh my God, what if my baby's been hurt!* she panicked. Suddenly an overwhelming anger surged within her. She wanted to know what was going on and right now. She got to her feet.

"You mean he hasn't called home?" Brian asked.

"No," she snapped. "So tell me what the hell is—"

"We're on our way over there." Brian hung up the phone.

She-She stood in the doorway, looking concerned.

"Auntie, is Malik okay?" she asked.

The question boosted Liz's anxiety. "Why didn't you tell me about that boy pulling a gun on Malik?"

Dismay leapt into She-She's eyes. "I didn't know," she wailed. "I seen a gun but never saw Derrick point it or pull it on Malik."

Regret swam over Liz. She didn't mean to snap on her. "I'm sorry."

"That's alright." She-She became teary-eyed. "Is Malik alright?"

"Everything will be fine." Liz thought about what to do next. "Write down your home address." She gestured toward the pen and notepad on the bed.

She-She jotted down the info. Liz pulled on jeans, a blouse, and a pair of kicks, then called Wanda.

"I'm coming over," Wanda said before Liz could finish telling her what was going on.

The twins showed up twenty minutes later. Their hardened expressions and heavy leather jackets gave Liz an ironic sense of security. The boys weren't about to bullshit with finding Malik's whereabouts. At the moment, Liz needed to feel their strong energy.

Wanda arrived minutes later and volunteered to stay at the house with She-She.

Liz pulled on her coat and followed the twins out of the house. They climbed into Brandon's Caddy truck and set out for the destination.

91

Liz planned to play no games. Somebody was going to tell her where Malik was. She wanted answers, and by any means necessary, she would get them. Tonight! "Where's the gun?" she asked from the back seat.

The twins glanced at each other, speechless. Brandon made a right onto Dre's block. Liz impatiently leaned forward over the front seat and patted around Brian's waistline area.

"What's up, auntie?" Brian laughed, surprised at her.

"I'm not slow," she said, feeling the steely lump under his clothes. She reached in his coat, lifted his shirt and took a hold of a rather large pistol. Its heaviness didn't intimidate her. She wanted answers.

Brandon slowed down in front of a rundown house. The whole block looked dark, foreboding.

"This should be the house right here," he said. He studied the address on the paper Liz gave him. "Yeah, this is it."

Liz searched for Andre's Chevy. Brian bent down and retrieved a small gun out a stash spot in the dash. Brandon drove up the street and parked. They simultaneously exited the SUV. Liz clinched the gun handle inside her coat pocket, as they marched toward the house.

"Hold fast, auntie," Brandon cautioned once they approached the porch. "We still need to be on point," he said. Liz pushed past him, ascended the stairs to the front door, knocked and rang the bell. The twins clicked the safeties off their guns and cloaked them inside their jackets. Liz gripped her weapon tighter, wondering how many guns the twins carried at one time. She kept hers tucked away.

There wasn't an answer at the door.

Liz banged on it this time. She was all hyped up and wanted answers.

"Ain't shit else poppin' till tomorrow," someone yelled from inside the house. The voice spoke aggressively—clearly a man's.

Brandon stepped in front of Liz, saying, "Say, Drizzle asked me to drop this loot off to his mother or little sister."

A pause.

"It's late as hell to be—" the doorman complained, opening the door, "coming by," he continued before seeing them standing there. They invited themselves inside.

"Come on in," the man said sarcastically. "Janice!" he called toward the back and looked across the living room where another guy was on a couch waking up. "Derrick, get up," the doorman said quickly.

Derrick rose up and stared timidly at the twins. He tried to ease toward the floor model TV. Liz spotted a gun on top of it. Brian accosted Derrick, gun drawn. Derrick froze in his tracks. "Too much movement, nigga," Brian warned and pushed him back on the couch. "Keep yo' soft ass real still or I'll help you to."

Brandon walked over and grabbed the gun off the TV.

"What is going on here?" the doorman wanted to know. He looked bewildered.

"I take it you're Jesse?" Liz asked him. She stood closest to him. She stepped back, clinching the gun in her pocket. Before the doorman could confirm that he was in fact Jesse, Brian was directing Derrick to the floor. Derrick went crashing onto worn carpet after he hesitated for just a moment longer than necessary.

"And I assume you're the punk Derrick who upped on my little cousin earlier?" Brian interrogated. Derrick choked in answering, clearly strangled by fear. Brian asked him, "Is that the gun, coward?" and kicked Derrick, then leveled his cannon on him.

Brandon stepped next to Liz, mugging Jesse.

"Janice!" Jesse yelled out.

"Where is my son?" Liz asked. She watched Jesse closely, then eyed Derrick.

"Janice!" Jesse called out again.

93

"What is it, baby?" Janice asked, walking into the room groggily. A raggedy nightgown hung tenuously off her painfully thin frame.

"Are you She-She's mother?" Liz asked. Janice stared around at everyone.

Brian clucked Derrick on the head with his gun. "I said be still," he snarled. Derrick groaned.

"What the hell is—" Jesse snapped. Brandon aimed his weapon and Jesse calmed down swiftly. "Be cool," Brandon told him coldly. "Too much movement will get you cut down," he admonished.

Jesse slumped his shoulders and gazed nervously toward Derrick.

Janice acted oblivious to the situation. "Yeah, I'm She-She's mama," she addressed Liz. "Who you?"

"Malik's mother," Liz said. Jesse flinched and froze up. Liz caught him and Derrick exchanging quick glances. The twins gave them the evil eye. An ominous silence passed through the living room where they stood.

"She-She is at my house," Liz spoke up. "And my son isn't."

She looked at Derrick. He lay cramped over on the floor holding his abused head, avoiding eye contact with Liz. Jesse avoided eye contact as well. The twins stood poised over both men, waiting on Liz's call. Liz's sweaty hand still clinched the gun in her pocket; she tightened the grip, bringing her attention back to Janice.

"Did Malik come back over here after he left with She-She?" she asked, tempted to display her weapon.

"No," Jesse spoke up quickly.

"He never came back through here," Derrick seconded, speaking up for the first time.

Brian yanked him by the shirt collar and dragged him over to Jesse. "Shut up and bring your soft ass here. I'm leaning toward letting the air out of you."

94

Jesse moved, and Brandon helped him to the floor with a pistol smack to the chin. Brian stomped Jesse in the stomach, then kicked Derrick. "You upped on my cousin, sissy?" he grilled them.

"It wasn't like that!" Derrick pleaded. Brandon punched blood from his mouth.

Liz was ready to leave. The situation was getting too crazy. "Wait, y'all," she said to the twins as they continued punishing their victims. "Let's go, right now." She pulled Brian away. Janice looked petrified. Brian's entire body, his every feature and gesture indicated a murderous desire. He wanted to kill. Liz felt it so strongly coming from him that she started shaking. She didn't let Brian's jacket go until he was by the door. Brandon came along on his own.

Janice stared at the whole thing in total silence. Jesse and his nephew sat awfully still on the floor. They knew they were narrowly escaping death.

"Next time one of you think about touching or threatening my son in any way, you better kill yourself first," Liz warned.

Brian started back toward them, prepared to inflict more brutality. Brandon stopped him. Brian made his disappointment obvious. Derrick's and Jesse's faces begged for mercy. The only movement on them was the sweat beading on their foreheads. Liz grew angrier but kept it to herself. She told Janice that she meant her no harm. Janice nodded.

"I'll send She-She home tomorrow," she said, then led the twins out the door. They rushed up to the Escalade truck and got inside. Brandon started the engine.

"Wait," Liz said, spotting Janice footing it up to the SUV.

"I'm sorry," Janice uttered weakly through the back window. She looked pitiful, standing there barefooted, in the same tattered nightgown.

Brandon slammed the gear into drive.

"Please keep my baby safe," Janice told Liz. "She don't need to come back around this. Tell her I love her. I'll come get her when I get straight—I

95

mean get clean," she stuttered. "The devil is getting the best of me right now. I need time to get back to God."

"Auntie, we gotta bounce," Brian cut in. "Them cats might be on something."

Janice's gaze locked on Liz's. The woman looked beat, defeated. Liz started to invite her into the truck.

"We're ghost," Brian said, scanning the block.

"I'll take care of She-She," Liz called out the window as Brandon smashed off, leaving Janice standing alone on the curb.

"That broad should be ashamed of herself," Brian said. He stashed the gun back in the dash.

Liz handed over the other one. "She is," she said more to herself than to him. They rode back to the house in silence. Oddly enough, Liz's thoughts reviewed Tessa's last impromptu sermon about "time" and "God" and "Satan." Plus, the eerie look, the sadness in Tessa's eyes favored Janice's tonight.

Brian's cell phone chimed. "Hello," he answered. Brandon had just parked behind Liz's car. "Hold on." He handed her the phone.

"Malik?" Liz said.

"Yeah, Ma," he said. Liz breathed normally for the first time in hours.

CHAPTER 15

"Where are you at, boy?" Liz breathed in Malik's ear. His mother sounded pissed but also relieved.

Malik swallowed air. "I'm at a friend's house." He walked to the kitchen. Brianna was asleep on the couch, and he didn't want to wake her.

"It's almost three o'clock in the damn morning. Get your ass home right this minute."

"Hold on, Ma." "I lost track of time."

"You don't lose this much track of time, 'Lik—"

"I got robbed," he blurted louder than he meant to. He looked into the living room, then walked over to the kitchen sink. "I got carjacked and my friend came to get me."

Liz didn't say anything to that. Silence. Malik had played his trump card.

"They jacked me at the gas station on 55th and Center," he added.

Silence.

"Hello?" he said.

"Where are you, Malik?" Liz's tone softened. "What is your friend's address?"

He had planned to stay over at Brianna's house till daybreak. This wasn't even an option now. He didn't dare suggest it. "I'll get dropped off," he said.

"No, you won't," Liz said. "I'm with Brandon and Brian. We've been out looking for you." Wanda had already informed Malik of this. "What is that address?" Liz asked. "We're coming to get you right now."

Malik gave it to her and they hung up. He took a seat at the kitchen table. *Trouble wasn't the word.* The gravity in Liz's voice forecasted major drama. He shook his head and released a deep breath, slumping back in the

97

chair. *Nana's big mouth*, he lashed out, thinking about Wanda's mention of "a girl calling" saying, "The car got stolen." Malik checked his thoughts and got up. He was just looking for someone else to blame and be mad at besides himself. Nana held no responsibility for him staying out so late.

He went to wake up Brianna. He stood near the couch admiring the sleeping beauty. The TV screen gave off the only light in the dim living room. It shined on her. She looked so peaceful curled up sleeping there. He studied her gorgeous face, her locks, her pretty little feet. The last four or five hours they'd spent together were special. She'd cooked him a little meal of fish sticks and cheesy macaroni: treated him to first rate hospitality. The mood had taken a hold of Malik once they kicked back on the living room rug, listening to music and conversing. With Usher singing about how he 'got it bad,' Malik got so caught up in the vibe that he told Brianna straight out that he had it bad for her. She acted deaf. Another brush off. This time it irked him, and she had picked up on it.

"What? Now you call yourself having an attitude?" she said, standing up. Malik got up from the floor as well, taking his time answering. He became self-conscious, wondering if he was acting immature. He finally said, "Naw, I'm cool."

"You can't even say what you feel," she'd accused. "A little too cool, huh?" Her sarcasm ticked him off further. It came out of the blue.

"I've tried to express how I feel," he said, "but your brush offs are non stop. Guess what i'm saying don't count for much, or you're too cool to hear it." He smirked. She frowned. He chuckled. She frowned harder. He accused her of getting an attitude then.

"What do you think you want out of me?" she'd asked him. The emotion in her voice caught him off guard. It was sudden, totally unexpected. For the first time, he detected some vulnerability. She turned away and picked up the CDs off the floor. But it was a little too late; Malik got his first glimpse of the little girl inside her. He began helping collect the CDs. She avoided eye contact, not saying anything. He didn't push it. He waited for her to break the silence; it didn't take long.

"You don't know me," she up and said, staring him in the face.

"I'm trying to," he said calmly. "You're shutting me out. I'm feelin' you fo' real."

"You're feeling an infatuation," she countered. "A teenage boy thinking with his penis. That's all."

The slug penetrated his ego, although he pretended it didn't. He still busted back at her. "It's not me thinking with my 'little dude'," he said. "If I was on that, trust me I wouldn't be over here."

"Meaning?" She crossed her arms over her chest. He smiled inside. They were in the midst of their first fight. He found her feistiness sexy as hell. Her eloquent mean mug enticed him into tapping out. He moved to assuage her, smiling, sweet talking. "Meaning I feel you, wanna keep it real with you and build with you." He eased forward but got fended off.

"Move! I'm serious." she maintained her attitude.

"Me too."

She stomped toward the kitchen. He trailed her, still kissing up, Usher still singing in the background. "Come on, Bree," Malik pressed. "You know I can't win unless you permit me victory." She turned on the sink faucet. He watched as she poured dishwashing liquid into the water. He kept kissing up until she suddenly spun around and dashed him with suds. Within seconds, an all-out water war ensued. They drenched the kitchen and each other. All tension had died by the end of their battle. They ended up entangled on the floor, soaked and laughing. Their chemistry reborn, Brianna stripped him down to his boxer shorts and threw his clothes in the dryer. For a minute, Malik hoped this would lead to make-up sex. It turned out to be a tease. While his pants, shirt, and socks dried, Brianna popped in a movie. Next thing Malik knew, he was waking up at 2:30 in the morning—way past his curfew. His first instinct was to call home. When Wanda answered on the first ring, Malik knew he was in a world of trouble.

What a night, he thought, still watching Brianna sleep. He didn't want to wake her, but he had no choice once he heard a horn blow outside. He peered out the window and saw Brandon's Escalade in the middle of the street.

"Bree?" Malik whispered, gently tapping her shoulder. Her eyes opened slowly... peacefully. She sat up.

"What time is it?"

"The wee hours," he said. "My family's outside." The horn sounded again.

"I could've taken you." She stood up.

"It's cool. Just give me a hug before I bounce," he said, half joking, fully hoping she would.

To his pleasant surprise, she sashayed right into his embrace. Their bodies pressed together like a soft, slow grind. "Call me later, 'Lik," she said sweetly in his ear. He did not want to leave.

"I had a good time tonight," he said.

"Me too, boy. Call me if you need a ride to see your friend tomorrow—" she thought about it. "or later today, I should say."

"No doubt." The urge to kiss her seized him.

Brianna led him to the door.

Malik walked out of her apartment, happy with a jolly-cool pep in his step. He exited the building with another stride. The walk to the truck felt like a walk to the electric chair. His mother sure wasn't going to grant him a reprieve. He opened door and climbed in back. Liz sat there, smileless.

CHAPTER 16

Last night's events played on repeat inside Liz's mind as she prepared to leave. She now regretted opting to work on her day off. Unable to get a full night's sleep, she was dead tired and fatigue brought on a headache. She wanted to rest.

Liz walked to the kitchen, popped a couple of Advil, and swallowed them down with two glasses of water. She was yet to confront Malik. They hadn't spoken after she and the twins picked him up from his friend's house. Liz needed time to deal with her emotions. For the first time in years she cried herself to sleep when they got back home. It was all too much. Her baby's life had been threatened twice in one day. She couldn't fathom why Malik didn't tell her about the incident with Derrick. Why tell the twins instead? Then he turns around and gets carjacked. Why didn't he call home first? Liz couldn't understand it. What did her baby plan to do with the twins last night? Handle Derrick's threats? How? The voices asked more questions and offered up cynical theories.

Liz rinsed out her glass and replaced it on the sink rack. Exhaling an extended, drawn-out sigh, she went to wake Malik. He had some explaining to do. His bedroom door was ajar. She walked quietly inside and found him fast asleep in bed, on top of the covers, with all his clothes still on, including his shoes. Liz stared at her son. What if he'd accompanied the twins to Janice's house last night? Liz hated to think of what might have happened. The twins' merciless brutalizing of Jesse and Derrick indicated nothing good. Liz's conscience convicted her. For years she frowned on Brandon and Brian's wild ways. But the moment she needed their thug services, she condoned those wild ways. She despised hypocrisy, and knew that last night she personified it. And to protect her baby, she didn't doubt she'd do it again. Guns were not foreign to her. Kevy kept a heavy arsenal back in the day and gave Liz two for her own protection. "Thirsty cats won't hesitate to run up in this house," Kevy often warned her. "They know I got money and believe every hustler keeps a stash at his babymama's crib." He also taught Liz the mechanics and use of the pistols. She got rid of them years ago, wanting to put that life far behind her. Last night taught her how quick the past—and its influences and instincts—could run up into the present and threaten the future.

Liz nudged Malik's leg. "Baby, wake up," she said. His eyes sprung open.

"Huh?" He turned over and staggered, groggily, to his feet. She wondered if he was having a bad dream. His face wore a look of panic. A manliness appeared to be overtaking the boyish innocence in her baby already. His face still had its youthful appeal but Liz saw something manly.

"Brandon said he'll take you to visit Andre," Liz said, placing twenty dollars on the speaker. "Here's money for him."

Malik sunk onto the bed. "Alright," he said. Then, "I might get a lift from Brianna instead."

"Is that the girl's house we picked you up from?" she felt a trickle of jealousy.

"Yeah."

"Why didn't you call me first, 'Lik?" she asked. "You get robbed, you supposed to call home before anywhere." She fully displayed her disappointment. "Then you call the twins. What was y'all plan last night?"

"Nothing, Ma," He didn't look at her. "I didn't want you worrying over it, that's all."

"Well, you almost made things worse," she said. "And don't try to trivialize what happened."

"I'm not."

She sat on his bed. "I went to see Janice last night too."

His eyelids shot wide open. "What?" He sat up.

Liz looked toward the door, then back at him, lowering her voice. "You never told me how messed up Andre's mother was on that stuff."

"Mama, you shouldn't have gone over there," he chided her. "That ain't no place for you to be."

102

"You don't tell me what isn't a place for me to be," she snapped at him. "Especially when I don't know where you're at past two in the morning. And the twins calling looking for you, me finding out you were threatened with a gun, that other girl calling saying that car was stolen. Then I found out you fought with a grown man." Her temperature skyrocketed as she vented. "I met Jesse."

"What happened?" he asked, paying close attention.

She stood, calming herself down. "Nothing you need to worry about." She hoped She-She was still asleep. "You just stay from over there unless Andre is with you. She-She will stay with us until we figure something out." She started for the door. "Make sure she eats breakfast."

Liz went to her room to get her work bag and keys. Thinking about it, she changed her mind.

"Matter of fact," she said, re-entering Malik's room, "I don't want you going over Andre's house at all until further notice."

CHAPTER 17

When Malik called Brianna for a ride, she was on her way out the door. "I forgot last night that I was scheduled to do my friend's hair today," she said regretfully.

Malik understood. "Don't trip. I'll hit up my cousin for a ride."

After a short pause, Brianna said, "No. I promised to take you, so I'm on my way."

When Brianna showed up shortly after, she told Malik the plan. "You drop me off and take my car to see Drizzle. By the time I'm finished doing hair, you should be back." He promised to be back to get her around noon. He dropped her off, then shot straight up to the group home with She-She.

"Shit is out of control!" Drizzle sneered after being told about the carjacking. "Dawg, I'm not staying in this punk ass place," he told Malik. She-She got up and went to the vending machines.

Malik listened patiently as his homie vented over the bad news. Besides She-She, they were the only ones in the small visiting room. The other group home residents were away on weekend passes.

"I'm going AWOL," Drizzle decided. "Tonight." He spoke in a stubbornly determined tone. "All I need is a ride," and he laid out the plan.

Malik nodded his complicity. The group home wasn't a locked down facility, so all Drizzle had to do was walk out and disappear from the area before any staff noticed. They had it all plotted out by the time She-She returned, cradling an armful of snacks. She wasn't made privy to the conspiracy.

"I got you covered," Malik said, vowing to be at the spot later.

Drizzle could hardly maintain his composure. His anger regulated his body language. "I'ma find out who poked you, too," he guaranteed Malik. "Milwaukee is too small and dudes talk way too much." He shook his head in an anxious, sinister gesture, adding, "and when I do…" he balled and unballed his fist. He didn't need to finish the sentence. Malik already knew.

Malik was at a point where he'd swallowed enough bullshit too. Yesterday left him feeling like a victim. Twice! He renounced the turning-the-other-cheek-love-thy-enemy doctrines. A man fell easy prey to the vultures if he was stigmatized as "busta," "coward" or "sweet." Malik wanted his respect, and it appeared the only way a nigga got respected in the concrete jungle was by being a guerilla. By playing it thug and keepin' it gangsta. By making the predators think twice before running up. Malik had fought off this thinking for years, viewing it as the slave mentality. But now, at the very moment he sat in the visiting room, he struggled to digest anything else besides the street philosophies on survival. Any concepts to the contrary appeared romantic. In one night, it all started to change for him. The street reality showed up and shook up his whole belief system. All the studying he'd done, all the discussions he had with Liz, Kevy, and others about the streets, the struggle—it all started to clog his emotions. He felt torn. Split. He tried to stave off the disillusionment. His belief system looked less believable, less tenable; a revamped set of beliefs began manifesting inside his mind, challenging what he once embraced.

As Drizzle and She-She conversed and gobbled down goodies, Malik thought back on a heated debate that he had had with Brandon at their grandma's house last summer.

"Niggas ain't trying to unite," Brandon had declared once Malik spoke on the importance of Blacks coming together. The twins, especially Brandon, attacked what they considered Malik's distorted perspective and dreams. "We're too busy gettin' at each other's jugulars," Brandon continued spewing. "Too suspicious of one another's motives to come together. That shit got embedded in us during slavery, cuz, and it still cripples niggas 'til this day. You read that Willie Lynch letter. That punk predicted our dissension and distrust centuries ago. We've lost or let go of all that once kept us bonded together. We lack any sense of history. So how the hell can we know where we need to be or go?"

"By overthrowing that slave mentality and re-instituting Afrikan consciousness," Malik had jumped in. "By not surrendering to defeat. Each generation is responsible for itself. We lose by accepting the status quo. If Harriet Tubman had surrendered to slaves' horrid plights, our asses might still be on plantations gettin' whipped and worked from sun up to sun down."

This only kindled Brandon's impatience. "What?" he scoffed. "We are still on plantations, gettin' whipped, mostly by other niggas."

"That's exactly what this beast wants us to believe," Malik asserted. "Keep us blaming each other for all that's happened and is happening, so that hostility destroys us. Divide and conquer. The real enemies—"

Brandon snapped. "Look," he leered. "Who shot my mama and daddy?" His contorted face glowered in pure anger. "Niggas killed them, that's who," he answered his own question. "Another nigga is the reason me, Brian, and our baby sister grew up parentless, without a damn thang but each other and that pain. Ain't no Klansman caused that. Our so-called own kind did. So when you start talkin' that Black, White, Red shit, you better recognize this real shit: the enemy also lies right inside our own ranks. Honkies can kick back now and let us do each other in." He stared hard at Malik, falling quiet and waiting for him to say something else. Malik had become so shocked and frustrated by his cousin's outburst that he felt unable to contend any longer. Brandon's tirade pissed Malik off, partly because of its superficial truthfulness.

"Bet ol' Willie Lynch is in hell dancing on flames," Malik had finally spoken up. "Straight jubilant."

Brandon ignored the comment. He dialed his cell phone and strode upstairs.

"Y'all dudes are too intense," Brian said. He hadn't commented till then. He lay back on the sofa. "I'ma tell you what the business is," he smiled his famous smile at Malik. "Grab a shovel and dig this, homeboy."

Malik stared at the TV screen. He already knew Brian's words weren't going to come across any better than Brandon's had.

Brian blazed up a spliff. "The only niggas gettin' respect are gangstas, cousin," he exhaled a glob of smoke; it glided through the air. "This is a gangsta nation, baby boy. From the President's domain down to the peons'.

Cats ain't honoring anything else but this gangsta shit. If niggas don't aggressively assert themselves, they're burnt up. It's 'bout respect and it's about gettin' that paper, that dust, that skrilla, that loot, those euros, ducats, shillings, yen, pounds, rupees, those, as the Mexicans say, those pesos."

Malik's face could only bear a despairing frown. Brian tended to take the most serious shit as a joke. Malik had been in no joking mood.

Brian kept getting blowed and bumping his gums. "You better listen to Brandon." Another toke of the weed. "'Cause," he choked on the smoke, then went on, "'cause if you come to niggas in the streets with that 'peace-unity-let's-come-together-my-Black-people' rhetoric, those same negroes will eat yo' young ass alive, shit you out, then turn 'round and piss on you." He chuckled scornfully.

Malik got up and went upstairs. He'd wanted to choke the twins that day. But their positions never ceased echoing inside his memory. He later presented those same positions to Liz, and wrote Kevy about them. It wasn't that Malik felt tempted to internalize the twins' cynical attitudes. Malik more wanted his own convictions re-affirmed. He needed his hope re-invigorated. Liz and Kevy helped in this respect. While Malik's mother motivated him to focus on his future, his father sent him searching in the past. Kevy recommended him certain books, sent articles, and wrote letters elaborating on the premise of each. In one letter, Kevy wrote:

> "... to understand the present struggle, you'll need to know the true, un-whitewashed history behind it. There's an ancient Akan word, Sankofa, which means 'Go back and fetch it.' You go back to move forward... the confusion develops when we view ourselves and our history through the eye of the enemy. It's important—crucially important—that we have our own interpretations of our past and present reality... and understand this, Malik: you can't drag a man's thoughts into a vision that transcends his mentality. An individual can see no further than his scope of observation allows. If folks only see pain and hopelessness in their past and in their present, then what else can they imagine for their future? You keep victory in your scope and reach for it."

Malik heeded his dad's more positive words. If the twins only wanted to dwell on symptoms, that was on them. Malik sought to dissect the disease. He wanted to move forward, onward, upward. He understood the unlimited possibilities in resisting, persisting, struggling, and striving until true freedom was won.

At the same time, he often felt like the lone fish in the sea willing to battle the hurricane. He tried to engage his peers in dialogues on the struggle, but few showed interest. If the subject wasn't about rap, rims, fashion, celebrities, or the latest good gossip, it didn't appeal to too many of them. Malik and Drizzle had some good discussions on a wide range of things. And Drizzle would seem down for the cause. But then some drama at home or in the streets would push him back into G-mode.

Now Malik sat thinking about all this. He found himself slipping further and further away from that hope. Maybe the twins were the realists, he thought. He wondered if he'd been the delusional one. It pained him to entertain this notion. The recent drama with Jesse, with Derrick, with being carjacked, with Drizzle being locked up were wearing Malik down. Life was really starting to test, and teach, him. One thing he'd grown adamant about within the last 24 hours: he absolutely refused to be or become anyone else's victim. He didn't care who it was, whether Black or White. Last night really showed him how vicious the enemy in his own ranks demonstrated. Never again. The twins never got robbed, messed with, or messed over, and Malik knew why. Brothas like Prophet Kemet never got toyed with or victimized in the streets, and Malik knew why. The streets respected their gangsta.

"Hurry up and come home," She-She hugged Drizzle as they wrapped up their visit. Malik watched her cling to her brother. Underneath She-She's sassiness, a deep love abided.

"You make sure you mind Liz," Drizzle instructed her. "I'll see you soon." He turned to Malik. "Every goodbye ain't gone," he said, the conspiracy in his smirk.

Malik gave a short hug. "No doubt. Call me at 7 o'clock sharp."

Drizzle said, "Tell ya momz good lookin' out on the loot and for taking my sister in. When we blow up with this music, she can retire."

108

CHAPTER 18

"Count it all joy, my brethren, when you meet various trials, for you know the testing of your faith produces steadfastness," Tessa biblically quoted as Liz wheeled her up to the table.

It had been a tedious Monday so far, and Liz wanted it to be over. Twenty minutes before her day hit the halfway mark.

Meanwhile Tessa hummed "Amazing Grace" and swung open her Bible.

Liz made up the bed. "Do you need anything to drink, Ms. Tessa?" She tucked the sheets under the mattress.

"All I need is the living water of Christ Jesus," Tessa testified. "With the Lord my cup runneth over."

Liz sighed. All the holy talk annoyed her. The old lady lipped religiously all yesterday while Liz worked. And she was back in the zone today. She seemed to speak indirectly to Liz, as if she knew something.

"Do you want anything non-spiritual to drink?" Liz asked with strained courtesy. She didn't come to work to get preached to. *Hell.*

Tessa gazed toward her. "It will be alright," she spoke softly, pity in her expression.

Liz finished making the bed. She felt fatigued and irritable. The situation from the other night still weighed heavily on her conscience. And it was like Tessa read the stressful thoughts on her mind—yesterday and now again today. This made Liz uncomfortable. Her impatience went deeper than the woman's holy talk.

Tessa must have sensed this, too. "It'll be alright, Liz," she repeated softly. "Keep faith and recognize His holy presence. That's all the Lord wants you to do is recognize Him. Submit to His will. He wants you, Liz. Go to Him before your life spins out of order. Give him the control. Let go and let God."

Liz's insides stirred: She sat at the foot of the bed. Tessa's words had struck a chord.

"I'm fine," she told Liz. "You will be fine, too. Take your troubles to God, so that Satan can't mount them up too high and push you too low." She resumed humming the gospel song and ran a wrinkled brown finger down a Bible page.

Liz walked out of the room.

Later that evening, Liz sat in class, heavy-eyed and yearning for solitude and rest. Her sleepless weekend continued to burden her energy. Time dragged. *Thank God the day was almost over.*

Class ended. Liz gathered her technical writing books. She eyed her mostly younger classmates as she rose to leave. She felt a little envious of their youthful vibe. They appeared so full of hope for the future while Liz felt fearful of what tomorrow might bring. Several weeks till graduation, and all of a sudden she felt her thoughts and emotions regressing. Stay optimistic, she told herself. She'd be able to get better employment using the new credentials. Progress was in motion. She strode toward the exit doors growing hopeful.

"How are you, Liz?" he asked as she stepped out of M.A.T.C. into the chilly night.

Liz tensed up, recognizing the voice. "Fine," she said, turning toward Marvin. "How about yourself?"

He stood there, handsome as ever, sporting a quarter length leather coat, holding a leather briefcase and smiling, his brown eyes beaming into hers.

The strong winds gave Liz good excuse to move on toward the parking lot. He fell right in step beside her. "I've been hoping to catch up with you," he said. "I want to pass on some information." He hoisted his briefcase to chest level and opened it.

Liz slowed up. The frigid winds pressed against the back of her coat and breezed angrily through her hair.

He extended a business card. "He's expecting your call," Marvin said. "A good job opportunity there for you."

"Thank you." She pocketed the card. "It's cold out tonight, isn't it?"

A brief pause. An awkward moment passed between them.

"Okay," he said. "Be sure to give that brother a ring." He abruptly turned away and walked off.

She didn't want to be rude. "Wait, Marvin," she called, starting toward him. He approached his SUV and disarmed the alarm. She caught up with him as he set his briefcase inside.

"I don't want to give the wrong impression," she said. He stared at her. She stared back. "Give me some time." She continued. "I'll be in touch. Right now I'm dealing with a lot. I promise to call you in time."

"No need to promise," he said.

"Seriously, Marvin," she said. "I appreciate you and the times we've spent together. I hope we can become good friends."

"Friends," he said. His stare grew resentful. "I'd naively assumed we'd reached the good friends level the night—" he stopped short.

Liz saw where he was about to go. "I'm talking about good friends on a platonic level." She shivered from the cold.

Marvin got inside his Range Rover. "That's cool," he said icily. "And don't dial my number until you figure out what you want. I'm too grown for games." He pulled shut the door. She waited there as he backed out and drove off. She walked to her car. That little situation was no longer an issue. Hopefully.

CHAPTER 19

Drizzle's AWOL came days later than originally planned. Brandon had suggested they wait. On weekdays all the other group home residents would be there. Drizzle's sudden disappearance wouldn't stick out with more boys to keep track of. Malik saw the logic in this, and things later fell right into place. The escape went smoothly.

"Dawg, I need my wig faded and some gear," Drizzle said as Brandon wheeled the Escalade down Water Plank Road. He sat low key in the back seat.

Malik sat up front, on alert for the slave catchers. Aiding his comrade's escape gave him a rush. Malik knew all was copacetic once they made it to the eastside.

Brandon turned onto his block and parked behind Brian's Infiniti truck. "Come on, lil' bad ass niggas," he said, killing the engine.

They hopped out and trudged up to the twins' house.

"Cousin," Brian greeted Malik over the loud music.

"What's crackin'?" Malik said. He and Drizzle exchanged handshakes with Brian.

Brian lounged back on a sectional, lit bazooka blunt dangling from his lips. "So you're on some fugitive shit, huh?" he addressed Drizzle.

"Yeah, B," he replied. "That group home living ain't for me when it don't have to be." He took a seat on the La-Z-Boy chair, reclined, and stared at the 42 inch plasma screen on the wall. A music show played on BET.

"I hear you," Brian said. He puffed the blunt, its fiery head blazing, then dimming. "They couldn't ever keep me in one of those places, either." He blew smoke and coughed. "Not even for a day," he coughed again. "My ass ran away like Kunta Kinte every chance I got. We want us free."

They laughed.

112

Brandon went in his bedroom. The twins lived in style, Malik noted. *Livin' it up fo' real.* The cherry wood and leather furniture sat lavishly in the living room, accompanied by an alcoholic's dream mini bar and an all- BOSE beast of a sound system. A pool table sat smack dead in the middle of the dining room, looking like it'd never been played on. Malik planned to visit more often. Brandon and Brian were free and on their own; no curfew, no problems that Malik saw. And their main loyalty was to each other.

Malik took all this in as old school Scarface classics thumped deeply and crisply out of the surround sound system. Drizzle leaned forward, watching the tube.

Brian said, "Drizzle, you be rappin' too, don't you?"

"A little bit," Drizzle sounded overly modest.

Malik refused to let him slide. "Family is savage," he bragged, smiling at Drizzle.

Brian called Brandon into the living room.

"What's up?" he said, coming in, counting a few racks.

Brian lowered the volume of the music by remote. "Check out lil' AWOL," he told Brandon. "He say he's next to blow out the Miltown."

All eyes fell on Drizzle. "What y'all wanna hear?" he asked, rising from the chair.

Brian said, "Kick some gangsta shit." Brandon leaned back on the pool table and observed.

"You wanna beat?" Malik asked.

"I'm straight," Drizzle said. "I'll do this verse a capella. I wrote it the other day when a cat wanted to battle me at the group home." He spit:

> I'll be a real ass nigga till I pass away/
>
> change my name become the greatest like Cassius Clay/
>
> cops pull us over, scream 'no luv' and we all fire/
>
> fuck livin' behind walls caged by this barbed wire/

113

> I was raised by fiends and surrounded by scavengers/
> dressed in all black packin' fo-five calibers/
> Pac turned you out but me an' my dawgz been thugs/
> yeah, you cats got nine lives but I got ten slugs/
> If the tek jam I pop out the clip and mug at you/
> I take the bullets out and just throw the slugs at you/
> Chase yo' ass home and I'ma slang some mo' shells/
> have you hidin' like a Jehovah Witness rung da door
> bell.../"

A burst of throaty laughter muzzled out his voice.

"Time the fuck out!" Brian piped, making a referee 'T' sign with his hands. "What the fuck?—this little nigga is a beast."

"—hiding like a Jehovah Witness rung da door bell," Brandon grinned.

They gave Drizzle mad props on his rap skills. Malik's admiration for him soared. He heard a redoubled hunger in Drizzle's voice.

"Kick something else," Brandon said. "In another direction. Go street with some political mixed with it."

"Are the two separate?" Malik asked rhetorically.

Drizzle didn't miss a beat. He jumped right in the zone, spitting:

> "Call me a crook but y'all the real villains/
> dropping bombs on Iraqi children/
> Bush got nerves/
> and yeah, onna low, the CIA got birds/
> raw flake Peruvian product/
> draconian schemes to pawnshop us/
> ya put guns in our hoods then build more prisons/

frame and kill black militants that show resistance/

then trap sistahs on general assistance/

Don't care my mama cook scraps for dinner/

but you quick to go to war 'bout a world trade center/

that's why my soul lie froze, inside me it's

cold old man winter/

money rolls and power is my summer/

so I spit out of cold hunger/

Promise to keep it street, young gunners/

guaranteed to do it wit' no blunders /

till my song catalog become the 9th wonder/"

A respectful silence fell between them. Drizzle had spit with such authority, such conviction. Brandon spoke up first. "You should be strictly in the studio," he told Drizzle. "You're a sure thing."

"In real life," Brian agreed.

"No doubt," Malik added. He was even surprised by how Drizzle got off on the verse.

Brandon put his loot down on the pool table. "You make me wanna start a record label just to see you blow up," he said.

"The game ain't ready," Brian said, standing to his feet. "We'll invest if you fo' real 'bout the grind," he told Drizzle.

Drizzle smirked, glancing at Malik. Malik eyed the twins for any sign of insincerity. He saw none. His cousins had the capital to fund Drizzle's come up. They also had the street respect to make it happen without the haters obstructing the path.

Drizzle didn't flinch. "Let's get it," he said, giving Brian dap. "Get rich like Suge Knight and the '90's Death Row."

115

"Fuck Suge," Brian jacked. "He so 20th century, we 'bout to usher in a new era, 'ya dig?"

For the next two hours the four of them planned, plotted, and strategized. They talked about starting up a record label, taking the industry by storm, and locking it down. The forming vision looked promising. Malik was gung-ho and ready to go. With the twins on the team, the money and muscle were in place. Shady producers and conmen in the game would think twice before stepping to them. Malik knew the twins had zero tolerance for funny business. They were guerillas. No doubt! But what was understood needed not be spoken on. Malik kept his thoughts to himself.

Brandon put a grand in Drizzle's hand and advised him to stay low key, out the streets, and to keep writing his rhymes. "Don't trip, we're gonna make it happen," he assured Drizzle.

Brian tossed Malik a set of car keys. "Y'all can push my Astro van until Drizzle's car turns up," he said. "I'll keep my ears to the streets. Most likely someone will be try'na sell the rims and music out the Chevy. I'll put the word out that I'm lookin' to pay top dollar for them."

Malik and Drizzle left the twins' house feeling nothing but gratitude and glee.

"Fam, you got some good people," Drizzle said as Malik backed the van out the garage. Malik drove cautiously. He wasn't accustomed to driving anything other than regular-sized cars. Drizzle could drive anything but it was too risky for him to get behind the wheel. More than likely, the cops had a warrant out for his arrest already.

"Go by my crib right quick," Drizzle suggested. "I wanna check on my momz."

Malik didn't want to go by there for more than a few reasons. His mother had told him not to, for one. For two, he hadn't let Drizzle know about Derrick and the drug dealing out of the house. She-She mentioned Jesse's presence there, but she kept the rest to herself. Malik had advised her to. Now couldn't be a worse time to confront all this, he reasoned.

"I think you should lay low for a few days, at least," Malik said, stopping at a red light on Sherman Blvd. "You know the po-pos will look for you at ya momz house first."

Drizzle thought it over.

"Plus, Jesse will snitch you out with the quickness," Malik continued.

He agreed. "No doubt," he nodded. "I'll wait. The police is probably waiting on me tonight."

The light turned green. Malik breathed a stealthy sigh of relief and mashed the gas. Drizzle would eventually go home, and Malik knew, things were bound to hit the fan.

Drizzle clicked on the radio. "I need to borrow some gear from you so I can get fitted and fresh and go holla at Kila. I'm fiending for some feminine affection, ya feel me?"

Malik laughed. "Ain't no secret." He was already on his way home.

CHAPTER 20

Liz's kitchen smelled of buttery garlic bread, roast beef, and sweet potatoes. It took her over an hour to throw down on the meal, and she was poised to get her grub on. She expected Malik any moment now, so she set the table with him in mind. "Dinner's ready," she called out to She-She. For the last forty-five minutes or so, the girl had been cooped up in the bathroom. Liz figured she'd come down with a bad case of the runs.

After making their plates, Liz went to see what was the holdup.

Liz tapped on the bathroom door. "She-She? Is everything okay?" She waited patiently when no answer came. A second knock got She-She to say, "One minute."

Two more minutes passed before She-She finally, and slowly, opened the door. Tears streamed down her cheeks. She backed up to the toilet as Liz stepped inside.

Liz, confused, asked, "What's wrong?" then gasped, her confusion mutating into shock upon seeing the blood. It was on the floor, all over the toilet seat, and dripping down She-She's legs. She-She held a bath towel tightly around her waist.

"Are you having your period?" Liz asked. But she knew it wasn't that. This was too much bleeding for a regular menstrual flow.

"Oh my god!" Liz said, seeing a thick glob of blood resting in the toilet. Her temples pulsed in sharp aches. She felt a stab of sickness in her stomach. She tried to process what she was seeing.

She-She wailed: "He said I couldn't get pregnant." Her body shook, tears continued to rain down her panic-stricken face.

"Who said—" Liz choked. The voices whispered "Malik." She shuddered, closing her mind to their sick suggestion. "Who have you been sexually active with?" Heartbeats went wild inside her chest. Fear mounted.

She-She lowered her head in shame. "He said—"

"Who said?" Liz demanded.

"Derrick!" she wailed.

"Derrick?" Liz felt ashamed. She'd feared the voices' suggestion. Then indignation snuffed out her shame as the realization hit her. *That bastard*, she thought. "The Derrick at your mother's house?" she asked.

She-She's non-response confirmed Liz's assumption.

"Stay here," she said, "while I call an ambulance."

Liz snatched up the kitchen phone and dialed 911.

She hung up before the first ring. *Think*, she told herself. The food on the table nauseated her—its smell and sight. If She-She was raped, the hospital would contact social services. Liz rushed back to the bathroom. "Did Derrick force himself onto you?"

"I told him to wait, at first," she said in a shaky voice. "He said he couldn't have kids."

Liz asked her to explain exactly what happened. She got a clean bath towel, ran it under warm water, and listened. As She-She went into vague detail, Liz cleaned up some of the mess. It all seemed dreamlike to Liz; she had a hard time deciding on what to do next.

She-She broke down. "He kept saying don't tell anyone."
Liz consoled her, helping her into the bathtub. But she fumed inside. Derrick manipulated and molested She-She. Liz wished Brian had beat him to a pulp last weekend. She had to figure out what to do. A lifeless fetus lay in her toilet. It was at least a month old. A pregnant thirteen-year-old having a miscarriage. Calling the cops seemed the normal choice. But then social services? Between Janice's state and She-She's rape, everything would crumble for the family. The cops were sure to visit and likely arrest Janice. Liz's only concern and sympathy resided with She-She. Janice could go to

119

jail, for all Liz cared, but that would only turn things further upside-down for the children.

Liz didn't know what the hell to do. She called Wanda.

"I'm on my way," Wanda said, once again displaying true sisterhood.

Liz schooled She-She on what to say to the medics and possibly the police. She refused to permit the system to get another Black child.

Liz called 911, requesting an ambulance. Then she went back to the bathroom. She spoke with She-She about what was about to happen. While they talked Liz heard someone coming in the house.

"Malik?" she called, leaning the mop against the sink.

She-She tensed up. "Please don't tell him," she begged.

"Wait here and finish getting cleaned up." Liz walked out, pulling the door shut behind her.

She was surprised to see Andre standing there with Malik. "They let you out?" she asked.

"Not exactly," Andre admitted.

Liz read both boys like an open book. "You ran away from that place?" she asked.

Malik stepped forward. "Chill out, mama," he said. "He's going to—"

"Andre can speak for himself." She frowned Malik into silence. Andre looked as guilty as sin. All Liz could do was shake her head. Now wasn't the time to get on them. A more urgent matter demanded their attention.

"I'm disappointed in you two," Liz stated flatly. "Andre, you shouldn't have left that place. But right now there's something else to deal with." She told them to take a seat. "And don't get loud when I tell you what's going on." She glanced toward the bathroom.

"What's up?" Malik asked.

120

Liz said, "She-She is a little shaken. I've already called for an ambulance." Before she could go into what happened, Andre leapt to his feet and darted to the bathroom.

Liz let him go. Malik asked her what was up again. She told him about the miscarriage and Derrick's pedophilia.

"What!" Malik scowled, jumping up. His eyes filled with utter disbelief, anger. "That nigga is a grown man," he sneered. "Messing with a 13-year-old. That's rape."

"Hush," Liz said. "And watch your mouth with that N-word."

Malik paced the floor. Liz told him to calm down.

"'Lik, we're—"

She-She's sobs echoed. The shadow of malice clouded Malik's eyes, his face becoming a stone of hostility.

"Help Andre make the right choice," Liz told him. He didn't speak or look at her.

Wanda and the ambulance arrived at the same time. Liz led the medics to the bathroom.

She-She kept telling her brother, "I didn't wanna do it, Dre."

Andre told his sister not to worry. He walked out of the bathroom with the same stone-faced visage. Liz saw darker clouds in his eyes.

The medic took one look at She-She and the bloody toilet and knew what had happened. They prepared her for the ride to the hospital. Liz said she'd follow. Wanda got instructions from one of the medics and helped with the deceased fetus.

André and Malik stood in the kitchen speaking at a low pitch between themselves until Liz came inside. "Y'all stay here till we get back," she told the boys. They didn't look at her, nor did they respond.

Liz climbed in the car with Wanda. They trailed the ambulance up to St. Joseph's Hospital. The whole time, Liz worried about what Malik and his friend might be thinking… about doing.

121

CHAPTER 21

Malik didn't hesitate to disobey his mother. As soon as Liz pulled off behind the ambulance, Drizzle asked for a ride to his cousin P-Nut's house. They hopped in the Astro van and bounced. During the drive, Malik told him everything about Derrick and their encounter. Drizzle seethed in the passenger seat. He wanted to meet this "punk Derrick." The drug dealing out of the house played a minimal role in his anger. His baby sister's sexual assault is what enraged him. Neither of them said anything about Janice, but there was an unspoken acknowledgement.

Once they made it to P-Nut's house, Drizzle ran inside. Malik waited anxiously in the van. He had strong reservations about involving P-Nut in what was about to go down, although Malik didn't exactly know *what* was about to go down.

Drizzle came back outside and got in the van. "I'ma lay back over here," he said. "Gone home befo' ya momz get back, fam."

"What's up?" Malik asked.

Drizzle shifted impatiently in the seat. He said, "Nothing. I'm gon' chill over here tonight. I'll holla at you tomorrow."

Malik recognized Drizzle's spin move. A moment passed by without comment from either boy. Drizzle stared out the window. Malik slammed the gear into drive. Drizzle shot him a puzzled look. Malik hit the gas.

"Dawg, what the heck you doin'?" Drizzle gripped the door handle like he was about to jump out of the moving van.

Malik drove on, whipping the wheel to the left and right, swerving off of P-Nut's block. "Pull over," Drizzle demanded.

Malik hit Wisconsin Avenue and smashed harder on the gas pedal, dipping in and out of the side lane. He made another right onto 35th Street, to avoid stopping at the red light. Drizzle kept yelling for Malik to stop the van.

"You on some brand new shit all of a sudden?" Malik finally said, "so I'ma get on some new shit too." A sharp turn right on 35th and Juneau.

"Alright!" Drizzle said. He let go of the door handle... "Slow your roll."

Malik glanced over, his face full of conviction.

"Slow down, for real," Drizzle said. Malik drove another block for good measure, then pulled over on a side street.

"I'm about to go sweat this bitch ass nigga Derrick," he told Malik.

"And?" he challenged. "I know you don't expect me to let you push by yourself."

"P-Nut goin' with me," he said. "It might get real ugly at my crib and I don't want you part of it."

That sounded condescending to Malik. "Don't want me part of it?" he frowned. "I'm already part of it. We family. My enemies are your enemies, yours are mine. This ain't no part-time thing."

Drizzle said nothing.

"And P-Nut?" Malik said. "He ain't cut like that. Dude bound to lose his grip under pressure. Cousin or no cousin, a cat's character is what it is."

Drizzle remained quiet, thinking to himself. Malik battled to recover from the blow to his pride. Did Drizzle think he was soft? If things did get ugly, what did that mean? Like he couldn't handle himself like P-Nut. Malik felt disrespected by the insinuation. He waited for his emotions to settle before he said, "If we need to handle something, then we will. But our emotions must be in order. If we're not thinking clearly, we're moving recklessly on some Kamikaze shit."

Drizzle nodded. "No doubt."

Malik pulled back off. "That cat Derrick is bogus," he said. "Ain't no way around that fact. Whatever drama comes to him is justified. The slimiest niggas touch underage girls."

Drizzle asked, "So now what?"

123

Malik headed for the east side. "Don't trip. I know how to play this," he assured, adding, "and I'm convinced that we can't demonstrate with P-Nut. Not on that level. The last time he went to jail with Tim and Tone on that robbery, he was the only one that didn't get charged, and the police mysteriously received information against Tone and his brother on two other robberies. So you do the math." His words lingered for a moment. "My pops and cousins warned me about stool pigeons. P-Nut fits the profile."

Malik left it at that. He hit the east side of Milwaukee, focused on the destination. It wasn't no turning back once he made it to the twins' house.

As soon as Malik parked behind Brian's Infiniti truck, Drizzle spoke up. "Let's gon' back to your crib," he said. "Wait for She-She and your momz to get back first."

Malik felt partly confused, partly relieved. Drizzle's about-face wasn't expected. Malik didn't argue though. He drove off and clicked on the radio. Another close call.

CHAPTER 22

The bland smell of the hospital room bored Liz. She gazed disinterestedly at the TV, having a hard time relaxing in the chair next to She-She's bed. It had been a long, eventful night and Liz was ready to go home. Upon arriving at the hospital, she'd posed as She-She's mother and also signed Janice's name on the paperwork a nurse handed her. Good thing it was a busy night in the emergency room. The hospital staff was too preoccupied with other things to suspect Liz of anything but being a caring parent—or better yet, a concerned mother. Wanda had teased her, saying "If they call the police and snitch you out, I'll bail you out. We'll tell the judge it was justifiable criminality." Liz hushed her and stayed on point for any fishy business by the personnel. After two hours of waiting, a doctor had finally come out and said She-She would be fine. It remained up in the air if Liz would dodge impersonation and forgery charges and if She-She would duck social services. The threats lingered as they waited for She-She's release

Liz shifted to the left arm rest. The hospital chair was very uncomfortable. It was hard to concentrate on the *Nightline* special on ABC. She felt an impulse to call home and check on Malik and Andre. They were a little too quiet before she left the house. Plus, the voices kept in a zone, trying to brainwash her into believing the worst. She wished they'd vacate her head once and for all.

Malik ain't left that house, Liz refuted them. *He know better.* The pessimistic voices rebuked her. She struggled in blocking them out. She was just too tired to argue with herself. She summoned to mind the day Malik was born. That joyous day her little brown bundle of beauty slid into the world. *Not exactly slid*, she thought in retrospect. But she'd forgotten all about the hard labor pains once the nurse handed over her infant son. His first cry was the sweetest melody. She and Kevy's lovely creation; their bond for life. She'd laid eyes on Malik and experienced a profound swelling of pride. Nothing but high spirits upon cradling a life that developed inside her womb. That short moment of celebration soon gave strength to the fear of failing at her parental duties. This particular fear still lived inside her heart till this day; till this very moment.

Liz wasn't a stranger to fear. Ever since early childhood, a foreboding spirit hounded her. This spirit had always lurked, even during the happiest moments of her life. It was like an innate phobia that sometimes hit her with fierce impact; other times it only brushed up inside her like a gentle but ominous breeze. There'd been those moments she knew the exact source of the fear; then there were those instances she was totally clueless—she only felt the forebodings, unaware of their causes. And sooner or later, she'd find out. She always found out. Months before Liz's mother succumbed to breast cancer, Liz had felt something ominous looming. She hadn't known it was connected to her mother's impending death. But she felt it; she'd felt something. She just knew calamity was going to strike. And it did. It always did. Those premonitions were yet to mislead her. She sometimes wondered if there was something she could have done to prevent the misfortune, or in her mother's case, tragedy. Regarding her mother's death, the doctors said there wasn't a thing that could be done. The breast cancer had reached the incurable, inoperable point a year earlier. A pastor told Liz that the Lord sent the sign to forewarn and prepare her. She accepted their theories; she believed she needed to in order to move on.

Kevy's arrest, and later conviction, was much harder for her to swallow. Months prior to the police showing up, Liz had felt the spirit of doom all around her. The foreboding shadowed the days leading up to the raid on their house. She knew it alluded to Kevy's criminal hustle and the possible consequences of it. Later when those ramifications manifested, Liz never experienced the exculpatory acceptance inside. Deep down, she truly believed that had she ...*nothing*, she checked her thinking and glanced toward the hospital bed. She-She lay there, her eyes closed, face full of mixed emotion. Liz wondered if she was asleep. She doubted it.

One thing was a definite. Liz was ready to go home. *What's taking these folks so damn long,* she complained to herself, shifting back to the right armrest. The chair was not user-friendly. And the should've-could've-would've started up. She did not want to start grappling with the past again; she could neither reverse nor change it. Kevy was in prison and that was that—until the courts freed him. Mulling over what she should've or could've done was senseless. What was done was did.

126

As Liz told herself this, memories of those earlier years stubbornly tickered across her mind: Kevy's marriage proposal (she still wore the engagement ring sometimes) and his passionate promise to go totally legit by the date of their wedding. *Good times back then.* She'd been overly eager to become Mrs. Elizabeth Freeman. And boy-oh-boy had she anxiously anticipated their honeymoon in Jamaica, and living happily ever after. Disquieting clouds had stalked those sunny prospects from the jump. The more she disregarded them, the thicker, more menacing they became. As the wedding approached, the skies darkened and darkened, descending on their brighter tomorrows. But Liz's love for Kevy, her longing for future family solidarity and stability, had blinded her to recognizing this until it was too late. The voices had been there too, telling her about how stupid she was being. She'd blocked them out and doggedly focused on the wedding plans. She only half-heartedly demanded Kevy stop pushing the product. The whole time she was well aware of her reckless selfishness. She had wanted to have her cake and eat it too. She wanted to splurge some more of Kevy's dirty loot; she wanted Kevy's hand in marriage and all the things his money afforded. In the end, she lost in a major way. No wedding, no Jamaican honeymoon, no happily ever after. The voices habitually uttered the "we-told-you-so" mantra.

Liz released a deep breath and stared over at She-She. The girl's eyes were now open, watching the TV. Hurt, shame, and confusion showed on her young face. A profound sympathy surged through Liz for her. Maybe God wanted Liz to see something, to understand something, to demonstrate something. Kevy's past of dealing poison. Janice's addiction to it. The cause and the effect. The extended consequences burdened She-She's life, Andre's life, countless lives. Liz condoned Kevy's pollution of the community back then. *Just plain 'ol selfish,* the voices spoke up, accusing. She didn't try to refute them. The movie "Beloved" came to mind. Liz wondered if her own past deeds hunted and haunted her present life. Had they shown up through She-She—or had they not shown up yet, but were going to through some calamity? Instead of murdering her child, like Sethe in "Beloved," had Liz killed her chances for future happiness or future peace? Was she trippin', overanalyzing? Or had she already fallen too low?

Liz sat up in the hospital chair. What was done was done, she paraphrased herself. Although that recurring foreboding had been creeping

127

back into position, Liz wasn't havin' it. *Not now!* Accomplishment was too close. So she couldn't allow herself to go back to fretting over yesteryear's madness. *Ain't no way!* Today and tomorrow are what mattered now, she determined, as she sat in the *bogusly uncomfortable chair*, waiting for *this slow ass nurse* to come discharge She-She so they could leave. *The past meant diddly unless it taught lessons.* It—the past and all its drama—had already happened, she reminded herself again. Done. Over with. Destiny called. Now. Damn it! And Liz would answer. As she made herself this promise, a renewed spirit of optimism ballooned up inside her.

Liz rose to her feet. "The doctor said you'll be fine," she said. She-She looked at her and nodded. Liz yawned and stretched her limbs. She wanted to get home, get some sleep, and awaken to the beginning of the rest of her life.

Right on cue, the nurse entered the room. "Y'all are good to go," she smiled at them.

On the ride home, She-She rode up front with Wanda. Liz leaned sideways in the back seat, dozing off.

"Why do people get high?" She-She's question pierced the air. Wanda took a hand off the steering wheel and turned off the radio. They were cruising down 55th street, about ten blocks away from Liz's house.

Liz, wide awake now, sat up in her seat, searching for the best answer. "Many reasons," she managed to say. Her conscience grew a bit heavy. Wanda glanced up in the rearview mirror at her.

Liz continued, "Usually it starts off as so-called fun and games. Recreational. Partying."

"Peer pressure and curiosity also," Wanda added.

Liz's leg fell asleep. "Because some fool convinces them to try or says it's cool or will make them feel good." She felt so fake saying this. She-She maintained a forward gaze. Liz captured her image in the side mirror. She-She's face reflected sorrow, consternation, indignation.

"One thing about messing with drugs," Wanda spoke up, "one drug usually leads a person to try more addictive ones. A sure path to rock bottom."

She-She shook her head, frustrated. "Why then?" she said, emotion thick in her throat. "Why keep doing it, seeing how it's destroying you? And why crack?" Tears cascaded down her mocha cheeks.

"Weed isn't any better," Wanda pointed out. She glanced at She-She. "It often starts with a little marijuana. Then cocaine. Next, they're strung out. Gone." She said this with a touch of scorn.

"They're always chasing that first high," Liz added.

"And they never catch it," Wanda said. "All they end up doing is losing their sense of self during the pursuit."

Liz came down with a headache. She-She wanted to understand, make sense of her mother's addiction. And Wanda? She was well acquainted with the effects of drug abuse. Her older brother, Kurt, had chased that first high for over a decade now. Wanda and her family exhausted themselves, trying to get him off crack. Their efforts were in vain. Kurt stayed on and off and back on his mission, pushing away family and friends alike, often avoiding the ones he'd swindled or stole from to support his habit. Wanda was the last one to throw up her hands on him. After he stole thousands of dollars worth of jewelry from their mother two years ago, Wanda disowned him.

Liz and Wanda shared many secrets. Their deepest ones involved Kevy, Kurt, and a murder. The same murder that Kevy went to prison behind. The same murder that Kevy had had little to do with. But Kurt had everything to do with it.

Kevy and Kurt had grown up together in Milwaukee and were super close. They were figuratively joined at the hip, embracing the same few friends and beefing with the same foes. One night, everything changed between them. It was the very night the police kicked in Liz's front door to arrest Kevy. Hours before the raid, Kurt had run into a guy named Stokes who they suspected of being involved in the home invasion/murder of Kevy's brother and sister-in-law: the twins' parents. Kurt spotted Stokes in a bar, but didn't confront him right away. Instead, he left and called Kevy, who was way across town on business. Kevy told Kurt he'd meet him at the bar asap and to keep an eye on Stokes in the meantime. This Kurt did, by parking in the lot of the bar. On stakeout for roughly twenty minutes, Kurt saw Stokes exit the bar with another man. Unbeknownst to Kurt, he just so happened to be parked right next to their car. As Stokes and his partner approached, they caught sight of Kurt. Stokes recognized him and spoke as if all was good. It all turned bad when guns were drawn and a shootout erupted. Stokes lay dead moments later; his partner fled the parking lot on foot with a bullet to the neck and shoulder. Kurt was without injury. A witness at the scene later told the police that she had seen an unknown man hop into a black sports car and speed off after the shooting. She memorized the plates; they belonged to a Mustang registered in Kevy's name. After the shooting, Kurt went right out to Liz's house. Kevy was home, just about to leave on his way to the bar. Kurt told Kevy all that had transpired. Liz stood in the kitchen, eavesdropping on their whole conversation. Kevy and Kurt talked for about an hour, then left. Kevy came back later that night like nothing had happened. Liz didn't question him. They made love and went to sleep. Hours later, the police were barging into their house. Stokes' partner and the other witness identified Kevy as the shooter. Kurt disappeared until after the trial.

Liz hated Kurt for not coming forward. Then her anger turned toward Kevy for not telling on him. She felt that his loyalty to her and Malik should have superceded his loyalty to Kurt. As time went on, and the courts shot down several of Kevy's appeals, Liz grew angry at herself for not pressuring Kevy to do what was best for their family. She'd held her feelings to her chest, hoping that the courts one day freed Kevy.

"Call me tomorrow, girl," Wanda said as they pulled up in front of Liz's house.

"Alright," Liz reached for the door handle. She-She broke out in tears. "Why don't she just stop smoking that shit!" she cried out.

Liz couldn't even look toward the side mirror this time. She didn't want to see the hurt on She-She's face. It would be her own shame staring back. *Do I deserve to feel guilt?* she wondered.

Wanda moved across the seat to console She-She. A hollowness invaded Liz's stomach; she hated this shit! It was becoming too damn much. A 13-year-old girl had no business being burdened with a grown woman's pain.

Wanda wrapped an arm around She-She, pulling her close. As Wanda caressed her shoulder, saying, "It's going to be alright," She-She bawled and asked them, "Why do she keep doing it?"

"It's difficult to quit, baby," Wanda said. "It's hard to get back up once you hit bottom. Your mom needs help, especially through understanding." She-She buried her teary face in Wanda's warm embrace.

Liz sat in back, feeling small, inadequate, empty inside. "I know Janice loves you and your brother," she said, leaning forward and placing an affectionate hand on She-She's shoulder. "I saw that in her eyes last week when I went over y'all house."

She-She sniffed and sniffled. They gave her time to gather herself.

CHAPTER 23

Malik slouched in his seat, struggling to stay awake in math class. A lack of sleep the night before had left him jaded. He and Drizzle stayed up till three o'clock in the morning, choppin' it, listening to music, and waiting for She-She and Liz to return from the hospital. She-She said little once they did make it back home. Although she admitted Derrick hadn't forced her into sex, that still didn't vindicate him in Malik's eyes. Statutory rape was rape, period. To Malik and Drizzle, Derrick's sick deed was tantamount to first degree sexual assault. He needed to be dealt with for his crime—and so he would be.

Liz admonished the boys against retaliating and getting into trouble. They heard her but weren't listening. Their vow for vengeance had already been made. Malik's blood simmered just thinking about it. Derrick pulling out the gun and threatening him could have been forgiven. But what the sicko did to She-She was unpardonable.

All these thoughts weighed down on Malik's eyelids as he felt himself dozing off in class. He caught himself, jerking his head forward. He checked the wall clock. *Hurry up and end, class.* His head started backward again… but a light tap on his shoulder saved him from fading out. He sat up and turned around to see Jennifer's smiling face.

"You were noddin', Mr. Freeman," she whispered, giggling with a few other students.

Malik rubbed an open palm over his face. "Good lookin'." He sat up straight.

"About twenty minutes to," she said. Malik peeped her desire to start a conversation. He leaned in his seat, ignoring her.

"Are you goin' to Kemet Quarters this Friday?" she asked.

The question got his attention. *What this girl know 'bout K Quarters?* He thought, turning sideways. "How did you know I kicked it at the

132

Quarters?" he asked. He figured talking would keep him from dozing off. "You must've went to the first couple teen nights?"

She blushed. "You know it," she smiled. "I've went since teen night started. I saw you there too. While you and Kila 'n 'em chilled in V.I.P., I was out there with the little people."

Malik offered up a smirk.

"Probably why you didn't see me," Jennifer continued.

"Don't hate," Malik teased.

She gently shoved him on the arm. "Never that, dude," she assured. The contact created an awkward moment between them. She looked unsure, embarrassment coming into her eyes. Malik grinned.

Jennifer relaxed then, saying, "I was feelin' your guy Drizzle's performance, and his skills are tight. He's grimy and keeps it real in his lyrics like he puts a lot of heart into what he writes."

Malik was taken aback. "Grimy?" he said. "What you know about that?"

Her smile widened. "See, you think I'm justa square little white chick, don't ya?" She spoke in jest but her question rang with truth. It didn't surprise Malik that she listened to rap music. Nowadays, who didn't?

"Naw," he said. " I always suspected you had a little flava." A blush by her. "I'm just trippin' over your comment about my nigga's lyrics." Right away he regretted letting the N-word slip out his mouth. This was like the first time he ever used it around a white person. He never wanted to make any of them feel as if they were entitled to say it, no matter what context it was spoken in.

"I look for the balance in music," she said. "I don't go for the overly commercial or the super thug stuff. I'm in the center, I guess. Some witty rhymes, slick metaphors and reality in the music and I'll cop the CD every time."

133

Malik dug her preference. Her appreciation for balanced music mirrored his own to a certain extent. It had never occurred to him that they had this in common.

"Who else do you listen to?" he asked, genuinely curious.

The bell rang and interrupted their convo. They grabbed their books and filed out of class with the other students.

"I like Common, Nas, Jay-Z, of course..." Jennifer was saying as they stepped out into the hall. "Love Wayne, Eminem."

Nana walked up with two buddies. "What's up, brotha?" she greeted Malik.

"What's up?" he replied. He turned back to Jennifer. "We'll get to holla some more," he promised her.

Jennifer nodded. "Okay, nice talking to you, Malik," she said. "See you later." She headed down the hall. Nana rolled her eyes, smacked her lips. All the theatrics irritated Malik.

"Careful in the jungle," Nana warned him. "You might contract an incurable fever, Black man," putting emphases on "jungle" and "fever" and "Black man."

Malik's patience with her had just about run out. "You look silly acting so childish," he said, about to walk away.

Nana blew up. "Nigga, you know what?" she snapped. "Fuck you and that white tramp." Her big mouth resonated through the hall. Frustrated, Malik walked on off. Nana followed him and kept up her show. "You might as well switch sides. At least they're accustomed to short, short men. Your little dick will fit her, hand in glove." Some of the students present snickered.

Malik halted in his tracks and turned. Nana stopped and backed up some. He felt a powerful urge to smack her for the disrespect. She was lucky he had a mother who'd kick his ass if he ever hit a female.

"Your mouth is just like your legs," he got at her, "you can't keep it shut and when open, nothing but foul shit comes out." The spectators found

134

this even funnier, laughing loudly. Nana flew into a tirade. Malik walked away, leaving her to fume. He was done with her. For good!

CHAPTER 24

Liz decided to swing by Janice's house the next day on her route to night school. She pulled up and parked, then climbed out of the car. The neighborhood didn't look as ghetto during the day. Liz attributed this to the kids arriving home from school, running around, adding their playful energy to the block. She knocked on the front door.

As soon as Derrick appeared in the doorway, Liz grew jittery, sensing trouble. "Is Janice home?" she asked him. She stood in a brave posture and stared him directly in the eyes.

Derrick, a shit-eating grin on his face, stepped outside with two other boys, who wore tilted ball caps and looked like bulldogs ready to pounce.

"Janice ain't here," Derrick said. There was an undertone of hostility in his expression. "But where are those twin bitches you came by here with last time?"

Oh, now they're bitches, huh? Little punk, Liz thought, but said, "Just tell Janice I stopped by to talk with her about She-She." She watched for his reaction. *Nothing.* She turned, starting off the porch. The foreboding spirit engulfed her, flooded through her. She heard the boys following behind her. She climbed into the front seat of her car.

"Say, ho, don't you hear my folks talkin' to you?" one of them said. Liz shut the car door and fumbled for the ignition key, her hands shaking. One boy positioned himself directly in front of the car. Derrick stood outside the driver door, grinning even shittier. He asked her to lower the window. The other boy posted up next to him.

"Let me holla at you for a sec," Derrick said kindly.

Liz put on a brave front and lowered the window. "Yes, what is it?" she asked.

Derrick leaned forward, saying, "My nigga didn't mean no disrespect." His arms rested on top of the car. "Check this out though. I need you to give those twin niggas a message for me, alright?"

Liz keyed the ignition. "What's the message, Derrick?"

"You gone give it to dem?" He smirked. The other boy came from the front of the car and stepped next to Derrick.

Liz started the engine. "Depends on what you want me to tell them." The skies darkened, descended...

"Tell dey bitch ass..." Derrick sneered as Liz felt a sharp sting on the side of her face, the smack echoed in her ear.

"Bitch!" One of them yelled. They spit and punched through the open window, attacking Liz!

She gunned the engine, dazed, but forgot to put it into gear. She threw it in drive and stomped down on the gas, and drove in a panic, her vision blurred by tears and the boys' saliva. A terrible fear gripped her. *Were they chasing her?* She dreaded, speeding out of the neighborhood, toward home.

Liz wheeled up to the curb, haphazardly parked and leaped out of the car. She ran up to the house and found the door unlocked. *Thank God*! Slam! She locked it, dead bolted it, slid on the chain, then collapsed against the wall and sank to the floor.

She-She came out of the kitchen. "Auntie, I cleaned—" the cheerfulness fled her voice. "What's wrong, Auntie?" she screamed out, panic-stricken.

Liz stood up, wiping away the tears. Malik bolted out of his bedroom. "Mama, what happened?" he cried out. Liz grabbed her son, hugged him tight. Her tears sprinkled onto his shirt.

"Them niggers jumped on me!" Liz wept. "They put their hands on me—I'ma damn woman and they put their hands on me, baby!"

"Who?" Malik's voice pulsated with rage.

He walked her to the bedroom.

****

137

Liz woke up later that night in bed. She couldn't remember what she dreamed about, but it somehow calmed her nerves. Laying there under the covers, she recalled the attack. *Bastards!* Anger overtook her fear. Then came some regret. She chided herself for the emotional outburst in front of her son. That was a no-no. She always strove to be a paragon of strength and self-control for him. Up until today, she had been. Burning hatred for Derrick overwhelmed her heart. The sons-of-bitches probably would've killed her if she hadn't got away in time. *Cowards!* She couldn't really remember what happened after the assault. The wild drive home turned up hazy in her memory. Almost dreamlike now.

The Lord is my sustainer... a very present help in trouble. Tessa's voice of conviction suddenly popped up in Liz's head. *Our refuge and strength, a very present help in trouble.* The devout sister loved quoting this verse to Liz for some reason. Liz slowly closed her eyes and imagined angels ministering to her, pulling and pushing her, tripping and picking her up, gathering and forming a protective shield around her. She took a deep breath and reopened her eyes. The bedroom was dim. She thought about her mother and granny. A deep yearning to be with them developed within Liz. She missed their love, their warmth, their strength.

Keep faith and recognize His holy presence. Tessa's sermon again. *Submit to His will...* Religion wasn't really Liz's thing. She prayed sometimes but that's about it. She hadn't attended church since childhood. *Take your troubles to God so that Satan can't mount them up too high and push you too low.* Liz got up and headed to the kitchen.

The house was quiet and dark. She hit the light switch and poured a glass of water. A little refreshed by the cold drink, she went to the sitting room, which now served as She-She's bedroom. The girl was fast asleep on the sofa bed; the TV played without sound. Liz turned it off and pulled a blanket over She-She.

She went to Malik's room. The door was open, lights out, and his bed looked empty. She flipped on the light switch. The bed was definitely empty.

The clock on his stereo player read 12:24 a.m. Liz hadn't realized how late it was. She went to check the bathroom. Malik wasn't in there either.

"She-She." Liz nudged her awake.

"Huh?" she rose up.

"Did you see Malik leave?"

"No. I thought he went to sleep."

Liz asked, "Did Andre come over while I was asleep?"

"Not that I know of," she said. "He did call. He was at his girlfriend's house. He said he was spending the night over there."

"Did Malik speak with him?" Liz felt the jitters coming on.

"Yeah," She-She said, then asked, "Is something the matter?"

"Did you overhear what their conversation was about?"

"Malik had went to his room and closed the door," She-She informed her. "I know that him and my brother were mad about what happened to you earlier."

"Call Andre," Liz said. "Call any number that you believe you can reach him at."

CHAPTER 25

"Cuz, you ever bust a gun befo'?" Brian asked Malik from the back seat of the van. Malik pulled up in front of Kila's house and blew the horn. Answering Brian's question seemed frivolous; more grave matters warranted their attention.

"I'll do this solo." Brian yanked back the .45's chamber and released. "You don't need to participate."

Malik's impatience mounted. "Fuck that," he snapped, blowing the horn again. "That punk put his hands on my momz. Mutha Fucka 'bout to feel it." His insides boiled lava—all fear, all restraint, all mercy were in ashes. Malik had never seen his mother so terrified, so emotionally distraught. To compound this, he felt partly responsible. *Time to right all wrongs.* He was about to bring heat to Derrick's ass. "This nigga is bogus," he sneered. It was on.

Drizzle charged up to the van and got up front. His malicious mug and anxious posturing sent Malik's adrenaline into overdrive.

"Wassup, 'lil awol?" Brian greeted him, acting as if they were about to go to a concert or party instead of war. "Here ya go." He handed the cannon to Drizzle. "The fo'-five caliber like you rapped about."

"Damn this punk bogus, fam," Drizzle raved. "You don't touch a nigga's mother or baby sister unless you're absolutely beggin' to die." He gripped the pistol, keeping it on his lap. "I feel guilty as hell 'bout all this. It could've been avoided if I hadn't changed my mind last night." He shook his head. "Let's do this."

Malik smashed off.

"Y'all young niggas 'bout to do it gangsta, huh?" Brian teased.

Drizzle raged on. "Dawg, I swear whoever this cat Derrick is…" His cell phone sounded. He read the screen and handed it to Malik. "This your crib, 'Lik."

Brian said, "Auntie gone kill you. Don't say you're with me."

140

Malik's mind centered on vengeance. That's it, that's all. No time to hear any Martin Luther King-inspired sermons about non-violence and forgiving the enemy. "This won't take long," Malik said as he pushed toward Drizzle's 'hood. He tossed the cell on the dash.

"Good idea," Brian said. "Leave that phone in the van. I've seen too many cats drop their IDs and shit at the scenes of crimes. No world's dumbest criminal episodes on us," he laughed. "Ya know?"

Malik wished his cousin took this more seriously. Everything seemed a joke to Brian.

Another phone chirped. Malik glanced up in the rear view as his cousin checked the screen on his cell. The smile on Brian's face disappeared, quick. "Damn, 'Lik, this your mama." The jovial tone in his voice vanished too.

"Don't answer it," Malik told him.

"I bet Brandon caught her call and cracked under pressure," Brian said. He sat the phone under the seat. "I know she called the crib first. Darn it, dudes."

Malik parked around the corner from Drizzle's crib.

Brian put on black leather gloves. "How y'all prefer to put this down?" he asked. "I'll do it solo. In and out in no time flat. Bap, boom, bam, he's dead, maybe paralyzed." He chambered a bullet in his Glock. "Shall I, gentlemen?"

They disregarded his question. For Malik, this was personal. There'd be no change of mind this time. He'd promised his daddy a long time ago to look after and protect his mother. What he planned to do to Derrick fit that job description, he rationalized. "Give me the strap," he told Brian.

"Put these on first." Brian handed him a pair of dark gloves. Malik put them on. Brian removed a black Tech-9 from a pillow case. "This will open him right up, cousin," he bragged. "Unless you want this?" he offered Malik the Glock. "Already locked and loaded."

141

Malik took the Tech-9 and chambered a bullet. "Come on," he clicked off the safety.

"Guess ol' 'Lik wanna air something out," Brian grinned. "Cool. I'll demonstrate with this lil' Glock niner."

Doors opened, and they filed out of the van together. Drizzle led the way through a yard. They walked out into the alley and got surprised. Flashing police lights danced all around Drizzle's house. The cops were all over the place! Two undercover police vans sat parked outside the garage. Malik spun around in the opposite direction as another car hit the alley, its headlights flashing on him. Malik stood there frozen like a deer, the Tech-9 partly cloaked in his jacket. "What the--," he choked up. Brian snatched him by the sleeve. "Come on, cousin!"

The three of them took off back through the yard. They hustled up to the van, stumbling over each other, rushing through the side door. Malik accidentally dropped the gun. It clunked to the curb and slid next to the back tire.

"Get on in," Brian said, reaching down to retrieve it. Malik, breathing hard, dove into the driver seat, pressed the ignition forward, and slung the gear into drive. Brian jumped in and slammed shut the side door. "Push out," he commanded. Malik jetted off. Drizzle fell back into the back seat.

Malik hoped and prayed that the cops weren't on their trail. He tore down the block, swung the steering wheel left and floored the gas. Then he swung to the right down another street. He glanced in the rearview. No cars in pursuit.

Brian was the most calm. "Drizzle, that was the ATF," he said. "They must've raided y'all crib." He looked out the back window, adding, "a few seconds earlier, we would've been straight caught up, with guns smoking." A chuckle. "Burnt up."

Drizzle climbed into the front seat. "'Lik, ride past the crib," he said.

Malik slowed the van. "We got guns with us, fam," he said, knowing they'd just gotten super lucky. He was in no mood to push it.

Brian tossed the guns back inside the pillow case. "We can stash the straps somewhere then go see what's up," he said. "Drizzle, you duck low though. They're already looking for you."

Malik turned off into a dark alley and slowed up next to a garage. Brian surveyed the area, then got out, pillow case in hand.

"My momz goin' to jail, dawg," Drizzle said in a low, disappointed tone. Malik didn't know what to say. The struggle worsened for his homie.

Brian got back in the van. "Let's roll out."

As soon as Malik turned onto Drizzle's block, they spotted a slew of cops and their vehicles outside the house. A small crowd gathered across the street, looking on. Drizzle eased down in the car seat.

"Definitely the task force," Brian said as they rode toward the scene.

Drizzle peeped up over the dash. "You see my momz?" he asked.

Malik slowed down and caught sight of Janice, Jesse, Derrick, and two other guys. They were being marched out of the house in handcuffs. "There she go," he told Drizzle. He drove on past down the street. The whole scene evoked memories inside Malik's mind of the night Kevy went to jail. He stole a glance at Drizzle. The look on his homie's face said it all. Malik empathized. He knew the hurtful feeling of helplessness from watching a parent in cuffs, being hauled off to jail. Drizzle must have felt worse. At least Malik still had his mother; she was there to catch him.

Malik meditated on this during the ride back to Kila's house.

"I'll holla at y'all tomorrow," Drizzle said. His hurt was evident.

Malik parked the van. "You alright, fam?" he asked.

Drizzle grabbed his cellular off the dash. "Life goes on," he nodded. "We'll pull through it." He opened the door and stepped out. "I'll tell She-She the news about momz myself. Love."

"Love." Malik responded.

Brian got into the front seat.

Malik pulled off. "You want to go get those guns now?" he asked his cousin.

Brian dialed his cell phone. "I'll have my bitch take me. Drop me off at the crib." Then, "What's up, baby" he spoke into the phone. "Meet me at my house ASAP."

Thought her name was 'bitch'? Malik joked to himself. He dropped Brian off on the east side.

"Remember, you wasn't with me tonight," Brian said before getting out of the van. "I don't want your mama calling interrogating me."

Malik headed home. He knew his mother was anxiously awaiting his arrival. He rode up to the house and parked directly across the street. The porch and living room lights were on. The apprehension hit Malik straight in the gut.

Before both his Nike Airs could step through the door, she was at him.

"Where in the hell have you been, boy?" Liz glared, her mug the most vicious he'd ever seen it. He slowly shut the door and locked it.

"I went to pick up my friend," he lied. "He needed a ride." He did go pick Drizzle up. *Didn't really lie.*

"How?" she blocked his path. "You don't even have a car."

"Brian lent me his van," he said. "I told you that before."

She stared at him, angrily, suspiciously. "Do not start this mess, Malik," she breathed. "Not right now. It's too much happening in my life. I don't need you adding more."

She took a breath. "Next time you want to leave this house after curfew you get my permission first."

Malik nodded.

"Do you hear me?" she asked with force.

"Yes, mama, my fault."

"Now get your ass in bed so you can get to school on time," she commanded. "Almost two o'clock in the damn morning…"

****

Liz double checked the front door locks. She-She came in the living room, looking concerned.

"I apologize for waking you up again," Liz told her.

"That's okay, Auntie," She-She replied. "I'm glad Malik's alright. I was worried too."

Liz cut off the lights and went to her room. She collapsed back on her bed, exhausted. The bond with her son felt like it was slipping into estrangement. She knew he'd lied to her about giving a friend a ride. Her intuition convinced her of this. She lay back on the pillows. A welter of thoughts sloshed around in her head. The closer she got to the new chapter, the more troublesome her story became. Conflict. Conflict. Conflict. She wanted the resolution. The peace. *The Lord is… a very present help in trouble,* and there came Tessa's scriptural voice again.

Liz remembered going to church as a pre-teen. Her grandma came every Sunday to drag her off to 'da house of da Lord.' Granny used to always say, "Chile, Gawd luv little girls' praises. Y'all are his angels on earth." Liz loved when she said that. She loved being called 'da Lord's angel.' She loved her sweet granny even more. And when she died unexpectedly from a stroke, Liz's attendance at church died too. She did continue to pray, periodically. It was mainly to talk to her deceased grandma in heaven. By the time she reached her mid-teens, Liz gave up on prayer and God. Too much started happening around her, in her life. The brutal murders of the twins' parents hit Liz hard back then. Why would God allow those kids to be left without a mother and father, she wondered. *Why did God leave me the same way?* Although Liz's parents died later in life, it still didn't seem right. It made her doubt God's concern for her. Those doubts gathered strength over time. Some of the doubts also helped to appease Liz's conscience. She'd fallen a long way

145

away from being 'da Lord's angel.' Not to mention how she now frowned on the church's apathy toward the ills of the Black community. A quote pertinent to this issue hung framed on her living room wall:

> We will have to repent in this generation.
>
> Not merely for the hateful words and actions of
>
> the bad people but for the appalling silence
>
> of the good people.

Words of Dr. Martin Luther King himself, a man of the cloth. Liz heard the same 'appalling silence' today. The young dying younger, the rich getting richer and the broke becoming broker and more broken.

And all preachers seemed to tell people to do is pray. *The meek and impoverished shall inherit the earth.* They inherited the earth alright, Liz thought. *Heirs of dirt.* Liz felt that folks needed to roll up their sleeves and work for blessings. *Ain't no way,* she'd just pray, pray, pray, and let any ol' thing befall her or her son. Only the strong survived while the weak got treated like lames.

The Lord is my sustainer… keep faith… recognize… Holy presence… troubles to God… Satan… mount them up too high… push you too low… Chile, da Lord luvs little girls… praises… y'all… angels… on… earth…

Tessa's voice, granny's voice, the voices babbled away inside Liz's dome. She turned over on her side and kicked the blankets off her. The room was getting hot.

Sustainer… faith… Holy… Presence… Troubles… Satan… God… God… luvs… praise…

The words surfed the fringes of her mind. *Pray*, the voices suggested. *Where was God in all this craziness?* she wanted to know. All the deaths? Malik's car jacking? She-She's sexual assault? Her own assault?

Liz got up and cut on the TV. *God ain't thinking about me*, she thought half-heartedly. *I'm far from an angel, grandmama.* She clicked off the TV and lay back down. "I'm trippin'," she giggled, closing her eyes, drifting off to sleep.

146

CHAPTER 26

"Congratulations," Marvin said upon seeing Liz standing in the doorway of his classroom.

"Thank you," she replied, smiling tentatively. This was their first encounter since she'd officially broken things off with him. It being her last day of school, she wanted to stop by to clear the air.

Marvin stood behind his desk looking over some paperwork.

"I gave Mr. Spicer a call," Liz said. "We set up an interview for next week."

Marvin parked his butt on the edge of the desk. "Good luck," he said. "He's a good brotha and treats his employees fair." He eased his right hand into his pants pocket.

"I'm grateful for your recommendation," she said. The moment felt odd. She struggled to find something to say, and his aloofness toward her wasn't making things any easier. Moving farther into the room, she said "He also spoke highly of you."

Marvin stared at her. "We have a long history," he said without much feeling. "Old high school buddies." He wanted to say something to her; Liz sensed it. *Get it off your chest,* she wanted to tell him. The discomfort further discomfited her. Did she take advantage of him? Should she have taken his feelings into deeper consideration? It wasn't her intent to lead him on, then abandon what they had. *Or what he thought* they had? *Selfish,* the voices accused her.

"Look, Marvin, I just wanted to stop by to see you," Liz said, not too sweet, not too harsh. "I truly want us to remain friends."

"The friends thing again," he huffed. Wrinkles spread across his forehead and bespoke his displeasure. "If you wanted to just be friends, why didn't you play it like that?" He kept going before she could utter an answer. "You know, I tried to come up with excuses for you, rationalize your actions.

147

But nothing solid held. You were self-centered. You led me on whenever it suited you. Whenever a night got too lonely, you called. It was all about indulging your desires."

"You have it all wrong, Marvin," she defended.

He stood and gave them some distance. "Do I?" he said. "I could just imagine it if our roles were reversed. Then I'd become the stereotypical Blackman-as-dog." His feelings poured. "So what does this make you?" he asked.

No he didn't just insinuate that I was a bitch, she thought.

A young woman appeared in the doorway. "Mr. Jackson, is this a bad time?" she asked Marvin. He regained his composure and moved toward her.

Liz walked over to a window to give them some privacy.

What does it make me, huh? she thought of his snide question. She wanted to get pissed over it, but couldn't. His little outburst had resounded with truth. Liz couldn't deny it any longer. She'd been selfish. *Once again*, the voices added. She'd used him, knowing full well his feelings were invested. *Selfish.* Now those feelings lay trampled over. *Selfish.* Wanda was always complaining about Black men portraying canine mannerisms in their relationships with women—about how too many brothas didn't appreciate strong, intelligent sistas. Liz never envisioned the day that a good Black man would make a similar complaint against her. And what if she did decide to tell Marvin her reasons? What difference would it make? He still wouldn't be introduced to Malik or know about Kevy. That was her personal business. Hell!

Marvin and the woman finished their conversation. As he headed back to his desk, Liz jotted down her home number on a sheet of notebook paper.

Marvin returned to his crusty attitude. Liz came over, tearing the paper out the book. "Call me when your anger subsides," she said. "I'll explain some things to you." She extended the piece of paper.

He acted reluctant in accepting it. "There's no anger," he said. "I'm disappointed."

148

"So, are you going to call?" She felt like such a manipulator. He didn't answer. Instead he stared at her. She smiled, lightly. He looked away, pocketed her number, and picked up a folder from his desk.

"I'll understand if I don't hear from you," she baited him. He stared her way again, his eyebrows arching.

"But," she added, "if your heart is in this, then you'll give me an opportunity to explain things." They engaged in a silent stare-off for several seconds. Then Liz walked away.

CHAPTER 27

"Cuz, is yo' mama there?" Brian asked Malik over the phone. Malik was just about to leave the house to pick up Drizzle.

"No," he replied. "What's good?"

"Run outside and meet me in the alley," Brian spoke fast, energetically. "I got someone with me that you've been dyin' to meet again." There was conspiracy in his cousin's voice.

"'Lik, what's happenin', Dawg!" someone yelled in the background. Then laughter.

"Who is that?" Malik asked Brian.

"That's Maniac," he laughed. "Hurry up and meet us out back."

"Right now?" Malik's suspicions budded. "Where y'all at?"

"Fam, trust ya cousin," Brian urged. "I'm out back, right outside inna alley, waitin', so hurry up."

Malik slammed the receiver in its cradle and darted out the back door. He cut through the yard into the alley.

Brian and Maniac stood near the garage beside a crashed up, dusty black car. A Monte Carlo. It looked vaguely familiar to Malik. Particularly the large dent in the door. He frowned in confusion at his cousin, then at Maniac, then back at the car. Then it hit Malik: it was the same Monte Carlo he saw the night he got carjacked.

Brian smiled his menacing smile and stood in a triumphant posture. Maniac, no smile on his dark face, posted up by the driver's door.

"When you get back out?" Malik asked Maniac. The last he'd heard, Maniac had caught an attempted murder case.

"Jail can't hold us," he boasted as Brian signaled for Malik to follow him to the rear of the car. His cousin wore black gloves. Malik noticed that Maniac had on a pair of gloves too. His heart rate quickened.

150

"What y'all on?" Malik said, stepping next to Brian. Maniac surveyed the area as if he was on security.

Brian looked around in a circumspect motion. "Let me know if you recognize this stud," he told Malik, then popped open the trunk. Before lifting it, he removed a Glock from his waistline.

Malik jumped back upon spotting a body. "Dawg, have y'all lost y'all mind?" his voice shook with disbelief.

Brian chuckled at his reaction. "Look," he gestured toward the man who was hogtied inside the trunk. "That's the nigga who carjacked you, ain't it?"

Malik hesitantly peered inside it again. That was definitely the dude who robbed him. Only now the tough guy façade was gone. The punk was all fears and tears now.

"I'll give the car back, plus some loot, rims, and whatever," the captive promised in desperation. "I got plenty stuff I'll give y'all. Please, dawg, I didn't know," he begged for mercy.

Malik's shock and unease subsided. Now the roles were reversed.

"Shut ya punk ass up," Brian sneered and jabbed the hostage in the mouth. "This him, cuz?" he asked Malik again. Maniac stood calmly in the same spot, looking up and down the alley.

"That's him," Malik confirmed, his anger igniting. "Yeah," he spit in the hostage's face.

"Hold up, cousin," Brian laughed. "Spit is DNA evidence," he joked, dramatically smacking the hostage's face extremely hard, wiping off the saliva. The nigga kept begging for mercy.

"Shut up!" Brian ordered, crashing him in the temple with the Glock. "You robbed a Freeman, Nigga." Another pistol smack, this time to the forehead. "That's suicide, pussy," Brian raged against him. "You're that nigga's son who killed my mama and daddy, I bet," he accused.

A deep terror sprang into the hostage's eyes; sweat and tears saturated his face. "My daddy dead," he said.

151

Malik backed up. Brian was acting too crazy, again and again thwacking the dude with the tube of the gun.

Malik pulled Brian away. Maniac rushed over and slammed the trunk down on the hostage's head. It buoyed back open.

"Time to bounce." Maniac slammed the trunk again, this time it locked shut.

"You rollin' with us, 'Lik?" Maniac asked.

Malik wanted to yell "Hell naw, you nut!" He wanted no part in whatever they planned to do next.

Brian replaced the gun in his waistline. "We got this," he smiled like it was all a comedy skit. "'Lik ain't ready for this gangsta shit."

Sho' ain't! Malik couldn't agree with him more. No way was he going anywhere with them. They started getting back inside the Monte Carlo.

"Hold up," Malik called to his cousin.

"What's up?" he said, halfway into the passenger seat. Maniac climbed in behind the wheel.

"Don't murk dude," Malik urged his cousin. Brian frowned at him like he was crazy.

"This nigga stuck you, could've killed you, and later bragged around the city about it, not knowing you was my family. So fuck him. He's 'bout to give me Drizzle's car, all his stuff, plus extra. After that, I might consider letting him live."

"Come on, B," Maniac called out the window. He stared around, on alert.

"I'll holla," Brian got in the car. Maniac smashed off.

Malik stood there until they turned out the alley. He felt somewhat sorry for the fellow in the trunk. No telling what Brian and Maniac had in store for him. Malik did know one thing; that gangsta life was not for him. Not on the brutal level that Brian played it. His cousin acted straight loony. *A damn nut.* He couldn't do it. Acting that reckless, crazy, retarded. Malik couldn't ever see that for himself. No matter how angry he got.

Wait till I tell Drizzle 'bout this, he thought, heading back in the house to lock it up.

CHAPTER 28

When Liz went to visit Janice at the Milwaukee County Jail, she expected to see the same pitiful woman who she first met several weeks earlier. But Janice had cleaned up well, didn't really look the same at all.

Liz took a seat in the visiting booth and studied her through the thick glass partition. Janice's mocha colored skin exuded a rich, healthy glow and five neat French braids cascaded down over her shoulders. She smiled and lifted the phone receiver off the wall.

"How are you doing in there?" Liz broke the ice. She knew Janice couldn't be doing too well locked up facing multiple drug and weapons charges, along with revocation.

"My baby didn't come with you?" Janice sounded disappointed.

The question irked Liz. "No," she said. "I wanted to speak with you about a few things first."

"Is my son still in that detention center?" she asked.

Liz's frustration festered. *All of a sudden you're so concerned for them. Woman, please.*

"They're both fine," Liz told her. A short pause. "They really need you right now," she said forwardly, "especially your daughter. She's worried, and very confused and hurt."

Janice's expression grew remorseful. "I know my baby needs me," she spoke softly. "That's why I'm really going to try this time."

"Try?" Liz could hardly contain herself. "I think it's about doing. You need to get it together, Janice. You see where you're at, what you're facing. Look where your lifestyle has landed you." She gestured around the small visiting booth, then said, "Your actions don't only affect you but also your kids and others. How do you think She-She and Andre feel, seeing their mother high and now locked up?"

154

Janice slumped back in her chair. Liz suppressed any sympathy for her. The woman needed someone to tell her about herself.

"It goes beyond trying, sister," Liz said.

"I know," Janice tried to sound so damn pitiful.

Liz wouldn't be moved. "Do you know that your 13-year-old daughter hasn't slept since your arrest? She's up worrying all night."

"I know—"

"Then act like it," Liz said sternly.

"Look!" Janice screeched angrily, shamefully. "I realize my shortcomings, okay?" she glowered at Liz. "I don't need your perfect ass comin' down here pointin' them out. You don't know my life. You don't know what the hell I've been through."

"So damn what, you've faced challenges in life," Liz wasn't backing down one bit. "You can't keep blaming and making excuses. You grow stronger. Without struggle there's no success." Most likely the other visitors heard them, but Liz didn't care. "Your little girl was taken advantage of," she went on. "Right under your roof. By the same man that you let peddle drugs out of your home."

Janice quieted, her icy gaze melted into savage shock. "What do you mean—"

"Yes," Liz fumed, "by the same bastard who assaulted me and threatened my son with a gun. You were walking around spaced out while that coward Derrick, that child molester Derrick, whispered sweet nothings in your baby's ear, misleading her into believing he could fill a void in her that you helped leave empty."

Janice shook uncontrollably. "You didn't have to come lay all this on me."

Liz corrected her. "I didn't lay it on you. Your irresponsible behavior did this."

155

Janice banged the phone receiver against the glass window, leapt out of her chair, and cussed Liz out. "You kiss my ass…"

Liz stayed seated and let her rant and rave.

"I can't deal with this right now," Janice burst out into tears.

"What?" Liz said as sheriff's deputies appeared behind Janice. "You're going to run once again? Grow up," Liz said. Janice dropped the phone and stormed out of the booth, past the deputies.

Liz got up and walked out, ignoring all the backward stares from the other visitors.

CHAPTER 29

"I'll be glad when I get to play in your hair," Malik flirted as Brianna gave him a haircut. He was seated at her kitchen table, secretly hoping she didn't mangle his waves or maim his hairlining.

Brianna changed the guards. "Be still, boy."

"You hear my question, lil mama?" The clippers buzzed in his ear.

"Loud and clear."

"Well, when?"

"When you get your barber's license."

He said, "You don't have yours yet," and threatened to get up. "So—"

She twisted his ear. "Be still."

Malik stilled himself back into his seat. "Alright, alright," he pleaded with her. "This is abusive barbering." *Why in the world did I let her practice on me?* he lamented inside. *The things a brotha subjects himself to for the love of a sistah, I tell 'ya.* Although Brianna was set to graduate cosmetology school soon, he still had reservations about her barbering skills.

"You're lucky I'm feelin' you," he said, "cause if I wasn't…"

"You'd still be real still or get your wig split," she finished his sentence.

He laughed.

"Come on, before I mess up," she griped after he moved again.

"My fault, dang," he muttered. "Don't see why you need this schooling anyway. Somebody seems to already be taking good care of you."

"There you go again, trying to pry in my business on the sneak tip."

A guilty grin. "You think you know me, don't you, woman?"

157

"I just know when your butt is being nosy." She pushed his head to a side angle. "Now be still before your lining ends up dented up."

Her ample breast stared him right in the face as she stood in front of him, working the trimmers.

"So you're saying some sugar daddy ain't dishing out the dollars?" He rolled his eyes up at her when no response came. There was a slight shift in her facial expression. Did she take his comment the wrong way?

"You alright, Bree?" he asked thirty quiet seconds later.

She wrapped up his haircut and took a seat at the table. "I had a little sister who passed away a while back," she revealed.

He stopped brushing the loose hair off his shirt. "Straight up. What happened?" he asked, staring at her with sympathy.

She swept down the clippers with a tiny brush. "We lived in these low income row houses in St. Louis after the projects were torn down." She continued, "Most of the residents who moved there were out the projects too. Later we found out that the whole complex was just as toxic as the PJs, only it was infested with asbestos." She cleaned her barber tools absent-mindedly. "The people who owned the property knew about it before we moved in. We sued, won the lawsuit, and I lost my baby sister."

"That's crazy," Malik said, shaking his head.

"Sis died of lung cancer caused by the asbestos," she said. "My mother lost herself watching helplessly as my sister succumbed to death. Soon after, she turned to dope to escape the pain of it." She stood up.

Malik remained seated, listening.

"The owners never spent a minute in jail either. They knew about the health hazard to us, but figured no one else would find out. Just a bunch of broke people living there, so I guess they assumed…" she let it go. The rest wasn't hard for Malik to figure out.

Brianna gathered her barber equipment and left the kitchen. Malik got up and grabbed the broom. As he swept up the hair, the stereo came on in the next room.

Brianna soon returned, clutching a hand mirror. "Tell me what you think, and don't candy coat it since you've heard my sob story," she said cheerfully. Malik took the mirror and checked out his 'do. He rushed to the bathroom to get a more thorough look. She trailed him.

"What do you think?" she asked.

"You butchered it," he messed with her. She rolled her eyes, gave him the hand and headed back to the kitchen.

"I'm just jackin' at you," he laughed, following her. "you know you hooked me up—superbly." He took the broom from her and resumed sweeping the floor. "Let me work off my bill."

"You do that," she smiled, admiring the haircut. "I did hook you up, didn't I?"

"You did alright now. Don't get all big headed," he teased.

"Just bring me some clients when I open my salon up." She exited the kitchen.

"Just don't think I'm gon' be on the cleanup crew," he called after her. He finished sweeping, then called up Drizzle, who was over his cousin P-Nut's house.

"I'm 'bout to come scoop you," Malik spoke into the phone.

"My mama called over here 'bout an hour ago," Drizzle mentioned. "She's taking the fall for all the drugs and guns they found in our house."

Malik already figured that. "Straight up?"

"Jesse, Derrick and those other two cats put it all on her. She's 'bout to do some time in the joint." A pause. "It might help her get her mind right. I'm not trippin'," he said with cool indifference.

"So those other niggas go scot-free, huh?" Malik said.

Brianna walked back in and went to the fridge.

"Somebody needs to let the air out that punk Derrick," Malik said. "He keep gettin' away with bogus shit."

Brianna spun around, frowning at him.

"What?" Malik asked her.

"Huh?" Drizzle said.

"Talkin' to my wifey," Malik smiled. "She's looking at me crazy all of a sudden."

"Still ain't got the pussy, I bet," Drizzle teased him.

Brianna looked pissed.

Malik told Drizzle, "I'm on my way," and ended the call.

"What you mean by that 'letting the air out that punk' comment?" she asked, both hands on her hips.

Malik pulled on his coat. "I'll holler at you later," he told her. He didn't feel like talking to her about Derrick. "Good lookin' out on the haircut."

"So you're on that now?" she pushed it. "All of a sudden you talking like a gangsta rapper?"

"You shouldn't comment on things you know little about," he said, zipping up. "Dude put his hands on my mama and molested Drizzle's sister. He deserves any punishment that comes to him."

"Okay, gangsta," she kept it up. "Go on out there and get yourself locked up or killed behind something stupid."

"Something stupid?" he frowned. "What's stupid about what I just told you?"

"What's stupid is what you said on the phone, what you got on your mind concerning Derrick."

"He'll soon—" Malik caught himself. "Nothing. I'm out." He started for the door.

"I guess you're about to fall right into the b.s." she followed him. "Go ahead and act out the stereotype. You'll do Black folks real proud."

He bounced out of her apartment, saying, "I'm not try'na hear that garbage you're talkin'."

160

"You won't have to," she yelled down the hallway at him. "Don't call or come back here since you wanna be someone you're not. Be yourself!"

Malik kept it moving. The cold wintry air hit him in the face as he stepped outside.

I won't call no more, he thought, getting in the van.

CHAPTER 30

Kemet Quarters teemed with lively teens while the monstrous sound system pounded out hip hop cuts. It was a frenzy on the dance floor. The partygoers got loose, grinding their gyrating bodies against each other, or simply doing their solo steps. The rest of the young patrons lounged around the club, socializing and trying to blend in.

Malik chilled at the bar, sipping on a cherry Snapple and observing the spectacle. He mainly scoped out the young eye candy strutting their stuff all around the place. *Oh, what a feeling*, thought Malik. Drizzle had really rocked the mic tonight with flawless stage chemistry. All week, he had tried to convince Malik to be a part of tonight's performance. But Malik declined, preferring to stay behind the scenes. This particular show had been a crucial one because Prophet Kemet invited a local producer to watch, telling Drizzle that the man had major music industry connections.

Malik browsed around the club for the producer, wondering who he was.

Jenny popped up out of the crowd. "I see Drizzle had it jukin' up in here this evening," she said, sliding onto the adjacent barstool.

"Fo' sho'," Malik nodded.

"The crowd loved him," she continued, and started grooving to the music.

"Am I feelin' groupie vibes from ya?" he teased her.

She shot him a lame glare. "Forget you, dude," she pouted, backhanding his bicep. "You never called me either."

He smirked. "You didn't get my message?"

"No, because you didn't leave one."

Kila and Nana weaved their way to the bar.

"Hey, 'Lik," Kila helloed, then said, "Hey, girl," to Jenny. They returned greetings. Nana only offered up attitude. The tension between her and Malik persisted.

"Hi, Nana," Jenny spoke, and got disregarded. "Oh Kay." She got up to leave. "Well, I'll see you guys later." She then headed off.

Nana's funky stares tailed her. "You don't have to bounce on account of me," she yelled after Jenny. "I'm not try'na stop a playa from holding his trophy."

Malik paid the snide comment no mind.

"Prissy little skank," Nana added.

Kila frowned. "Stop acting so damn petty," she told Nana.

Malik addressed Kila. "Where Drizzle?" Nana had spoiled his whole mood.

"Whatever, Nigga," she hissed at him. "You're salty I offended your little white jumpdown?"

"Nana, bounce with that nonsense," Kila said.

Malik bridled his tongue.

"Whatever," Nana huffed and stomped off.

"She's just mad you're not giving her any attention," Kila said. "That girl needs to grow up."

"Ain't no secret," Malik agreed. He took a sip of his drink.

"Drizzle and P-Nut are in my uncle's office meeting with Jeff," Kila said.

"Jeff who?"

"That producer dude," she said. "Personally, I don't trust the nigga. He seem shady."

Malik nodded. "The sharks are prowlin' already, huh?"

"Thirsty and eager to eat off someone else's talents," Kila added.

163

"Family!" Drizzle appeared, behind Malik. They exchanged daps, then Drizzle threw an arm around Kila's waist. "Your uncle wants you in his office, asap," he kissed her on the neck and whispered something else in her ear.

Malik could see their puppy love flowering. The open affection Drizzle showed her got Malik to thinking about Brianna. He missed her, but pride stopped him from picking up the phone. Malik hadn't spoken to her since their argument. She hadn't called him, he hadn't called her.

Kila sashayed off with a lovey-dovey smile plastered across her face.

"You love that girl," Malik teased Drizzle.

"Cut it out, fam," he laughed. The smile vanished after something caught his attention.

Malik turned and saw the source of Drizzle's displeasure. P-Nut and Nana stood over in a corner, openly flirting and being touchy-feely with one another. She glanced toward Malik and rolled her eyes.

Drizzle sneered. "Look at this super sucka," talking about his cousin.

Malik looked away, untroubled. "It's all good and gorgeous," he assured Drizzle. "I hope he keeps her away from me."

"P-Nut knows the business," he said anyway. "Nana try'na use him to get to you. I'm 'bout to stand on his ass." He marched off to confront P-Nut.

Malik didn't move. He could care less who Nana messed with. Shit was comical to him.

But Drizzle didn't find it funny at all. He tongue-lashed P-Nut all the way back over to the bar.

Malik spun off his stool. "Told you I'm not trippin,' fam," he told Drizzle.

Drizzle still had the last word, giving P-Nut another stern warning about playing into Nana's "punk ass games."

P-Nut said he needed to go to the bathroom, then walked off. Drizzle calmed down and started telling Malik about the meeting with the producer,

Jeff. While they chopped it up, a group of female fans came over seeking Drizzle's autograph. They also complimented his rhyme skills in a coquettish fashion.

Kila appeared out of nowhere and wrapped her arm around Drizzle's shoulder. The girls got the picture and strolled away. Malik cracked up inside over the whole situation.

"Control ya groupies," Kila warned Drizzle. "I don't dig their cold stares."

The in-house DJ announced last song, and the clubbers prepared to leave.

Malik beat the crowd to the door. He walked outside, got in the van, and pulled around to the rear of the club, so they could load up P-Nut's music equipment. The doors were still locked. He waited awhile, then walked back around front to see what the holdup was.

People were already filing out of the club, packing the parking lot.

"That's out of order," someone complained. Then came other words of discontent—and laughter—throughout a gathering. Malik went to investigate what was going on. He cut through the small crowd and saw Jenny's Pontiac Grand Am. She was standing next to it with two of her friends. All three girls looked very upset. Malik soon found out why. Jenny's car leaned to the side on two flat tires, and 'White Tramp' was scrawled in red lipstick across the windshield. Malik had a strong hunch who the vandal was.

Several boys stood by, laughing uproariously at the damage. Malik didn't see any humor in it at all.

Jenny stared at him as she held a cell phone to her ear. Malik offered the three girls a ride, which they accepted. Drizzle and Kila came over and Malik told them what had happened. Nana was missing-in-action. Kila was genuinely pissed over the whole ordeal. P-Nut thought it funny until Drizzle checked him.

Kila offered to drop P-Nut off since Malik was giving the girls a ride. Drizzle rode with Kila as originally planned.

165

Jenny called AAA to come get her car. The Grand Am was loaded up on a flat bed thirty-odd minutes later. She paid the service man up front for the tow and made arrangements to pick up the car the following day. She didn't want to wait around for the tire repair.

Malik dropped off her buddies first, since they lived the closest. Jenny asked him to take her out to her grandparents' house. They lived on the outskirts of the city in Waukesha. Malik didn't enjoy the prospect of driving out to the suburbs. It was late and he knew he'd stick out like an Arab at the airport. *A brotha with a snow bunny, on his way to a lily white area,* he rued his potentially Emmett Till-like predicament. *At night*! Oh how he wished the van windows were limousine tinted. *Fo' real!*

Jenny asked, "What's so funny?" after he chuckled over the scenario.

"I'm just envisioning certain images, that's all," he said cryptically, driving at a modest speed up 60th Street.

"Images of what?"

"Of strange fruit hangin' from Southern trees," he grinned.

"Huh?"

He laughed at her puzzled look. "Nothing. It's a black thing."

"I wouldn't understand, I know," she replied with a pinch of bitterness.

Malik leaned over and turned up the radio.

"Thanks for giving me a lift," Jenny said, "although it's sort of your fault that your psycho girlfriend trashed my car."

"My ex-girlfriend," he corrected her. "If she could be called that."

Jenny stared out the side window. "She must be something to you because her attraction is gettin' fatal."

He laughed. "Don't jinx me."

They went without speaking for several minutes. Malik entered Caucasian country and kept a vigilant eye out for the Klan.

166

"Make a left on 95th", Jenny instructed. Following her directions, he turned onto a wide, quiet street.

"Y'all live out in the boondocks fo' real," he said, checking things out, on alert. Huge trees cast shadows over the street. Finely-built homes with immaculate lawns lined the block. Parked at the curb and in spacious driveways were newer-model cars, vans, and SUVs. Malik was far from the 'hood; this was a neighborhood!

"Where in the world have you brought me?" he uttered.

Jenny giggled. "My grandparents live out here," she said. "I stay with them when I wanna stay out late on weekends."

"You're gonna get my ass lynched," he said.

"Stop it, 'Lik," she laughed. "These folks are very friendly."

"That's to their white neighbors."

"Now you sound like Nana," she said, then pointed. "Park right behind that Lincoln."

Malik slowed down in front of a huge brick house that resembled a mini mansion. Night lights dimly shone across the manicured front yard. "I see your grandparents are livin' it up," he said, parking. A big body Cadillac sat in the driveway next to a Jaguar. *Probably inherited their wealth from y'all slave master ancestors,* Malik joked secretly to himself.

"'Lik?"

He looked over at her. "What it do?"

Some hesitance. "What is Nana's problem?" she asked. "I mean, why does she get so upset over us being cool? Is it only because I'm white?"

Malik shifted the van into park. "Nana has issues," he said, "and she just uses your race as a pretext to lash out."

"So if I was a black girl, she would still trip?"

"She'd find something else to get at you about. She's just hatin', but this isn't to say that some black chicks don't get genuinely salty over brothas dating white chicks."

167

"But we're not dating," Jenny shook her head. "And why is that? I mean, why is my color always a factor?"

"History designed our todays," he replied. "It's the American way, although people pretend we've grown beyond it. Like the nation has become this big happy melting pot of diversity, seasoned up with tolerance." He paused a moment. "See, you might not feel how much race influences things because you're part of the dominant culture. But blacks feel it all the time. We confront racism on a regular basis and still feel the effects of it from the past."

"And I don't?" Jenny flushed. "I felt it tonight when Nana wrote that racist garbage on my windshield. I feel it often when I'm the lone white person in the room." She was emotional. "I feel it from you too, 'Lik." Her voice lowered. "I really feel that you ignore me at school because I'm white."

Malik snickered to hide his self-consciousness. "We're talkin' now, aren't we?" he pointed out.

"Yes, but we're alone," she replied. "What about tomorrow or when we're in school or out in public and people are watching. Then how social will you act toward me?"

Malik thought about it. His mother always admonished him against becoming what he hated in other people. Was it even possible for him to be a racist? Prejudiced, bigoted or biased—yes. But racist—no. It took cold-hearted military and political power to dominate and disenfranchise a whole other people. Malik lacked those kinds of resources. Plus, he didn't hate white people. He hated white oppressors. And black oppressors for that matter. And niggas like Derrick!

"I can't exactly break it down for you to understand," he said to Jenny. "Race is a complex issue. Maybe I did shun you at school those times because you're not black."

"Because I'm white," she asserted.

He nodded. "No doubt." Then he smirked. "It's all good though. And rest assured, I love all pussy—black, white, red…

She blushed. "Malik!" Embarrassed.

168

He laughed. "I'm saying—"

She slugged him in the abdomen. "I'm being serious," she recovered. "This issue really does bother me."

He held his stomach. "Me too," he said with a straight face, then burst out laughing again. She joined in.

"Fo' real, Jennifer," he said. "We're cool. Maybe it's for us to grow together and set an example in our little part of the world. At least that possibility is there, right?"

She considered it. "Right."

"Plus, you're fair for a square white girl," he teased.

"Please, dude, I'm far from a square." She sounded cheerful.

"Well, let me bounce before the Gestapo catches me with you." He leaned forward, glancing out the window into the side mirror. "Your friendly neighbors might've called them by now."

She giggled. "Okay. You'll call me soon?"

"Can I get a hug?" he bargained.

"You mean you're not ashamed to touch me?" she asked.

"I told you I like all pussy," he grinned. "Better hurry before the wrong people see me."

"Stop it." She reached over, and they embraced.

"That's all I'm talkin' about," Malik said, feeling her stringy hair against his head, her warm face against his cheek. The mood swooped down on them as they slowly disengaged. And stalled. And gazed in each other's eyes.

Kiss her fool, he heard the internal order. The moment felt right but kind of awkward.

"You've never kissed a white girl?" she smiled, their lips close and waiting for it to happen.

"You never even kissed a black dude," he replied. She moved in... then a light flashed through the back window. They turned as a car approached and rode on past. Malik fell back from Jenny, spooked by the interruption. She looked confused, then disappointed, then resigned.

"I'll just talk to you later," she said, opening the door. "Thanks again for the ride, and much gratitude for our talk." A smile of appreciation.

"No doubt," he said. "I'll call you tomorrow."

"Looking forward to it." S he got out and headed up to the house.

Malik stayed on point till he made it back to his side of the tracks. He reflected on what had happened—and almost happened—between him and Jenny. It didn't take long for Nana's sarcastic comment to replay in his head either. *Careful going inna jungle, brotha. You might contract an incurable fever.* He couldn't stand her loud mouth ass.

CHAPTER 31

She-She ate with her head down at the kitchen table. She and Liz were having supper—chili dogs, seasoned fries and corn. Liz matched the girl's slow pace on purpose. They needed to talk but it couldn't be forced, Liz decided.

Ms. Hill, She-She's school principal, had called earlier that afternoon to inform Liz of She-She's three-day suspension for skipping English class. Liz shot right up to the school to pick her up. When she arrived, she met privately with Ms. Hill. The principal explained that She-She and a male classmate were found hanging out in the boys' bathroom. Liz alluded to some of the recent drama She-She had been dealing with, and Ms. Hill sympathized, saying that she could return to class the next day. Liz thanked her and promised to give She-She a good talking-to later.

"We'll visit your mom again on Saturday," Liz spoke across the kitchen table.

She-She said, "Alright," and took a small bite from her chili dog.

Liz neither judged nor justified the misbehavior. She-She was old enough and smart enough to know better. But Liz did try to place things in the proper perspective. The girl hadn't had the best parental guidance.

"Are you telling Andre and 'Lik?" She-She asked.

Liz got up to get the pitcher out of the fridge. "Telling them what?"

"What I got suspended for." She flashed Liz a shameful glance.

Liz poured them glasses of Kool-Aid.

"What happened?" she asked, taking her seat again.

She-She dipped a fry in ketchup. "I got caught skipping class…" she dropped the fry on her plate, "…with a boy from my class."

Liz eyed her.

"In the boys' bathroom," she admitted.

171

"Who is this boy?" Liz asked.

"Sean."

"Sean?"

"My boyfriend," She-She said.

"Why would your boyfriend have you in the boys' bathroom?"

She-She hunched her shoulders. "Stupid."

"That's a smart way to look at it," Liz said. "You need a new boyfriend because it sounds like Sean isn't for you. Sounds mannish."

"He is," she confirmed.

"You believe that he really respects you?"

She shrugged and went back to picking over her food. "I never asked him."

"You shouldn't have to," Liz said. "When a boy likes and respects you, he'll show it in his deeds. Anyone can talk a good game but all don't walk it. If he's asking you to disrespect yourself, then he's not respecting you at all." She let it sink in some. "Most importantly, respect yourself. Love and respect you first. You're a pretty girl, so knuckleheads like Sean will come along with their sweet jive trying to get you to do certain things. But if you want their respect, then remain a mystery. Your body is precious. No one has the right to violate it."

She-She looked on in agreement.

"And dump Sean," Liz advised her.

She giggled. "I am."

The ringing phone disrupted their little chitchat. Liz went to answer it.

It was Marvin calling. This was his first call since the classroom episode weeks earlier. "Hold on a sec," Liz told him, glad to hear his voice. "She-She, take care of the dishes, and I won't mention anything to Andre or Malik."

172

She-She got to it. "Bet." They exchanged cunning smirks. Liz retreated to her bedroom with the phone.

CHAPTER 32

Jeff the producer contacted Drizzle the following weekend to set up a meeting down at his recording studio. When Drizzle showed up at the scheduled time with Malik and the twins, a big burly brother named Mook welcomed them inside, introduced himself, and said "Jeff will be here inna minute, fellas," in a gravel baritone. He led them into a small reception room to wait, then returned to whatever he was doing on the computer.

And the four of them waited.

"Who is this Jeff cat?" Brian asked, obviously ticked off over the producer's tardiness.

Drizzle leaned sideways in an upholstered chair with his leg swung over the armrest. "I met him through my girl uncle." He toyed with his cell. "Ol' boy who owns Kemet Quarters."

Brandon's eyebrow jerked upward. "Prophet Kemet," he said. "That's ya girl uncle?"

Malik said, "Yup," and plopped down on a small couch. The twins glanced at each other.

"I know of that old school nigga," Brian acknowledged. "He did a bid back in the day, got out, and flipped the script on some straight legit grinding. He's havin' that bacon!"

"I remember when his case got overturned," Brandon nodded reflectively. "I was locked up at the time in Fox Lake. He got acquitted at the new trial. Gave those crackers back a seventy-year sentence, walked scot-free. They hated it, but the real niggas loved it." He smiled at the memory.

"What he go to prison for?" Malik asked.

"For bank robbery and shooting it out with the police," Brandon said. "The case was all over the news. The streets had counted him out. He came from up under it, though."

Malik's thoughts flew to Kevy. He imagined his daddy coming home after so many years on lock. "What do y'all think had the biggest influence on Prophet's success on appeal?"

"Money!" the twins chorused. "He had the loot to cop a competent lawyer. Plus, I heard that he learned the law himself. That's probably why he hasn't saw the inside of a jail cell since," Brian soloed.

"You can believe the feds got him under heavy surveillance 'til this day," Brandon chipped in.

"'Lik, we need to get rich and cop yo' pops a legal dream team," Drizzle said. "He's been in for a minute."

"No doubt," Malik replied, just as Jeff finally decided to show up. He walked through the door with two other dudes, who were dressed thuggish and gave off tough guy vibes.

Jeff appeared all about business. "Apologies for the delay." He shook Drizzle's hand and flashed Malik and the twins sideways glances.

"Are these your homeboys?" Jeff asked Drizzle.

"Naw," he stated proudly. "They're my family."

Jeff introduced his two companions. "This here is Chill Will." He gestured toward the lanky one, sporting an L.A. Lakers ball cap over a nappy afro. "He's a monster on the mic," Jeff claimed about Chill Will, "and this is Ronnie C.," he said of the other guy. "He's a monster inna booth too."

"Inna streets too," Ronnie C. jacked. Chill Will chuckled without smiling.

Malik picked up on the hint. Jeff would've preferred that Drizzle came without them. This was indicated by the way Jeff focused on Drizzle, basically ignoring Malik and the twins.

"Your family can kick back out here," Jeff told Drizzle, "and we can step into my office and talk bidness."

Brian gave Jeff an icy once-over.

P-Nut slipped through the door. "Did I miss anything?" he asked anxiously. "I got sweated by the po-pos."

Drizzle shot him an evil eye. Malik appreciated the brief distraction. Jeff assured P-Nut that he'd made it in the nick of time, appearing more receptive to P-Nut's presence. "Y'all come on in my office," he welcomed the two cousins as he moved in that direction.

"I'll be at ya inna moment," Drizzle replied. The producer stopped and turned back around. Chill Will and Ronnie C. mimicked his motions.

Jeff looked impatient. "Okay, brotha," he told Drizzle, and led his two stooges away.

"Dawg, why you all late and shit?" Drizzle snapped at P-Nut.

"You see how that punk straight up ignored us," Brian sneered.

"Chill out, B," Brandon told his brother. "Let Drizzle find out what he talking about."

Brian frowned and took a seat.

"Drizzle, y'all go ahead and see what's up," Brandon said.

"Watch dude too, fam," Malik warned. "I get funny vibes from him and those other two cats."

Drizzle led P-Nut into Jeff's office.

"I don't like this punk Jeff," Brian complained. "I'm tellin' y'all now."

Brandon took a seat. "You're going to encounter all sorts of people in life that you won't like," he said. "But that doesn't necessarily mean they can't benefit you. That's what should matter."

"Respect matters mo' than anythang," Brian said stubbornly.

"Prophet said ol' boy got major plugs in the industry," Malik said. He picked up a Don Diva magazine.

"I don't give a fuck if he knows Russell Simmons," Brian said, "he better learn to show mo' respect to real niggas." He rested a hand on the bulge under his Pelle jacket.

176

Mook remained tightly squeezed in a chair at the reception desk. Music played out of the computer speaker as he focused on the screen and poked at the keyboard. He paid Malik and the twins little attention.

Malik glanced at the lump on Brian's jacket.

"B, it's a new method of dealing with situations in the music industry," Brandon said. "You'll need to develop a thick skin and press pause on yo' street instincts."

"These so-called legit hustlers are just as cutthroat as niggas in the streets," Brian said. "They just rob people with pens and paper instead of pistols. They're paper gangstas."

That made sense to Malik.

Brian continued. "If they find a sucker, they'll swiftly try to stick a hard dick in him. No Vaseline. Give him a legal dickin'."

Malik laughed at his cousin's metaphoric rhetoric.

"Yeah, think it's funny," Brian snickered at him, "just don't get bent over, cousin."

Malik didn't see the humor in that. The twins laughed at his long face.

Drizzle and P-Nut came back out.

"That's all good, cuz," P-Nut enthused. "Sign with dawg!"

Drizzle wasn't as celebratory.

Malik and the twins stood to their feet.

"What's the business?" Brandon said.

"Dude offered me a contract," Drizzle said. "He wants me on his label."

"Hell, yeah!" P-Nut was just gangbusters over the whole idea. "He got pictures of himself with all kinda famous rappers. We'll be doin' music videos and everything."

"So he claims," Drizzle sounded skeptical.

177

"Tell that cat you're not signin' nothing," Brian said.

"Are you familiar with contracts?" Brandon asked Drizzle. "Dude might be peddling dreams."

"Ain't no secret," Drizzle said.

Mook stood up as Jeff walked back out with Chill Will and Ronnie C.

"You ready to blow like the twin towers, playboy?" asked the producer-cum-CEO.

"Me and my fam need to go over the contract," Drizzle said. "We'll holler at ya inna day or two."

Jeff's impatience resurfaced. "Brotha, the first rule of this game is always keep bidness and family separated," he schooled. "Now if—"

"Nah, Brotha," Brian cut in, stepping next to Drizzle. "The first law of any game is making sure you know who the opposition is, lest he pose as a friend and destroy you."

Jeff blew off Brian's comment, saying, "Say, Drizzle, what you wanna do, playa? I got other bidness to attend to and don't have time to chase the wind. Do you wanna slice of the money pie or prefer to stay stranded in this city with crumbs and crumb chasers." He said all this in one final breath.

"Cuz, you should…" P-Nut began before Drizzle flicked him a 'shut-the-fuck-up' mug.

"Fam, if you can't peruse the contract, it isn't worth signing," Malik told Drizzle.

"Who is you, this nigga's lawyer?" Chill Will confronted Malik. Ronnie C. and Mook cackled like hens.

Brian unzipped his Pelle. "Who do yo' tissue soft ass think you talkin' to?" he started at Chill Will. Brandon grabbed his brother, then stepped forward.

Chill Will huffed and puffed up. "Whoever you want me to be talkin' to," he challenged Brian.

"I'll handle this, Will," Jeff said, pushing Chill Will behind him.

178

"Yeah, Willie Chili, you better let him handle it before you end up fatally handled," Brian threatened over Brandon's shoulder.

"I'm not fuckin' with this," Drizzle decided. "Let's bounce, fam."

"Be gone, you—" Chill Will was saying until Brian's gun barrel greeted him. Silenced him.

"You what?" Brian dared him to complete the sentence.

Jeff, Mook, and Ronnie C. jumped back with their hands up. Brian directed them up against the wall. P-Nut got out of the way. Malik and Drizzle maintained their positions as Brandon backed up his brother.

"Lil' AWOL, come here," Brian said, steadying his Glock on Chill Will's chest. Drizzle moved next to him.

"What's up, B?" he asked.

"Willie Chili wants to tell you something," Brian said. He inched the cannon closer. "Don't you, chump?" he asked Chill Will.

A part of Malik wanted to play peacemaker. But Brian seemed to have things under control.

Chill Will's tough guy demeanor descended into fear and trembling.

"What do you have to say, chump?" Brian poked Chill Will's ribcage with the muzzle. Brandon frisked all four guys for weapons.

"I was just jackin'," Chill Will said with a nervous chuckle.

"Apologize, punk," Brandon told him. "Tell my family you're sorry for the disrespect."

"And it better be sincere," Brian threatened.

Chill Will uttered, "My bad—" then Brian bopped him on the ear with the burner.

"That don't sound genuine," Brian said.

"Come on, brothers," Jeff pleaded.

Brandon shoved him back against the wall.

179

Brian stayed at Chill Will. "Now say you're sorry because you're a gay ass nigga try'na act hard," he instructed. Chill Will held his ear, looking a lot less thuggish.

Malik and Drizzle smirked at each other. P-Nut stood near the door glancing back and forth, nervous.

"Say it," Brandon urged Chill Will.

"I'm sorry, dawg," he spoke loud, clear, convincingly.

Brian smiled The Smile. "What else?"

Chill Will looked mortified. He muttered, "and I'm gay—"

"I said say 'gay ass nigga,'" Brian reminded him. "No ad-libbing. Follow the script, fag."

Malik suppressed his laughter. Brian was a fool!

"Cause I'm a gay ass nigga try'na..."

Drizzle burst out laughing. Malik let go too.

"Come on, B," Brandon pulled his brother away.

Brian reluctantly complied, warning Chill Will, "Next time I'm leaving you stiff."

Ronnie C. and Mook breathed gratitude as Brandon backed Brian, Drizzle and Malik up toward the door. P-Nut exited first and fast.

They all went and hopped inside Brian's truck, except for P-Nut. He got in his mother's old, raggedy Malibu.

"Brandon, you messed up my movie directing," Brian joked on the ride to the east side. "I was practicing."

Malik and Drizzle laughed up a storm in the back seats. Brandon drove without comment.

They made it to the twins' house and exited the SUV. Brandon and Brian started toward the house. Malik and Drizzle waited near the curb while P-Nut parked and got out.

"Yo' cousins are wild, 'Lik," P-Nut giggled, approaching. Drizzle glared at him.

"Y'all come on in the crib," Brandon called from the porch. They headed up to the house, entering. Drizzle and P-Nut dropped down on the sofa. Brian strolled out of the kitchen snacking on a bag of strawberry licorice. His Glock rested on the pool table.

"That cat Jeff is sheisty," he said. "He tried to pull a move on you, Lil' AWOL." He turned on the stereo and collapsed back on the La-Z-Boy chair.

"I'm already knowin'," Drizzle said.

Brian reclined. "See what I'm saying," he said. "It's all cutthroat, don't matter if you're legit or not." Then The Smile. "I started to strip all four of them for old time's sake. Y'all think they had some loot?" he asked.

They laughed and P-Nut laughed the loudest.

Brandon came out of his room. He looked disappointed. "Forget dude Jeff," he told Drizzle. "You'll find another plug. Can't jump out the window at anything."

Malik took a couple licorices from Brian.

"Fo' real," P-Nut said.

"What you talkin' about 'fo' real'?" Drizzle got at him. "You was ready to let me sign the first piece of paper he shoved in my face?"

P-Nut closed his mouth.

"Better believe everything that glitters ain't gold," Brandon said. "Don't trip. I'll holla at my guy about some beats and studio time for you."

"He got a studio?" Drizzle asked.

Brandon grabbed his keys off the coffee table. "It's not state of the art, but it's workable," he said. "At least for now." He palmed his cell and left out the front door.

P-Nut was really checking out the twins' pad. Malik just did *not* trust him.

Brian and Drizzle started debating over which famous R & B chick was the finest. Malik envisioned Brianna. They still hadn't spoken, and it was getting harder for him not to call her. He wondered if she missed him. He missed her. He knew she cared. That's why she'd got so upset over the comment he made to Drizzle. She didn't want him getting into trouble, and he respected her for that.

"I'm about to bounce," P-Nut announced.

Drizzle got up too. "I'll catch a ride with you," he told his cousin. "I need to go check on my Chevy down at the shop."

"Your car straight, Lil' AWOL?" Brian smiled, knowingly.

Drizzle returned the smile, then followed P-Nut out of the house.

"I'm up too," Malik said. "Can I roll the Infiniti truck?" he asked, semi-serio*us.*

Brian gazed toward the front door. "Go ahead." He gestured at the keys on the speaker. "Keep my cell with you and answer when I call."

Malik tried not to show his excitement. It was definitely time to call Brianna.

"Another thing," he said to Malik. "Don't trust that nigga P-Nut," he warned. "He's shady and shows blatant signs of a coward."

Malik already knew. "No doubt."

CHAPTER 33

Liz stood quietly in the doorway of Bobcat's room. The old fella didn't notice her for all of two minutes. He sat gazing out his window at the snowflakes swarming down from the gray sky. Once he finally did turn to see her, he perked up and greeted, "Look who the cat has dragged in." A weak smile, "no pun intended."

Liz gave a warm smile. "Hey you." She took in the familiar smell and sights of the place, and felt a slight distance from it all now. A full month had elapsed since she'd resigned to start the new job at Technology Enterprises. She had no intention of returning for a visit this soon, until the unexpected call came from Amy, her former supervisor at the nursing home. She wanted to know when Liz planned to pick up a box of stuff that Tessa left for her to have. At first Liz was confused. *Tessa left me what stuff?* she wondered.

Amy had assumed Liz knew about Tessa's death and attended the funeral the day before. The sad news was very disheartening to Liz. She showed up at the nursing home less than an hour later, and found most of the residents in a reflective mood. Bobcat wasn't even his ol' mischievous self. "How's Lizzy been?" he asked. His puffy arms rested crisscrossed on his pot belly.

"I'm making it." she replied. "What about yourself?"

"You know the cat," he grinned, "Just squeezing out these last few days of living."

"You have more than a few days of living left," she told him.

"The new gig going well?" he asked.

"Yes," she said. "I'm still adjusting to working third shift though."

A little more small talk followed. Bobcat made her promise to come back to visit again soon. "Try not to wait until another one of us bites the dust," he said. Liz waited for a dirty joke or a request for Viagra. But he kept it clean. She gave the old guy a hug, then left to finish making her rounds. She went to see Amy last.

The supervisor was at her desk reading over some pamphlets.

"Knock, knock," Liz said to get her attention.

Amy looked up. "Hello." She seemed a little puzzled at first. "Oh, come on in." She stood. "You're here for Tessa's things, right?"

They chitchatted for about five minutes. Liz asked about Tessa's family. Amy said that she could only find one phone number for Tessa's sister, but it was no longer in service.

Liz left the nursing home, brooding on her own mortality. When she made it home, she placed the box of Tessa's things in the closet. She wasn't quite ready to open it. She gathered up some unwashed laundry, and lugged it down to the basement. As she separated the colors from the whites, she thought about Tessa. It made no sense. Where were Tessa's siblings, children, grandchildren, great grandchildren? Why did they leave her in a nursing home to die all alone? *I guess all Tessa had was the Lord,* Liz concluded somberly, somewhat bitterly.

Liz often struggled through her lonely nights, but at least she still had loved ones to love and to love her back. She wanted to believe that they would never abandon her, or drop her off somewhere to be cared for by strangers. Malik. Wanda. Kevy. Other relatives. They all loved and cared for her. Marvin even cared. *Don't go there,* the voices butted in.

Life, love, death. Liz meditated on these concepts until she started feeling depressed. She exited the basement in a lonely mood. She got the book that Marvin had gifted her shortly after their first 'hotel visit.' A novel by Octavia Butler. She lay down on the living room couch and cracked it open. The concentration just wasn't there. Liz's thoughts zigzagged all over the place. She tossed aside the book and turned on the TV. Soap operas and talk shows, the very programs she took little delight in watching. *Boring junk.* She turned the idiot box back off.

I wonder if he's at home? The phone winked at her from the table a few feet away. Calling to see seemed so attractive right now, Liz entertained. She waited for the voices to protest. They kept quiet.

Liz picked up the phone. Dialed. Marvin's voicemail answered three rings later. She left a short message and hung up. *Ah hah*, the voices taunted her.

"Whatever," she said, picking up the novel again. She began reading…

Liz found herself tiptoeing down a dimly lit hallway. "Where is everyone?" she whispered, realizing she was back at night school. She sought out any sign of human life. None. She felt isolated, alone. She approached the computer lab and peered inside. Empty of human life too. Rapid heartbeats and strained breaths echoed in her ears from within her. She appeared in front of another classroom, then another, then another and another, finding each one vacant. She reversed direction and ended up at Marvin's classroom. Inside danced the shadow of a flame. She moved deeper into the room to investigate it. The lonesome feeling squeezed her tighter with each cautious step she took. The building suddenly darkened behind her. She reached forward in fear of bumping into a desk, a bookshelf, a cabinet, a wall. Marvin's classroom seemed much larger than Liz remembered. The flickering image of the flame stretched over the walls, the ceiling, the floor. The closer she tried to get to the flame, the more distanced it became. It was enchanting. Liz stopped and snapped out of its spell.

She looked back over her shoulder. Pitch darkness rushed her eyes like a fierce wind gush. Her heart pounded harder, breathing grew more strenuous, heavier. The door had disappeared in the blackout. She swung her focus back toward the fleeing flame. She proceeded toward it, and it flittered farther away, appearing to die out. The deepening flutters of Liz's heart rattled her whole body. The lonesome feeling squeezed harder.

"Liz?" his voice whispered. Liz darted her eyes in search of him.

"Marvin?" she cried out. "Where are you?" Her words echoed.

"What is it you want, Liz?" he called back from a distance. "What do we have together? I need to know now." She heard the remote rings of what sounded like a telephone.

185

Liz hastened toward the dying flame, toward Marvin's voice. They were leaving her behind. "Wait," she cried. "Marvin, I can't see you. Don't let it burn out." She felt sweat pouring. The flame scooted away as she pursued it. Liz picked up speed, hoping not to collide with anything. She started gaining on the flame. Almost… she got within reach as it fizzled out. Liz buckled at the knees and sank to the floor. The engulfing darkness prevailed.

"Mama?"

She leaped back up to her feet. "'Lik?" her voice cracked. "Baby, where are you?"

"What?" Malik called out from the dark. She looked around in a panic.

"Mama." He sounded closer.

"Malik!"

"Mama, wake up."

"Come here, Baby." Liz no longer felt alone.

"Mama."

She opened her eyes and saw her son standing there, looking confused.

A dream! It was all a dream, she realized, rising up on the couch—the novel fell from her lap onto the floor. "What time is it?" she bent down to retrieve the book.

"About seven o'clock," he replied. "You alright?"

She was covered in sweat. "Yeah, turn the damn heat down."

"It is," he said.

"I need you to go pick up She-She from Wanda's house."

Malik stared at her like something was on his mind.

"You wanna talk?" she asked. "What's new with you?"

"Nothing too exciting," he said with a tittle of attitude. "Anything new with you?" he asked.

"Not really." She stretched out and yawned. "Have you written your daddy lately?"

"Have you written him?" More than a tittle this time.

"What's on your mind, boy?" she asked in a tolerant tone.

A momentary pause. "Who is this dude Marvin?" The accusation surfaced in his eyes.

"What?" she asked. "Why you ask? Did he call?" she faltered, acted guilty. *Must've called while I slept*, she assumed. *Dammit!*

"Is he your new nigga?" Malik asked.

"Watch your mouth before I slap you in it," she snapped.

His defiance loomed over the entire living room.

"Did he call here?" she asked again.

"Apparently so," he spat out.

Liz said, "Marvin is a friend that helped me get that new job," volunteering information. *I don't need to explain myself.* She could hear Wanda's chiding mouth. *I'm grown. The mother. He's the child.*

"You go get She-She," she said with authority.

He mumbled, "Wonder if my pops know about this friend," walking out the house. He slammed the door behind him.

"I'ma hurt that boy," Liz said to the empty house, "Acting silly." She reached for the phone.

****

"Ummm… ummm… ohh!" Liz's lustful moans resonated throughout Marvin's bedroom. They sexed it up with freaky abandon between the sheets, giving one another body rockin' pleasure. His coordinated long strokes helped to release her pent-up stress, and she hungrily welcomed each satisfying thrust.

"Tell it to me," he groaned, and she responded in salacious chants. The friction had their bodies feverishly dewy. "Tell it to me," he said again and again with mounting manly affection. She told him, too. And he stroked longer, deeper, spreading her thighs wider until her heels edged off each side of the bed. She swung her legs up around his back, squeezing their bodies together. She wanted to be fucked like this—she needed it hard and rough and plunging and eager—*no slow romantic shit.*

And Marvin delivered, with sweating, smacking intensity. Each forward thrust inside her felt like he was absorbing portions of stress, relieving her of it with each retreat.

"I'm tellin' yoooou!" she cooed and laughed out.

He slowed up. She slid from under him, whipped the sheet aside and climbed on top. She reached down and guided his member inside her wetness. It felt marvelous, ecstacy with tingles of pain. Liz rode him wantonly, wildly. He palmed her hips in a firm grip. She liked the extra touch. The tension, the stress, all the emotional build up, came with at least one perk and Liz was now taking full advantage of it.

The orgasm sucked her breath away. "Goodneeesssss." Sent her crashing into his chest. She rolled over onto the mattress thoroughly satisfied. He leaned over and rubbed his moist lips across her right nipple and got out of bed.

Liz lay there staring up at the ceiling, thinking. Marvin had really come through for her this time, on both the sexual and intimate tip. His affection soothed the tension she had been feeling inside over the last few months. The new work hours hadn't been all that easy to adjust to either. This feeling felt better than cashing a check. *Some things money can't buy.* She loved it. For an ironic instant, she empathized with Janice. *Drugs. Men. Both can become addictions--escapes.* She thought about the dream. Whatever Liz's dream meant earlier, she knew one thing: It would take some torrential rains to extinguish the flame burning between her and Marvin.

188

CHAPTER 34

The crowd went absolutely bananas as Drizzle performed. Malik hyped them on, bouncing around the stage, mic in hand, rapping along here and there. He, Drizzle, and P-Nut had practiced all morning and part of the afternoon for tonight's set. Now their chemistry breathed new spunk into Drizzle's stage show. They had Kemet Quarters jukin'!

Malik never knew what he'd been missing until now. Electrcity flowed between them and the audience. He scanned the crowd, trying to spot the twins. Folks were everywhere!

Barely even breaking a sweat, Malik and Drizzle ended their set, throwing up the deuces to the party people. The cheers and hometown love sent them offstage feeling like ghetto heroes.

"Didn't I tell you, fam'?" Drizzle beamed, giving Malik a passionate double pound.

"I might start rappin' after this," Malik returned. "They were lovin' it."

"Didn't I tell you?" Drizzle celebrated.. They were geeked. After knocking fists again, they went into playa-mode and strutted out to the main floor.

Drizzle went to join Kila in VIP. Malik shot to the restroom to take a leak.

The pungent odor of weed smoke hit Malik as he entered. A small circle of guys hung out, sharing a slim blunt and shooting dice on the tiled floor. Malik stepped up to a urinal to relieve himself.

"That cat Drizzle is sho' to blow," one of the gamblers commented. "That boy is a beast."

"I wanna hit his dame Kila," another boasted. "I'll do damage to her thick ass."

Malik listened. They had no idea who he was.

189

"That broad is in love with dude," someone else said. "You're better off try'na knock her buddy Nana. I hear she a boss freak."

The word is officially out, thought Malik. He finished up and stepped over to the sink to wash his hands. The weedheads offered him a hit of the blunt and another invited him to join the crap game. Malik nodded in the negative, dried his hands, and exited the bathroom.

"Cousin!" Brian called out as Malik approached the booth. He knocked fists with his kinfolks. The twins kicked back like celebrities in the far corner of the club. Brandon, geared up in a crispy tan denim 'fit and matching timbs, observed the crowd. Brian sported gold and ice on both wrists and around his neck; his outfit: dark jeans and a polo golf shirt. The females standing nearby overtly solicited their attention.

Brandon said, "Drizzle set this joint on fire tonight! Prophet gotta start comin' out his pockets."

"Straight up," Brian said. "They came to see Lil' AWOL."

A young lady came over and sexily interrupted them. "Which one of y'all is Brandon?" she asked. The Baby Phat attire she wore accentuated her physical features quite erotically.

"I am, baby," Brian swiftly lied. "What's up with you?" She stepped over and put a hand to his ear, whispering something that put a lustful smile on his face.

"I can believe every word," Brian assured her. "Each vowel and consonant. Now please tell me you're over eighteen." He stared with hopeful anticipation.

She whipped out an I.D. "Nineteen and some change," she sassed. "Far from jailbait, baby."

"That you is, that you is," Brian laughed. "I'm grown too. That makes us compatible."

She handed him her phone number. "Call me later and we'll see."

Brian smiled at the piece of paper. "I'll do that. Promise you."

190

"What made you ask for my brother Brandon?" Brandon asked her.

She eyed Brandon. "I heard that you were the wild twin," she smiled, not knowing she'd just handed her info to the wild twin. "The streets talk and I listen." She strolled off.

Malik and Brian burst out laughing after she disappeared into the crowd.

"Wish I was a balla," Malik uttered. "Y'all crazy." He thought how strange—and fun—it would be to have a twin.

Jenny walked by. "Hey, 'Lik," she greeted. He nodded in her direction. She kept it moving toward the dance floor with her three buddies.

"Never thought yo' pro-black ass would be drawing with a young pink toe," Brian teased him about Jenny.

Malik flew into denial. "I'm not messing with her like that, B," he defended, trying not to sound so defensive. "She's cool but it's strictly buddy-buddy cool. That's it." Since the night he dropped Jenny off and their lips almost locked, Malik did entertain the thought of them going there. He kept this to himself though. When they spoke on the phone, which they had done almost daily for the last month, or chopped it up at school, he enjoyed it. She really was a cool chick. The attraction was mutual; she made hers obvious, and he hid his, only flirting when they talked in private. He fought the feeling because he didn't want people spreading rumors. *Malik's dating that white girl Jenny,* he could hear the gossips gossiping.

"'Lik, I can't understand why you're all self-conscious," Brandon said. "Nothing wrong with white broads. They'll keep it more real than sistahs if you groom 'em right."

Malik grimaced. "You crazy as hell," he asserted. "That's a myth that should've gotten dispelled after the O.J. case." He hated hearing such stupid stereotypes. "You can believe the hype if you want to," he continued. Talk like Brandon's further discouraged Malik from exploring the other side. He'd never even thought about it until he met Jenny. Sistahs suited him just fine.

"You keep lettin' race blind you," Brandon said. "Niggas better step out that box. We complain about racism and fail to see our own bigotry."

191

Malik cut in. "History justifies our attitudes toward white people."

"Dawg, y'all hold that down," Brian said. "We at the club. Save it for Sunday table dinners. Damn. Let's talk about all these hot heifers running around here."

Brandon ignored him. "I'm saying, Malik," he said, "it's the 21st century. Niggas gotta ally with white, brown, yellow, and red if we want to get that green."

Drizzle came over. "What upper, family?" he plopped down next to Brian. "Y'all ready to bounce?"

"Yeah," Brian said. "These dudes over here acting like they're at a black forum or something." He twisted out of his seat, staring at the piece of paper again. "Plus I got a late light with Tangy."

P-Nut joined them, and they headed for the exits. On the way out of the club, Malik caught a glimpse of Jenny. She was near the bathrooms with another girl, eyeing him. He averted his gaze and followed his fam' out the doors.

Outside, the frigid air encouraged them to make haste toward the rides. P-Nut and Malik climbed inside Drizzle's Chevy—Malik behind the wheel. Although Brian wasn't able to get the rims back—the carjacker-turned-hostage claimed he'd already sold them—he did get all the music equipment back along with the Sony Play Station, TV and full replacement money for the rims. Brian also demanded a hefty interest fee on the debt. He called it "Die another day taxes." Malik was just relieved that Brian let the dude live.

"'Lik, hit it!" P-Nut panicked. "There go them niggas from that studio." He scooted down in the passenger seat.

Malik followed his fearful gaze and saw Jeff, Chill Will and two other goons walking up on Brandon's Escalade. Drizzle and the twins had just climbed inside it.

Malik's heart jumped over itself as he hopped out to alert them of the threat.

Brian had already peeped the foes; he sprang out the SUV ready for war.

"Bring it now," Chill Will sneered, holding a huge black burner.

Malik ducked behind the Escalade. Drizzle crept around the other side, a small semi-automatic in hand.

"Get back in the Chevy," Drizzle whispered to Malik. "We got these cats."

Chill Will and his goons scattered as shots rang out. Drizzle ran out and started gunning.

Malik ran and plunged inside the Chevy. P-Nut hid way under the dash, his knees bent up to his chest, his neck scrunched over on his shoulder.

Malik stayed low in the seat until the shooting stopped.

"Hit it, dawg!" P-Nut begged, squeezing himself farther under the dash.

Malik threw the car in gear. "Shut yo' scary ass up," he lashed at P-Nut. "Stop acting like a bitch under pressure." He zipped out of the parking lot. The Chevy jumped the sidewalk and wheeled bumpily off the curb onto the street. P-Nut's head smacked against the underside of the dashboard.

Malik sped non-stop for two blocks.

P-Nut slithered back up into the passenger seat. "That was drama," he said bravely. He stared out the window, the heebie-jeebies all over him.

Malik dipped off into a Walgreen's lot. "I gotta see what's up," he said, making a U-turn.

"What the hell you doin'!" P-Nut screeched like a girl.

Malik stayed on the lookout for Brandon's Escalade as traffic rode past from the opposite direction.

"We don't got nothing to protect ourselves," P-Nut whined, his eyes searching for danger. "Those niggas might spot us and gun us up."

193

Malik could no longer stomach it. He skidded over to the curb and gave an ultimatum. "You either shut up or get out." Kemet Quarters was right up the street.

"I got weed on me," P-Nut claimed. "We can't—"

"What you gonna do?" Malik took on a stronger tone.

"This bogus." He opened the door and got out.

Malik reached over, pulled the door shut, and smashed out. He got back to the club and saw people coming out. Heavy traffic crowded the streets. Malik circled the block and came back around from another direction.

The cops were showing up. "Time to go," he said to himself. On the way past the club, he spotted Jeff, the shady producer, limping up to a burgundy Cutlass Supreme. A chick cut right in front of the Chevy, forcing Malik to slam on the brakes. She ran out the streets. Malik had halted right next to the Cutlass. He noticed a painful expression on Jeff's face. One of the goons wrapped Jeff's arm around his shoulder to help him inside the car. "He's shot," a female screamed to a cop riding past.

That's when Malik caught sight of the blood soaking Jeff's pant leg. *It's really time to go.* He got out of there, racing for the eastside.

He drove up and stopped in front of the twins' house. No sign of the Escalade or anyone else.

He wheeled around to the alley. "Good," he relaxed upon seeing Brandon's truck backing into the garage.

Brandon stepped out the yard. "Park around front," he instructed Malik. Drizzle lowered the garage door.

"Where's Brian?" Malik asked.

"In the crib already," Brandon said.

Malik parked around front. When he got in the house, Brian greeted him with an evil grin. "See Lil' AWOL sweat those chumps?"

Brandon and Drizzle came through the back door.

194

Drizzle was still a bit amped up. "Why dude run up like a killa then only shoot in the air?"

"I think you hit at least one of them," Brandon said. "I saw somebody stumble to the pavement."

"Boohoo for dude," Brian said, walking to his bedroom.

Malik fell back on the sectional. "Jeff caught a hot one fo' sho'," he revealed. "I seen him bleeding from the leg when I rode back thru."

Drizzle zeroed in on Malik. "Straight up?"

Brandon asked about P-Nut.

Malik frowned. "He probably at home scared, hiding under the bed with a pillow over his head." He told them about P-Nut's scary ass reaction.

Brandon shook his head in amusement. Drizzle shook his head in disgust.

Brian prepared for a late night with his "newest flipper," Tangy.

"It's a possibility that Jeff will mention names and give descriptions to the police," Brandon warned Malik and Drizzle. "Remember you don't know nothing about nothing, in case you end up in interrogation. No matter how many threats, cigarettes, chips, or Sprite sodas in Styrofoam cups they offer you—keep your mouth shut," he schooled "Y'all don't say nothing, they won't know nothing," was his final statement on the issue.

Brian strutted out of his bedroom looking fresh to def in a brand new outfit and pair of J's, drippin' in jewels, and smelling sure of himself. "What better way to top off the night than with a hot shot of twat." He pulled on his Pelle jacket. "I'll holla at y'all in the morning. Tangy promised to keep me busy tonight. All night." He left smiling.

Brandon laid back in the La-Z-Boy chair, reading *The 48 Laws of Power*. Drizzle was at the kitchen table writing lyrics in his book of rhymes. Malik reclined on the sectional thinking about Brianna. He still hadn't called, although he kept promising himself that he would. He missed her so much it moved his gut at times…

195

Malik had started to talk to his mother about the situation. But then the call came from Marvin; or was it Melvin? Didn't matter. Just the thought of her creeping with another man made Malik cringe inside. Wouldn't any wannabe Don Juan character be welcomed in their house. Malik wasn't anyone's stepson. Never would be. Kevy was the one and only suitable suitor for Malik's mama. Surely not some ol' Barry White-talking negro named Melvin. Or was it Marvin? Didn't make any difference.

Malik got up and grabbed Brandon's cellular off the pool table. He stared at the dial pad a moment before punching in her digits.

"Hello," the sweet, sexy voice answered on the second ring.

"'Bree?" Malik replied, and slipped off into Brian's room, feeling all aflutter.

CHAPTER 35

Liz and Wanda entered the Y.M.C.A. and took in the active scenes. Men and women, engaged in a variety of exercises, busied themselves at different machines and modules. They stretched, pulled, pumped, pushed, paced, took measured breaths, and perspired. House music thumped out of the sound system. The scent of air freshener competed with a blend of deodorants. Liz, a little intimidated, acted unfazed.

"Girl, look at all those Tonka truck machines," Wanda totally exaggerated. Liz had invited her to come, mostly for the company and support. This was their first visit.

"You got to be crazy." Wanda stared around at the machines like she had an attitude toward them. She was not encouraging Liz to stay the course. They posted up at the threshold looking cute, clad in their new Adidas sweat suits and sneakers. Liz's energy dwindled by the second.

"Hey now," Wanda's tone switched to a livelier one. "I see a couple prospects," she enthused. "Young, strong, and handsomely complexioned. My hubby might be up in this joint."

Liz followed behind her. "Keep stalking and they gone kick you out," she giggled. They stepped next to an unoccupied universal machine.

Wanda's eyes continued to roam around the room for male goodies. "So this is where y'all stallions been hiding," she whispered.

Liz shook her head. "And you call me fast." She placed her towel on the weight bench. An instruction manual hung on the side of it. Liz read it over.

"Try not to strain anything," Wanda said as Liz sat down on the bench. She stuck the weight pin on one hundred pounds.

"I'll try sets of ten," Liz said, sounding confident, like she knew what she was doing. She wanted to get into it before the drive drove out of her.

"This is going to be good," Wanda snickered and watched.

"Shush!" Liz laid back on the bench. Both hands on the bar grips, she heaved up about halfway, then froze and let go under the overwhelming pressure. The weights slammed back into place with a loud clap. "Damn," Liz uttered under her breath, mortified. Folks glanced in their direction.

"Okay, She-Ra," Wanda laughed.

Liz got up. "Forget you," she laughed at herself. "That just tickles you to death?" she took hold of the towel. She wasn't quite ready for the bench press.

A brothah came over to offer assistance. "You ladies need some help?" he asked cordially.

"Yes, we do," Wanda said, poring over his chiseled frame.

He questioned them about their workout goals. Liz quickly made some up, and he pretended to believe her. Wanda eyeballed him as he explained different machines, which muscles they worked, and suggested how much weight to set them on. Liz listened closely to what he said, while Wanda paid close attention to how he moved. She smirked when he wasn't looking, and asked questions when it appeared he was about to leave them. Liz laughed inside at Wanda's playful hanky-panky.

"Could you demonstrate on this machine?" Wanda asked. As he obliged her, she flashed Liz a naughty smile.

The man doesn't have a clue, Liz thought.

He got them comfortable with the leg press and left them to it.

"I might need a personal trainer after this," Wanda giggled, referring to the brothah, who'd mentioned he was one.

"You're something else," Liz said. They casually worked out on adjacent leg machines, talking, man-watching, and laughing at basically nothing.

"If you worked that machine like you're workin' your eyes every time a guy strains a little, you might just get in great shape," Liz commented.

198

Wanda embellished her breathing. "I am workin' it, girl. Look." She picked up the pace. "Get it. Come on!" she laughed, frowned, and arrested her leg movement. "Okay, I feel a tendon sting," she ouched. "That's it for me." She limped to her feet.

Liz stayed on the move. "Cut it out."

"I'm serious—" Something caught her eye. "Look at Black Stallion— far left, third row, shirtless, chiseled chest, and pumping hard," she said in military fashion. "Good Lawd."

Liz shook her head. "You're a mess," she laughed, but got up and stole a glimpse of Black Stallion herself.

"I know what your butt is up to too," Wanda said. "You're try'na tighten up for ol' messy Marv."

"Please," Liz dismissed. "It's not that serious. If anything, he'll tighten up for me."

"Or y'all will tighten up each other," Wanda retorted.

Liz stretched and rubbed her taut calves. "I'm feeling it already," she said. "And I'm not thinking about Marvin. No man, period."

"Right now."

"I wonder why the freaky stuff is on your mind so tough lately," she said. "You wanna tell me something—or 'bout someone?"

"Who?" she shot Liz a sideways look. "You know ain't no shame in my game. I'd tell you in a flash."

"Sho' you right," she acknowledged.

"I do know one thang," Wanda said. "I need to do something. Mess around and cross over to the other side if brothers don't present themselves."

Liz thought about Marvin, the little classroom spat they had months back. "It's some good ones out there," she said sincerely. They headed over to the treadmills. "Give yourself more room to roam and see what you see," a pause. "And stop being so picky. A man will need to wear stilts to reach your high standards."

"You doggone right!"

"Maybe he's at the circus," Liz replied.

"I guess I'll go get his clown ass from there, then," Wanda assured. "Stilts and all."

They mounted adjacent treadmills.

"I work too hard to settle for less," Wanda continued, "you know that."

Liz increased the speed a few notches. "Well, your biological clock is ticking, sis," she pointed out. "I know you want to have a kid or two."

Wanda decreased her pace. "I already have a son and daughter," she said. "I could end up with another child at the rate you're going."

Liz looked over at her like she'd just spoken Arabic. "What you talkin' about?"

"I'm talkin' about 'Lik and She-She," Wanda clarified. "They're my babies too, and will do as long as I can't find anything more than a sperm donor."

"You can have 'Lik's stubborn butt," she said. Something hit Liz, "and what you mean 'another child' at the rate I'm going?" she wanted to know.

Wanda said, "I'm talking about a Marv junior or juniorette," and stared her up and down. "you have put on a couple pounds."

Liz stepped off the treadmill. "Now I know you're crazy," she said.

Wanda giggled.

"You shouldn't even play like that," Liz said, not joining in on the laughs. She got back on the machine and quickened her pace. "Bad enough Malik been acting all stuck up since Marvin called." She started to perspire from the workout. "It's like that boy knew the business right away."

"And," Wanda frowned up. "So what?" She stopped and leaned on the control panel. "He'll get over it. Just don't rush it with him."

"Nothing to rush," she said. "I'm longing for something a lot more fulfilling than what a man can offer. I thought it would come after I finished

200

school. Then when I got this new job. Now that I've accomplished those goals, I don't exactly feel what I thought I'd feel. It's like I'm bipolar."

"Your spirit is just talking to you," Wanda said. "Calling you to a higher purpose."

Liz thought about it.

"I know that feeling," Wanda continued. "Once I finished college I just knew the millennium was on its way. Then the career job would bring happiness home. After awhile I realized I searched outward for something that's inside me. I'd let others influence my decisions as far as what would make me happy. I had to figure out for myself what brought me fulfillment."

Liz stepped off the treadmill. She wiped her face and neck with the towel. "So what have you figured out?"

"Example," Wanda said. "I love mentoring kids. I love helping them discover their beauty. My preference is the young sisters like She-She. When I'm with her, there's this genuine exchange of fondness. She's so genuinely grateful to have someone care about her. That's what touches me."

Liz was getting acquainted with that feeling.

"Maya Angelou said that 'you have to love yourself enough to allow it to spill over and support others.' Lately, I've really grasped what she meant."

"Lord knows our people need more self-love," Liz said. "More of us actually caring for ourselves and each other."

"And the brothers gotta get more involved with community-building."

"And set better examples for the younger brothers," Liz added. "It's hard for a boy to mature into a good man if he doesn't encounter any good men to pattern himself after. The mess our kids are falling into these days is mind-boggling. I fret every time my baby leaves the house."

"I'm sure you do," Wanda said. "A strong male role model will do Malik a lotta good." She stared over at Liz, asking, "You know any?"

Liz picked up on the hint. Wanda was alluding to Marvin. It was obvious that he would be an excellent mentor for Malik. The only complication was that Marvin and Liz were lovers. Although Malik didn't know that, his suspicions were on high alert due to the phone call. Their communication had been left strained and basically one-sided because of it, with Liz doing most of the talking when they did speak and Malik giving flippant, curt replies when she asked him questions. She tolerated his funky attitude and waited patiently for it to freshen up.

Liz and Wanda lolled around the gym awhile longer, then decided to head on out. Wanda joked about adopting She-She. Liz laughed but something told her that Wanda would if she could. She and She-She had grown pretty close over the last few months. She-She talked about Wanda constantly, sometimes referring to her as "my Ma Dukes." Liz was glad to see them bond. Wanda was having a good influence on her. She-She's attitude, how she carried herself, her behavior at school, her grades, all started improving. She'd also dumped the knucklehead Sean. Liz and Wanda encouraged her to keep up the good work, and she promised to. They promised to make sure she did.

Wanda dropped Liz off at home and said she'd call her later. "Or tomorrow," she smiled. "You might get in too late tonight."

"Bye," Liz said, knowing what Wanda was getting at. She had dinner plans with Marvin this evening. She got into the house and made a beeline for the bathroom. She ran a nice hot bubble bath and settled down into the sudsy water. It felt scorchingly wonderful. She reclined, feeling it, appreciating the alone time, meditating, moving closer to herself.

CHAPTER 36

Mr. Golden, the school principal, entered the chemistry lab with a no-nonsense look on his chubby, copper-colored mug. The entire class ceased all activities as Mr. Golden strode past and approached the teacher's desk. A troubling hunch struck Malik. He edged down some in his seat and braced himself. After formal greetings, Mr. Golden spoke with Ms. Emily in a low tone. The teacher's cheerful countenance turned grim. Whatever Mr. Golden had told her seemed quite disturbing, and it disturbed Malik after they both looked his way. He sat up in his chair. The other students stared back and forth; Ms. Emily looked on sympathetically as the principal moved toward Malik.

This ain't good, he thought.

"I need you to come with me, Mr. Freeman," the principal said.

Malik reached under the seat and gathered his books. Mr. Golden guided him to the door. Malik kept up a fearless front until he stepped outside the class.

Two black detectives waited in the hall. Malik's heart began pounding dents into his chest plate.

"What's up?" he wanted to know.

"We need to ask you a couple of questions," one of the policemen said. He looked serious, sounded stern, and appeared to be a veteran.

Malik eyed him and his younger partner, whose hardened expression wasn't nearly as convincing.

Malik turned defiant to hide his dismay. "Questions about what?" he asked. "I don't know nothing 'bout nothing—" he stepped back and before he knew it he was being manhandled and slapped in handcuffs.

Mr. Golden said something, but Malik didn't understand it because he was too busy arguing with the detectives. They escorted him down the hall and out of the school.

"I need my coat," Malik complained. The winter chills nibbled on his bare forearms, head, neck, and then breathed through his button-up. "If I catch pneumonia, I'm suing," he threatened.

The veteran shoved him in the back of an unmarked squad car and slammed the door shut. His rookie partner climbed behind the wheel and started the car. Malik was grateful when the vents started blowing heat.

Mr. Golden appeared with Malik's coat. The veteran searched through the pockets and tossed it on the seat next to Malik.

"This is some garbage," he complained, "I wanna talk to a lawyer." The veteran got in front and his partner pulled off. Malik felt cramped in the back seat. He shifted sideways trying to get comfortable. That seemed impossible with his hands cuffed tightly behind his back. Nausea formed in his stomach; jumbled thoughts swamped his mind. He wasn't with this situation—at all! His grumbles basically got ignored by the pigs. He asked, "What the hell is this about?"

"I thought you said something about an attorney," the veteran reminded him. "Remain silent until you get one."

"This is bullshit," Malik said.

The rookie went to bumping his gums, saying, "You one of those wannabe thugs, huh?" he chuckled. "Thugged out, huh? Wait 'til you hit prison and see how real thugs trick and treat little wannabes like you."

Malik wanted to spit right in his lopsided afro.

"They'll love your little cute ass in the cell halls up in Green Bay or Waupun," the rookie continued taunting him.

Malik reflected on Brandon's counsel.

Ask for a lawyer and say nothing else. But curiosity was getting the best of him. He ran through the possibilities in his head. Did the kidnapped carjacker rat on him, Brian and Maniac? How much sense would that make? *I didn't put him in the trunk. And the nigga robbed me.* Malik had only reported the Chevy stolen, but the carjacker didn't know that. *Naw, it can't be about that*, he concluded. *The fight with Jesse? That happened months ago.*

204

Can't be. Shit! Malik figured it out. The shooting up at Kemet Quarters! It had ended up on the news and the people in the area were trying to get the club closed down. *It must be about the shooting*, he realized. The sick feeling deepened in his gut.

They made it to the 7th district and pulled into the parking garage. Malik stared out the window at the various police vehicles. The rookie parked in between a paddy wagon and squad car.

"What is this about?" Malik finally broke his silence.

They got him out the back seat and into the station house, draping his coat over his shoulders.

"First of all," said the veteran, "for an attempt to flee. We only wanted to ask you some questions before that."

Malik glanced sideways at him. He had a large build, high arching forehead and bushy salt and pepper mustache.

"I never attempted to flee," Malik asserted.

"Yeah you did," the rookie backed up his partner. They moved Malik down a bright hallway.

"That's just a bogus pretense to get me down here," Malik said. The trumped-up charge really got him heated. "Just like an ol' Uncle Tom," he mumbled.

"Shut up," the veteran snapped, shoving Malik down onto a wooden bench. His aggression left Malik temporarily stunned. The seven or eight other officers in the room glanced their way.

Malik kept his mouth closed. The veteran uncuffed one of his wrists and locked the loosened handcuff to a steel loop attached securely to the bench. "You little disrespectful punks are always letting that Uncle Tom epithet come off ya tongue," he scolded Malik. "But look in the mirror. Y'all are the quintessential Uncle Toms. Y'all are the main ones betraying the community and killing off each other. Young, dumb, ignorant, silly little shits." He glowered with bona fide contempt.

Malik didn't utter a word, didn't budge one inch until the brother walked off.

About twenty-five minutes later, a much nicer police woman came and got him. She told Malik to remove his shoe strings, belt and everything in his pockets. He obeyed without the least bit of resistance and respectfully answered all her questions, giving his name, D.O.B., address, phone number and what not. She had him stand against a wall, then snapped his picture.

"Any tattoos?" she asked.

"No, ma'am," he replied.

She escorted him to an interrogation room and locked him inside. He stood there alone. The room was small with only a metal table and two chairs bolted to the bare concrete floor. The door was carved up with gang signs, names, racial slurs, police bashing statements, and other sloppy inscriptions. Malik felt claustrophobic, helpless, apprehensive, trapped. He paced back and forth in the tiny space. He wanted to go home!

"What the hell is this?" he said, exasperated, still taking baby steps back and forth. Then he took a seat on one of the hard chairs. No comfort whatsoever. He switched to the other chair. Just as bad. He tried the table. Even worse. He got back up and paced, wished someone came and hollered at him. Told him something.

Time dragged on. *An hour? Maybe two?* Malik could only guess how long he'd been trapped in the ugly ass room. He sat. He stood. He paced. He collapsed on the chair. He slid onto the table. He leaned against the walls. They started closing in on him, the space shrinking right before his eyes. He wanted his mama, the comfort of her protection. He heard voices, people talking and laughing outside the windowless door, somewhere. Somebody needed to come talk to him before he went crazy or snapped out! He listened intently as the voices and chuckles faded. Were they talking about him, laughing at him? *Thinking this shit is funny?* Were they somehow watching him? He looked around at the walls for any peepholes or hidden cameras. All he saw were dingy walls that apparently hadn't been washed in ages. He spotted something green and slimy-looking on one of the chairs… it looked like dried snot and clustered boogers! He backed away from the mucous-smudged petri-dish of a seat.

Malik paced. He wanted to go home. He wanted to know what time it was. He wanted someone to talk to. He wanted to apologize to Nana for embarrassing her at school; he wanted to tell his mama that he loved her, that he had no right to question her about who called the house; he wanted to thank Brianna for caring enough to get on him for acting—faking like—talking like, some type of thug. He wanted to speak with Jenny in front of whomever, whenever. He wanted out, out, out!

Malik sat down on the table, exhausted. Time seemed non-existent; he hadn't the vaguest idea how long he'd been cooped up... *inside this ugly, unsanitary room!*

The voices came back on the other side of the door, the jingling of keys accompanied them. Then they faded out. Then the voices and key jingles returned and faded, came back and faded again and again, and no one ever stopped at the door to open it and tell Malik what the hell was going on. Each time any sounds came from the other side of the door, he stopped pacing—or hopped to his feet—to listen, his ear kissing the door; he knelt down and tried to look out the slit at the bottom. *Impossible*, he lamented.

Damn it, he sighed, depressed. He was in jail—he couldn't believe it. *I'm in jail!* He thought about his daddy, their county jail visit months ago. Malik remembered how remorseful Kevy was.

He paced and got sicker, saltier. Thinking about it now: His daddy hadn't been there to help him grow up. *His ass should be sorry. Allowing himself to go away to prison, knowing he had a son to raise?* Malik thought bitterly.

The resentful feeling overtook him. His sentiments fluctuated from blame to justification. Then back to understanding.

Malik took a seat back on the table and tried to compose himself. He was out of order. Never had he blamed his pops like that. All those years, Malik never even thought to feel anger or disappointment toward Kevy. Nor did he ever doubt his father's love.

Malik hoisted a foot up on the table and fumbled with the tongue on his laceless Nike kicks. The guilt erupted in his heart. He'd thrown a fit, cracking under pressure, acting soft... like... acting soft like... like P-Nut. "P-Nut!" he piped, jumping back to his feet. *I bet he sent these people at me.* He started doing the math. Drizzle did mention that P-Nut had caught a weed case recently. Malik hadn't seen P-Nut since the night of the club shooting, when he kicked the nigga out the chevy for acting so scary. *That coward must've volunteered information,* he suspected. *Snitch!*

Malik heard footsteps approach the door. Keys jingled. The door finally opened. In came the rookie and the veteran.

"Take a seat," the vet ordered.

Malik moved to a chair. The rookie sat down in the booger-infested one.

"Been down to Kemet Quarters lately?" he asked, staring across the table at Malik. The vet posted up near the door.

"When is 'lately'?" Malik asked, buying time.

The rookie glanced in amusement at his partner. "I know you're ready to get out of here." He rubbed his trimmed goatee. "The fleeing charge could go away. You need to tell us what you saw on the night of the shooting. Your homeboy already said he was in the car with you as the bullets flew. What did you witness? Help yourself like he did."

Filthy rat, Malik considered P-Nut. "I saw nothing that night besides the path I took out the parking lot." *Stop talking.* "If dude lying ass told y'all differently to get out of that weed case then he lied."

The detectives eyed Malik like he was Cain in Menace II Society during the interrogation scene. "Can I go?" Malik asked.

"Go where?" the rookie chuckled, "out to the juvenile detention center on fleeing and obstruction charges?"

Then came additional threats, but Malik stood firm and kept claiming to know "nothing about nothing."

208

The detectives exited the room after their interrogative tactics failed at breaking him down.

Pride filled Malik as he waited out their little games. They didn't have anything on him, Drizzle or the twins. P-Nut couldn't have witnessed too much. Not enough to incriminate Malik or his fam. *Too busy hiding under the dash.* Malik rested his arms on the table like a pillow and rested his head.

"Freeman," the voice jolted him out of his doze.

Malik looked up. "Yeah," he said, jumping up upon seeing the policewoman at the door. She was the same one who processed him earlier.

"Come on," she said.

Malik walked out of the room, relieved. He gazed toward a window; it was still daylight outside. He'd assumed that it was late at night.

"Where am I going?" he asked.

She escorted him into a room full of police and other personnel. "Wherever your feet take you after you leave here," she said. She handed him his property bag.

Malik could've kissed her. The pressure vanished. He was on his way home! He ripped open the bag and removed his stuff. He bent down and laced up his kicks.

"You stay out of trouble," the policewoman advised him. "Next time you come through here, you might not go home for awhile," she warned. "Surround yourself with positive people and do something productive with your life. Miles of potential inside you. Try not to throw it away on foolishness."

He stared up at her. She turned and went about her business. Malik looped his belt, pocketed his stuff, and went to the pay phone. He called Brianna for a ride.

****

209

Malik and Drizzle caught up with P-Nut later that night outside Nana's house.

"You Snitch!" Drizzle snapped on his cousin. "You shouldn't have said shit. You shouldn't have mentioned no club, no name, no nothing! What did you tell them?" He had P-Nut pinned against the Chevy.

Malik, Kila, and Nana stood by, looking on.

"What did you tell?" Drizzle demanded to know.

"They just wanted to question 'Lik," P-Nut said, scared and humiliated.

Drizzle shoved him in the face. "They wanted to talk to 'Lik because your rat ass gave them his name." He socked P-Nut in the head, sending him slipping on the icy snow and crashing against the car door, cracking his head on the side mirror. Drizzle kicked him in the chest.

Nana jumped between them and helped P-Nut back to his feet. The side of his face and head dripped wet with slushy snow.

"Y'all supposed to be cousins, Drizzle," Nana ran her mouth. "You're fighting your family over some other nigga," she lectured him.

"Nana, stay out their business," Kila said.

P-Nut glared Malik's way. "You act like he mean more to you than me," he whined to Drizzle.

Drizzle charged forward. "You ain't shit to me," he said, and tore into P-Nut's jaw with two stiff jabs. Right. Left. The impact knocked P-Nut into the Chevy; Nana slipped in the snow trying to leap out the way. No one helped her back up.

Malik wanted to contribute to P-Nut's beat down but instead decided to let Drizzle deal with his own family.

P-Nut, up on his feet again, backed out into the street, and threw his dukes up.

This only stoked Drizzle's anger. He charged after P-Nut in heated pursuit, swinging a wide haymaker at his head and missing. Then Drizzle

210

caught him with a quick, solid uppercut to the chin. P-Nut staggered over to the curb, seeing stars.

"Come on, Dre," Kila said. She pulled him away.

"You ain't shit to me no more," P-Nut wailed dizzily, clamping his bruised chin. Nana linked her arm with his and rolled her eyes at Drizzle. "You should be grateful," she told him, "he was the main one helping you, letting you stay at his house when your mama went to jail. A good way to repay him for feeding you." P-Nut tried to lead her away before she said another word.

Drizzle took off. "You told this hoodrat lies, gossipin' with her about my business?" he began choking P-Nut, both hands around his neck. Malik stepped in and broke it up.

Nana jumped out the way as Drizzle turned his fury on her. "And you don't know nothing about me, slut, so keep my name out yo' mouth." Malik released him. "Don't no nigga feed me," Drizzle spat at her.

"Anyway," Nana replied. "You can gon' somewhere with that disrespect."

Kila and Malik restrained Drizzle.

"That's the problem," Malik told P-Nut, "You can't stop talking," then included Nana in the address: "Y'all two make a good, talkative couple."

P-Nut got tough with Malik. "You're just jealous she didn't wanna mess with you no more," he said. Nana steered him away.

Malik didn't dignify the retarded accusation with a reply.

"Let's bounce," Drizzle said. "Real family," he regarded Malik.

Kila got in the back seat of the Chevy; Drizzle hopped up front in the passenger; Malik slid behind the wheel and drove off.

211

CHAPTER 37

Peace and quiet. Liz exhaled as she rubbed on cocoa butter cream. She strolled into the living room, considering what to do with the next several hours. She had finally adjusted to the late shifts, and being free during the day was a pretty nice respite. She made it home from work each morning at around six o'clock and usually prepared breakfast for Malik and She-She before getting them out of bed for school. Once the kids were out of the house, Liz crashed out until noon. From then until nine-thirty at night, she was free to do whatever she pleased.

Marvin's daily schedule didn't jibe with hers, which was probably a good thing. She didn't want to get carried away with seeing him. Some times on the weekends, every blue moon on the weekdays, when time and energy permitted, would suffice for them.

Liz needed to focus mostly on herself, and on Malik. The phone message from his school last week, informing her about the police picking him up, had unsettled her. When Liz interrogated Malik about it, he acted like it was nothing. "They just asked me a couple questions about something that wasn't my business and I didn't have anything to do with," he assured her. She decided to believe him and let it go. Plus, she noticed an attitude adjustment in him lately. *That trip to the police station probably spooked his butt*, she assumed.

Liz opened the blinds to let the daylight in. It snowed heavily outside. Thick flakes poured down on everything. She appreciated the wintry scenery—but Lord knows she couldn't stand the cold.

She went to the kitchen and made a cup of hot chocolate.

Carrying the steamy mug back to the living room, she took slow, light sips, the tasty liquid scorching her tongue a bit. She turned on the radio and surfed the AM stations, stopping on a discussion that caught her attention. She sipped her drink and listened.

"It's unbelievable, ridiculous with these people," a lady ranted out of the speaker. "I mean, the parents need to instill better values in their children and give the appropriate discipline..."

These people, Liz wondered who the woman meant by that. She sipped and listened to find out.

"... the crime in our city is terrible, the inner city, urban area has become a frickin' jungle," the caller carried on. "The state and local government need to bring the pound down on these wild hooligans. I say lock 'em up and melt the key in the keyholes of the cells. Whatever it takes to eradicate the domestic terrorism and restore Milwaukee back to the peaceful city it once was."

The radio host eagerly agreed with his caller. "We're on one accord, Debbie. It's alarming, and what's more alarming are the talks about budget cuts at a time when the crime rate is soaring. The liberals want additional social giveaways. I believe that only fuels the problem. There must be accountability, responsibility. If you commit a crime, you go to prison. If you don't want to go to school, then work, earn a decent living. My tax dollars will not go toward enabling your laziness and dependence. It's not society's responsibility. But it is the government's responsibility to keep us all safe. So if we need to build more prisons, get tougher on crime, bring back the death penalty—then let's go. I'll call my congressman, you call yours, and let's demand they act. Thanks for the call."

Liz's insides flared up and it wasn't only because of the hot chocolate she was sipping.

Caller after caller phoned in and vented about the 'crime' in 'the city' and how it continued to spread to 'outer areas' and how the 'urban youth' needs to be sent a 'stern, uncompromising' message... and how some of 'the parents' don't seem to take on their responsibilities in 'the home.'

Liz felt like karate chopping the radio. It pissed her the hell off how they were judging—most likely from a distance, living in some suburb, getting all their understanding (or misunderstanding) from the nine o'clock news—and generalizing with such damning audacity. All they advocated to eliminate crime was tougher laws and additional prison construction. *A bunch of self-*

213

righteous conservatives, undercover racist hillbillies, Liz seethed. The host encouraged people to call and weigh in.

Liz snatched up the phone as another caller stated her bullshit opinion.

"I'm a substitute teacher," the caller said, "and I often work in the inner city public schools. A lot of these young people, from elementary to the high school level, come to school angry, insecure, with low self-esteem, and often don't focus on the lessons. I struggle a great deal with getting them to understand the importance of educa—"

Liz turned down the radio. She kept getting busy signals. She redialed and redialed until she finally got through to the radio station.

"Chuckie Walker," the host came on line, "You're on."

Liz clenched the receiver. "Hello," she said.

"Yes," Chuckie the host said. "Do you have a comment? You're on."

"You're damn right I have a comment." Liz had a lot to say. "I've stood here listening to you and your callers narrow-mindedly place blame and generalize about folks in the inner city of Milwaukee. First off, I want to address the last caller, the substitute teacher, who insinuated that *these* kids can't learn like the ones in the suburban schools. Has she ever considered that maybe she's not competent enough to teach the lessons to them?"

"Okay," Chuckie said.

Liz stayed at it. "Maybe she needs additional schooling or cultural training," a quick breath. "And Chuck, or Chuckie, you point out the crime rate as if that comes about in a social vacuum."

"Well," he cut in.

"And," Liz cut him off, "you, nor any of your callers, ever mentioned the causes of crime. Let's be blunt instead of all the coded, politically correct language. When the teacher spoke on urban students vis-à-vis her suburban student darlings, she was really talking black and brown students compared to white ones. Just say who the urbanites are, why don't you?"

214

"They're urban," Chuckie claimed. "No one race. Whites, Blacks and Browns—as you call our Hispanic citizens—all live in the inner city. A Webster dictionary will define to you what urban means and it'll say nothing about ethnicity, I'm sure."

"Listen here," Liz said. "You know what the word indicates. It's subtle racism."

"What do you mean?" Chuckie chuckled.

"Ask what it means to those state elites who stick you in the middle to demonize the lower class, the poor and forgotten, the very poor people who fill those prisons you talk about, and the other prisons you want to build. The prisons that benefit the people in the predominantly white rural areas of the state by creating jobs for them. Why don't you open a discussion about that, Chucker? Talk about the corporate schemes and the private prison hustle, and who really profits from the tougher laws and exploding inmate population."

"It's not that simple."

"I know. But it's easy to blame one segment for all the problems, right?" Liz said. "Talk a little about the poor schools and measly funding they receive. About the lack of programs to help less fortunate citizens develop and how the racist media, like the Chuck Walker show, stigmatize people and spews misinformation to distort the reality of their situations. Learn more about why those 'urban' kids grow up angry after—no," Liz said on second thought, "talk about the parents who love and do their best to raise—"

"Spoken like a true liberal," Chuckie said and hung up.

"And you listened like a true bigot," Liz yelled at the dial tone. She slapped the phone receiver into its cradle. "Disrupted my damn mood," she griped, chest heaving.

Liz needed to recapture some peace. She put on a soul Classics CD and forwarded it to Marvin Gaye's 'What's Goin' On'. The irony of the name Marvin, she thought, going to her bedroom to straighten out her closet. Tessa's box remained in the same place on the floor. Liz hadn't touched it since she first brought it home.

She picked it up and carried it over to the bed. Two slabs of masking tape crisscrossed over the flaps. She squeezed a nail underneath the tape and peeled it off.

Tessa's black leather-bound Bible sat directly on top of the contents. An eerie feeling came over Liz. She picked up The Good Book and ran a hand over the worn cover. She couldn't recall the last time she'd read any scripture. She fingered the wording stitched on the spine. A stringed bookmark dangled over the side; it was stuck near the middle pages. She opened it there. *Proverbs,* she noted, and browsed down the page. She came upon a highlighted verse and read:

Trust in the Lord with all your heart.

Do not depend on your own understanding.

In all your ways remember Him. Then

He will make your paths smooth and straight.

CHAPTER 38

Brianna parked her Maxima down the street from the Black Holocaust Museum. "Come, come, brotherman," she said to Malik. Keeping his disappointment to himself, he climbed out the passenger seat.

Earlier that morning, Brianna called and asked Malik to come over. He was supposed to spend his Saturday with Drizzle and the twins, helping them move music equipment and furniture into a building that Brandon owned and planned to convert into their studio/record label. But Brianna's unexpected request—and in the tone she asked it—was just too enticing to resist. Malik reneged on his fam'. He had to go see his "future wifey."

When he made it to Brianna's apartment, she asked him to ride with her, not divulging their destination. Malik hopped in her car with the cool quickness. He just knew, just knew, that his stars had finally aligned themselves. *Cherryland, here I come*, he'd secretly rejoiced, his hormones abuzz. Instead of going to the hotel or the motel, like he fantasized, she brought him to the museum.

Now, as they jaywalked across Martin Luther King, Jr. Drive, Malik peeped out her little scheme. *Callin', talkin' all overly sexy.* He felt duped. Bamboozled. Hoodwinked through his horny longings. Brianna's come-hither voice over the phone had been a lure, and he had swallowed the bait, hook, line, sinker, whole rod.

Brianna flashed him a foxy smirk as they entered the museum.

"You think you're so slick," Malik said.

She grabbed him by the hand. "No," she replied, "I'm so sincere."

"I guess." He took a look around the place. Only a sprinkling of visitors was present.

Brianna led Malik over to a photo display on a wall. The dim lighting in this part of the museum added an eerie effect.

"You know who he is?" Brianna directed Malik's attention to one of the photos.

He got a closer look. "That's Frederick Douglass, isn't it?" he asked, easily recognizing the ex-slave, orator, and author. Staring at the image brought to mind the veteran detective who'd roughed Malik up last month at the police station. The vet's bushy salt and pepper mustache resembled Frederick Douglass's tousled Afro.

Brianna examined the different portraits. "Can you imagine how it felt to live back in those times," she said, "enslaved, degraded, enduring that oppression?"

"Hell, naw," he said. He had read enough about southern slavery to know this, undoubtedly. "Those crackas would've had to noose me before I Hebrewed from sunup to sundown. Freedom or death. Nat Turner, fo' real."

She pointed to another photo. "Harriet Tubman, too," she said proudly. They stared at Harriet's solemn expression. "She was a woman warrior, fo' real, fo' real," Brianna admired. "Drove ol' massa and his minions crazy tryin' to catch her. Put in essential work for the struggle."

"No doubt," Malik nodded.

"And she stayed strapped up with an old rusty revolver," she added, "but she carried it only for protection against the bloodhounds, slave catchers, and milquetoast negroes whose feet turned cold as they made their escape through the underground railroad."

"And she never lost a passenger during her numerous conductorships to freedom," someone spoke up from behind them. Malik turned around to see an old school brothah standing there in African garb, smiling warmly and sporting a thinning afro and full beard. "I'm glad to see that you know your history, young lady," he smiled warmly at Brianna.

Her smile was the same temperature. "I know just enough to know to keep learning more of it," she said humbly, respectfully.

Malik's attention fell on a photo that made him wince. "Damn," he uttered, eyeing it. The image was that of a Black man's bare back. The grotesque flesh from the nape of the neck to the bottom of the spine was

218

thoroughly slashed and scarred up, criss-crossed with a legion of welts. Malik read the caption below the picture.

"That's Crandon," the brothah enlightened them. "He was a freed slave from Baton Rouge, Louisiana. Lived in the 1800's, fought for the Union against the Confederacy in the Civil War, and also became a corporal."

"I hope he found the person who mutilated his flesh like that," Malik said. "That's crazy."

"It's brutal," the man said, "and he was one out of many blacks forced to suffer under the whip and endure other terroristic assaults in those days. It is important for us to know, be exposed to that history. Our people can't afford to ignore it, no matter how ugly it is at times."

Brianna nodded. "If we lose sight of our origins, we fall dead to purpose."

"Correct," the brothah agreed. "It's up to you young folks to claim that torch. To take it up with pride, dedication, and determination. *A luta continua.* The struggle continues. Your generation has to stand tougher, love harder, and march forward toward deepening liberation."

A romantic thought, Malik deemed. "These nig—" he began, but quickly changed up his language. "My generation ain't try'na embrace consciousness or heed the call," he said, feeling an emotional tear inside. "And love?" he scoffed at the notion. "Showing the wrong person love will get you got."

A shade of disappointment fell over Brianna's face. The brothah's expression stayed the same. They both stared at Malik.

"Disloyalty didn't originate in your generation, young brother," Old School said. "There were Africans in Africa who sold their own brothers and sisters into slavery, there were blacks who informed to their white masters about planned slave revolts throughout the diaspora, there were negroes who fought to preserve their own oppression." A pause. "But you also had the freedom fighters who fought on. You had Toussaint L'Ouverture in Haiti, Frederick Douglass, Harriet Tubman, Sojourner Truth, Denmark Vessey. Later came Garvey, Ida B. Wells, King, Malcolm. The list goes on and on.

Some known and many more unknown sheroes and heroes. Undeterred freedom fighters who faced much deeper oppression and opposition back then than we face today. It hurts when your own kinsmen betray you. It's painful. Cuts deeper than anyone else's back stab. But we've always known that those disloyal persons didn't reflect the whole nor stop the rest from struggling on." He considered something for a moment. "The historical enemies of our people continue to push for our collective defeat. It's important to always remember this."

His words struck a nerve in Malik. They jostled his consciousness, caused a stir in his conscience. Malik understood Brianna's look of disappointment over the cynical comment he made. He felt overwhelmed by guilt. Then anger and frustration. And also irritation. He wondered what Brianna's ulterior motives were for bringing him to the museum.

By the time they left, Malik had drifted off into his own little world. He barely said a word to Brianna on the way back to her place.. *Don't I have good reason to feel how the fuck I feel?* he rationalized. *Niggas put their hands on my mama*, he couldn't forget. *Nor forgive.*

Brianna parked in front of her apartment building. "You comin' in?" she asked.

"I need to go help my fam do some movin'," he said, and got out of the car.

Brianna got out. "Call me later, okay?" she said.

"Yep," he said without any feeling. *Should've stuck with my original plans,* he thought. He got in Brian's van and hit it.

220

CHAPTER 39

Liz and She-She entered the church, bedecked in their Sunday best. "Good morning, sisters," the young usher welcomed them. He smiled, handed Liz a program sheet, and motioned toward the inner sanctuary.

"He healed my body, and told me to run on..."

The choir's spirited rendition of "Can't Nobody Do Me Like Jesus" jibed nicely with the live instruments, lifted voices, and handclaps of the congregants. Liz's grandma had loved the gospel classic. The lyrics and melody, the church's scent and scenery, conjured some distant memories. The moment wrapped Liz in a blanket of *déjà vu,* as if she was the granny and She-She the grandchild.

Predominantly women and small children filled the pews. Liz led She-She to one in the back, and they slid in next to a senior sister with a flamboyant hat nestled atop her head. "This is the day the Lawd has made!" she greeted with gusto. "Praise his glorious name!"

Liz offered up a polite smile and looked around. Members continued to arrive, smiling, hugging, shaking hands, joining in the singing and praising. Many of them wore their best faces, although some of their stress and weariness was too heavy to hide. Lying smiles, telling eyes. *What are you people watching for anyway?* the voices got at Liz. *Need to be focusing on God and your self.* She didn't dare argue with them.

A sister came in and caused heads to turn as she made her way down the middle aisle. She slowed up a few feet from where Liz sat and greeted several folks. The sister exuded grace, warmth, confidence. Liz sized her up on the low-low, estimating her age at late thirties. *Maybe older.* She wore a classy skirt suit, stylish gold frames, and a laid-out hairdo. *You go, girl,* Liz silently cheered when the sister strode up to the pulpit and mounted it.

Still at it, huh? the voices got on her some more. Liz couldn't help but notice the blingy wedding ring on the sister's finger. Manicured nails, radiant

221

chocolate skin, svelte figure… girlfriend appeared to have it goin' on, Liz admired, gazing down at the program sheet before the voices could start up again. She came across the name "Pastor Diamond U. Banks," and knew it belonged to the sister. Liz was glad to see a black woman in a leadership position.

The choir quieted and took their seats. Pastor Diamond, as Liz decided to regard her, placed her Bible on the lectern and asked the flock to stand for prayer. Liz stood and bowed her head, too. A short, passionate prayer was given, igniting praises all around, followed by a chorus of amens.

"Please be seated." Pastor Diamond opened her Bible. But instead of reading from it, she stared around at the congregation.

"Praise God," someone sang out. Several other worshippers repeated the statement. Hand claps spread around.

Pastor Diamond removed her glasses, a pensive look coming into her features. It became apparent that she was about to speak on a serious matter. She placed her glasses next to her Bible and addressed the latest tragedy to hit Milwaukee, the black community in particular. A local minister, a sister, had been killed. The story dominated the city's news and left folks saddened and thoroughly outraged. The cause of death was a stray bullet to the neck; it happened as the minister drove home from a Friday night Bible study class.

Liz's heart went out to the family, and her anger poured toward the 15-year-old suspect who was now in police custody. She was also upset with the community, including herself. Something had to be done to stop the cycle of violence. *A shame the women of God ain't even safe,* Liz kept thinking. She was sick of all the craziness. But it wasn't enough to complain. And as bad as she wanted to do something about it, she didn't know how. She'd begun studying the Bible every night, randomly reading the passages Tessa left highlighted. Each one seemed to talk directly to Liz. Eventually she ended up in the Book of Ecclesiastes, chapter three. From there, she backtracked to chapter one and read and re-read and read again, all of Ecclesiastes, appreciating the wisdom. It fed a hunger deep inside her.

Then came the news of the minister's death. Liz needed help in comprehending the meaning in what seemed like meaningless mayhem. She decided to do something she hadn't done in decades: go to church.

Pastor Diamond acknowledged the deceased minister as a close personal friend and mentor. She was on the verge of tears as she directed everyone to the book of Proverbs 3:5-7.

Liz opened her bible and found the passage highlighted.

> *Trust in the Lord with all your heart.*
> *Do not depend on your own understanding...*

Liz read along and felt a visceral nudging. Was God winking at her... she ceased with the speculation and re-focused on the Word.

Pastor Diamond stepped from behind the lectern. "This morning I plan to talk directly to my sisters in Christ," she said. "God put you on my mind."

Liz could've sworn the Pastor looked right at her before continuing.

"Grandma, Mama, Auntie, Sister, Daughter, Girlfriend, Wifey," she addressed them all. "The heart of the 'hood, backbone of the community..."

She-She inched over closer to Liz.

"We're troubled and in trouble, sisters," the Pastor continued. "And why?" The question lingered over the flock. Pastor Diamond gazed at the different faces, familiar faces, the social masks on too many dishonest faces, the faces uttering words of agreement, but no answer to her question. "Why, sisters?" she asked again.

"Jesus knows," proclaimed one of the sisters up front.

"So why don't we know if His Spirit is in us and we in Him?" the Pastor asked no one in particular. "Now I know we love to front like everything is alright," she strengthened her tone, "when it's really all bad." She stared around knowingly. "Fakin' the funk and only foolin' ourselves."

"Tell it!"

"Bring it to us!"

223

"Come with it, sister!" they encouraged her.

"Not this morning." She told it. "The façade comes down!" She brought it to them. "It comes down so we can be about our Father's business, our family's business, our community's business. It's time to re-build what's been left in ruins. Re-build our relationships with God. Re-build our home bases, re-build our neighborhoods. We can't do this if we're perpetrating a fraud. God has no use for pretenders," she got loud.

She-She got closer as a couple sisters leapt to their feet. Amens and guttural utterances sounded throughout the pews. Pastor Diamond kept coming with it, and Liz was feeling it but stayed quiet and seated, listening and looking on, mask still on.

"We know how to get suited and booted, don't we?" Pastor Diamond was saying. "Our hair whipped up, faces dipped in makeup. Made-up and looking good. I mean looking *good*." She smiled, waited, and erased it. "All these ornamental externals." A pause. "But what about the internals. The indwelling. The spirit that connects us to each other and the eternal source. It's easier to deal with the outside, isn't it? Yet and still, all this covering can't hide the results of our neglect of the spiritual life. Too bad we can't cover up the consequences. Too bad our kids' future is being forfeited while we're frontin' like everything is alrighty right. Too bad our elders aren't safe, our warriors aren't ready, and our women aren't united and standing together, battling the devil with everything inside us, because we're scared to look inside and reconnect with God and claim the responsibilities that come along with that divine kinship…"

The passion in the message, the way it was delivered, tugged at Liz's core. She squeezed her hands into fists as tears welled up inside her.

"So I ask again. What about our internal nature? The indwelling?"

"Preach, sista!"

"No matter how much we look outward, if we're not right inside, right with God, we'll feel forever shortchanged in life," the Pastor preached, while congregants endorsed her with shouts, gestures, murmurs, stomps, and tears. "We finally accomplish this, achieve that, try'na get closer to what we think will provide us with happiness. We think if we nab that man, land that better gig, make more money, buy that house, that we'll realize fulfillment. Then we later

224

find out we're no less of a mess. All those things did was distract us away from the gaping emptiness in our souls…"

Liz wiped away a tear to make room for another one. Over in the aisle, a sister stomped and tossed her hands toward the heavens, flailing her bony arms and crying out, "Why, Lord Jesus, why?"

Liz felt way out of her comfort zone. She held still but felt the chords that the Pastor struck tightening. The sister spit fire and the heat provoked folks to their feet left and right, front and back. The senior sister and She-She weren't exceptions. Only Liz was until the force made it impossible to stay seated.

"… we call our secret someones for late nights, go get that so-called sexual healin', tryin' to escape that hollow feelin'…" Pastor Diamond strutted forward a few feet and zeroed in on sister after sister after sister. "But it's transitory. After the temporary pleasure, returns the aches and pain. So we go back to him…" a pause to look around, "or back to her," she said boldly, stared knowingly. "Or both him and her or it." This provoked heightened responses from three or four congregants. "God knows all our business," the Pastor said. "So don't act like you don't know what's goin' on. Creepin' off to do it again. Feeling guilty afterwards and doing it again to escape that guilt and that void. Just like junkies seeking escape. We escape through materialism, through dope and alcohol, through clubbing, synthetic lovin', whatever and however. All routes to try… I said 'try' to escape, to only realize that void never left us. You can't use something ephemeral to deal with something eternal. Flesh is at odds with spirit. They're not coming together for your good…"

Liz was caught up in the whirlwind, weeping openly and too in the moment to care who noticed. She was being talked to, talked about. She wanted to leave. She needed to stay.

"Sister, in order to reach fulfillment, you need something of substance, of depth, without the abuse," the Pastor said after the shouts became murmurs, sobs became silent tears. Quiet "yes, Lords" danced around.

"We're troubled and in trouble," Pastor Diamond said in a soft sigh, standing front and center of the pulpit. "Why?" she asked. "Purpose answers a lot. It gives meaning to all pain, all suffering, all turmoil. We must understand this. Understand that we're all here for a reason. To do something. Mean something. Matter to somebody. There's the individual purpose and the collective purpose, sisters. And you can't always know it here," she tapped her left temple, "especially when you haven't accepted it here," she touched her chest, gesturing toward the heart. "But we always feel it, don't we? And when we don't understand in the mind what we feel deep in the heart, depression breaks out in the soul. So what's the mediator? Who is? God is. Faith in God will release his substance in us." She walked to the lectern and re-read, "'Trust in the Lord with all your heart. Do not depend on your own understanding,'" from her Bible. "That trust leads us through any darkness. That trust lights our paths. That trust acquaints us with what our mission is. The chaos around us, in our homes and community, activates something within and communicates a demand. The spirit calls us to do something, to move against the bedlam. And if we don't answer, there are painful ripples within our being. That's the disconnection taking hold in our soul. We're turning away from purpose, from self, from God. God is trying to work through us and we're running away like the prophet Jonah, trying to escape, only to wind up in a deeper mess."

"Talk to 'em, sistah," a brother piped.

"I'm talking to all of us," she assured him, "I'm talking to myself as well. The grassroots are us. Our collective efforts are God working through us. These children are our responsibility, whether they're doing us proud or causing us pain. The police and politicians won't heal our personal or social ills. Their basic remedy is the penitentiary for our troubled youth. Lock up our future. We can't have that, so it's time to get out the house, out the club, out the mall, out the church and rush up to the frontlines. Mobilize. Isn't that what Christ did?"

Agreement all around.

"As Christians, we're obligated to follow his lead," Pastor Diamond continued. "Jesus didn't wait around for a government to change things, to change hearts, to change perspectives. Nor did He stay cooped up in some church. He was out and active in the community. His spirit is in us, demanding that we do the same…"

Liz nodded and clapped. "Thank you," she whispered to God.

226

"Lil bad Twon down the street, selling crack, acting out," the Pastor said, "he's my son, your son, our kin. He's our responsibility. To shun him is treachery. Lil fast Shalonda is our family as well. To act self-righteous and only judge or disregard her is betrayal. To feed her our love so she'll know she's worthy of it is obeying God. Loving her is saying yes to God and no to the devil. Loving her is loving all of us and Christ." She raised her voice, adding, "True love erases self and expresses higher self which is connected to the whole body of Christ. Sacrifice is an essential feature in—" she was interrupted by a commotion that arose at the rear of the church.

Liz followed everyone's gaze when someone yelled, "Call an ambulance, this boy is shot!" The young usher who'd earlier welcomed Liz inside the church held a young man in his arms. A crowd formed around them as Pastor Diamond squeezed her way down the aisle. The usher laid the young man down on the carpet. "He's shot and bleeding bad. Call for help!"

Liz caught a glimpse of him and could've sworn… She shoved her way through the frenzy. She saw the boy's sweaty forehead and wavy hairdo; and she buckled at the knees right next to him. She reached out and felt the warm blood seeping through his clothes. She found the wound and placed a hand over it to slow the bleeding. His cry of agony pounded her ears and tears blurred her vision. He turned and looked up at Liz. "Help… Ma," he choked out, his distraught face resembling… His eyes begged Liz for help. She cradled his head as the wild quakes in her chest echoed up to her head.

"Malik!" Liz cried, "Baby, what's wrong?"

"Auntie, that ain't 'Lik," She-She screamed somewhere nearby.

"Help him dammit!" Liz demanded. Someone gently moved Liz's hand away from the bullet wound to press a towel against it, causing the boy to roar in pain. Liz held him, doing all she could to comfort him. "Help is comin'," she whimpered. Liz couldn't see his face clearly through her tears and she was afraid to let him go to wipe them away. But then she felt him let go, his body going limp inside her embrace.

227

CHAPTER 40

Malik navigated into Kemet Quarters' parking lot and parked next to Prophet's BMW. He wasn't all that confident about meeting with Kila's uncle, let alone asking for his assistance. But he had to do whatever it took to help out his cousin—and time was of the essence.

Last night the 5-0 had nabbed Brian, questioned him about the club shooting and claimed to have a credible witness placing him at the crime scene. Brian asked for a lawyer and smiled and waited. Two hours later he was transported from the police station to the county jail. He hadn't been charged with anything, but his parole agent slapped a P. O. hold on him for some undisclosed reason. Brian peeped the ploy. "Stall tactics," he told Malik over the phone. "They're hoping to either come up with some flimsy evidence against me, or" –a pause and voice change, "hoping someone points me out in a lineup."

Malik read between the lines. He never told the twins about P-Nut's loose lips and advised Drizzle not to either. Malik couldn't trust his cousins' reaction, and didn't want P-Nut's blood on his hands. But now he questioned his decision. Although P-Nut was too far under the car dash to see who'd done what, his cooperation could still prove detrimental. Then there was Jeff and his boys. The cops could easily pressure one of them into viewing a lineup. Out of everyone, P-Nut remained the strongest possibility, especially since his humiliating beat down in front of Nana's house. Malik asked Drizzle to get in touch with P-Nut to see if he knew anything about Brian's arrest. Meanwhile, Malik had given Prophet a call, and he told Malik to come down to the club so they could talk in person.

The heat on Kemet Quarters had simmered down, but, Kila told Malik at school, there remained a group of area residents calling on their alderman to get it shut down. Prophet compromised with them by canceling teen night and promising to close his doors for good if any more violence erupted in or outside his club. Malik couldn't help but feel a little guilty about some of this as he walked into Kemet Quarters. It was quiet and the lights were down inside the club. It didn't really feel the same without the music poundin' and people

228

everywhere. It kinda felt like a trap... a mob hit. Malik imagined Prophet, Jeff, Chill Will and some other goons surrounding him on the dance floor, rolling out the plastic so no physical evidence would be left behind.

Prophet was behind the bar talking on his cellular. He saw Malik and gestured for him to come on over.

"That was Jeff on the phone," he said, placing his cell on its charger.

Malik took a seat on a bar stool. "We'll hit his hand with whatever," he said.

Prophet moved to the end of the bar and fetched a case of alcohol from the floor. He wasn't exactly frowning, but he definitely wasn't smiling. He returned and proceeded to stack bottles of bubbly. He took his time responding to Malik's proposition.

"It's not about hitting his hand. " He dropped the empty case on the floor. "Nothing to do with bribing anyone." He stared across the bar at Malik. Malik stared right back at him. "That's the problem nowadays with y'all young brothers. Thinkin' it's all about money without any true notion of respect. Mutual respect."

"Me and my fam expect respect and give it up to the point we're disrespected," Malik replied.

Prophet released an intolerant breath, shaking his head. "Your fam that's sitting in jail need not worry about Jeff cooperating, so tell him to be cool and wait it out. The police are just bluffing. As for who implicated him, that's something y'all will have to figure out. Must be a weak link on your end."

"That possible weak link is no more," Malik said. He didn't appreciate the "y'all young brothers" comment nor the tone of it.

Prophet leaned forward and rested his elbows on the bar top and eyed Malik. He began rubbing his chin as a reflective expression came over his face. "What's your position in the world?" he asked, studying Malik.

Malik eyed him closely. "What you mean 'my position'?"

Prophet stood erect. "I mean what position do you play? Do you spectate and let shit happen around you, to you, without applying yourself? Or do you participate and work to shape yourself into the man you want to become? And work to shape the world that you want to see develop one day? I mean, are you controlling ya' own destiny? Or do you let mediocre shit and situations influence you into ruining your tomorrows?" There was an undercurrent of frustration within the questions.

"I strive to control myself first and my own destiny second," Malik said. "Both are tied together, matter fact."

"How do you go about that?"

Malik had a hard time answering, and Prophet hit him with another question. "In striving toward that, what's one of the main things required?"

Malik said, "Opportunity," unsure of his answer.

"Opportunity is a part of it," Prophet said. "But what about surrounding yourself with the right people? People who promote your growth and development? This gets tricky because you'll have those niggas acting like they're on it with you but aren't at all. Defeated niggas who only aspire to deter, discourage or distract you away from what you're try'na focus on. Controlling yourself is necessary. Controlling your surroundings is just as necessary. Hand in hand. And if you can't also control your impulses and ego, then you'll end up fucked inna game. What you don't control, controls you." He stopped speaking and poured himself a shot. He downed the brownish liquor without a wince. "Review that situation with Jeff for instance," he said, plopping down the glass. "Petty and avoidable."

Malik cut in. "That popped off 'cause of Jeff and his little clique," he defended.

"Doesn't matter," Prophet shook his head. "The situation held no meaning. It contributed absolutely nothing to y'all cause and could've contributed to y'all downfall. If Jeff or anyone else had gotten killed that night, all y'all would've had a case to fight. Not just who pulled the trigger. Every last one of you would've got charged with party-to-the-crime. Outta there." He let it sink in a moment. "Now look. Drizzle lost a venue to perform at. He blew the opportunity to build a stronger fan base. Over some silly shit. Cemeteries and prisons are packed with niggas because of something that started over silly shit."

Malik felt that shit, fo' real.

"I know how it is at yo' age," Prophet continued. "The tests, the temptations, the hunger to be recognized and respected. I've also been through a fire you really don't wanna feel." He replaced the bottle of liquor into its slot. "Trust me, you do NOT wanna feel the agony of sitting in front of a judge and receiving a jail sentence that surpasses your life span."

The mere thought of it troubled Malik. Prophet walked over and turned on the sound system. When he came back, Malik asked him how he was able to give back so much time.

"I wonder about that myself," Prophet admitted. "Had to be God 'cause the courts wanted my head. And I'm the miraculous exception. For every one nigga who gets his case overturned, there's a multitude who get denied. You better believe it wasn't easy. I could still be in prison, wasting away. Alone. So understand when I say you don't wanna experience that. Death offers more comfort. Take it from a nigga sentenced to die in a cell." He spoke the last line with a faint tremor in his voice as a split second of dread blazed in his eyes.

"I overstand," Malik said. Prophet's words reflected something Kevy had once written him: *Prison is pain*, he had warned Malik in a letter last year. *I'm talking not the physical. It's a psychological torment, son.* His father always told him about the harsh reality of life behind bars. "Did you know my pops?" Malik asked Prophet. "Kevy Freeman. He was—"

"Kevy is your –" Prophet said really loud, the awareness impassioned his features. He slapped the bar top with an open palm and said, "Say it ain't so," staring at Malik in bewildered disbelief.

His reaction had Malik trippin'.

"Do I know your pops?" He came from behind the bar.

"What's up?" Malik jumped to his feet, smiling nervously. The man's excitement was serious.

He stopped just short of hugging Malik. "Boy, I knew yo' ass looked familiar the first time I saw you. And your name rung a bell."

"You know him?" was all Malik could think to say.

231

"I've known Kevy since grade school," Prophet frowned proudly. "We got it in together back in the day and later wound up in the same joint. Your father helped me fight my case and taught me some law." He went into a lengthy narrative about their history, how real Kevy was and how much love and respect they had for each other.

Malik listened, unable to keep from smiling. For a cat like Prophet to speak so highly of his pops had Malik brimming with pride.

"I haven't been in tune with Kevy for years," Prophet said. "The last I heard he got sent to one of those private prisons in Tennessee."

"Oklahoma," he corrected him.

"Your father used to talk my damn ears off about you when we were cellies up in Waupun. He's crazy about you."

That sent a mushy feeling through Malik. He'd always believed that Kevy loved him, but hearing Prophet say it with such certainty added strength to that conviction. Malik had to send his pops a kite.. All the recent drama in his life had disrupted their correspondence. *Then again*, he reconsidered, *that's just an excuse.* Malik resolved to write Kevy tonight and stay consistent.

"What's the latest on his appeal?" Prophet asked.

"He's still fighting," he replied. "He had an evidentiary hearing several months ago. I visited him at the county jail."

"That case is so bogus," Prophet said. "The courts should've overturned it." The reflective look returned. "It hurts to be a solid brother."

Malik wanted to ask him about Kevy's case. "He's gon' come from under it," he assured. "Even if I have to get rich and sacrifice it all."

Prophet reached over the bar. "Write down his information." He found a pen for Malik. "I'm out of pocket for not staying in tune with him."

Malik wrote down the address on a napkin. Prophet gave him four different numbers and an address for Kevy to reach him at.

"We can hit the highway and visit him," he promised Malik. "Tell him to send me a visiting form if you speak with him before he receives my letter."

Malik left the club and shot right to Kila's house to holler at Drizzle. It was a small world!

CHAPTER 41

"She-She, your mom is on the phone," Liz announced. She-She appeared in the doorway of Liz's bedroom seconds later, expectation highly visible in her expression.

"You can take it in the living room," Liz said. She-She uttered an excited "Alright," and dashed to the phone. Liz hung up upon hearing her come on the line.

The girl had been anxiously waiting to hear from her mother. This was the first time Janice had called since a hard-nosed judge sentenced her to three years imprisonment and one year of extended supervision. Days before the final court date, Liz and She-She knelt beside each other and prayed that God would move the judge to send Janice to a drug treatment center instead of prison. They soon found out that God had other plans. Liz accepted the outcome with modest disappointment. She-She shed a full night's worth of tears but understood, because she also asked the Lord to do whatever it takes to get her mother off drugs for good.

Liz set aside the Iyanla Vanzant book she'd been reading before the phone had rung. She rose from bed, slipped on her house sandals and started for the kitchen.

She-She stared out the front window as she talked happily on the phone. It moved Liz to see mother and daughter bonding. The months in the county jail were like detox for Janice. She had sobered up and regained enough focus to see how far she'd fallen away from herself and her children. Liz took She-She to visit on a weekly basis. Janice teared up on almost every visit, showering apologies and promises in her daughter's ear. Liz surveilled the mother for any signs of insincerity. On more than one occasion, the exchange between She-She and Janice became so emotional that Liz found herself fighting back tears. She-She had let loose on Janice several different times, expressing hurt, anger and embarrassment, and demanding answers. To Janice's credit, she respected She-She's feelings and seemed to truly seek her forgiveness. And while mother and daughter worked on healing their relationship and one another, Andre took a detached stance, stubbornly unmoved by Janice's apologetic gestures. Due to

234

his fugitive status, he couldn't visit her at the county jail, so their only outlets of communication were through phone or letter, or a third party. Whenever Liz or She-She conveyed one of Janice's motherly messages to him, Andre acted downright indifferent. This sometimes aggravated She-She, who was apt to remind her brother, "You ain't been a saint yourself, boy." He remained aloof to his sister's allegation. Andre's attitude hadn't offended Liz like she might've assumed. It was the boy's right to feel how he felt. Janice needed to understand the pain she put her children through. Hopefully, it would help her think twice before doing anything to hurt them again. If it was up to Liz, the family would already be healed and back together, but this wasn't something she could pull off. What she would do is keep the three of them in her prayers and trust God to bring about the best outcome.

Liz clicked on the kitchen radio and looked in the freezer for dinner. It had been a long, troublesome winter and she was relieved that spring was on its way. The coming season would probably introduce a fresh share of adversities, but Liz still looked forward to the change in weather, and hopefully in fortune.

The church tragedy continued to cause her grief and dismay. *In the house of God.* She couldn't get over it. Death and violence honored no boundaries, showed no favoritism. The young man's murder had come right on the heels of the minister's. Both victims of gun violence. One bullet aimed, one bullet strayed, each resulting in death, pain, leaving families in mourning, a community hurting and searching for answers to the absurd. Liz wondered about the two killings' connection to the church. Her granny used to often caution her to watch for 'signs', to read the 'signs of the times.' What in the world was Liz supposed to read in the most recent tragedy? It was the closest she'd ever been to death.

Witnessing life depart the boy's brown eyes, holding him in her arms as he took that final breath was sure to haunt Liz for a very long time. She could still feel the warm blood on her skin and hear the desperate voices crying out for help. And what wicked trick of the devil made her mistake the dying boy for Malik? Signs, the voices whispered. He'd died so young and full of life, and with an insatiable hunger to live. Liz saw it in his eyes, on his confused face--it pulsed in his plea for help, in his sad plea for his mother. Youth gone. Taken. Stolen away. *And for what?* Liz wanted to scream out. *A set of fuckin' car rims!* The killer confessed a week later while in police custody on an unrelated robbery. He was just as young as his victim. His own life just as gone.

Liz cut thin slices of potatoes. She decided to cook a simple meal tonight—Polish sausages, seasoned oven browns and corn. Marvin's oven brown face barged in on her mind, and she shoved the image right back out of her head. Soon came the memory of the nightmare she'd had four nights after the boy died in her arms. In the terrifying dream, Malik was dead, and Liz was viewing her son in his casket through the window of a county jail visiting booth. She cried and beat on the glass desperately trying to break through it. She came back to her senses only after seeing him alive and fast asleep in his bed. She returned to bed, unable to sleep and not really wanting to. The following morning, she concluded that the dream was just an outgrowth of her unconscious fears concerning Malik. It was best she confronted her worst fears in dreams rather than in real life.

As Liz unloaded the Polishes into a pot of boiling water, something dawned on her. The dead boy wasn't only the same age as Malik but he had also been carjacked. Although it happened right down the street from a church in broad daylight on a Sunday morning, and ended in the young brother's death, Liz couldn't help but think about the parallels and possibilities. *My baby could've been...*

"What's up, Ma?" Malik's voice saved her from insanity "Yeah, right on time." He smiled at the stove top. "I'm sho' hungry." Liz was set at ease to see her child home and safe. She wiped off her hands and reached out and hugged him. He smiled, obviously puzzled by the spontaneous show of affection.

"Is you alright?" he asked.

Liz returned his smile. "Yeah, I'm good," she said. "Just glad to see my baby.

"The mid-life crisis is coming on." A wary nod. "Aw, hell..."

She pushed him away. "Okay, 'mid-life,'" she said. "I'm too young for that."

"In denial too," he taunted. "Time for therapy."

He opened the fridge. She watched him drink straight from the Kool-Aid pitcher. Instead of getting on him, like she usually did, Liz actually appreciated the moment.

"Let's kick it," she said. "What's going on with you?"

"Huh?" he shot her a curious look.

She-She entered the kitchen.

"School been going alright?" Liz questioned him.

"Yeah." His eyes filled with suspicion as they shifted to She-She, then back to Liz.

"Brianna, Jenny, and some other girl called," She-She informed him.

"Did they say how much they missed a playa?" he jacked his slacks and spread a cocky grin.

Liz frowned. "Okay, playa." She went back to making dinner.

"Jenny sounded like a white girl," She-She busted him out.

His grin vanished, replaced by a glare. "What, you're a racial voice expert?" he got at She-She.

"Whateva," she smirked.

"Since we're on the subject of girls," Liz reentered the conversation, "Who is this Brianna?"

He got his swagger back. "First off, she's not a girl," he assured. "She's a grown woman."

"How grown?" Liz wanted to know.

"Grown enough to recognize a playa when she see one," he slick talked.

Liz looked him up and down, making a mental note to have a little talk with Ms. grown woman the next time she called the house. "Your butt better be careful and keep your little thing wrapped up," she advised him.

"I'm gone," he told her, and got out of there.

"Boy, where you going?" Liz asked. "Did I say I was done talking with you?"

He stopped outside his bedroom. "Y'all trippin'," he accused.

"When one of those girls breaks your little heart, I bet you'll wanna do a whole lotta talking," she said.

"Ain't that the truth," She-She backed her. "Playa!"

"Yeah, right," Malik walked on into his bedroom.

She-She shot to the kitchen door and warned, "And the Lord is watchin' and aware of all that you do. Better keep this in mind when ya with grown lady Brianna or White girl Jenny."

Malik's door slammed. Liz and She-She laughed and slapped each other five.

CHAPTER 42

The June sun beamed down on the people-packed grounds of Summerfest. Drizzle and Malik bounced around on stage performing in front of the largest crowd ever. This was the first time Drizzle had opened for a major artist, so they rocked the mic with all their might. Drizzle's raspy voice delivered a high dosage of uncut lyrical cocaine, and Malik was getting the hang of being a hype-man without really feeling like one. The beat slammed through the concert speakers like King Kong stomping. Malik fed off of the crazy energy of the crowd and experienced a rush like never before. He loved it! And Drizzle spit with a passion:

"Everybody's packin' heat so I'm keeping da metal/

hoppin' in my front seat, put my foot onna pedal/

gunshots and sirens, it's hard to sleep in da ghetto/

maybe I'll catch a couple Z's when all this beefin' is settled/

say I'ma die young—at least I'ma rebel/

at least I got heart, at least I got webbos/

and on my word you ain't reachin' my level/

you do dirt, I dig deep wit' the shovel/

toss you a blunt, here get chief'd wit' da devil/

tell him to light it, my niggas just got indicted/

tell 'em to fight it/

don't let jail hold you/

or them honkies railroad you/

just stand toe to toe with every blow life throws you"/

Malik and Drizzle kicked the hook two more times and dropped their mics, extended deuces to the sky, and strutted off stage.

"I said the game ain't ready, fam!" Drizzle boasted as they celebrated with daps and hugs. "We're comin'," he promised, "on my daddy's grave!"

"Ain't no doubt or contradiction," Malik seconded his confidence. "The Miltown's finest!"

"Buck City's grimiest!" Drizzle mean mugged victoriously. They calmed down some, then went and hobnobbed back stage. A couple of nationally known rappers were present and propped Drizzle on his rhyme skills. One down south producer offered to sign him on the spot. But Drizzle wasn't havin' it. Instead, he accepted the producer's number and promised to get in touch. It all seemed to be coming together, and Malik couldn't feel more pride and joy. Ever since the local clubs and radio stations put a couple of Drizzle's joints in rotation, the buzz had spread broader throughout the town and surrounding areas. Fortunately, the right person got wind and called somebody who called somebody who contacted Prophet and asked him to reach out to Drizzle. They were interested in letting him open up for the annual Jam for Peace concert. Malik was ecstatic. Drizzle was skeptical. "I think they're try'na set me up for capture," he told Malik.

Malik had laughed at his paranoia. "Set you up? Dawg, it's not that serious," he replied. "You're Awol, not wanted for a homicide. The holice wouldn't waste the resources. Plus, they could've snatched you up at one of the clubs you've performed at recently. You trippin'." The twins basically pointed out the same things and encouraged Drizzle to take advantage of the opportunity. He listened.

Now Malik messed with him about his paranoia as they headed out onto the Summerfest grounds to find Maniac and the twins. "Stay on point for the jump-out boys," Malik taunted.

"It ain't too late," Drizzle smiled. They made their way through the sea of people. It was beautiful weather, not too hot, not too cold; the perfect temp with the ideal breeze. Malik couldn't think of a better way to enjoy the summer than with his fam. Performing at an outside concert in their hometown was an added bonus. Life was good!

"Lil Awol," Brian saluted as Malik and Drizzle mounted the bleachers. Brian, Brandon, and Maniac were kicked back, parlaying on the periphery of the crowd. "Your come-up is imminent," Brandon congratulated Drizzle.

"No doubt," he replied in super cool dude mode.

Malik perched next to Maniac. "The town showed love," he said.

"We just got off all the CDs," Brandon mentioned. "Sold like hotcakes before y'all set ended. That's a clear indication that ya on ya way."

Drizzle corrected him, saying, "On our way. Ain't no 'I' in fam. It's us."

That brought a rare smile to Maniac's sinister mug. "I dig young dawg," he expressed his respect for Drizzle. "Fidelity is law in fam. Blood in, blood out, stand fo' it or tap out."

"No doubt," the fam chorused.

The next set of performers emerged on stage and attracted everyone's attention. Malik rose to his feet and cast his eyes over the animated gathering. The initial reaction was comparable to the one during Drizzle's set, Malik noted. But then a bolt of energy thundered through the audience for the rap stars on stage once the beat dropped to their recent hit.

Different associates of the twins, Maniac, Malik, and especially Drizzle, stopped by the bleachers and paid homage. The ladies came through and hollared, too. Malik stood off to the side and took in everything around him, bobbing his head to the beats and savoring the occasion. It felt good to be a part of it all.

The concert wrapped up a little over an hour later. Malik and the clique took a final slow-paced walk around the Summerfest grounds, flicked up, stopped and got some grub, kicked it until they got bored, then set out for the main gates to leave.

"Hey, Drizzle," a girl called out from behind. Malik turned around to see a nice-looking sistah with a mean stride following them into the parking lot. She accosted Drizzle for his autograph.

241

"Got something to write it on?" he replied after some hesitation. The request surprised him, although he tried to hide it from her.

She whipped out a fifty dollar bill and Maniac supplied the pen.

"Who am I making this out to?" He flirted, smiling humbly at his fan.

"Bangin'," she said her name.

"Yes, you is," Maniac said from the side line. Bangin's body language screamed nothing but sex to Drizzle. "Make it out to 'Bangin' with love'" she said. He scribbled exactly that right across Ulysses Grant's bloated face.

"Now, where can I cop yo' CD?" Bangin' asked, accepting the bill back.

Right then, Kila appeared out of nowhere like a ghost. "Hey, husband of mines," she greeted Drizzle without acknowledging his female admirer. Malik moved back some, just in case the cat fight jumped off. Bangin' gave Kila the once-over, then redirected her attention to Drizzle, telling him "I 'preciate the autograph, baby," and sashayed away with striking sway in her switch.

"Control ya groupies," Kila warned Drizzle once again.

He grinned and swung an arm around her. "I'll meet y'all on the eastside later," he said to the fam. "I'ma roll with the wifey somewhere right quick." This got Kila to relax her frown. Malik gave him dap and caught up with Maniac and the twins on the other end of the parking lot.

They were posted up outside their rides. The two pimped-out trucks sat up pretty right next to each other, charming the onlookers. A gathering of fine-looking honeys formed and flirted with the twins and Maniac. Brian started up his Infiniti and let Drizzle's CD pound out. Some of the ladies started dancing to it like they were at the club.

The night is just gettin' started, Malik thought. Jenny's Grand Am rolled up, the horn sounding. Malik walked around to the driver's side to speak.

"Is it okay to say hello?" Jenny said out the window. She had two friends in the car with her.

242

Malik said, "Only if it's okay for me to say something freaky in ya ear," picking up on the sarcasm. She didn't blush behind his insinuation this time. Deep desire twinkled in her gray-blue eyes as the lids fluttered. Malik had to look away, glancing at her buddies who gawked in the twins' direction. They commented on the parking lot party and improvised dance show the ladies were putting on.

"I see ya, cousin," Brian said over the loud music pouring out of his truck. "Get it in, brothah," he teased Malik about Jenny.

Malik tossed up the middle finger at him.

Maniac crept over. "What's poppin', lil mamas?" he greeted Jenny's buddies. The girls shrunk back in their seats and exchanged nervous looks. Maniac bent down to get a closer view of them. A crooked smile etched across his hardened midnight features as he ogled the girls. "Which one of y'all niggas ain't treatin' ya right?" he attempted to woo either one of them.

Malik laughed at the girls' false claims of having boyfrieinds who treated them like queens. Maniac's persona intimidated them, and Malik could see why. Maniac had a fearsome aura about him, bolstered by a six-inch scar that snaked over his lower jaw. He sported a superfly perm straight out of the 1970's and two tattoo tears dripped below his left eye. Even his attempts to charm with a cordial demeanor came off threatening. He eyed the girl in the back seat like potential sex prey.

Malik urged the girl to, "Holla at my fam," and laughed. "He doesn't bite."

"Unless they wanna nigga to," Maniac said suggestively.

The back seat girl fumbled on her cell and dialed like she didn't hear him.

"Stop it, Malik," Jenny whispered.

"What?" Malik grinned innocently. "I'm try'na hook up ya girl—" is all he got out before vaulting out of the way of a station wagon that flew up and braked within inches of hitting him. Malik landed halfway atop Jenny's hood, narrowly escaping the collision.

"The fuck you doin'!" he shouted at the driver. "Watch where the hell you're goin!" He slid back to his feet, chagrinned and glowering.

All four doors on the station wagon swung open and a quartet of thugs exited and encircled Malik. None of them looked very happy. Malik backed up a step. Derrick came forward.

"How it do, snitchin' ass nigga?" he confronted a boggled Malik. "Thought dat shit wasn't gone catch up, huh? Karma my main ho, nigga."

Malik winced from the tension and got on guard as Derrick and his goons closed in on him.

"'Lik, just walk away," Jenny called out the car window.

"Bitch, pull this muthafucka off," one of her buddies demanded.

"Come get in the car with us—" Jenny said to Malik.

Maniac and the twins stormed over like troopers. Malik told Jenny to leave.

"Y'all niggas don't wanna get left out here tonight," Maniac assured Derrick and the others. "So jump back in that beat up bucket and be gone befo' life start flashin' befo' ya eyes."

Villainous recognition broke out on Derrick's mug. "Aw, it's been one," he leered at the two brothers. "Here dem twin bitches go right--," Brian walloped him in the mouth with a jaw-breaking right fist. Derrick pirouetted like a punch-drunk ballet dancer and dropped.

The rumble was on from there. Malik charged at Derrick with a flying kick to the gut. The nigga groaned like Master P: "uugh!" Malik bent over and unloaded a heartfelt battery of combination blows on him. Brian tag-teamed with Malik for a few seconds, then locked horns with another cat. Malik wanted Derrick, attacked Derrick, mindless of the goon that was swinging on him. Brandon took care of that one for him, knocking him out. He fell asleep next to Derrick.

Malik could hear Jenny arguing with her buddies. He turned to tell them to leave, but Maniac distracted him by scooping an opponent off his feet and super-slamming him onto the trunk of Jenny's car. The girls' screams

244

harmonized with the agonized wail of the guy who was sure to need a good chiropractor after tonight.

Malik saw one of the foes run over and duck off inside of the station wagon. He started to give chase until the cat re-emerged brandishing a firearm. He zeroed in on Malik.

"Don't run now!" he said and started blazing. Malik turned to run and what felt like balls of fire seared into his chest and torso. Another volley of gunfire rang out. Malik clinched his stomach to put out the flames. The fire spread throughout his entire body and smothered his breathing. Another volley of shots echoed and echoed, fading into the distance. Malik closed his eyes hoping to die just to escape the unbearable burning and suffering. He envisioned his mother's face. She wore the same traumatized look he saw on her face that day Derrick and his boys assaulted her.

Malik's eyes shot open. He couldn't die now. He heard the slamming of car doors, the revving of engines, the admixture of various voices, the burning rubber of tires. The sky fell, its dark blue twirling around white clouds, looking peaceful, contrary to how he felt. The serenity of death beckoned Malik. But something inside resisted, pushed him to live on, to capture his mama's smile, to hear the love in her words, to feel the warmth and comfort of her embrace. He could smell her in the air. Blood scorched his skin, soaked his shirt. *The pain,* he gasped as it throbbed and squeezed him, asphyxiating his consciousness. His eyelids grew heavy. The sky dimmed. Darkness fell from the clouds and engulfed him. Someone touched him, pulled his arm, stoked the inferno in his chest, stomach. Maniac's face flashed into view and faded out..

"Take him to the hospital!" The voice sounded like Brian's.

"Wake up, Malik!" The scream sounded like Jenny's. *Or was it Brianna's?* He willed his eyes open and caught a quick glimpse of Jenny's panicked expression, the back seat of her car. A door slammed. Malik faded out again. He forced his eyes back open for another second. Jenny's buddy cradled his head, tears dripped off her cheeks onto his forehead, cascading into his eye. The car jerked forward. Malik faded out. He heard incomprehensible cries. He forced his eyes open again, stealing snapshots of blurry images in motion. His breaths were strained, painful and running out. It sounded like the girls were singing, then screaming over each other. He gasped and gagged on the hot liquid filling his throat and mouth. He couldn't get out the yell for help, for his mama; the effort burned the air out of his lungs.

"… mouth to mouth… " Those three words introduced Malik to a dark, dreamless sleep.

CHAPTER 43

Liz's hands trembled on the steering wheel as she maneuvered her car down Lisbon Avenue. "Come the hell on, dammit!" she yelled at a Volvo in front. She honked the horn, riding its bumper then veered into the side lane. She stomped harder on the gas, passing two other cars. Up ahead the light went from green to yellow, and Liz flew right on through as it blinked red.

Malik and his cousin have been shot... those terrible words had rocketed over the phone and blown Liz's world apart. *This can't be happening,* she couldn't stop thinking as the torturous contractions in her bosom deepened with each extra second it took for her to reach her baby. *Can't be happening.*

She made it to St. Mary's Hospital, parked near the emergency room doors and sprang from the car.

"My son was shot," she addressed the nurse at the reception window. "I need to see him."

"Name?" she asked routinely.

Liz almost snatched the frail heifer up and demanded she move faster. "Freeman," she voiced vehemently.

"Are you Malik's mom?" a young white girl asked, appearing behind Liz.

"Yes," she said. "Where is he?"

"He's in surgery," she said. "I'm Jenny, the one who called." Resentment came into her voice. "These people aren't telling us anything."

Brian rushed over. "Auntie, Brandon and 'Lik got shot. That nigga got on some bullshit down at Summerfest." He shook with outrage. Liz noticed the butt of a gun peeking out his waistline. She pulled his shirt down over it.

"Calm down," she said, although she was in a panic herself. Maniac came over. "Take him over there," Liz told Maniac, gesturing toward the sitting area.

247

He guided Brian away. Liz went and drilled the nurse for information on Malik's status.

A short Asian doctor with a receding hairline came out and approached Jenny. She directed him straight to Liz.

A sickening feeling gripped Liz's intestines. "My son?" she asked. The doctor's sullen gaze had damn near pushed Liz over the edge.

"Who is your son?" he sounded regretful.

"Malik Freeman," Jenny answered for Liz.

The doctor swallowed, saying, "He just made it through surgery." He raised a hand in a gesture of comfort. "Ma'am, your son should be fine."

"What do you mean by 'should'?" Liz asked.

"I mean he suffered some internal damage that'll keep him bedridden for awhile. But he'll recover fully in time."

"Thank you, Jesus," Liz took a relieved breath. Jenny reached out and hugged her.

Brian stormed over. "What's goin' on with my brother?" he accosted the doctor. The surgeon's hesitance heralded bad news. Liz didn't have to hear him say it to know.

"I'm sorry," the doctor said. "The internal bleeding was too much."

Liz lowered her head. It was like time stopped in that moment.

"Fuck that!" Brian raged. "You're 'bout to help my brother." He took on a desperately determined look.

"We did all we could," the doctor pleaded as Brian seized him by the collar. "Please, sir."

The people present winced and skedaddled to safety. Liz regained her composure. "Brian, you turn that man loose," she ordered.

"Freeze now!" A slew of policemen stormed through the emergency doors with weapons drawn.

"Hands up!"

248

Liz moved to grab Brian. "Wait," she said as a policeman tackled her to the floor.

"He's armed," another cop warned.

Liz lifted her face off the carpet and spotted the gun in Brian's hand.

"Back the fuck up!" he directed the cops, pressing his pistol against the doctor's neck, ready to use him as a human shield.

Additional law enforcement showed up. They stopped short upon realizing the hostage situation.

Firearms nosed in Brian's direction from all angles. "Please, don't do this, baby," Liz tried to reason with him. Cops dragged her away, cutting short her pleas. Then a knee stabbed her back and cuffs clamped around her wrist. "They're gonna try and kill you," she screamed to Brian. "Surrender, baby, please!" She was yanked from the floor, shoved through the emergency doors, and marched outside, up to a squad car. Liz was frisked and pushed by the head into the back seat, the door slammed in her face.

A gathering of spectators formed around the perimeter of the parking lot. Police vehicles continued pulling up, lights flashing, sirens wailing.

Sharp pangs led an assault on Liz's temples. She shut her eyes for relief and prayed for release from this terrible nightmare. "Jesus, bring us out..." Emotion obstructed the passage of her words. She let her heartbeats complete the prayer. She feared that gunfire would erupt inside the emergency room at any second. She watched the sliding doors. Civilians exited, officers entered, everyone moving in a controlled panic. The cramped back seat confined Liz into a state of helplessness. The metal cuffs bit into her thin wrists. "Don't you kill him!" she yelled at the officers passing by the squad car. Her words bounced off the window back down her throat, and choked her into fretful silence. They ignored her appeals. Liz's thoughts were in a tizzy. Malik was somewhere alone. On a hospital bed. Hooked up to machines. Tubes sticking all over him, wondering why Liz wasn't by his side. A worse scenario: The doctor got it wrong. A mix-up... Brandon had actually survived. Malik had... The back seats, the humidity and confinement smothered Liz. The dying boy in the church interrupted her thoughts. The image. The blood crawled on her skin. The awful memory remixed itself. The face of the

249

deceased young man turned into Brandon's face… then Brian's face… then Malik's face. The scream stuck in her throat. Perspiration bubbled out her pores. Feelings rioted in her chest. Liz's head fell back on the seat. The pangs stepped up their assault on her temples. *Life wasn't worth this shit,* she grieved. The hurt, the despair. The hell with it. With faith in things unseen and seen. With all the hope rhetoric of religion. Things had only worsened since Liz started praying and attending church again. Her spirit plumbed the depths of turmoil. She was sick and tired of all the teasing God did. Making it look as if things were getting better while setting up something worse. She opened her eyes to the chaos around her. It reflected the reality inside her.

She saw the emergency room doors slide open. A jolly white giant of a policeman escorted the doctor out and to a waiting ambulance. Liz pulled up in the seat, watched the doors, waited for… They slid open again and out came Maniac in handcuffs. Two cops marched him over to a waiting paddy wagon.

"Thank God," Liz exhaled, seeing Brian alive. A gaggle of officers led him out the hospital in restraints.

The media showed up and directed their recorders and cameras. Liz sank down in the seat a peg. An officer opened the driver's door. The night air helped Liz breathe. He spoke with two of his colleagues about something, then got behind the wheel. Liz braced herself to hear about all the trouble she was in.

"Your full name?" he asked without a look back or in the rear view mirror. She repressed the instinct to tell him to kiss her black ass.

"Why the hell was I dragged out that hospital like some damn road kill and treated like a criminal?" she snapped out.

"Get used to it because you'll soon be a convict," he said in the snidest manner. "Your name?"

"Ask your partner," she sneered at the back of his bald ass head. "He took my fuckin' I.D." She was beyond pissed off.

"Keep it up so I can keep adding on the charges," he threatened, and refused to give Liz the respect of looking at her.

"While you're at it with your charges," Liz vented, "go find the bastards who shot my son and murdered my nephew and charge them."

"I probably will once I'm done wasting time with your silly ass," he said, finally looking up in the rear view at her.

"Kiss my ass, you devil," she shot back.

"Pull down your nasty ass panties and I will, bitch," he disrespected. Liz lost strength, lost the will to speak. He laughed at her tears. She longed to go be with her son.

CHAPTER 44

Malik pressed the control button, adjusting the hospital bed to a better sitting position. He grimaced the entire time, struggling to balance the physical and emotional pain. The two bullet wounds—one in the lower stomach, another right below his right armpit—sweated heavily underneath their thick bandaging and suffocated all solace. Anger and anguish had double-teamed his sleep for the past week, only allowing short, sporadic naps throughout each day. The battle with insomnia kicked off the night he awoke from surgery. He daydreamed more than anything else, spending hours and hours trying to wrap his mind around what happened, how it happened, why it happened. And why his kin? Grappling with Brandon's untimely death exhausted Malik, and although he survived the shooting, part of him had died with his cousin.

To pour acid in his wounds, neither he nor Brian got to attend the funeral. Malik worried about Brian's predicament. The courts were gearing up to hang him over the hostage situation. The case had garnered too much publicity in the news and most of the state of Wisconsin—probably most of the region—knew Brian Freeman's face and about the allegations against him. Getting a fair trial or impartial jury seemed far-fetched, thanks to the excessive media coverage.

Malik sighed out of mental fatigue and frustration and pent-up animosity. Derrick's life lines had run out. In Malik's mind, the nigga was already dead and just needed a violent shove into a cold grave. The responsibility now weighed on his shoulders and he anticipated executing justice. *Couldn't wait!*

His intimate brush with death didn't sidestep his awareness. It could've very well been his wake and funeral this week. He vaguely remembered being shot. It came back to him like a choppy dream: Maniac lifting him off the pavement... Brian ordering Jenny to drive him to a hospital. After that, he drew a blank up until the time he came out of surgery.

"A teaspoon of blood and God's mercy spared your life, young man," one of the doctors had claimed. The full impact of Malik's near-fatal dance with the reaper was yet to hit him. The hurt and loss of Brandon served as a distraction, a temporary cushion. He owed Maniac and now truly understood why the twins embraced him like they did. He owed Brian. And Jenny and her buddies. He really owed the nigga Derrick and his guys and couldn't wait for pay back. Principal and interest: capital punishment.

"Happy birthday, dude," Jenny greeted as she entered the room. She approached Malik's hospital bed in sneaky steps. "I hope I don't get indicted for smuggling you outside food." She fetched the contraband out of her carry bag. The aroma of Pizza Shuttle pizza awakened Malik's appetite from its coma.

"Good lookin'," he said, tempted to thank her a third time for driving him to the hospital while he bled all over her car seats.

"Your mom said she'll be down here after Brandon's burial. The funeral was really emotional." She stared at him for a sympathetic moment.

"No more sadness and tears," he said and positioned his slice of pizza on the sliding bed table in front of him.

She smiled and perked up. "Hey, I got you..." she reached in her bag again, "a little something for your b-day," and she pulled out a small gift box.

He mustered a smile, accepting it. "Mighty kind of you." He stared at the Movado watch inside it. A deeper depression sank into his soul. *Not a damn thing happy 'bout this birthday.*

"You like it?" She expressed uncertainty.

"Of course I do," he assured her. He forced a mannish smirk and added, "Now all I need is some nooky."

She blushed. "You might prefer that from Brianna."

Malik laughed for the first time since he'd been shot. It hurt; he winced.

"You alright?" she moved closer.

He recovered. "Yeah." He placed the watch on the table. "Why you throw Brianna's name at me?" His smirk returned.

"She's your lady, isn't she?"

He took a bite from the pizza.

Jenny shrugged. "Plus, I get the feeling she doesn't really care for me. I'm not here to complicate y'all thing."

"What are you here for?" he asked.

"Do you want me here?" she replied.

"You can't answer a question with a question."

"Why not?" she said with another shrug. "You don't want me answering other people's questions."

His appetite fell back asleep. He set down the pizza and picked up the cup of water, guiding the straw to his lips.

"Did the detectives come again?" she lowered her voice in asking this.

"They will but we still won't know nothing," he said. Their eyes met. On the night of the shooting, both Maniac and Brian warned Jenny not to speak with anyone about what she saw, including the cops. Later she'd told Malik and asked his advice. He told her the same thing. "Say nothing." And she didn't, which clearly bothered her. He sensed it then and sensed it now.

Jenny looked down at her hand. Malik stared up at the TV.

"I don't understand," she spoke up. "Why would you let those guys get away with what they did?"

Malik pulled up farther in bed. Pain shot through his belly up to his head. He grimaced longer than he needed to. "Leave it alone," he said.

"Leave it alone?" she raised her voice. "They killed your cousin and left you for dead. Don't you want justice?"

"Yeah," he replied. "Street justice. That's where it began, that's where it'll end." His words sounded hollow, even to himself.

She glowered with frustration. "Then what?" she shook her head. "What's proven?"

He thought about that. Deep down, he shared her frustration with him. He preferred for the police to handle the situation. Malik was sick of all the drama. "Some things you'll never understand," he said ruefully.

"I saw Derrick run over and grab the gun from the boy who shot you and then shoot Brandon. Me and Nelly saw him."

He stared at her. This was a revelation to him. Nothing would stop him from killing Derrick. "Y'all didn't see nothing," he said in a final tone.

Jenny's bafflement reached a boiling point. "I saw you almost die," she snapped, rising out of her chair.

"Look," he snapped back, "I know what the hell happened. I am the one it happened to."

"I could've gotten shot too," she frowned.

"So what, you didn't. I did."

"Fuck your so what," she fumed.

"Suck my so what."

"Suck your own so what, asshole," she stood over him in a brazen posture. She looked possessed.

"Asshole?" he laughed in her face. Again he exaggerated his grimace to get her to back off. She stood down, falling back onto the chair.

All of ten minutes passed while neither one of them spoke a word. Malik really didn't want to hear it. All the preaching from everybody was starting to bug him. He didn't expect anyone to understand besides the streets. Surely not some suburban white girl. *Caucasians always try'na tell niggas how to live.* The bitter sentiment lingered and dissolved into a gust of guilt. He was bogus for thinking about Jenny like that. Breaking the silence, he said, "Got me trippin' on you on my b-day," in a lighthearted tone.

255

"I'm not trippin' on you trippin', 'Lik," she composed herself. "I'm trippin' on you goin' about dealing with that situation in the wrong way. Help me to understand your reasoning."

"Don't assume it's for you to understand," he said. "Certain shit in life will never make sense to you unless you live it. Same goes for me, for everybody."

"Okay, so you heal and go carry out your 'street justice,'" she said with a sliver of derision. "Then what, you give them another chance to kill you or someone else you love?"

"Leave it alone." She was making his head hurt. Worse.

"Who wins in the end, Malik?" she pushed it. "You wanna throw away your life and hurt those who care about you?"

"Listen," he lashed at her. "Stay on the other side of the tracks where shit is Laverne and Shirley. Let me live how I live and deal with my shit how it has to be dealt with. Dealing with it like you and yours isn't always an option."

She shut up and turned away. Hurt and offended. Two minutes passed. She leaned back in the chair and mumbled, "Must be one of those black things that my white self just don't understand."

"You don't know shit about being black," he lost it. "Nothing about it so don't speak on it. You think listening to hip hop and dressing like a sista makes you *bona fide*. You can only act black while we live it."

She leapt to her feet. "Act black?" she seethed tears.

"Did I stutter?"

She got her bag. "Well, I guess you're acting like a grand wizard of the KKK when you go out and—"

"Get the fuck out of my—" he choked on the bile in his throat. She was out the door by the time he swallowed it.

He wouldn't digest the disrespect for a very long time, if ever. He reclined on the pillow, madder than a mutha fucka! The "KKK" slug was the third shot he took in a week, and this time the bullet ricocheted off his ego and wounded his pride. "KKK," he grumbled at the door. "This time the niggas brought it on themselves."

His rationalization only pushed the bullet deeper into his chest. He thought about Brandon. The enmity stripped his emotions. Derrick had to suffer. Period. *Out of chances, nigga.* Malik wasn't hearing shit from anybody.

"Happy Birthday," she cooed, chasing away some of Malik's bitterness. "Why are you looking so mean?" Brianna asked as the door closed behind her.

Malik beheld her beauty for a minute. The sistah was soothingly gorgeous, dressed in a dark silky head scarf and ankle-length sun-dress. She planted an intense kiss right on his lips. "Cheer up," she smiled.

He grinned so hard his teeth hurt. "Do that again," he requested, and she did, spicing it up with a shimmer of sensuality. His nature gave a standing ovation.

"One more time," he pressed his luck

It had run out. "Here, boy," she handed him a gift bag with two books in it. He thanked her and read over the titles: *Know Thyself* by Naim Akbar and *Spirit of a Man* by Iyanla Vanzant. He browsed over their inside jackets.

Brianna presented him with an Afrocentric birthday card and a written poem. "You wrote this?" he asked. She nodded in the affirmative. He fell in love and read it:

Live 4 me, Black man

so that our 2-morrows can add up

2 one nation standing

advancing and demanding the next day

plus 24-7-365-eternities

Live 4 me, Black man

defy the devil's lures

257

feel the contours of your destiny

hand me my blues back

gift-wrapped in our dreams

open it up and show us what it means

2 live 4 purpose

make the struggle worth it

Live 4 us, Black man

our veins are runnin' dry

the blood spill is depleting the promise

don't let us perish!

Live 4 us, Black man

lose the stagger in ya swagger

fuel the vim in ya rhythm

take it back from them

no more dis-ease, swallow the symptoms

no more sick feelings, digest the healing

Live for you, Black man

noose the nigger in U

let him die!

let him die!

let him die, so you can

live 4 our 2-morrows 2-day

and beyond the beyond of

what's beyond...

Malik's throat grew dry. He swallowed the airy build-up and exhaled. They gazed into one another's eyes and communicated without a word being spoken. Brianna's physical beauty captivated Malik, but her essence lifted him up even as he lay there in the hospital bed. He loved her far more than he could ever hate Derrick. Letting the cops step in seemed within reason now. A sistah's love can save a brotha from himself, he heard himself think.

"Knock, Knock," his mother converged with their flow. She walked over, a smile on her face, sorrow in her eyes. "Hi, Brianna."

Brianna stepped back from the bed. "Big Sister."

Two of the most important women in Malik's life hugged each other and injected him with a shot of joy. "Where's my hug?" he pouted playfully.

"Happy birthday, baby." His mother hugged him, and didn't let him go. When she pulled back, tears were in Liz's eyes. Brianna exited the room quietly to give them some privacy. Liz hugged him again. "Don't you dare leave me," she whispered. Her warm tears dampened the right side of his face. "You hear me?"

"No doubt, mama," he said. The hurt, the anger, the sense of loss, it all welled up within him with a passion. He held on to his mother, disregarding the physical pain.

CHAPTER 45

Liz breathed easy now that her son was back under her roof. The past three and a half weeks had taxed her emotions beyond calculation. Seeing Malik laid up in a hospital bed all that time kept her world spinning on a wobbly axis. That level of depression and pressure hadn't hit her since Kevy's arrest. Any drama in the past seemed like a cakewalk compared to the recent rough ride. Liz had literally broken down during each visit to the hospital and wept on those mornings she awoke and looked in Malik's room at his empty bed.

She had almost lost her only child.

The mere thought of it weighed too heavily for any portion of peace to settle over her life. *Something had to give—and soon!* Milwaukee was a death trap, and Liz planned to mount an escape ASAP. *But how?* She stared out of the screen door at the kids playing cans on the sidewalk. Two boys launched a basketball back and forth while another boy and three girls stood nearby on the sidelines. It was a sunny day and everything appeared peacefully good in the 'hood. But Liz distrusted appearances. Storm clouds lurked right around the corner. Maybe just up the block. Today the kids played with balls, tomorrow it might be pistols. Dangerous products of their environment.

Thanks to Liz's sympathetic boss, she would be able to stay by Malik's side for another two weeks. She looked forward to playing nurse-mom during his convalescence. This offered the much-needed opportunity for them to discuss things, like moving out of the city. She also wanted to keep a close eye on him until the police solved Brandon's murder. Liz was far from a fool. Malik's uncooperative attitude toward the police left the red flags fluttering in her head. *Somebody knew something.* Liz remembered what Brian said about Derrick the night in the emergency room. So his and Malik's claims of not seeing who did the shooting or who was involved were bullshit. She smelled it. And she considered it a good thing that Brian remained locked up in the county jail, even though it didn't quell all of her worries. Malik would eventually get out of his bed and out of her sight. Lord only knew what vengeance brewed in her son's heart.

"Ma," Malik called from his bedroom.

"Yeah," she answered, closing the front door. "Here I come, baby."

'Shoot 'em up with the Glock' music greeted her as she entered his room. She walked over and turned it off.

"What you doing?" he complained. "I was listening to that."

She gathered up some clothes that lay messily on his floor. "I don't wanna hear that mess," she said, "and I prefer you not either." Cleaning up after him reminded her of the nursing home gig.

"It's just music," he downplayed it.

"Too bad others don't always see it like that," she said. "And often try to live out what they hear in those songs."

"Reflects reality," he defended.

"Creates reality, too," she said.

"Movies do the same thing, but I don't hear people attacking Hollywood like they attack rap."

"It's a difference between seeing a movie one or two times and hearing the same violent lyrics over and over and over again, day in and day out," Liz asserted..

"You sound like one of Bill O'Reilly them," he accused. "Fox News got you too, huh?"

She stared at him like he'd lost his mind. "What I sound like is a mother whose son happens to be recovering from some of the same violence that rappers love to glorify in their music."

"You just had to go there." He diverted his attention to the TV screen.

Liz tossed the clothes in a basket and sat down at the foot of his bed. "I'm thinking about moving soon," she said. "Time for us to get out of Milwaukee."

261

Malik knitted his brows. "Time for *you* to get out of Milwaukee," he said stubbornly.

"I said 'we,'" she insisted. "It's too much negativity in this city."

"I'm stayin'," he stated flatly. "If you move, be sure to come back and visit sometimes."

"We can move to the south. Maybe Atlanta. That way we're closer to where they got your daddy at."

"Don't try'n' play the daddy card on me," he said.

"I don't need to play any cards," she said. "Your butt will move where I say move."

"Think so?" he challenged.

"I know so," she assured. He huffed a sigh and directed his attention back to the TV. She got up and turned it off. He frowned and stared at the blank screen. Liz couldn't knock his attitude toward the idea of packing up and leaving a place he'd always called home. Milwaukee was all he knew, they both knew. The city had its good, but lately the bad and ugly had taken a formidable lead. Liz's seven-hour stint in jail had embittered her. It was the most degrading thing she'd ever experienced. "You're lucky," a black female officer had told Liz at the precinct. "The county jail is a lot worse." They issued her a disorderly conduct ticket and let her go. Liz felt wronged, violated, and disrespected. To top it off, the desk sergeant on duty had had the audacity to flirt with her, first while he delivered the citation to the interrogation room she was thrown in, and hours later when he finally came back to tell her she was free to go.

One thing was for certain: they didn't ever need to worry about her committing any crimes. She paid the fine the very next morning. Never again! She was scared straight.

"You don't feel it'll be good to get away from all this?" she said, breaking the silence between them. "A fresh start inna healthier environment for black folks."

262

"America ain't healthy for black folks," he upheld his resistance. "And you talking 'bout heading to the south?" he went on. "They'll kill ya quicker down there. white and black folks."

"I didn't say anything about anyone getting killed," she said. "I'm focused on living. You're set to graduate next year, so it's important to start looking into some colleges. A southern one is likely your best bet. You've always talked about going to an Historically Black College."

He stared down at his stomach. "A lot has changed since then," he said, his mood growing somber.

"The need for you to plan for your future hasn't and never will change." She considered something. "I won't be here forever. You're at the threshold of manhood. Prepare to live without me always being around to handle things."

"You not gon' be here forever?" he asked. The acute concern that took over his expression was touching. "How you gon' say something like that?"

"Anything can happen," she replied. "Life should've taught you that by now. Tomorrow isn't promised to none of us."

His leg moved under the sheet and made contact with her hip. It was an unconscious gesture, Liz assumed.

"So," she went on, "It's high time for you to decide what you're gonna do with your life. Those who fail to plan, plan to fail."

"Don't even trip," he said. "I got plans."

"Productive plans?" she asked. He took way too long to answer, so she continued. "God is writing something on the wall for you to read, Malik. Pay attention and heed the signs of the times. Your cousin is in jail and will likely be going to prison for a very long time. He'll miss out on some of the most precious years of his adult life. And worse is his brother." She paused for effect. "Killed unexpectedly." A beam of anger flickered from his eyes. "He didn't get to start a family. Didn't get to have any children to carry on his name. Neither twin did for that matter."

Malik asked, "Why does God let these things happen if He's the one writing the script?"

"Maybe to get our attention," she reasoned.

He twisted up his face. "If that's true, then God is a sick dude," he said. "That makes him an accomplice to murder, robbery, rape, child molesta—"

"You can't look at it like that, boy," she interrupted him. "You're using human reasoning to figure out a spiritual matter. Search deeper for the answer."

"Right now all I'm dealing with is human drama in this human reality. Not using my mind to reason will leave me where Brandon is. I'll focus on the spiritual when this world becomes a little more peaceful."

"'Lik, you can't always depend on your mind," she said. "Over-thinking will drive you insane. God will provide you with the best angle if you lean on Him."

Malik picked up a book off his night stand. "Yeah, I sure gotta holla at God to see why He don't like niggas," he said.

She let him slide with the N-word this time. "God didn't make any of us niggers," she frowned. "That identity was thrust on us to break us in and break us down during slavery times. This is why it's so sad for any black person to refer to himself as one. A nigger is the invention of some white man, not God. It's a stigma, a state of mind that ruins a person's humanity."

He looked up from the book. "It's crazy how people get offended by the use of that word but don't seem to fight as hard against being treated like a nigger. I know what nigga means to me and what being treated like a nigger is. I'm not accepting nigger treatment from anyone ever again. People better respect me or get their faces ripped off. Believe that."

The fire in his words disturbed Liz a great deal. There was heat in his conviction. She felt it. "While you're demanding respect from people, make sure it doesn't cloud your judgment, or worse. Your purpose in life is the only thing worth the risk of your life and liberty, and the demand to fulfill your purpose is placed strictly on you."

264

"What's your purpose?" he asked firmly. Liz was caught by surprise and left speechless. What *was* her purpose? She never really invested a lot of time in figuring that out. She'd set goals, had goals, achieved goals. But an actual purpose?

"Right now it's you," she said to her son. "It's helping you mature into a strong, productive man. You are my purpose and I won't get off your butt until my mission is complete, mister."

She got up and bent down to plant a warm kiss on his forehead.

"No doubt," he said. "And right now you'll be my purpose in return."

She smiled at her baby boy. "We all we got," she reminded him. Nothing will ever come in between this here," she pointed at him, then back at herself. The innocence eased back into his features. *It never left,* she realized. *Just was buried.* She froze the image in her mind.

"I feel 'ya, Ma," Malik said.

"No doubt," she said with a hip hop swagger. They laughed.

"Now run down to Jake's and cop me a corned beef sandwich with extra pickles, good lookin'," he ordered.

"Yo' butt ain't gone be runnin' me all around town like I'm ya worker," she warned.

He cracked open his book. "I might have to do the same for you one day," he teased. "Set the example now so I'll know how to—"

She waved him off, saying "Please!" and exited his room. She grabbed her keys and pocketbook to go get her baby something to eat.

CHAPTER 46

Malik posted up on the front porch, glad to be out of the house, back on his feet and fitted in all new gear—from the Jordan trainers on his dawgs, to the Jordan classic tracksuit draping his frame, to the matching Jordan headband hugging his noggin. The boredom from being stuck in the house bedridden had been a burden. It took Malik over a month to recover from his injuries and to use his limbs without grimacing. Getting shot just wasn't cool.

He did enjoy Brianna's daily company and phone calls. Their intimacy had grown deeper within the last month. He believed that he was making strides with his future wifey, although she refused him any more kisses on the lips like she'd given him on his b-day. Cherryland remained off limits to Malik. He assumed she felt uncomfortable getting too touchy-feely in his mother's house. He'd test this theory later when he stopped by Brianna's crib for an evening visit. Malik smiled thinking about the slugs Brianna shot at him about "the little white girl." When he mentioned his debt to Jenny for driving him to the hospital, Brianna responded by saying, "God saved your life, so that's who you praise and give the glory to." Malik had left it alone. Throwing Jenny in her face wouldn't benefit him any because Brianna was a black woman through and through, and he respected her too much to try to manipulate her emotions.

Malik checked his Movado wrist wear and gazed across the street. Some of the neighborhood homegirls hung out in their front yard talking with three dudes who rode up in an old school droptop Cutlass on 24" wheels. One of the girls named Shakeris yelled "What's up, 'Lik" and waved. He tossed the deuces up to her as the dudes turned and looked. He ignored the attention and stared up the block.

Jenny hadn't contacted him since their heated argument. He knew he'd hurt her feelings. But what she said highly, highly offended Malik. *Actin' like a KKK Grand Wizard...* He just couldn't get over the disrespect. His ego had a hard time letting it go. Jenny was out of pocket, he kept telling himself, not wanting to admit that he sort of missed the girl. Reaching out to her first was out of the question though. Only Brianna had his nose that wide open; he'd chase her to the end of the earth and then carry her in his arms back to the altar. *Brianna Freeman.* He liked the ring of that. All he needed to do was figure out a way to get his ring on her finger.

Malik felt a warm, gentle breeze caress his neck and face. Today was the perfect day to get out and about again. Too much of his summer vacation had been wasted already. It was time to kick it.

Someone's slammin' car system approached. Malik stepped off the porch thinking it was Drizzle. An oyster-white Yukon Denali hit the block and rocked it. The ballers across the street checked it out along with Shakeris and her buddy named Babygirl, who inched toward the curb. The driver of the Denali slowed down and gawked at her. Babygirl approached his door and they started talking. One of the guys standing near the old school didn't appear too happy about that.

The Cutlass crew climbed into the drop top and pulled out behind the Yukon, which blocked their exit. Their horn blew. Babygirl frowned. "Stop hatin'," she yelled at them. Tension developed once the driver in the Cutlass got out to check Babygirl.

"Bitch, I know you ain't try'na front in front of these niggas," he disrespected.

The doors on the Denali flew open and five guys exited. An argument ensued. Malik eased back on the porch ready to dash to safety in case a gun battle erupted.

The driver of the Cutlass leapt forward and smacked Babygirl. The Denali guys got back in their vehicle and left.

At some point during the assault on Babygirl, Shakeris had run into the house. She returned with a Louisville slugger. Babygirl stormed over, snatched the bat, and went after her assailant, who jumped in his car and tried to get away. But Babygirl was quick on her feet. She went wild with the bat, whacking him on the shoulder one good time with it before he could burn rubber. She slung the bat and it flew right over into the dropped top of the Cutlass and plucked one of the back seat passengers on the crown of his head.

267

Malik looked on in silent cheer and amusement. "Okay, Babygirl," he whispered, glad to see her fight back. With the drama over, everybody present out on the block went back to minding their own business. Babygirl, Shakeris and their other buddy went in the crib. Malik thought about the times when Babygirl had asked him to hook her up with one of the twins. He never did because he knew what type of chick she was. Or he thought he knew. It wasn't a secret that Babygirl sought out any hustler rollin' slick and havin' it. Malik witnessed no less than five different dudes driving five different cars— all dressed up with baller vehicular accessories—either pick her up or drop her off on the block within the last several weeks. And these were only the times Malik had just so happened to hear their car systems and looked out the window. So her slut-status made the ghetto grade and she flaunted it. To go with that dishonor, she could also swing a mean bat at a nigga's head, Malik joked. Good thing he never played matchmaker with her and one of the twins.

Malik soon realized that it really didn't matter anymore. Brandon was dead... and Brian locked up... Maybe that was the reason Babygirl hadn't sweated him about the twins lately. Guess she had no use for a jailed baller. At least Shakeris carried herself with greater respect, and Malik respected her for it. She'd come to see him when he first got out the hospital to extend her condolences. "'Lik, you stay focused and don't let the streets steal you away from you," she had told him. She also spoke on the scholarship that she recently received. She was scheduled to attend an Alabama college   this coming semester. He congratulated her and let her know she'd done the 'hood proud.

Malik stepped off the porch and waited for his ride. He planned to visit Brian at the county jail tomorrow morning. They spoke on the phone daily. Usually Malik made three-way calls for him and listened while Brian either tongue lashed some female or spoke sweetness in her ear; it all depended on his mood or attitude during each 15 minute period. He called three or four times a day and periodically had someone drop off money to Malik for the phone bill.

He kept Malik updated on his case. The DA and judge wanted to hang him. Brian was a realist, so he began setting things up for his stay upstate. Malik hoped for the best, but still expected the worst.

Kevy had started flooding Malik with letters since the shooting. His father hit him with some of the realest, most heartfelt, and insightful wordage ever. Malik had responded to every letter and told Kevy about the drama and about the conflicting thoughts and feelings he was experiencing. Kevy helped him make some sense of it; however, most of Malik's issues remained unresolved. He still wanted to kill Derrick.

Prophet had visited him at the hospital a couple of times and called weekly once Malik was released. He asked about the shooting, and Malik told him little. Since Prophet and Kevy were back in tune with each other, Malik assumed his dad had asked Prophet to keep an eye on him. Prophet had also questioned Drizzle about the incident. Drizzle claimed ignorance, and he later shared a theory with Malik. "I bet any money yo' pops told Prophet to take care of who shot you and Brandon." Malik suspected the same thing.

On a brighter note, Prophet got Drizzle to sit down with Jeff, Chill Will, and the other guys. They all met up at Kemet Quarters, agreed to let bygones be bygones and put the possibility of working together back on the table. A week later Jeff called and invited Drizzle to travel out to New York with him. Drizzle accepted without his normal cynicism. "You don't think dude is up to something?" Malik had asked. Drizzle said he'd already posed the same question to Kila's uncle, and Prophet assured him that "everything was on the up and up." Malik and Drizzle figured if Prophet put his stamp on it, then it was all good. Jeff probably wouldn't have been as forgiving had he known Drizzle was the one who had put a hot one in him. "What he don't know won't irk him," Drizzle said on the night before the trip.

Malik couldn't wait to hear all about the New York adventure. He expected Drizzle to arrive any minute now.

Just like clockwork, Brandon's 'Lac truck bent the block with Kila behind the wheel. Drizzle leaned sideways in the front passenger seat. As Malik made his way toward the sidewalk, he noticed Babygirl magically reappear outside.

"Say, dun," Malik greeted Drizzle in a bootleg New York accent.

Drizzle laughed and embraced him. "The trip was ill, god," he came back in the same east coast slang. "They told me I'm the new John Blaze, kid."

"Word."

"Word, kid."

Kila got out and handed Malik the keys. "Y'all need to stop," she laughed. "Call me later," she kissed Drizzle and walked over to a Buick Century that pulled up. Malik stared through the windshield at the driver. She looked like a woman he wouldn't mind getting better acquainted with.

"Who is that?" Malik questioned Drizzle as Kila got in the car.

"That's Kila's cousin." Drizzle lowered his voice and dropped a bomb. "She got that package. You don't wanna fuck around."

"Straight up?" Malik asked in disbelief. He took one last gander at her. She looked too good to have HIV or AIDS. "Damn."

"Let's ride, fam," Drizzle said, getting in the truck.

Malik got behind the wheel. An eerie feeling passed over him. This was his first time back in Brandon's ride since the shooting.

Babygirl popped up outside the driver's door and asked Malik about Brian. "I wanna write him," she claimed.

"Babygirl!" Shakeris called. "Here he come!"

Babygirl turned, spotted the droptop Cutlass zooming her way and broke toward the house. The car skidded to a stop next to the Escalade.

Drizzle got on point. "Who is these cats staring all up in our shit?"

The three dudes mean mugged for about 10 seconds and pulled back off. Malik relaxed and smashed out into traffic.

Drizzle began telling him about the trip. "Dawg, New York is a whole new time zone in grinding and rhyming. Those cats made me feel slow but I still held my own and made my presence felt. People were everywhere. You had chicks doing it harder than the niggas in certain instances. And everybody got a hustle. It's crazy. Niggas out selling anything that can be sold. One

270

Jamaican cat tried to sell me a damn piece of wire with a skeleton of a baby chicken on it talking about it'll keep *'trouba ub offa ya, mon'.* " They cracked up.

"But this punk Jeff definitely got some plugs," Drizzle went on. "He had me flowing for people who worked at Def Jam, Jive, and some other record label I never heard of."

"Straight?" Malik shared his excitement. "What they say?"

"They wanted to know how much I was selling locally and regionally. I learned a lot these last couple days," he said. "A nigga can be a beast inna booth but if he don't have hits in the streets, in the clubs, and making hella noise, then it don't mean shit to the big companies. It's mostly 'bout ya grind, homie. The talent is only 10% of the equation. The rest is hustle, game, and recognition. But I'm not deterred. Jeff threw me some beats earlier and tonight I'm hitting the studio and not leaving that bitch until I record a classic."

As they rode through the Miltown, they chopped it up about their next moves. New York had left a deep impression on Drizzle. "We gotta do this for the twins."

Malik nodded. "No doubt."

"It's a rat race to the top though. We can't let up when playing catch up, fam. You with me?"

"One hundred," Malik said. "Losing isn't an option."

"Naw, it ain't."

Malik stopped at John Red Hots on 27th and Fond du Lac. All the talking and excitement made him hungry. "So what's next on the agenda?" he said, parking in the small lot.

"Jeff still runnin' that contract spiel on me," he said, "although very respectfully." They both grinned knowingly. "What it is is that he's try'na get a national distribution deal for his label and think he's gonna use me to make that happen. He know Chill Will and the other artists he has now won't get him in the door, but believes that I can. He even asked me to collab on a

271

whole album with the cat Chill Will. But I'm not feeling that at all. I'm not about to carry a nigga I don't respect."

"Keepin' it real," Malik said, "I still wanna do what we planned on doing before Brandon got killed. Start our own label and push the music out the truck until we catch. The town is gonna hold you down regardless. We're gonna have to spread our hustle throughout the state, the region, and eventually beyond. If the parent companies want numbers, let's show 'em numbers and make 'em come to us. Brian already said he's leaving me everything. We can liquidate some of those assets and invest the proceeds in the vision."

Drizzle rocked with confidence. "Dawg, get out my head. I've been thinking along similar lines. You just articulated it a lot better than I could've. That's why I call you my brains. We won't settle for nothing less than a distribution deal. Until then it's the Indy 500's. We'll keep our real plans between us. Jeff has a role to play but his position will stay below ours, even if I need to sell him a dream."

Malik switched subjects. "You know Brandon owned that house on the eastside? Brian wants me to pick up the keys from his girl and play caretaker. You can stay there with me. I'll get you an extra set of keys."

"That's love there," Drizzle said. He shook his head. "I just hope Brian overcome that case. Niggas heard about that hostage situation all the way out on the east coast. I miss him and Brandon, fo' real. Those are some good dudes."

"Take it one day at a time and stay focused," Malik said.

"Fam died in the midst of trying to support me and my dreams," Drizzle said. "I plan to show my gratitude in everyway." They looked at each other. Both knew that "everyway" didn't only pertain to the rap hustle. Derrick and his boys and the consequences of their acts fell into that category also.

But what was understood needn't be spoken on. They got out.

272

CHAPTER 47

The visiting room at Taycheedah Correctional Facility for Women was well organized with low tables, plastic chairs, several vending machines, a guard's desk and station, a picturesque corner where inmates took photos with their loved ones, and a small children's area with toys and two bookcases. A sprinkling of inmates easily distinguishable in their state-issued khakis and gray tees sat talking with their visitors.

This was a familiar scene to Liz, except for the gender of these prisoners. She sat with She-She at their assigned table and waited for Janice to come out. This would be their first prison visit. She-She's apprehension showed as she fidgeted with her wristwatch and repeatedly glanced at the inmate entry door. All of the previous visits to the county jail had been non-contact. She-She hadn't touched her mother in over six months.

"I'ma hug her when she comes out," she said. Another inmate had just walked out and kissed and hugged her family.

"She'll like that," Liz said. "I'll give her a nice warm one too." She tried to imagine life behind bars: the women inside their cells, how they functioned with so little privacy, the lesbian liaisons. She had heard stories about women being turned out and coming home representing the rainbow, some gay, some bisexuals. Liz couldn't see herself tied up in any of that. *Strictly dickly,* she thought to herself.

"De'Von, get your butt back over here," a slim sister with a low cropped hairstyle called out to a little boy. He obeyed her long enough to disobey her once she turned and refocused on the conversation she was having with her other visitor, an older woman who looked to be in her late fifties.

"Auntie," said She-She, "You think they have any Bibles over there?"

"They should." She watched De'Von as he hardheadedly eased away towards the toy area. "I'll go see if we can get one," Liz said and got up. She walked over to the desk where a woman C.O. sat looking like it would hurt for her to smile.

"Are these Bibles available to visitors?" Liz asked, noticing a set of them on a shelf next to the guard's desk.

"One per table," she said rather bluntly.

You don't have to be rude, heifer, Liz was tempted to say. *You lucky I found Jesus.* She rolled her eyes when the C.O. looked away. "Thank you," Liz said with intentional insincerity. She took a Bible and walked off.

Janice was already at the table hugging She-She when Liz returned. She placed the Bible on the table and waited while mother and daughter greeted each other with genuine love and affection. Then Janice turned and pulled Liz into a warm bear hug. What surprised Liz more than the unexpected show of sisterly affection was how good Janice looked. The weight gain rounded out her figure and gave her a great shape.

"Mama, you look so pretty,´ She-She said with a smile on her face.

They took their seats.

"Girl, who hooked up your 'do?" Liz asked, admiring the new style. "It looks like you just stepped out of the salon." Janice's hair was laid out in a silky style of pressed curls and braids.

"My cellmate is a beautician," she said. "I hit her with some canteen items and she plugged me."

"Tell her to look me up when she gets out," Liz said. "She'll have a loyal client in me." They laughed.

The mood stayed cheerful among them as they fell into conversation. She-She picked up the Bible and shared some passages with her mother. This filled Liz with pride.

Over the recent months, Liz had become more involved in the church, and She-She was with her every step of the way. They attended Sunday services and sometimes had their own private Bible studies together at home. She-She also joined the youth choir and a Bible study class held at the church on Wednesday evenings. Liz found inspiration in all of this. It gave her a sense of purpose. She-She was like the daughter she never had and always wanted.

274

"Mama, you want some goodies from the vending machines?" She-She asked. Janice said, "Yeah," and they got up.

"Y'all go ahead," Liz told them.

Once they left, Liz's attention wandered to the little boy, De'Von. He was back at the table with the two women but the sneaky look on his face indicated he was planning another escape. Slowly but surely, he started creeping off on them. Liz figured the older woman was De'Von's grandmother, the inmate his mother.

At first it looked as if De'Von's destination was the toy bins. But then he moved on to the guard's desk.

"You need to stay in your assigned area," the big masculine looking C.O. warned him sternly.

Woman, you're gettin' on my nerves with your shitty attitude," Liz wanted so bad to tell her, but once again practiced self-restraint. She grabbed the Bible off the table and headed over.

"I wanted to get another book," said De'Von, looking up at the C.O.

"You already have one," she said funkily. "Now return to your seat."

Liz slid the Bible back on the shelf. "Hey, lil man," she addressed De'Von, hoping to lure him away from the cranky guard.

He turned to Liz for a second then back to the guard, saying, "Can you let my mama come to my birthday party next week? I promise she'll come back."

A table of visitors nearby laughed at his request, apparently finding it cute. Liz's heart just about melted in her chest. De'Von looked around wondering what was so funny. He was so for real. The question had even moved the C.O. to contort her bloated mug into a crooked grin.

"I'm sorry but I don't have that power," she told him.

"Yes, you do," he accused. He sounded determined to get what he wanted.

275

The grin lost its hold on her face. "NO, I do not," she said coldly. "Maybe your mom will get herself together and not put herself back into a position to miss any more of your birthday parties."

Liz grabbed De'Von and frowned at the evil woman, saying, "That was crude, totally uncalled for and unprofessional." The other visitors nearby backed her up. De'Von ran back over toward his mother in tears.

"You fat miserable bitch, don't you ever cause my son pain," De'Von's mother said, confronting the C.O. "I'll slice your fat, disgusting throat."

The C.O. rose to her feet and hit a button. Liz restrained the sister and tried to get her to calm down.

"Ms. Sanders, you are being disruptive and your visit is terminated," the guard said as her co-workers rushed in the room. They surrounded the sister.

"Don't play yourself, honey," Liz told her.

"Ma'am, please return to your seat now," the C.O. directed Liz.

She-She rushed over. "Auntie, what's wrong?"

The sister was handcuffed and marched out of the visiting room by two other guards.

"I hate your fat ass," De'Von cussed at the C.O. as his grandmother escorted him past the desk and out the door.

Liz and several more visitors complained to a white shirt who came out. The rude C.O. went on the defensive. The captain politely asked everyone to calm down and return to their tables. "Or I'll have to ask you all to leave," he warned. Liz rolled her eyes at the C.O. and followed She-She back to their seats.

"How's Malik?" Janice asked, unconcerned with all the commotion. She was snacking on a bag of M&M's.

Liz decided to let go of the frustration. "He's back on his feet," she replied, sinking down onto her chair.

"Mama, the radio plays Andre's songs," She-She jumped in. "Do y'all get V100 F.M. up here?" She accidently knocked over her soda. "Dang."

Liz snatched the can up. She-She left to go get some paper towels. Janice moved the other stuff off the table.

She-She returned and wiped up the mess, then went to toss away the wet paper towels. Liz and Janice got back in their seats.

"I never thanked you for all you've done for me and my kids," Janice said. "You are truly a godsend."

"It's nothing," Liz replied. "We're sisters of the same struggle. It's our responsibility to help each other."

"I'll be back y'all," She-She called over. "I need to go to the bathroom." They watched her exit through a door.

"Plus, She-She has blessed my life in many ways," Liz said. "She and Andre are special kids."

Janice nodded in agreement. "I'm getting myself together so I can do right by them this time."

"It's on us," Liz said. "If we fail to step up for our children, no one will. All the system wants to do is stigmatize them."

Janice shook her head. "You're sure right." She took a deep breath. "I've been so selfish. And this has caused my kids pain. It's brought you and Malik all kinds of problems. I really, really apologize."

"You don't need to."

"Yes, I do," she insisted. "It's impossible for me not to feel some responsibility for Malik getting shot, your nephew getting killed, you getting assaulted, my baby getting sexually assaulted, and my son ending up in jail and now on the run."

"Your mistakes aren't any worse than mine in God's eyes," Liz told her. "Our roles could've easily been reversed." She exhaled. "I think we all have our own little prisons. The focus should be on getting free within."

She-She rejoined them.

277

They went on enjoying each others' company until the C.O. called out, "You have five minutes to wrap up your visits."

"Man, already," She-She complained.

"We'll be back next weekend," Liz promised. They stood to say their good-byes. Janice slipped Liz a piece of paper while She-She cleaned off the table.

Liz pocketed the note.

"That's Derrick's grandmother's address," Janice said. "He's over there quite often. Jesse wrote me last week and gave it to me. He asked to marry me now that he's locked up, too. I've led him on long enough to get his mama's address. He won't be hearing from me again, nor will he know I gave it to you."

"What about the charges against Andre?" Liz asked. "Can't he get them dropped?"

"Jesse's doing time on a burglary charge. He won't cooperate with the D.A. But just in case, I'll maintain contact with him until that situation is resolved. Good thinkin'." They embraced.

"Love you," She-She hugged her mother. Liz made her way over to the exit doors and watched the visitors say their goodbyes. She thought about Kevy. They hadn't hugged and kissed each other in years. The distance continued to widen the gap between them. Lately, Kevy hadn't written or called her. She hadn't written him either. Her involvement with Marvin further complicated the situation, and she felt she needed to tell Kevy the truth about him. It was time for her to stop running and deal with the whole situation. She only lusted for Marvin but loved Kevy. And since she'd started attending church again, her conscience constantly checked her about everything. The appetite for Marvin's touch ebbed and flowed and clashed with her self-accusing spirit. The devil was coming on stronger with his temptations. It had never been this difficult for her to abstain from sex. It had to be a part of the test. Liz prayed and prayed on it. She was tired of using shallow intimacy as an escape. *Sorry, Marvin.*

Liz exited the prison, promising herself to stay man-free until she was in a committed relationship. If Kevy couldn't forgive her, she'd move on. But for now, the relationship she had with the Lord would suffice.

She fingered the piece of paper in her pocket. There was another situation she needed to deal with, too.

CHAPTER 48

Popping sounds cracked and echoed in the distance as Malik lounged back in a chair on his front porch. It was a warm August night in Milwaukee. Malik could only wonder if the pop-pop-pop-pops were guns blazing or fireworks igniting. He hoped it was the latter. The summer had reached record temperatures in heat and hit record highs in homicides. Gunplay prevailed. Within the first 21 days of July, thirteen murders occurred. The local media dubbed the season 'Bloody Summer' and the streets referred to the city as 'Da Murda Mil' and it violently lived up to its moniker by the day.

In Malik's heart of hearts, he yearned for peace to caress the city. He held no illusions though. He'd torpedoed all romantic thoughts about the 'hoods coming together. Only God's almighty power could loosen the grip of despair. Malik now focused on survival. He'd spent most of the summer selling CD's, studying the music business with Drizzle, teaching himself how to operate the beat machines and keyboards Brandon had bought before he died, and hanging out at the house on the eastside.

Brian remained tucked away in the county jail awaiting trial. He'd entrusted Malik with every material possession that he and Brandon owned. Malik was floored when he discovered how much money the twins had stashed in their house. He knew they had hustle, but "Damn!" And for Brian to trust him with so much gave Malik more than enough motivation to keep it real. He didn't spend a dime out the stash without his cousin's consent. The temptation to borrow did arise on occasion. But Malik's love and loyalty held it at bay. After taking Brian's lawyer ten stacks, Malik stashed the rest inside his mother's sofa. Liz had no idea a piece of her furniture held more money than she'd made in the last seven years.

She-She and her friend Amina stepped out the house and accosted Malik. "Take us to Dairy Queen, 'Lik?" they double-teamed him with the demand. The girls had become close friends during the summer after meeting at church. Malik also knew Amina's big brother from the 'hood.

"Which one of y'all treatin' me?" he asked them.

They smacked their lips in unity and frowned. "You're treatin' us," She-She said. "You're the dude."

"On the real," Amina added her two cents. She-She puffed up into a cocky posture, warning, "Unless you want Auntie to know you're actin' less than a gentleman by try'na hustle two girls?"

Malik got up, and they jumped back. "It's a new day," he said. "Destiny's Child messed it up for y'all."

The girls frowned up their faces, then smiled and slapped fives before going into a broken rendition of 'Independent Woman,' with dance moves to match.

Malik gave them the thumbs up. "Now drive y'all independent asses to Dairy Queen." The suggestion halted their impromptu performance.

She-She rolled her eyes. "Can't stand you."

"Trip back inna crib then," he replied.

"Whateva," Amina said as She-She threatened to "tell every little hoodrat who call the house about each other and how you're playing them. Can't wait to holla at Brianna."

Malik grabbed She-She and hoisted her up on his left shoulder. "What you gonna do, little snitch?" he said. She rained down a clumsy combination of weak blows upon his back. "Put me down!" she screamed. "I'm tellin' Auntie."

Amina dashed off the porch, laughing. Malik let She-She go and she ran and joined her friend on the front lawn. They kept a safe distance and talked smack to him. He flinched like he was about to give chase, and they split toward the curb.

"Scary butts," he accused them.

A black Lexus pulled up and parked in front of Brandon's Caddy truck. Malik watched as none other than Maniac hopped out, leaving the engine running and sounds bumping Drizzle's first CD. "Fam," he greeted with a crooked ghetto smile. "Holla at ya nigga." He strutted over with a skinny blunt dangling from his lips. He wore all black fabrics.

281

"Y'all go get ready before I change my mind," Malik told the girls. He stepped off the porch and knocked fists with the homie.

"Check game," Maniac spoke out weed smoke. "I know that hoe ass nigga Derrick's locale. And who he's plugged with."

This gave She-She pause. Malik saw her summer joy dissipate into dread at the mention of Derrick's name. He pulled out his keys and chirped off the alarm on the truck. "Y'all get on in," he told the girls, passing She-She the keys.

"I need to get something first," She-She said and marched in the house. Amina followed her lead.

"Lock up the crib," Malik called after them, "and hurry up."

Maniac sucked another dose of high out of his blunt. "We can go punish his whole 'hood as soon I verify the info," he told Malik. His eyes screened murderous intentions.

Malik breathed out of his mouth, to avoid a contact, and considered Maniac's proposal. Lately, he'd tried to forget all about Derrick. But the deeper he missed Brandon and reflected on his death, the harder he thought about Derrick and all the drama. The indignant desire to avenge his cousin's murder agitated the hell out of Malik. He could never not think about Derrick and all the pain he'd caused. The hate was chiseled deeply into Malik's heart. He considered what the nigga did to Liz. "Where is this punk?" he asked Maniac.

"Suppose to be right on the eastside," he said. "Not too far from the twins' crib." His voice had a vindictive edge to it. "I've staked out the area but haven't spotted him yet. I can smell his pussy though. He's right in the city." He spoke this with a happy wickedness, as if he'd just won the lottery and would soon do evil with his winnings.

Maniac had exited the county jail last week, fully dedicated to hunting down Derrick. He had informed Malik that his P.O. hold was lifted once no evidence was found to link him to the hostage situation at the hospital. "They tried to get me to flip on B and tell who killed Brandon," Maniac told a stunned Malik that day. "But never." Then he vowed to sniff out Derrick. "It

282

doesn't matter if he's hiding out inna cave in the Middle East somewhere. I'm gone find him and send him to see Brandon so my nigga can torture the mog in the next life." So Malik was somewhat expecting him to show up any day with the recent update on Derrick's possible whereabouts.

"So you haven't seen him over there at all?" Malik asked.

Maniac deepened his mean mug. "What?" he choked on the weed smoke. Once he cleared his throat, he said, "We'd be speaking on that nigga in the past tense if I'da saw him already."

The girls came back outside. Malik waited for them to go get inside the truck before continuing the conversation with Maniac.

"Holla at me as soon as you verify his whereabouts," Malik told him. "I'm on deck."

Maniac took an extensive drag off his blunt and studied Malik through the marijuana cloud. Malik stared back without a blink, flinch, or twitch.

"I'll be at you the moment I know more," Maniac said. They knocked knuckles and nodded. "Love, fam." He strutted off to the car. Malik watched him settle into the Lexus and put a cell phone to his ear. Good thing Liz wasn't home. She would've flipped over the loud music, not to mention the open drug use, thought Malik. He went and made sure the house was properly locked up, then headed for the Escalade. As he stepped out into the street, a big Chevy Suburban rode up and stopped right next to the 'Lac truck, narrowing Malik's path. Before Malik knew it, the doors on the Suburban flew open and two masked men hopped out with guns aimed.

"Come up off it!" one demanded. He snatched Malik by the shirt sleeve and pressed the gun against his rib cage. The other armed man yanked open the driver's door of the Escalade, aiming his weapon at She-She and Amina. The girls' loud, terrified screams pierced the air.

"Where's the fuckin' keys?" he demanded to know. She-She tossed them into the front seat and jumped out the truck with Amina and ran. The armed man bent down and got the keys as his partner in crime searched Malik's pockets. Malik knew the routine. He stayed calm and compliant, but feared his chest would explode any second once the bullets penetrated his flesh. He repeatedly jabbed Malik in the side with his gun as he shook him down. "Start that bitch up, dawg," he yelled to his crime partner who was still in the Escalade searching frantically for the ignition key.

Malik stole a quick look inside the Suburban and saw a third masked man in the driver's seat observing the robbery. *Maniac?* Malik suddenly remembered and cut his eyes toward the Lexus. It was now empty.

The stickup man shoved Malik between the front of the Escalade and rear of the Lexus. "Fuck it, let's bounce," he said to his accomplice inside the Escalade. Malik glanced in the direction of the Lexus again, wondering… then…

A light blinked on inside the car, and Maniac, ducking low, crept out the front passenger door. Malik fell back on the curb, and the masked man left him and jumped in the Suburban, yelling "Fuck that truck, come on!" to the one still in the Escalade. Malik dove behind the Lexus and crawled over to Maniac.

Maniac showed him a beastly black cannon and whispered, "Hit it toward the crib. I got these niggas." Then he crept off toward the Escalade… almost unnoticed.

"Watch out, G!" the driver inside the Suburban yelled. Maniac popped up at the rear of the Escalade and started blazing at the Suburban. Malik hid behind the Lexus, his back pressed against the door. Multiple shots rang out. He heard slugs slapping into the car as the Suburban sped away.

Malik peeked around for She-She and Amina and didn't see them anywhere. He crept low over toward Maniac.

"Psst," he psst'd upon seeing Maniac crouched down next to the rear bumper. Maniac spun around, swinging his gun barrel in Malik's direction.

"It's me, fam," Malik said, falling back on the curb onto the grass. Maniac looked as if he was a millisecond from pulling the trigger before recognizing him. He sped a finger to his lip, signaling for Malik to keep hush. Malik crouched down behind him. Maniac turned back toward the street and peered out at something. "I think dude is still in the 'Lade," he warned in a low tone. He gestured up toward the back window. They rose up with caution

284

and peered inside, then ducked back out of sight. Someone was definitely inside the truck! Malik's heart acted a fool. "I seen him," he whispered.

"Let's ride," Maniac said, rising and running up to the open driver's door. "Fuck out!" he ordered, gun pointed. Malik came up behind him and helped pull the masked man out.

"Wait—" he pleaded, dropping the keys to the pavement.

"Let's go for a little ride, nigga," Maniac said, shoving him to the Lexus at gunpoint.

Malik got the keys off the ground and climbed inside the Escalade. It shocked him to see the gun laying on the passenger seat.

Maniac yelled for Malik. "Come on, fam!"

Malik grabbed the gun, got out, and slammed the door shut. Maniac pushed the masked man into the back seat of his car and crawled in behind him. Malik chirped the alarm on the truck and ran up to the Lexus.

"Drive," Maniac directed from the back seat. The key was already in the ignition when Malik got behind the wheel. He checked the side mirror and whipped out.

CHAPTER 49

Liz and Wanda rushed out of the movie theater when the call came with the urgent text message, saying "911—come home. PLEASE!" Liz's worries went crazy when she called home and didn't get an answer.

Wanda worked her cell phone in repeated attempts at reaching She-She or Malik. Meanwhile, Liz drove, with no respect for any traffic laws that hindered or slowed her down. She had to get home and fast.

"No answer," Wanda pulled the phone from her ear and hit the re-dial button for the umpteenth time. She kept getting the voice mail.

The moment was déjà vu for Liz. Here she was speeding through yellow and red lights, trying to get to the aftermath of some uncertain situation. She prayed Malik and She-She weren't in any trouble. Her intuition bustled with bad vibes.

The tires on the Ford Focus screamed as Liz made a hard right turn onto Sherman Boulevard.

Wanda clicked on her safety belt, then pressed on the dash to brace herself against the possible whiplash. Liz took a hand off the wheel and secured her own safety belt. "Hold on," she cautioned her friend. A couple more blocks, several sharp turns, and one near-collision with a parked Jeep Cherokee later, Liz finally reached her destination, dipping over into a parking space behind Brandon's Cadillac truck. Before Wanda could breathe her relief, Liz was out the car, sprinting up to the house. She fumbled the key into the lock.

"'Lik?" she called out. "She-She?" The house was eerily quiet; all the lights were off. Liz checked Malik's bedroom. No one there. "He should be here," Liz commented. "Brandon's truck is outside." She searched around the room for any clues.

Liz flipped on the light in the hallway. Her heart skipped a beat when she found the back door wide open. She closed the screen and scanned the yard. It looked dark and spooky out there. Liz shut the door and locked it. *What the hell's goin' on?*

Wanda gestured down the hall toward the bathroom door. It was shut. Liz's anxiety sent her tip-toeing in its direction. Wanda grabbed her by the hand. "Wait," she cautioned and led Liz to the kitchen. She quietly pulled open the silverware drawer and removed several butcher's knives. She handed one to Liz.

"What the hell is this for?" Liz whispered.

Wanda raised one up in the air and whispered back "Slice a sucka up if they don't live here." The huge blade glistened. Liz gripped hers and led the way out of the kitchen.

They took slow, measured steps, creeping down the hall, both of their knives extended. Liz's palm sweated on the wooden handle. She glanced over her shoulder at Wanda. "Don't stick me with that thing," she whispered.

"I got ya back, girl."

They edged up to the bathroom door and listened. They heard what sounded like low groans or mumbling, or something.

"Come out before you get hurt," Wanda threatened in a manly voice. Liz jumped sideways, scared shitless.

"Woman!" she frowned, dropping the knife.

Wanda turned into Super Sistah and pushed open the door. "Here I come," she yelled out and got back. "Ya' gon' get it now!" They had their weapons drawn, ready to inflict pain. Low cries came from the dark bathroom. "Listen…" Liz whispered to Wanda.

"Sounds like some damn chickens in distress." They moved closer, with caution. Liz reached inside and hit the light switch on the wall. The crying grew louder. Liz moved in and yanked back the shower curtains, and discovered the source of the noise: She-She and Amina lay hugged up in the bath tub, their tear-soaked faces drenched in mortal fear.

Liz dropped the knife in the sink. "She-She?"

287

Wanda put down her knife as well. "Babies, what's going on?" Both girls flew to their feet and into their arms.

"Auntie, they started shooting," She-She wept. "We thought y'all were the dudes with the guns."

"It's okay," Wanda consoled the shook up girls.

"What dudes with guns?" Liz asked. "Who was shooting? Where's Malik?"

She-She and Amina recounted the robbery and subsequent shooting. "… we ran in the back yard…"

"… I used my key to get in the house…"

"That's when we heard shooting…"

"I left the door open so Malik could get in…"

"We hid in the bathroom 'cause when I lived in Gary, Indiana my granny always put us in the bathtub when someone started shooting outside so we wouldn't get hit by a stray bullet…"

Liz cut in. "Malik never came in the house?"

"Not that I know of." She-She wiped her nose with the back of her hand. "I left the door open."

Wanda told Amina to go call her parents. Liz went and looked out the front door. Where was her child? And why was the Cadillac truck still out front if someone was supposed to have jacked it? Liz walked outside to take a look around.

The block was quiet for the most part. Nothing unusual caught her attention. She stepped off the curb and surveyed the perimeter of the truck. She noticed two spent shell casings near the back tire. Liz's stomach twisted up into knots.

Wanda came outside. Liz got in her car and hit the high beams.

"Those are bullet holes," Wanda pointed at the left rear fender of the Escalade. Liz inspected the two dime-sized holes. "What the hell happened?" She stalked back inside the house.

288

"Auntie, do you want me to call my brother?" She-She asked. Liz stared at the two girls. Something wasn't right about their story. They'd claimed to have run straight in the house and to the bathroom. So at what point did She-She send the text message?

"Didn't you text us?" Liz asked her. Wanda came in, closed the door, then peeked out the window.

She-She shook her head. "Yeah. Before all the shooting and stuff happened, because that boy Maniac came over and I overheard him tell Malik that he knew where Derrick might be at. I think he wanted Malik to go with him to see."

"Liz," Wanda signaled. "The police are outside flashing their lights on your car and that SUV." She pulled away from the window. "They just flashed on the house."

Liz instructed She-She to call Andre. "Let me speak with him as soon as you reach him." She went to her bedroom to check her drawer. The information that Janice had given her on Derrick was in the exact spot she put it a week ago. She returned to the dining room and warned the girls to stay out of sight until the police left. Then she walked out the door.

Two black policemen were shining flashlights on and around Brandon's truck. Liz observed them from the curb. A light soon flashed in her face. She raised her hand to block it out.

"Is everything all right out here?" she asked.

"You tell us," the heavier policeman said as his partner knelt beside the bullet-riddled fender. Liz stepped into the street and down on a shell casing, covering it with her left shoe. She couldn't be certain that Malik or Maniac weren't the ones doing the shooting.

"Are you the person who called us?" the cop asked, looking up at Liz.

"No, I did not," she said.

"Do you know who this SUV belongs to?" he asked. The other officer got inside the squad car to run a check on the plates.

Liz ignored the question. "What did the caller say happened out here?"

His eyes turned lustful. He moved closer and smiled. Liz held her position, not taking her foot off the potential evidence.

"We got reports of shots fired," he told her. "Your fine self ain't shot anyone, have you?" He put on the lame charm.

His partner got back out of the squad car. His bald head had a spit-shine. "You know the guy who owns this vehicle?" he asked.

"My nephew," Liz said.

"Does he know about these bullet holes?" Baldy cop asked.

"I doubt it," she said. "He was killed earlier this summer."

The officers glanced at each other. "What was his name?" Flirty cop asked.

"Brandon Freeman," she said.

"We got his brother downtown," Baldy mentioned. Liz assumed the question was a test. It had to be since he'd run the plates and likely got the answer already.

"Who's driving it now?" Baldy asked.

"I'm keeping it here until I figure out what to do with it" Liz said.

Flirty cop stared down at the customized rims on it. "You're better off parking this in a garage somewhere because it's a car thief's wet dream." He reached in his front shirt pocket. "If you decide to sell it, give me a call. I can help." His fake GQ smile irked Liz. His partner frowned as Flirty cop tried to clean it up by adding, "Or if you come across any information on the reported shooting."

Baldy cop shook his head and returned to the squad car.

Liz accepted the card.

"My private numbers are on the back," Flirty cop grinned. Liz walked off on him.

"Dre on the phone," She-She said as Liz got back in the house.

To Liz's disappointment, Andre claimed he knew nothing about the robbery/shooting. He did give her Brianna's and Jenny's phone numbers. "Brianna might hear from him before I do," he said.

"Ask him for Maniac's number," She-She said to Liz.

"I don't have it." He said. "I know where his girl lives. I'll stop by there."

"If you talk to him or Malik, y'all call me right away," Liz said.

CHAPTER 50

"Pull into that alley," Maniac instructed. Malik made a right turn and slowed down next to a garage. He threw the Lexus into park and killed the headlights.

"Murder me then," the robber-turned-hostage dared Maniac. He was literally asking to die. Malik looked up in the rearview mirror and saw Maniac snatch the mask off the hostage's head.

"You gone get yo' wish," Maniac said and walloped him on the ear with the gun. "Don't whine now," he told him. "Tonight you meet yo' maker, nigga." The death threat accompanied multiple pelts to the captive's dome. He called out to God through swollen, bloody lips.

"You better pray, punk," Maniac encouraged him.

Malik stared out the car windows around the dark alley. This wasn't a situation he wanted to be in.

"My mama is smoked out," the hostage declared. "I only pulled the move cause I was desperate. Me and my little brother out here starvin'."

"Fuck yo' hype ass mama," Maniac said heartlessly and clobbered him with the cannon again.

Malik turned and looked over his shoulder. Maniac opened the door, then ordered the hostage, "Out of the car," keeping the gun trained on him. As the hostage climbed out, he tried copping another plea for his life. Maniac yanked him by the shirt collar up to the side door of the garage and shoved him through.

Malik got out the Lexus, quietly closing the doors. He knew that he needed to somehow get the cannon out of Maniac's hand, or the man's chances for survival were slimmer than slim. He trekked up to the garage and entered. It was deathly dark inside. It took him a moment to adjust his eyes and make out Maniac's shadow.

"Gimme the burner," Malik said, acting like he wanted to use it. "This is me here, cuz."

"I'm begging y'all not to kill me," the hostage begged from the ground. "I'm begging y'all as brothers."

Maniac drop-kicked him. "Shut up," he hissed. "Here, fam," he pressed the gun into his hand. "Handle yo' business."

The hostage attempted to get up and run, and Maniac clotheslined him. He fell back against the wall and hit his head on the hardwood. Maniac proceeded to blindly beat the shit out of him. Malik backed up and tried to get a better visual on them. The semi-open door provided the only glimmer of light inside the boarded-up garage. Maniac's punches produced heavy-handed 'thwack'thwacks,' as he raged in the darkness. "Stick this up, pussy." Thwack! Thwack! Thwack! "Take this!" Thwack and thwack and more thwacks. He pounded away on the human punching bag.

As long as Malik held the gun, he'd let Maniac vent all he wanted. But Malik refused to hand it back over, and just to play it off, he stepped over to stomp the captive, but missed his mark, bringing his foot down on something else that stung like hell. He staggered backwards to recover. He hoped the ass-whopping would sate Maniac's murderous appetite.

The captive stopped moving, stopped begging for mercy, apparently knocked out cold. Maniac's hard breathing resonated. He stepped next to Malik. "Put him out his misery."

Malik tensed up. Thinking fast, he said, "Let's bounce. This cat felt us." He felt Maniac look his way. "Naw, he done living. Handle ya function or I will."

The gun in Malik's hand grew heavier by the second. The hostage shifted a little on the ground and released a weak whimper. Malik stared down at the shadow. If he pulled the trigger, that would be it. No turning back. No resurrecting the dead. He considered what the captive said about his drug-addicted mother, his little brother, their struggle.

"Go 'head," Maniac urged.

Malik inched toward the door. "He ain't worth a bullet. Let the streets finish him off."

"Fuck that," he said. "I got plenty bullets and we are the muthafuckin' streets, nigga. He came to yo' crib, tried to take yo shit at gunpoint, and put fam's little sister in harm's way. Yo' momz coulda been there too. Did he give a fuck? Fuck no! So he gotta go." His breath reeked of death; the lethal scent crawled down Malik's neck. For a split second, a fit of anger seized him. Then let go.

"Give me the cannon and go start the car. Make sure the music is subbing." Maniac reached for the gun.

Malik moved back. "Gon' to the car," he said. "I'll be out inna second."

"Gimme the keys."

"They in the car."

Maniac advised him to "Move back some and aim directly for the head. Wait 'til you hear the music." He slipped out the door.

The music soon came on outside. The air inside the garage grew stuffy and dry.

"Do it," the man groaned. "I'm tired of living in this world, anyway."

"Shut up!" Malik yelled. He shook and perspired.

"Do it, nigga. Kill me." He moved. "Do it—"

Malik jumped back, aimed the gun and fired. Pop! Pop! Pop! The kick of the cannon vibrated his whole arm. His trigger finger throbbed as he fled the garage.

"Jet out, fam," Malik said, getting in the car.

"Wrap that strap up." Maniac handed him the mask and flipped on the headlights. After riding for about five blocks, he pulled into another alley. They were deep, deep in the ghetto.

"Pass me that," Maniac said. Malik handed over the masked weapon. Maniac killed the lights and got out the car. Malik tried to relax. He watched through the windshield as Maniac tramped up to a sewer in the middle of the alley, squatted down and dropped the gun into the earth. He ran back and got in the car.

Malik almost forgot! He reached under the seat for the gun he found in the Escalade. "Toss this one too?" He showed it to Maniac.

"Where you—" he said, confused. "Dude had a burner on him?" He took it in disbelief and popped out the clip and checked the chamber. "Empty," he chuckled. "This clown went onna move without ammo." He got back out.

Maniac dropped it in the same sewer and returned to the car shaking his head. "The nerve of some of these idiots out here inna streets."

CHAPTER 51

Liz waited in McDonald's, reading through the Milwaukee Journal-Sentinel. It was time she put down her own investigation. The upcoming meeting with Jenny was the first step. Malik was withholding information, even potential plans that could lead to more trouble. He'd acted as if nothing major had happened after he finally got back home last night. The way he downplayed the robbery attempt put the jumper cables to Liz's already revved-up worries. When she questioned him about what She-She overheard Maniac say to him about Derrick, Malik claimed that She-She "didn't know what she was talking about," flashing her a you-talk-too-much look across the dining room, adding, "Shouldn't be so nosy anyway. What 'da Lawd' say about that?"

Liz wasn't falling for it. Somebody knew something and she wouldn't be kept in the dark. Hopefully Jenny could shed some light on the matter. Last night Liz called her looking for Malik, and the second the girl came on line, she sounded very concerned, as if she was expecting to hear some bad news. She mentioned her fall-out with Malik on his birthday but not what it was about. "We haven't spoken since then," she said. Liz suspected that Jenny wanted to say more, so she invited her over for a little chitchat. Jenny suggested they meet someplace else instead. They agreed on the place and time, and Liz arrived the next day at the fast food rendezvous half an hour early.

Liz closed the newspaper and checked her watch. 1:05 p.m. Just as she started to wonder if the girl had chickened out, in walked Jenny. Liz waved her over. They greeted and Jenny took a seat.

She asked, "Did he make it home all right?"

Liz nodded. "He's fine." They stared across the table at each other. "He got home shortly after I spoke with you."

Jenny exhaled and looked away. "Did something happen with him last night?" She sounded resentful but also a little worried.

296

"Yes," Liz said. "Someone tried to carjack him for his cousin's Escalade. There was a shooting involved."

"Unbelievable," she reddened, then slouched in her seat, exhaling a troubled breath.

Liz waited patiently. Strategically. "It might've had a connection to the guy who shot him."

"I wish Malik would just tell the cops on that monster." Jenny's exasperation oozed out. "I understand 'Lik's distrust of law enforcement, but in situations like--" she shook her head.

"Who are you referring to?" Liz tried hard not to seem too anxious. "Derrick?"

"Yeah, Derrick," she huffed with hostility.

"Did Malik tell you anything about Derrick's involvement in Brandon's murder?" Liz asked as a knot formed in her gut. Jenny's eyelids widened. "He didn't have to tell me. I know what and who I saw. I was right there when the shooting started. I witnessed Derrick kill him."

"What?" Liz leaned closer. "Why didn't you tell the police about this?" She could've just smacked the girl into tomorrow.

"'Cause 'Lik and Brian warned me not to, and their friend Maniac insinuated his threat."

"Are you telling me that you saw Derrick shoot Brandon and Malik?" Liz's heart felt ready to explode.

Jenny sat up. "The guy who shot Malik wasn't the same one who shot Brandon. I saw who shot Brandon. It happened after the fight broke out." She looked down at the newspaper. "I told Malik to tell the cops. This is what led to our argument and fallout."

Liz couldn't believe this shit. Here was a damn witness who could put Derrick's ass in jail! How could Liz have missed this in the first place? Jenny was the one who drove Malik to the hospital? And why didn't they want Jenny to cooperate with the police?

297

"Tell me everything about that night and your argument with Malik," Liz said.

Jenny recapped up to the part about Malik saying he was keeping it in the streets. Liz didn't need to hear any more.

She stood to her feet, keys in hand. "Come on," she ordered. "You need to speak with the detectives."

"What about Malik and this code of the streets," she snipped. Liz scoffed at her sarcasm, her impatience getting the best of her. Jenny saw this and got to moving.

"Are you absolutely sure you can identify Derrick?" Liz asked as they exited McDonald's.

"I believe so." Jenny hesitated.

Liz stopped in her tracks. "You just told me you saw him do the shooting."

"I did."

"Let's go."

CHAPTER 52

Malik laid low on the eastside at the twins' house. He needed the solitude to gather his thoughts and get a grip on what had happened last night. What started out as a peaceful summer evening ended with nothing but strife. It ended with Malik feeling less than real, feeling like the type of nigga he despised: A fake. A busta. A straight up wannabe thug. A sickly feeling settled upon his gut and formed a vacancy of depression. He could no longer concentrate on the game he'd been playing on the X Box. He tossed aside the joystick as the frustration overwhelmed him. He got up from the leather La-Z-Boy. *Stupid ass punk ass dumb ass niggas just had to test me, just had to try to take what wasn't theirs. What I got a sign on me saying: rob me, I'm an easy lick?* He fumed within, pacing over to Brandon's bedroom. He willed a deep breath.

Malik stopped outside the door. Neither he nor Drizzle had entered the room since the Summerfest shooting. Malik did not out of uneasiness and respect.

What did it matter now? He turned the doorknob. The light was off and all was still and quiet. Brandon's scent lingered. Malik peered inside, unbothered. He flipped on the lights. His reflection stared out at him in the dresser mirror. His eyes fell on a picture of the twins and Maniac. The airbrushed Benz background indicated they were at some club, posted up like ghetto stars. Brandon rarely smiled in pictures, and this one wasn't an exception. But Brian grinned like life couldn't be better for him. It was hard to tell if Maniac was smirking or sneering. He held up a drink in a toasting motion and leaned with it. "Crazy ass nigga," Malik mumbled at the image. He replaced the flick and lifted another one that he, Drizzle, and the twins had taken together last spring down at Kemet Quarters. In this shot, Brandon's face hinted at a smile, a peaceful one. Malik fell back on the king-sized bed. *Maybe cuz finally found peace in heaven*, he imagined. Although still a gangsta, Brandon had toned it down within the past couple of years. Malik noticed the change after his last bid. Brandon had stepped out the joint focused

299

on the money and the power, but this time he wanted it legit, and seemed to be on his way until…

Malik collapsed backward across the mattress and stared up at the ceiling fan. He was sick and tired of being sick and tired. Was too young to be feeling so sick and tired. Brandon was dead. Gone. The words kept popping up to remind him of the tragedy. The loss. And the killer remained a free man, roaming the streets and probably acting like the hero of his hood. Bragging within his inner circle about murking one of the Freeman twins. The streets couldn't keep a secret though. Derrick would surface and slip up eventually. Malik wanted the punishment to be swift and severe. The spirit of the point-of-no-return took hold of him. He felt strategically reckless. Not that he'd go about things sloppily. Brandon had schooled him better than that. Big cuz warned him about the cats who ended up in jail behind their own stupidity. "Most niggas aren't inna joint because the police are super smart," he had let Malik know. "It's mostly because those niggas are super stupid, careless and talkative." Lately those lectures stayed on Malik's mind. He wasn't about to go out like some goofy… Malik supposed it a good thing that some time had elapsed since the shooting. It would make him less of a suspect when… Soon it'd hit the fan, and his pain, She-She's pain, all of their pain would be felt and memorialized.

Malik rose up. He opened and removed the small drawer of the night stand next to the bed. Brian had asked him to do this weeks ago. The drawer contained some papers including several car titles. Then he stuck his hand down in the opening and felt the cool stainless steel. He lifted the .357 Desert Eagle out of the stash spot. Its heft filled Malik with a powerful sensation. He examined the triangular barrel. He yanked the slide, released, and heard a bullet lock into the chamber. He checked the safety for his own safety.

The doorbell rang.

Malik's heart jerked from the disturbance. He slipped the cannon under a pillow and replaced the drawer. He wasn't expecting any visitors and Drizzle had his own key. Malik went in the living room to investigate. He inched down a flap on the Venetian blinds and peeked out. The window only offered a view of the sidewalk and street. He didn't see Drizzle or Maniac or their cars. He went and peeked out another window to get another view. A

300

couple dudes stood on the porch, at the front door. Malik zeroed in on P-Nut and frowned. *What the heck is he doing here?* P-Nut's companion looked unfamiliar.

They rang the door bell again.

Malik pulled back from the window. P-Nut was out of pocket. Stopping by the twins' house like he was welcome. Bringing along some other cat too! Malik and Drizzle had cut his water off months ago after the situation in front of Nana's house. Malik hadn't spoken with P-Nut since, so for him to show up now and uninvited... Malik peeked through the blinds again. P-Nut was just stepping off the porch with his crony. They paused on the walkway, looking suspicious, dubious. They spoke and scanned the area for a minute or two, then proceeded to the side of the house and out of view.

Malik darted to a different window and got another visual on them strolling into the back yard. He skipped over into Brian's room. In full 007 mode, Malik crouched low by the window and surveilled the two trespassers.

P-Nut and his crony approached the back door. Malik dived sideward onto the carpet after P-Nut glanced over in his direction. He waited a moment, then repositioned himself. Another gander showed the boys at the screen door. P-Nut handed something to his crony, then stepped back. Malik strained to get a better look and peeped the screwdriver in the other guy's hand. P-Nut staked out the vicinity as his crony opened the screen door. He tapped on the door window with the screwdriver until it shattered.

"These niggas breakin' inna crib," Malik whispered to himself, adrenaline thumping, feet propelling him straight for Brandon's room. It was on! He reached under the pillow and grabbed the Desert Eagle and zoomed to the kitchen. Posting up by the fridge, he waited, listening, poised to welcome the intruders with a nice shiny surprise. He heard their sneaky whispers coming from the back hallway. He pulled back, moving over to the kitchen table. He quietly took a seat, rested an elbow on the table top and leveled the gun directly at the door. *The element of surprise,* he thought.

The sudden ring of the phone disrupted the plan.

He slid off the chair and advanced with stealth into the living room.

"Yeah?" he whispered into the phone, crouching next to the pool table.

"'Lik?" Drizzle said from the other end.

"Fam, where you at?"

"A couple blocks from there," he snickered. "Why you talking so low, dawg?"

"Smash the gas. The nigga P-Nut showed up with some other cat. They just broke inna crib. Hurry, gotta go." He dropped the phone receiver and dashed back to the kitchen. The intruders were just creeping in. Malik welcomed them. "Hey there, fellas, have a muthafuckin' seat," he yelled, the beak of the Desert Eagle pointed their way. The burglars froze up in their tracks, shocked like they saw 2pac.

"Come on, cowards."

They eyed the cannon. P-Nut spoke up first. "What's good, fam? I came through to holla about that little bullshit I pulled," he lied in boldface.

"Oh, that's why you broke inna crib." They jumped back against the wall. "Get the hell on the floor."

P-Nut gestured toward his crony, saying, "This clumsy cat knocked on the door too hard and accidentally cracked the window. I told him he gone have to pay for it."

Clumsy Cat mugged at P-Nut. "Don't try'n put it on me. You said this was yo' cousin's house."

"And what about the screwdriver in your hand, my guy?" Malik asked. No reply. "Drop it." The screwdriver tumbled to the floor. Malik flinched at them. "Didn't I say get on the ground?" he elevated the gun. "Now get flat!"

They got down with the quickness and started pointing the finger back and forth. Under Malik's anger, the clowns amused him. How easy they turned on each other. He took a seat and rested the cannon on the table top, aimed and ready. "So what was the plan?" he addressed P-Nut. "You figured Brandon's dead and Brian's in jail, so what the hell, a quick come up?"

Clumsy Cat scooted away from P-Nut.

"You like robbing graves?" Malik asked. His anger burned away the comic aspect. "You move one more inch and I swear I'll leave you slumped over," he warned Clumsy Cat. "Matter fact, y'all punks hug each other."

Clumsy Cat glanced at the door like he wanted to get froggy. Malik lifted the cannon. "Leap for it," he said. "I quadruple dare you." He stood over them. "Now hug."

P-Nut forced a grin. "'Lik, what you on—" He was cut off by the impact of Malik's Nike sneaker to his chest.

"Hug!" he ordered.

P-Nut's arm fell around Clumsy Cat's shoulder. "This ain't even cool, dawg."

"I'm not huggin' no nigga," Clumsy Cat defied the order. The approaching muzzle of the Desert Eagle changed his mind.

"What you ain't gone do?" Malik challenged.

Clumsy Cat showed P-Nut the unwilling affection.

Malik heard someone coming in the house. "Drizzle?" he called out, keeping a close eye on his captives.

Drizzle stalked into the kitchen ready for war. "What's poppin?" His sinister posture was intense. "Hardhead?" he recognized Clumsy Cat. "You and P-Nut—" he assessed the situation for a second. "Yeah, okay," he leered and launched an attack, going wild on both boys—kicking, socking right, left and left, right, right, right, left with a follow up kick and spit and cuss and slap and stomp to the stomach. "Y'all broke in our shit?" Another combo kick to P-Nut's right ear and jab to Hardhead's noggin. "Huh?" He raved and executed the simultaneous beat down without any resistance from either burglar. Malik waited for any defensive move by them, but kept the gun on safety. He had no intention of using it besides as a scare tactic.

The boys' remorseful cries echoed throughout the kitchen until Drizzle tired of punishing them. Once he caught his breath, he cussed them out and delivered a few extra kicks to P-Nut's torso. Then he commanded them, "Strip."

P-Nut looked pitiful, his face steadily swelling and tearful. "You supposed to be my cousin," he whined.

"Cousin?" Drizzle sneered in sheer contempt. "Cousin?" He gestured for the gun in Malik's hand. But Malik knew better and backed away. Drizzle didn't insist. Instead he seized a kitchen chair and clubbed P-Nut with it. "Cousin that, you piece of shit. Now strip right gotdamn now before I murk both you fags."

They complied, albeit with reluctance. Drizzle supervised and motivated them on with a sporadic smack to the face or earlobe. P-Nut literally cried like a baby as he removed his clothes. Malik assumed that Hardhead's anger and humiliation licked away any more tears before they could fall.

Drizzle handed Malik his car keys. "Go pull the Chevy 'round back. We're 'bout to drop these niggas off somewhere highly populated." Malik saw that Drizzle had his emotions back under control, so he gave him the cannon.

By the time Malik whipped the car around to the alley, Drizzle had already marched P-Nut and Hardhead out to the back yard. They both looked ludicrous standing there ass naked, cupping their privates, chagrined.

Malik suppressed his laughter and got out the car.

Drizzle handed Hardhead a towel. "Lay this across my seat," he said. "I don't want yo' shit stains on my leather."

Malik burst out laughing.

Drizzle smirked. "You too," he told his cousin.

As the nude dudes got in the back seat, Malik pulled Drizzle to the side. "It's too risky for us to be riding around with them naked as jaybirds. We'll just make 'em walk from here."

Drizzle agreed. "Y'all get out and kick rocks," he said.

"Cuz, don't do this to me," P-Nut pouted.

"Stop calling me cuz and getta truckin'." Drizzle tossed P-Nut's car keys on the pavement. When he knelt down to retrieve them, Drizzle kicked

304

him dead in the butt cheek. P-Nut staggered over and scraped a kneecap on the concrete.

The butt naked burglars barefooted it down the alley. Malik and Drizzle got in the Chevy and tailed them for several yards, honking the car horn in mockery until they cut through someone's back yard.

Malik and Drizzle parked around front and fell inside the house cracking up. They gathered the clothes off the kitchen floor and cleaned up any DNA evidence. Drizzle disposed of all of it, while Malik contacted a glass repair service and hid the Desert Eagle outside in the garage. The man at the glass shop said he would send someone out shortly. Malik gave him the address and waited.

"Check these bars out, 'Lik," Drizzle said, exiting the kitchen. He read from a sheet of paper:

> "Dey say the apple don't fall far from the tree/
>
> I disagree, look at them and look at me/
>
> dey ain't my family/
>
> I wish my momz never had me/
>
> I think she do too, that's why she always mad at me/
>
> so what am I to do, treat 'em like my enemies/
>
> but dey know I won't hurt 'em 'cause dey kin to me/
>
> like my pops, why the fuck you ain't bother, nigga/
>
> was always drunk, you wasn't no father figure/"

He stopped right there.

"Real shit," Malik nodded.

"Should I finish it?"

"ASAP, while the emotion is raw."

Drizzle bounced to the kitchen. Malik gave him his space. His homie had a lot on his mind and writing raps was therapy.

305

Kicking back on the couch, Malik surfed the TV channels. Nothing interested him on the tube so he put on some Curtis Mayfield and called up wifey.

"Beautiful black woman," he addressed Brianna, knowing she loved when he called her what she was.

"Huh?" The smile all in her voice.

"You heard me?"

They spoke for about ten minutes. Then Malik put it on the wood, saying, "We can't keep denying ourselves true happiness, Bree." A breather. "It's time to take it to the next level. Stagnation is the father of death, ya dig?"

Silence on the other end.

"Come on, baby," Malik worked the Berry White voice. "Don't be bashful. I know you hear me."

"Yeah and I'm not trying to hear that," she said. "You still want me to cut your hair later?"

"What we gone do afterwards?" He intensified the seduction.

"Bye, 'Lik."

"Alright, alright." The line clicked. "Hold on, baby." He clicked over and answered, "What upper?"

"What's up, young and thuggin'?" It was Maniac.

Malik's whole mood changed. "Chillin' wit' Drizzle."

"Good. I need to chop it up with y'all 'bout that business."

"You on your way now?" He tried to think of a quick excuse to give him.

"Right now."

"Don't come through ridin' dirty," he said. "We had a little situation here earlier and it might be hot."

Maniac asked for details.

"It wasn't nothing too serious. I'll holla at ya when ya get here." They ended the call.

"Took you long enough," Brianna said when he came back on line.

"I try to take things nice and slow, ya know?" He returned with the Berry White voice.

"What time you comin' over?"

"'Bout an hour or so. Turn the lights down low and wear that teddy with the—" She hung up on him.

Drizzle walked out the kitchen.

"Maniac is on his way over," Malik said.

"What happened last night?" Drizzle took a seat. "I'm always missing in action when the drama hits."

Malik and Drizzle had spoken that morning, about the attempted robbery and shooting, but Malik was yet to tell him everything. With Maniac on his way, Malik figured it a good idea to let Drizzle in on the rest of the story.

"I didn't tell you everything about last night," he admitted.

Drizzle turned his way.

Malik felt the shame coming on. "I demonstrated real crazy."

They locked gazes. Drizzle leaned forward. "What ya'-- mean?"

He told him about the drive to the garage. "I came in afterwards. Maniac is punishin' dude. I'm standin' there in the dark hearing it. Then Maniac turn around and tell me to handle my business. He left me in the garage with the nigga."

Drizzle was on the edge of his seat. "You whacked him, fam?" His voice had a shakiness to it. The conspiracy wrinkled his forehead as he eyeballed Malik. He bound to his feet when Malik didn't answer. "Did you?" His throat sounded dry.

307

Malik sank back onto the couch pillow and shook his head. "Naw," he confessed. "I faked out and shot into the wall over his head. He's still breathing but Maniac think I left him stankin'. Threw the burner in the sewer and everything." Drizzle clinched his chest and huffed out a deep sigh of relief. "Damn, nigga, you're tellin' me this shit all dramatically like you bodied the cat." He fell back on the couch.

"Maniac think I did," Malik mustered a chuckle.

"So," Drizzle frowned. "Let him. We don't need no homicide case hanging over our heads."

"And Derrick?"

"That's different," he said. "If it do come down to that, we won't do it onna humbug. Dude last night would've definitely been a murder case. As soon as the body got found, those other niggas would've flew right to the police and drop dime, quarter, and some."

Malik assumed the same thing, although that wasn't his reason for letting the boy live. He just didn't have it in him to take that life. His conscience convinced him of this last night, and wouldn't stop reminding him of it.

"After I shot Jeff," Drizzle said, "I was broke up. Straight shook. I never told you, but that situation stayed on my mind for weeks. I thought about how easy I could've killed dude and probably got shipped away for decades behind his murder. Everything lost. Look at Shyne Po's situation. A nigga sitting with all that talent in the joint. All that potential. Homie was on the escalator, riding toward the top and one fuck-up knocked him off. Back to the bottom."

"And it wasn't even his drama."

"It was Puffy's, and this nigga out and about not really thinking about Shyne. Life goes on and the industry hopped on the next hot rapper's wood. I think about that. I also think about the fact that I'm thinking about it after the fact. It's hard to think about it when you're in the midst of drama."

"One misstep will leave a nigga stuck, fo' real."

"Trapped and forgotten. I'm not try'na let me or you go out like that. Forget what another nigga talkin' 'bout."

"We still need to be on point for those cats," Malik said.

"No doubt," he replied. "But ol' boy glad to be alive right about now. He know how close he came to death. After crawling out that garage, he probably saw the light and ran to join the church or mosque."

Malik laughed.

"We'll lay low and focus on this music hustle. Forget that other nonsense. Those white folks already got enough brothers locked down. We takin' another route."

The doorbell sounded.

"And you don't need to worry about P-Nut going to the police," Drizzle assured. "He'll only incriminate himself in a burglary, home invasion, and anything else we can think up."

"No doubt." Malik looked outside.

"Who is that, the glass repairman?"

"Naw," he glanced over at Drizzle. "This Maniac."

CHAPTER 53

Liz left McDonald's a woman on a mission. She shot home first to get the information on Derrick and Flirty cop's card. Afterwards, she instructed Jenny to follow her downtown to the police station. She sensed Jenny's uncertainty but didn't have time to waste on motivational speeches. They could talk later. First Liz had to do what was best for her son.

They arrived at the station, and Liz instructed Jenny to ask for the lead detective on the case. Luckily, he was in and ushered Jenny straight to an interview room. Meanwhile, Liz's anxiety mounted as she waited out in the lobby. She checked her watch and the clock on the wall, gazing back and forth at each one by the minute. Then an intermission for a silent prayer to ask for direction. Minute after minute dragged by. She wanted Malik's confidence back and understood that this current move could very well push him further away. Faith. This was what she had to act on.

An hour passed and Jenny hadn't returned. Liz pulled out Flirty cop's card. She planned to exhaust all resources. The sooner Derrick was off the streets, the safer Malik would be. She flipped open her cell phone.

"Is this Travis Glenn?" Liz asked, reading his name off the card.

"Yes," he said. "Who is this?"

"This is Liz." A pause. "The woman you gave your card to last night after shots were fired." She imagined his fake GQ grin forming as he realized who she was.

"Oh," he sounded a bit more enthusiastic. "How are you, beautiful?"

She swallowed her irritation over his unprofessionalism. "I'd like to speak with you about a murder suspect and his possible whereabouts."

"Right, right," he said in a play-along tone. "When can we hook—I mean, meet up to discuss this."

Liz asked him to stop by her house in an hour and a half.

310

The eager arrogance in his voice alerted Liz to his hopes. On a romantic level, he didn't have a devil's chance in heaven. But he could think whatever he wanted as long as he assisted Liz's mission. She repocketed his card. When it came to protecting her son, the lines between right and wrong blurred. She counted on an all-knowing God to know her heart.

As she continued to wait, Liz remembered her drives home from night school, the sisters she'd see on the avenue walking the ho stroll. How often she wondered what drove them to that point of degradation. A drug addiction? She doubted that that was all of their reason. Some must've done it out of love for a loved one, out of a dire need to put some food on the table. Liz had a hard time justifying prostitution, but she was beginning to understand the desperation behind it. Inviting Travis over, knowing what he expected and knowing that she did nothing to get his mind out of that gutter, left her feeling a vague commonality with any and all women who did something questionable out of love for their children. At present, it didn't matter to Liz what that 'something' was. The voices spoke up, accusing her of whoring in her own special way, of playing on Travis' lust to use him. Liz shut them down. She wasn't trying to hear it.

Jenny finally returned with the detective. Liz read the apprehension on her face and hoped the girl followed the script.

"Are you alright?" Liz asked her as they left the station.

"I'm not so sure about this anymore," she replied. They approached Liz's Ford Focus.

Jenny looked scared to death. "Did you pick anyone out from the book of mugshots?" Liz wasn't going for the change of heart.

"Yes," she shook her head ruefully. "But I—"

"Was he the one who shot Brandon?" she cut in, "and could have and still wouldn't hesitate to do the same to Malik?" She knew she was wrong for throwing in the last part.

Jenny stared out at the passing traffic. "Did you know that Derrick belonged to one of the most notorious gangs in the Midwest region?" she asked, staring directly at Liz. "I'll have to appear in court and testify against him."

"All the more reason to get him off the streets."

"And his gangster friends?"

"Once he's out of sight, he'll drop out of their minds." She inserted a key into the car door. "You're doing the right thing, so lighten up, relax, and follow me home so we can get better acquainted."

Jenny didn't seem moved. "Why didn't you want me to tell the detectives about Malik's knowledge of the shooters?" The accusation stared out her eyes.

Liz really didn't have time to waste on this. "Look, Jenny, you do what you feel your conscience can handle. But a part of caring for someone is taking risks to protect them from external dangers and from themselves. You already have an idea of what Malik is set on doing and you can imagine what those boys will try to do to him. So it's on you to prevent something else from happening. Malik made his decision not to cooperate, so whether you told the police about his knowledge of the shooter or not, wouldn't matter." She opened the car door. "I have to get home. You can follow me and we'll talk there or you can go your own way and I'll understand."

Jenny looked indecisive, but said, "I'll trail you." Liz got behind the wheel and exhaled.

****

When they made it to Liz's house, she invited Jenny inside. They spent the next 45 minutes chatting, looking through a photo album full of Malik's childhood pictures, and sharing laughs. It didn't take long for Jenny to relax and open up about her feelings for Malik. Liz already knew the girl was feeling her baby; she recognized it by the time they left McDonald's. Even through all of the tension, Jenny's glow gave her away. Wanda had accused Liz of having a similar glow months ago. Liz did not want to imagine Malik making any female radiate. Not in the sense that Wanda meant. Malik *was* at that mannish age... Liz deleted the thought and made a mental note to speak with him in depth about it.

"It was nice talking with you, Liz," Jenny smiled as they stepped outside on the porch.

"You too."

"Now I better split before Malik comes home." The glow again.

"So what if he does?" Liz dramatized her frown. "You're here with me. His butt bet' not say anything slick."

This had Jenny all giggly.

"You're welcome over anytime. You have my number."

Jenny left with an uplifted spirit. Liz went back in the house feeling like the ultimate manipulator.

"Did Snow White get back in her chariot and leave?" She-She asked, entering Liz's bedroom. She-She had walked in the house thirty minutes earlier, saw Jenny all cozy on the sofa, and instantly copped an un-Christ-like attitude. She spoke to Liz and ignored Jenny before going to her room. The only time she came out was to tell Liz some girl called for Malik, making sure Jenny heard. Liz thought it was cute and funny and doubted Malik would think so.

"Yes, she's gone," Liz laughed.

"What did she want, anyway?" She-She asked.

"She means no harm." She fixed her hair up into a ponytail in the mirror. "Do me a favor and put the clothes in the dryer."

"I got you." She-She got to it.

Liz closed the door to make a private call. Once the police operator came on line, Liz said, "Yes, I want to report the whereabouts of a murder suspect by the name of Derrick Grayson."

"Would you like to speak with a detective, Ma'am?" the lady asked.

"No, I don't. I will not be involved any further than giving you this information." She read the address off the piece of paper. "Derrick will kill me if he finds out I snitched on him. He's extremely dangerous and will kill again if he's not apprehended soon. I pray for his speedy arrest. Good luck and may God be with you."

Click.

Liz called four other precincts and ran the same script. She impressed herself with the theatrics.

Travis was soon to arrive so Liz prepared for act two. She asked She-She to get in touch with Malik and Andre while she got dressed. She had a bone to pick with both boys.

"Auntie, telephone," She-She called from the kitchen.

Liz assumed it was Malik until...

"Hello, Sister." It was Marvin.

Liz walked over to the front door and stared out. "How you been?" She smiled with all sincerity.

"I'm making it." They settled right into an easy conversation and Liz found herself slipping. Just that quick!

"Would be doing a lot better if I was spending more of these sultry summer nights with a special someone," he winked through his words.

Stay strong. "I'm sure you'll meet that special someone in due time." She didn't mean a word of it. "Patience, brotherman, patience."

"Guess it's time for me to open myself up to some other possibilities."

Liz read between the lines. She had a powerful yearning to explore their possibility some more. She wanted to insinuate that the hope remained of them becoming an item. The temptation to do what she wanted to do often proved stronger than the temptation to do what she needed to do. Didn't help that the former temptation was right on the phone sounding delicious. She closed her eyes and envisioned the lit candle in the dream. The room. The flicker. The yearning. His voice. The flame wavered in her head. The

314

darkness, the loneliness engulfed her. The candle's glare scooted on away from her, dimming, dying out.

Liz's eyes shot open. This was reality, not a dream. And reality demanded she do what she needed to do.

"Liz?" Marvin said.

"She's out there, Marvin," she said. "And you're the best brother for her."

The conversation was pretty much over.

"I'll let you go," he said. "You and Malik will stay a fixture in my prayers."

"Thank you." *Don't say it.* "Call me sometime." *Why, why, why?*

"You take care."

No more than a minute after Liz hung up the phone, Travis appeared at the front door.

"Come on in," she welcomed him. He stepped in like he was stepping out for the night, dressed in a freshly creased pair of slacks and a silk button-up shirt and leather Stacy Adams. His cologne and confident smile complemented his style. He did smell nice, she admitted. *Lookin' all playa-playa.* Liz turned away from his lustful eyes and went to get the information on Derrick.

CHAPTER 54

Meanwhile, Malik and Drizzle were pulling up in the Chevy behind Liz's car. Malik knew that he was in for an earful. He hadn't called home all day although his mother had been trying to reach him ever since he'd left that morning without a word as to where he was going. But this was the least of his concerns. Earlier, Maniac told him and Drizzle about a chick who knew for sure that Derrick was still in the city. She said she saw him two days ago by her boyfriend's house. "I still need to check this out," Maniac had stated. "I'll get up with y'all as soon as I know more." Then he left. Malik secretly hoped that nothing came of the information. The deepening conflict within hadn't abated. His desire for revenge urged him to bring it to Derrick like Derrick had brought it to Brandon. Malik felt obligated to stand on the business. At the same rate, his conscience kept breathing on him too. It rebuked his emotions and pressed him to let the police step in. Malik preferred for them to before he was forced to step up.

Drizzle turned down the music. "This Maniac," he said, showing Malik the screen on his cell phone. A car alarm screamed behind them, its headlights blinking through the Chevy's back window.

"We setting off alarms and thangs," Drizzle boasted. They looked in their rear view mirrors. Malik didn't recognize the SUV so he disregarded the noise it was making.

"Wanna hit Maniac back?" Drizzle asked. "He might have a location on that chump."

"Yeah." Malik pulled the key from the ignition. "Most likely he's on his way over here anyway."

Drizzle shook his head. "Life is a trip," he looked out the window. "One minute things will start looking proper and promising, the next minute a situation pops up and tempts you to risk everything. Reminds me of something I read in the Bible. In the New Testament."

"What's that?" Apparently Drizzle shared Malik's mixed feelings. "Spit ya sermon, preacherman."

"I remember reading this passage while I was locked up in the Detention Center last time. It talked about how Jesus went in the wilderness to pray and fast for like forty days and how Satan crept up and tried to test him. Satan offered Jesus the world if only he'd bow down to him. The *world*, fam."

"Well," Malik said.

"And Satan tempted Jesus at a time when Jesus was 'bout to fulfill his mission and at a time when Jesus struggled with what he had to do. What spoke to me was how, right when a nigga 'bout to reach that next level, some test comes along. Comes down to what a man is willing to sacrifice to fulfill his promise."

"Real talk," Malik said. Right at that moment, the apparent owner of the SUV appeared out in the street and chirped off the alarm. Malik finished what he was saying to Drizzle. "Lately I've done a lot of thinking on revenge," he said. "Let's say a cat robbed you and later you catch up with him and sweat him and end up with a case for killing him. You go to the joint behind it. Is that really revenge?"

"No doubt. You got at him for what he did and he suffered for it."

"Yeah, but you're left to suffer as well. While he in the grave, no longer feeling the pain, you're left in prison and—"

The shadow outside the driver window got their attention. The SUV owner gestured like he wanted to speak with them. Malik frowned over the disturbance.

"What's up?" Malik made his displeasure obvious.

The man didn't appear very happy either. "Your loud music set off my alarm, didn't it?"

"My fault," Malik remarked in a saucy manner and looked away.

Drizzle leaned over and said, "And it's not safe to walk up on people like that."

The man bent down and stared into the car. "What do you mean by 'not safe'?" he wanted to know.

Malik waved him off. "Alright, man, gone 'bout ya business." He raised the window some.

"Keep it down next time or get issued a citation."

Who is this dude? Malik thought, and Drizzle asked, "Who, you think you is-the police or somebody?"

Another car came beating up the block and set off the alarm on the SUV again. Malik turned and saw Maniac drive up, dip around the man and park. The man swung around and cursed at the Lexus. Malik and Drizzle found it hilarious.

"This is bullshit," the man complained, chirping off his alarm. Maniac climbed out of the car and pimp strutted his way over.

"You don't have a problem with disturbing the peace?" the man confronted him. "Is that marijuana I smell on you?" he sniffed. Maniac looked the man up and down and glanced over at Malik and back at the man. "You joking, right?" he said.

Drizzle and Malik watched the drama unfold, getting a kick out of the whole thing. They shrugged at Maniac like they were clueless.

"Yo' momz onna porch," Drizzle signaled on the low.

Malik got out of the car pronto. "Chill out." he stepped in between the man and Maniac. "Go turn down the sounds. Momz on deck."

"'Lik, bring your butt here," Liz summoned.

Drizzle got out and went to the Lexus. Maniac and the man stood face to face in the street having words.

Malik braced himself for the third degree as he walked over to see what his mother wanted. "Huh?"

"Fam, who is this nigga?" Maniac called over to Drizzle.

"Huh, hell," Liz got at Malik. "You got some explaining to do."

The confrontation in the street progressed.

"Dude gone get himself hurt," Malik commented. Drizzle walked over to get Maniac.

"Boy, that man is the police," Liz said and rushed off. Malik tensed up. Liz called the man. Maniac stalked away to his ride.

"Dude the police," Malik warned Drizzle and hurried over to tell Maniac.

"Malik, you go in the house," Liz directed.

"I'm 'bout to get at this mog," Maniac got his chrome out the car. Malik pushed him back into the driver's seat. "Dawg is the police," he whispered.

Maniac came to his senses. "What?"

"Straight up," Malik said.

Drizzle came and got in the Lexus. "Let's bounce." He glanced out the back window. "I have a warrant."

She-She appeared on the sidewalk. Maniac moved in a flash, stashing the gun back in the console. Malik stared toward his mother and the man.

"'Lik, that girl Brianna is on the phone," She-She said.

"Time to move around before ol' boy call for back up," Maniac said.

"Holdfast," Malik said. "I wanna see what he wants with momz." He went to investigate. She-She repeated herself about the phone call. Malik ignored her.

"Mama, who is dude?" he questioned. A shady grin stretched across the man's face.

"It's all good, lil homie," he said like it really was. "This was a minor misunderstanding. I didn't know you were Liz's son." He extended a hand. Malik left him hanging.

"'Lik, go wait for me in the house," Liz said. The man withdrew his hand and slipped it into his pocket.

"Who is you?" Malik eyed him. He didn't like anything about him, how he dressed, the cologne he wore, how close up he was on Liz, or his phony fly guy bearing.

"This is Travis," Liz said. "He's an associate of mine."

"An associate?" Malik scorned. "Since when?"

"Go in the house like I said." She pointed for him to get moving. "Now."

Malik felt like knocking Travis' grin down his throat.

"Malik?" Liz got in his face. He stared .50 caliber slugs at Travis.

"Malik?" Liz said again. He mumbled "Whatever," and marched off to the Lexus, getting in the back seat. "Pull off," he told Maniac.

Drizzle stared at him. "Is ya momz straight?"

She-She rushed over. "'Lik, yo' mama said don't leave and I told you Brianna is on the phone."

"Pull off, fam," Malik said without acknowledging She-She.

"Move," Drizzle said out the window to his little sister. She rolled her eyes and stomped away. Maniac glanced over his shoulder. Malik nodded for him to leave.

Maniac pulled away from the curb. Their first destination was the southside to drop off the gun at his girl's house. Maniac wasn't taking any chances of getting sweated by Travis' cop buddies. "Wouldn't surprise me if dude called in my tags," he said to Drizzle. Malik was in his own little world.

After leaving the house on the southside, they went cruising around the city. Maniac spotted a car full of chicks parked outside Checker's Restaurant on 11th and North Avenue. One of them recognized Drizzle and acted the role of unashamed groupie with the other girls. Everyone got out the cars and kicked it in the parking lot, except for Malik. He stayed put in the back seat. The bass of the subs vibrated through his body as the gangsta music seeped into his brain, darkening his mood all the more.

Maniac got back in the car with Drizzle and dipped back into traffic. They continued their cruise. Malik hadn't paid much attention to where they were going until they reached the eastside. She-She was blowing up Drizzle's phone.

"This momz 'n 'nem again," Drizzle handed it to Malik. He dropped it onto his lap. He didn't have nothing to say to his mother and resolved to move out of her house asap. *The police got pops inna joint and she turn 'round and get down with one...* A so-called 'associate.' Malik steamed over the betrayal. *First some cat named Marvin, now Travis. Wonder how long this been goin' on, how many...*

Maniac stopped at a gas station located a few blocks from the twins' house.

"Y'all want anything up out of here?" Drizzle asked.

Maniac put the car in park. "I'm goin' in with you."

"I'm straight," Malik said. They got out. Malik slumped lower in the seat. The music infested his hostility, caused his head to ache. He reached in the front and lowered the volume. The illusions in his life continued to get stripped away. Day by day, one by one. Malik had taken his mother's loyalty to his father for granted. For years, he'd admired her for it and strived to live up to her example. When the man Marvin first called, Malik had overstated his suspicions, not really believing there was foul play. *We live and we learn though.* As much as it hurt to see the truth, he accepted it for what it was—and would live life in sync with it.

A candy apple red Blazer sped into the parking lot and swerved over to a set of gas pumps. Seconds later, two women drove up in a convertible Chevy Cavalier and parked beside the Blazer. At first, Malik paid little attention to the guys exiting the Blazer. Then the one strolling over to the left side of the Cavalier fell in Malik's line of vision. He assumed his eyes were trippin' when he saw who he thought he saw. Leaning forward to get a closer look, his heart caved at the sight of his archenemy, his nemesis: Derrick. The nigga was trying to get his mack on with the chicks in the drop top! The passion of Malik's hatred stirred him to trembles. Derrick didn't even see him sitting a couple feet away in the Lexus.

Drizzle and Maniac came back out of the gas station. They made it all the way to the car without recognizing Derrick. "Get in, get in!" Malik signaled eagerly, ducking down. "Y'all ain't gon' believe this."

They closed their doors. "Believe what?" Drizzle asked, snacking on a bag of Cheetos.

"Don't make it obvious but there go the nigga Derrick."

Maniac almost gagged on the soda he was drinking. "On what?"

"On everythang," Malik gestured. Derrick was up on the driver of the Cavalier, grinning and running game in her ear. Maniac reached for his stash spot, forgetting that the gun was no longer there. He was about to get out the car but Drizzle stopped him. "Not now. Run by the twins' crib."

"Right when I don't have a burner, I see this bitch ass nigga," Maniac glared.

"Run by the twins' crib so we can get 'em," Drizzle urged. Maniac hit it in reverse out of the parking lot undetected. He floored it down the street, through a stop sign, down another block, through another stop sign, and made a wild left turn. "I'm at this nigga." He turned full speed into the alley, nearly hitting a dumpster. The Lexus skidded to a stop next to the twins' garage. Drizzle beat Malik to the door. "Come on, dawg?"

"I got it." Malik found the right key and unlocked the door. They barged inside, tripping over each other. "Move, man," Malik said. "You don't even know where I hid it at."

Drizzle hit the light. Malik squeezed between the wall and the Escalade and bent down. He fumbled through a tool box and came back up gripping the .357 Desert Eagle. On the way out, he dropped the keys. "Dammit." Drizzle said, "I got 'em," and retrieved them. Malik had taken a second gun out of the tool box and passed it to him. "Go ahead. I'll lock up," Drizzle said.

Maniac blew the horn until Malik returned to the car. Drizzle could barely get all the way back inside before Maniac stomped the accelerator. Malik thought it was happening too fast. *Fuck it though*! He hungered for revenge.

322

Maniac drove like a maniac all the way back to the gas station. They stared around frantically. Derrick and the Blazer were gone.

"Shit." Maniac punched the steering wheel.

"Where--," Drizzle said.

"Couldn't 've got too far," Malik said.

"I know where—" Maniac said and slammed on the gas. "I bet they went to that house I told y'all about." His driving got more reckless as he sped down one block after another. Malik gripped the back of Drizzle's seat.

"Slow down, 'Ac!" Malik yelled.

"I told you I got this." Maniac hawkishly focused on the destination. Malik braced himself for the crash.

"'Ac, slow the hell down!,'" Drizzle piped out. "Or you gon' mess around 'n' kill us or get the police attention."

"There's the street," Maniac said, finally driving like he had some sense. Malik recognized the area. It was maybe about half a mile from the twins' house.

"Looky here," Maniac cocked his head in the direction of the red Blazer. It sat parked in plain view in the middle of the block. "There it go and here we come," he hurrahed.

Malik clutched the Desert Eagle and leaned over. The Blazer was empty. He looked around and didn't see Derrick or anyone else.

"They're in that brown house. The address matches the one 'ol girl gave me," Maniac assured. He pulled the Lexus around the corner and parked. Closure was closer for Malik.

"I saw a red light reflecting off the Blazer's windshield. All we gotta do is set off the alarm, and wait for 'em to come out and lay shit down." Maniac's bloodthirsty plot put Malik on a whole other edge. He wasn't feeling the 'lay shit down' part. Wasn't no telling who came out or if Derrick would even be one of them.

"Hold up," Malik said, "Derrick's the only target."

Maniac found this too funny. "Sound good," he laughed. "Hand me one of those burners."

"I'm fo' real," Malik said. "Ain't no tellin' who else comes out that crib."

Maniac shot Malik an extremely impatient look. "Dig this," he said. "Fuck dude and whoever else decides to die with him. Them niggas didn't give no fuck when they shot you and yo' cousin, so ain't no way I'm gone get all tender hearted towards any of 'em." He turned to Drizzle for support.

Drizzle didn't endorse his homicidal views. "We can't go off on no kamikaze type mission," he asserted. "'Lik gotta point. If we gon' go do this, our target is Derrick. Handle him and push out."

"I'm not try'na float up shit creek without a paddle," Malik said.

"In real life," Drizzle added.

"Y'all picked a golden time to get on this sensitive thug shit," Maniac huffed.

"Call it what ya want," Drizzle came back, "but I refuse to bury myself in the process of trying to deal with that chump. If we suffer try'na make him suffer then we might as well—"

"Suffer?" Maniac snapped. "Life is sufferin'. I've suffer'd more since my nigga died at the hands of this fag y'all defending."

"Ain't nobody defending him," Malik snapped. "Don't never let no stupid ass shit like that fly out yo' mouth."

Maniac locked gazes with Malik.

"Hold on," Drizzle said. "We need to take a breather and think."

"While y'all takin' breathers, those niggas probably leavin'," Maniac said. "I'll get down by myself. Hand me a burner."

"Naw, 'Ac," Drizzle recoiled away from him. "You're too emotional."

"Fuck this shit, man. Drop me off," Malik said. His mind was made up. "I'm not 'bout to burn myself doin' some reckless shit. I don't get down like that."

Maniac said "What?" with the meanest mug Malik had ever seen. "Give me that," he grabbed at the gun in Drizzle's hand.

Drizzle turned and deflected his hand. "Back on up," Drizzle warned. This further inflamed Maniac.

"Give me my nigga strap," he climbed across the seat.

"Calm the heck down," Malik shouted from the back seat as Maniac tried strong-arming Drizzle. "Maniac, what's wrong with you, dawg?" Malik leaned over the seat, fearing the gun would discharge in the tussle. Drizzle got the door open and fell out the car.

Maniac's focus darted to Malik. "'Lik, give me the D.E." Rage contorted his face. Malik eased a hand to the door handle.

"'Lik, come on," Drizzle snatched open the back door.

Maniac dived over the seat and went for the Desert Eagle. Malik couldn't move fast enough; Maniac got a grip on the barrel and began jerking it from him. "You gon' fuck 'round and shoot me!" Malik bellowed out. He held onto the Desert Eagle with all his might.

"Then let it go, nigga!" Maniac wasn't letting it go.

Drizzle aimed his gun at Maniac. "Let it go," he said sternly. His order betrayed no room for compromise. Maniac got the point and released the barrel and collapsed on the seat next to Malik. Malik did a hasty backwards crawl out the car and fell into the street. He regained his footing and moved behind Drizzle.

Maniac slouched, taking a hard breather, looking defeated. "You bitch ass niggas ain't no killas," he spoke defiantly. He climbed out the car, gross hatred in his eyes. They backed away.

Malik said, "You bogus, Maniac." He tucked the firearm in his waistline and pulled his shirt over it. Drizzle kept his weapon in his hand but lowered it.

Maniac opened the door. "Look at y'all bustas," he said, "ready to do me in but the nigga who killed fam is 'round the corner livin'." He got behind

325

the wheel, reached across the front seat and closed the passenger door. "Y'all just became my enemies." He tossed them one last glare and burned rubber.

Drizzle shook his head as the Lexus bent the corner and disappeared. "That dude need help." He pocketed his gun.

"Some medication or something," Malik said. "Let's bounce."

They started the journey to the twins' house. Malik acted cool as a fan but stayed on point for any car, person or shadow on the prowl. They would have to walk past Derrick's block on the way.

"Stay on yo' p's and q's," Drizzle warned.

"No doubt," Malik's alert system shifted into high gear as they quickened their pace. "Check out this car creepin' up," Malik said, glancing over his shoulder at the approaching headlights. It was coming down the street way too slow. Drizzle stopped and stared bravely at the car, his hand in the pocket that held the burner.

Malik realized it was an unmarked police car. "Them the detecs."

Drizzle swung back around and got to footing it.

They put plenty pep in their steps. The cop car flashed its light directly on their backs. They pretended not to notice. The car slowed down next to them.

"Time for us to break," Drizzle whispered. Suddenly cars zoomed out from two other directions. Malik stiffened when the red Blazer hit the corner right in front of him. Police lights flashed all around. Drizzle took flight as the cops sprang from their vehicles. Malik got a glimpse of Derrick inside the Blazer. The other occupants scrambled to get out. The cops ran right past Malik and swarmed the Blazer.

"Hands up!"

"Driver, let me see your hands now!" The red beams on the police weapons dotted the windows.

Malik tossed up his hands.

"Get out of here," One of the detecs ordered Malik and pushed past. The D.E. in Malik's waistline slid downward as he stumbled out of the way. He poked out his stomach to hold it in place. *Please don't fall.* Derrick's block became Malik's best escape route. He didn't want to risk the gun dropping out of his shorts so he paced his steps. Sweat-bubbles popped out of his pores. He felt the D.E. slipping lower and lower as he picked up the pace. Additional police vehicles flew past him. Malik crossed to the other side of the street. He resisted looking back until he got to the side of a house and out of sight. He stopped, secured the gun back in his waistline and kicked rocks through the back yard. Tires screeched somewhere behind him. Malik took flight through the alley, over a fence and through another back yard. He ran holding the pistol in place. It was a nuisance to carry but he wasn't about to stop and stash it. He followed the yard-alley-yard-street-side-of-the-house-to-another-back-yard routine for about four blocks, sprinting the whole way. He ducked and dodged any detection and prayed and swore to God to do right after tonight. *Just let me make it to the house.* He ran out of another yard onto another block, about to cross another street, but saw headlights beaming his way. He scampered for cover. The car drove on past. Malik took off. He ran on the side of a duplex and slowed up in the back yard to catch his breath some. His lungs felt constipated. He could've sworn he heard something move near the garage. Then he heard the growl...

"Oh, man!" he yelled as the shadow leapt across the grass at him. The monstrous dog charged, snapping its slimy teeth at Malik's legs. He slipped on the grass and the dog clamped down on his sleeve. Malik twisted out of the shirt as the dog's teeth sliced into his elbow. "Hell offa me!" he cried out in agony. He wrestled with the animal and the physical pain. The dog chopped and clawed at his flesh. The gun fell onto the grass. He blindly reached for it. The beast stayed on the attack. Malik got a hold on the gun barrel and clobbered the canine on the nose with it. Unfazed, the dog went to work on his arm. The sting excruciated him. Malik was losing the fight. He fingered the safety switch on the D.E. and rocked it, squeezing and squeezing the trigger. The dog shrieked out, whimpered, and limped away.

Malik broke out of the yard. He felt blood trickling from his wounds. His cuts and gashes felt like perpetual bee stings. He was bare-chested and running like a track star, D.E. in hand, mangled flesh dangling from his elbow.

****

Drizzle glanced back over his shoulder and didn't see anyone giving chase. Nor did he see Malik trailing and this caused him to slow his wild sprint to a sudden stop. He gave the area a quick scan and ducked off in between two big spooky-looking houses. His lungs wailed and writhed as he tried to recapture his breath. And catch sight of Malik. "Da hell is you at, fam?" he gasped in a low whisper through clinched teeth. His throat felt dirt-dry. Drizzle's left hand flew to the burner in his pocket when he heard the muted commotion coming from inside the Caravan parked at the curb. Sounded like a scuffle? He eased out onto the walkway to get a better look. *Ain't this a...* the occupants were in the back seat gettin' it on! All Drizzle saw was bare booty and legs, then a set of surprised eyes spotting him! He got ghost.

Where was Malik at? he kept wondering. Drizzle cut down an alley about half a block from the sex scene. Up ahead at the mouth of the alley on the far end, police lights flashed in a colorful frenzy. Drizzle soon realized he'd run full circle ending up back where he and Malik had somehow split in two separate directions. Drizzle hoped like hell that nothing crazy happened to Malik. The Summerfest incident burst forth into his thoughts. He and Malik had split up that night too, and Malik was almost killed. Drizzle had damn near lost it when She-She called him, crying. He broke into tears upon getting the news. Besides She-She, and maybe Kila, Malik seemed the only other person in the world who genuinely cared whether he succeeded or failed, lived or died. So when Malik got shot, the bullets also pierced Drizzle's heart. *It's like every time a nigga ain't around, some bullshit happens...* he felt. *Every time!* What made Malik getting shot up even worse for Drizzle was that he didn't get to see him at the hospital the night it happened. "The police are questioning everyone who shows up to visit Malik," Jenny had called to warn him. Drizzle didn't give a fuck. He made the trip anyway, too worried about his #1 comrade to care about getting knocked on the AWOL warrant. But then he showed up, made it all the way up to the floor Malik was on, and ran into a legion of law enforcement. Drizzle reversed his direction right back into the

328

elevator. He called Kila and sent her down to the hospital, then waited with She-She at Malik's crib. Kila called about an hour later and advised Drizzle to stay far away. "You'll get questioned and likely arrested if you show up," she'd cautioned. "Malik's going to be alright."

Drizzle still regretted not being there—that night at Summerfest, then later at the hospital. Then again last night during the carjack attempt... then again before that when they 'jacked 'Lik for the Chevy. And now once again, Drizzle wasn't there to make sure his fam made it out of danger.

Dropping the gun into the green city dumpster he'd taken cover by, Drizzle swallowed his hesitation and took off up the alley. He marched right out to the police swarm. All four doors on the red Blazer were wide open. Drizzle tensed up, wondering if Derrick and his boys got away—and possibly caught up with Malik? He weaved his way through the small crowd of onlookers. Four dudes sat on the curb in handcuffs, getting questioned by detectives. Derrick was among them; Drizzle remembered his face from earlier at the gas station.

An officer searching through the Blazer came out of it with a black semi-automatic. He held it up, careful not to corrupt any possible fingerprints. Derrick and his crew were then hustled off to different police vehicles and shoved inside. Drizzle didn't think to peer inside the cop cars for Malik. He stepped closer to check the back seats of the other ones. All empty. No Malik to be seen, *which could be a good thing,* he considered. Then came the flash of light in his face and the stern order to "Freeze and place ya hands above ya head." *Ain't this a ...* he took flight—or tried to—*bitch!* One-time gaffled him up.

****

Malik slowed down when he reached the twins' back yard. The keys? Drizzle had them. Shit! Malik tossed the D.E. under some bushes and dashed around front hoping that Drizzle had made it to the house already. He banged on the door and rang the doorbell like a madman. And waited. His elbow bled badly and hurt terribly.

329

Drizzle didn't answer the door.

Malik was desperate to get in. He checked the front door. Locked. He ran around to the back and checked the rear door. Locked! He kicked it in frustration and hurt his foot. "Aah!"

Malik limped back to the front of the house. *Think.* His elbow was killing him. He feared touching it would make it throb worse. Tears stalled in the corners of his eyes. He steadied the bloody elbow, thinking about what to do next. *Drizzle should've got here by now.* Malik feared the worst.

He glanced up and down the shadowy street. There wasn't a human in sight. The nearest pay phone was blocks away. With no shirt on and blood on him and on his clothes and shoes, he would definitely stick out to the cops. And cutting through any more yards wasn't an option. Malik checked for his watch and realized it was gone. The dog had robbed him of his jersey and Movado. He didn't give a damn about the material loss. He just wanted to get to a phone. The risk was there but the trip seemed his best bet.

He started the walk/run and ignored the spookiness of the neighborhood. He would be forever grateful if he could just make it through the night with no more drama.

Spotting the set of pay phones up ahead, Malik broke into a painful jog and kept his injured elbow extra still.

****

Liz got rid of Travis shortly after Malik had hard-headedly left with his friends. She couldn't believe his ass! Disobeying her like he'd lost his damn mind.

"And you told him what I said?" Liz asked She-She for the second time. She-She confirmed with a sad nod of the head. "Call and keep calling Andre's phone, texting or whatever," Liz said. She-She jumped right to it.

Liz stomped off into her bedroom, slammed the door and considered her options. She felt like she was on her last leg with Malik. *Just tired of all of this*, she ranted. What the hell did God want from her? What was the use of calling out to Him if He never answered? Only seemed to heap and heap and heap on more hell. Tears fell as Liz fell to her knees next to the bed. She closed her eyes and pressed together both hands and lowered her face all the way down to the carpet. In her head she heard Tessa's voice, Granny's voice, Pastor Diamond's voice, all kinds of voices talking over, preaching over, praising over each other. Liz arose from the floor with a face soaked in tears, reached up and spread out her hands to God. She went into her most fervent prayer over the medley of voices. She cried out, repeating the same one-line request: "Please let me hear your voice, Lord!"

****

Malik thanked God for the loose change in his pocket. He worked his one good hand, feeding the phone slot and dialing in the number. Brianna's sleepy voice came on line about five rings later.

"Hello?"

"Bree, I need you to come scoop me," he said. "Get up." He glanced over his shoulder.

"What?"

A squad car cruised by. Malik ducked deeper into the phone booth.

"Why didn't you come to the phone earlier?" Brianna asked.

"Bree, my fault, alright. Just come get me from the twins' house before I bleed to death."

"Are you for real? Don't be playing…"

"I'm serious," he said. "I need you."

"Where are you?"

"The twins' house. I'll be waiting outside."

"Here I come."

Malik dropped the phone and took off. The night breeze pressed against his bare chest. Some of the blood began to congeal. He slowed to a jog when the pain in his elbow flared up. He hoped Derrick and his crew got hauled off to jail and stayed forever! He hoped Drizzle got away. Malik hoped for a lot of things. His brain knocked against his skull. Thoughts and questions stomped through his mind with every step toward the twins' house. Actually his house. The air got chilly. He longed for warmth and relief. A car approached. Malik picked up the pace as the driver stared out the window at him and passed. Malik ran the rest of the way.

He made it back to the house and saw the lights still off on the porch. He rang the doorbell.

Still no answer. He worried about Drizzle. The chilly winds snaked around Malik's bare chest and legs and arms. What he wouldn't do to be in a warm bed. He rang the doorbell again. He paced back and forth on the porch to raise his body temperature. After awhile, he thought about breaking out a window to get in the house. He ran around back. Nothing to do it with, he lamented. The cannon? He grimaced bending down to get it out the bushes.

A horn blew out front. "Brianna!" Malik broke out in a sprint down the side of the house. Brianna got out of the car and rushed over. "'Lik?" She spotted the gun in his hand and stopped short. "What are you doing with that?" Then she spotted the blood. "Is that—"

He strained in pain. "Lay something over your seat so it won't get on—"

Panic swept over her. "Boy, are you shot?" She took the gun and led him to the car. He got inside, replying, "Worse than that."

Brianna rounded the car and got in. She placed the gun under her seat. "Who did this to you, Malik?"

"A dog. Tried to eat me alive."

She stopped the car at the corner. "What?"

"Straight up," he squeezed out a laugh. "I cut through the wrong yard."

"I'm taking you to the hospital." She hit the gas. "And I want to know why you have this gun and why you're out this late. This isn't making sense."

"No hospitals." Malik wasn't chancing it. "I shot the mutt and I'm sure the owners called the cops." It was unlikely that the police would go out of their way to catch a dog killer but with Malik's shirt and watch left at the crime scene and the bites all over his body, the preponderance of evidence solved the case for them. And with a pistol involved? Malik wasn't going down for animal murder.

Brianna put up a weak argument for him to go see a doctor. "Those injuries can lead to infection."

"And a felony conviction and prison if I'm found out." She didn't argue with that. Instead, she stopped at a 24-hour Walgreen's for medical supplies.

Malik felt better already. Sore and sticky, but better. The ride from the store to Brianna's house was a quiet one. She was upset with him and he was upset with himself. "I'll take care of the blood on your car seats. Maybe get yo' ride piped out in leather with your name stitched in the headrests."

Brianna said not a word.

They got inside her house, and Brianna sent him to the bathroom.

He uttered, "Damn," watching himself in the mirror. He was a hot mess. His new Nikes and shorts were ruined but the wounds didn't look as bad as they felt. And his waves set on his head with resilient perfection. He slowly pulled up his elbow and studied its gory reflection.

Brianna came in and directed him to the toilet. "Sit down." She frowned the entire time. Her hostility tantalized him through the pain. *Better I not mention that*, he thought

She dabbed his elbow with a warm towel. "Ah!" he winced. "That sucka hurts, girl." She opened a bottle of peroxide and applied it to his flesh wounds. The most she said was an ungentle "Be still" or two. Her attitude shouted though. Malik cracked wisecracks as she finished cleaning him up. She wasn't humored.

"Get undressed," she said. Malik broke out into a big smile. She went to the bathtub and ran the water.

"Ooh, all I needed was for a dog to attack me for us to—"

"Grow up," she said and stomped out of the bathroom. This pissed him off. He slowly stripped off his clothes and shoes and tossed them on the floor. "Stankin' attitude," he mumbled and dipped a toe in the bath water. It was a perfect steam. He sank in it. The hot water cast a tingly sensation into his wounds, a throbbing solace.

Brianna came and collected his clothes and left a pair of socks, a thick bathrobe, and a towel on the sink.

Malik marinated in the water until it cooled and he became drowsy. He toweled off and patched up his elbow with a huge Band-Aid. He was relieved that the lesions were only shallow. He pulled on the robe and socks, then went into the living room and lay down on the couch. Brianna walked past to the kitchen. She persisted with the silent treatment.

"I'd think we were already married," Malik said. Silence. He called Drizzle's cell phone three times. Voicemail. Voicemail. Voicemail. He tried Kila's. Voicemail as well. He left short messages and hung up.

Brianna came out and turned off the TV that he happened to be watching.

"Tell me how it happened." She crossed her arms over her chest.

"Huh?" Malik stared up from his relaxed position on the couch.

"The dog attack?" she said. "And why do you have that gun?" A fierce glint lit her big, brown eyes.

"I told you I cut through the wrong back yard," he offered. "The mutt came out of nowhere and got at me."

She uncrossed her arms and heightened her hostile stare. "And the gun?"

"What about it?"

The frown deepened across her gorgeous face.

334

"You evil-eyeing me like I got caught cheating on you," he joked.

"First of all, you can't cheat on me because you're not my man. And in order to be anyone's man you have to first *be* a man, without the boyish games."

That insulted his pride. "So you saying I'm a boy?"

"You saying you're handling yourself like a man?"

Malik started feeling self-conscious about his nudity under the bathrobe. "What am I doing here if you think so low of me?" He stood up. "You're the one playing games, sending mixed messages, goin' hot and cold. Then get mad and wanna throw slugs about the age thing like that makes you superior. That's characteristic of a girl," he accused. "A little girl."

They argued back and forth.

"I don't know what you thought," she shouted, "I was trying to extend my friendship to you. What I look like fuckin' with a dude who's afraid to march to his own drum beat." She was all up in his face.

"You think you know me?" He stood his ground.

"How can I know you when you don't even know yourself?"

Malik backed up away from her. "Soon as my clothes dry, I'm out. You won't have to worry about my ignorance."

"And when I tried to expose you to something real, you closed your eyes," she kept babbling. "Too lost in Drizzle's dream to see the reality of your own future and what you want to be in it. What do you want? What are you aiming for? Aiming to become? Huh? Another broken down brother? A castaway to prison? In the grave?"

"You don't know nothing about me," he mouthed. "You haven't seen what I saw and can't imagine what I plan to do with my life." He clinched the front of the robe and held it close. "I know what I want and where I'm going!"

"Where?" she challenged. "Where are you going, Malik?"

"That's my business!"

"Sure is," she said. "And what about your responsibilities?"

Malik turned away and sat back down. "I could've called my mama for a ride tonight if I'da known you was gon' get on this."

"Call Mommy, huh?" She derided him. "Boyish just like I said." She waved him off. He followed her to the kitchen.

"You think you know so much." His headache kicked in again. "You don't know a thang 'bout these streets and how cutthroat these niggas get."

She slammed the dryer door shut. "You're a nigga," she snapped on him. "Listen to you. 'These niggas.' This system considers you one of those niggas. So when you generalize, you're tearing down yourself, too. When you carry guns, you're acting out the role of one of those niggas."

"No," he replied. "I'm protecting myself. You haven't been shot and robbed. You ain't experienced none of that. And I be damned if I experience it again. I can guarantee that. Ain't nan other punk muthafucka catching me slippin' ever again."

"That's how you kill the problem—by becoming it?" she asked. "My mother is on drugs. My cousins have got killed. My friends have fallen victims. My mother is locked up and recently revealed to me that she's HIV positive, but am I using all that as an excuse to fold?" She teared up. The news about her mother's disease hit Malik right in the gut.

"I'll never let anything conquer or enslave me or my future," a tear dripped down her cheek. "And you need to grow up and stop making tired excuses."

Malik took a seat at the table. He was still trippin' off of the news about her mother and lacked any desire to drag out the argument any longer. Brianna left the kitchen. The mini-dryer next to the washer purred on in cycles. He pulled open the small door and checked on his clothes. They were still damp.

Brianna returned. Malik restarted the machine. She took a seat and spoke calmly across the table. "Malik, you need to understand that violence and betrayal have been a part of the world since Cain killed Abel. It'll remain when you're long gone. You gotta decide for yourself to react to it or act against it. Anyone can react by creating more of it. This distinguishes the male from the man. The male lashes out and acts the role of a thug. But a man buckles down under the pressures in life until he rises above them."

Malik considered the twins childhood tragedy. They were thrust into manhood—or malehood—at an early age and not of their own volition. How could boys make the best grown-up decisions? What, they were just supposed to suck up what happened to their parents and keep being happy-go-lucky kids? Malik knew he couldn't have. And Drizzle's upbringing wasn't much different. Thugs wasn't born thugs. "I feel you, Bree," Malik spoke up. "But it's some things that happens in people's lives that pushes them."

"Then push back," she said.

"What about the kids too weak to push back. The ones who don't have anything to push back with. I understand what you went through with losing your sister and the situation with your mother, but at least you were left with something to fall back on."

Brianna shook her head, irritated. "Before all of that, my daddy was killed. As a child you don't always have control. You don't always understand. But you learn to deal with it. You strengthen yourself within. Violence, drugs. I saw all of that by the time I reached 11 years old."

The conversation ended with Brianna saying, "Remember there's more than one way to run from your pain, shame or fears. Some of us use drugs. Some use alcohol. And too many brothers use thuggin'."

It was four o'clock in the morning when Malik retired for the night. Brianna brought him some blankets and went to sleep in her bed.

Malik lay down on the couch and closed his eyes. He was glad to be alone. This had been the longest year of his life. The longest, most exhaustive two days of his life. No telling what would happen tomorrow. The drama never ended. How long would Derrick be locked up? For the first time, Malik wondered about his childhood. Derrick must've seen some things and gone through some things that turned his heart cold, too. But Malik didn't care about the nigga or his upbringing. And wouldn't blink over the news of his death. He got salty at himself for even considering some type of mitigating factor in what Derrick had done to him. And Brandon. And Liz. And She-She. And whoever else.

The depression came over Malik. He lay there and sulked in it. He loved his mother and it hurt to think about the hurt he was causing her. Brianna too. His closest relationships were unraveling. He got the urge to get up and call his mother to apologize. The same urge to go and apologize to Brianna. He was too tired to get up. Too tired to go to sleep. His life was spiraling out of control. He came close to killing another black woman's son. Lashing out. All the drama had shoved him off his square. He hadn't buckled down like a man but reacted like a boy. A gangsta, he wasn't; a thug, he wasn't. His heart and soul fought against him ever becoming either. His mind and emotions only led him to believe the hype. The cracks in his heart splintered the more he reviewed it all. He played the role of the slave driver just like the elderly sister said that day in front of Drizzle's house. Malik had lost pity for any nigga that tested or tried to treat him, and he thought nothing about toting guns or using one on any nigga. Any nigga? *Listen to me*, he grew ashamed. What was a nigga? Some white man's invention. That's what his mother had told him. That must be what he'd become: invented. The concocted image of a sick mentality. Who was he to talk though? He searched for his buried hopes, dreams, vision. He saw the .357 Desert Eagle, the hours he spent in jail, the lack of sympathy for Jeff after Drizzle shot him; Malik saw the night the goon had shot him, the night Derrick murdered Brandon. He saw himself with Drizzle plotting revenge, plotting murder. Murder. Guns. Black on black homicides. black mothers crying at funerals. Cell doors slamming. The face of the judge sentencing his father to prison. Sentencing Brian to prison. Sentencing him to prison. Stereotype manifested. It hurt and shamed Malik even in his sleep, even as he slept.

CHAPTER 55

Heavy rain splashed against Liz's window pane. She watched it stream down for a moment. Then she refocused on the Scriptures she was reading. She got halfway through the eleventh chapter of Hebrews and set the Bible aside. Her attention returned to the window. Outside, dark clouds and gray streaks smeared the sky. Liz felt so alone. This morning's boring church service had done nothing but nudge her woebegone spirits deeper into hell. After the parting prayer, she sent She-She to the mall with Wanda. Liz drove to the eastside to speak with Malik. When no one answered the door at the twins' house, she came home. And waited. And contemplated letting her only child go. She couldn't keep doing this. Their bickering was tearing them apart and ripping her heart deep down the middle.

Liz hadn't slept much last night and couldn't sleep when she returned home this morning. She just watched the rain and wondered and meditated on things. Some good news did arrive at the break of dawn. Travis called and said that Derrick was in police custody. He'd been arrested on gun possession. Liz couldn't believe that that was it. "What about my nephew's murder?" she'd asked. Travis assured her that homicide charges would be filed soon. "The DA wants to run ballistics on the gun that we found in the vehicle they were in," he said. "But don't let it concern you. The evidence is piling up against him. One of his boys is cooperating." This news eased some of her depression. And before she got off the phone with Travis, he asked her out. He kind of hinted that he deserved the date for the role he played in the arrest. He flat out claimed credit. She never informed him about her string of anonymous calls to the precincts. None of it really mattered as long as Derrick was locked up. She prayed that he stayed locked up for a good long while.

Liz called Jenny after telling Travis, "Call me after church."

"Church?" the cocky confidence softened in his voice.

"Yes, church," she asserted. "Wanna come?"

He gave a lame reason why he couldn't and promised to call later. She accepted it because she wanted to stay updated on the case. Travis' hopes could fly to the moon, for all she cared. The police had already contacted Jenny by the time Liz reached her. She told Liz that they wanted her to view a lineup, to which she agreed. Jenny also volunteered to try to convince her two friends to come forward. "What two friends?" Liz questioned. Jenny hadn't mentioned them yesterday. But when Liz found out that there were additional potential witnesses, she silently thanked Jesus. With Derrick already in custody, she hoped the other girls would feel safe enough to cooperate.

The rain outside continued to fall. Liz went and put on a Mary Mary CD. The sisters' beautiful singing filled a small corner of her depression. Good Gospel music always soothed.

Liz poured herself an icy glass of lemonade iced tea. The stove clock read 2:30 p.m. Outside it resembled evening. She wondered how Marvin was feeling this afternoon. About her. She hoped he understood. *Should've let him go months ago*, she thought, reflecting on their phone call last night. She stood at the kitchen sink and stared out the window. Was she addicted to rain-watching? "Hope not," she said to herself. She sipped the tea and silently accused the showers of tampering with her loneliness, stirring up in her a desire to cuddle, to be cuddled. *Marvin probably thinks…* The phone rang.

The county jail operator's voice rattled Liz.

"… 'this Dre'… please press one to accept…"

She poked the #1.

"Auntie, is 'Lik home?"

Liz set down the glass. "No. He didn't come home last night. What are you doing in jail?"

"Police picked me up on that warrant."

"What you doing downtown?"

"They charged me with fleeing, too," he said. "Since I'm seventeen now, I got sent to the county. They might be taking me out to detention later for that other stuff."

"Why didn't you and Malik answer my calls last night?" she asked. He got quiet. She didn't push the issue. "Where is Malik?" she asked him.

340

"We split up after we left there yesterday," he said. "He ain't come home yet?"

"No."

"He should be over the twins' house then."

"I went by there this morning and didn't get an answer."

"Yeah, I called there right before I called your house," he said. "He might be over Brianna's house."

The doorbell rang.

"Hold on," she said and went to answer it. She opened the door upon seeing Malik.

"Where is your key at?" she asked as he stepped in out of the rain.

"Dre has them." He closed the door.

"Dre is on the phone. He's in jail."

He hastened over and lifted the receiver to his ear. "Hello?"

Liz noticed the faded stains on his shorts and shoes. And the scars on his legs and the bandage on his knee and the unfamiliar hoodie he wore, and how he kept his elbow bent and steady like something was wrong with it. She reached out and felt the dressing underneath. Malik winced from her touch. His hand was also bandaged. Scratches covered his wrist. *What in the world did this boy get himself into?* Liz wanted answers as soon as he got his ass off the phone. She picked up her drink and carried it to the kitchen. She strongly suspected that Malik's injuries and Andre's arrest were connected. She sipped from the glass. The ice had melted, diluting the flavor of the tea. She poured it out and stared out the window over the sink. Her goal wasn't to make things worse between them. But that little show he put on yesterday... Rude and disrespectful toward her and Travis... *he knew better than that... then left after I directed him not to. Didn't call or come home either. Completely unacceptable! Unacceptable.* Something had to give because Liz wouldn't put up with it any more. The self-talk failed her. She didn't want to risk losing...

341

"Bring yo' ass here," Liz ordered Malik once he hung up the phone and started for his bedroom. *The gall of this boy!* "What happened to you?"

He dragged his feet and attitude back around in her direction. "A dog attacked me," he muttered like he didn't feel like explaining himself.

"A dog?" she said. "Pull off that sweatshirt and let me see your arm.

He funkily pulled his arms out of the sleeves. "I cut through a yard and it came out of nowhere." He lifted the hoodie over his head.

"Did you go to the hospital?" She examined his Band-Aided elbow.

"It wasn't that serious," he said. "Brianna helped me clean it up."

"I told that girl to have you call me."

"She did." He made eye contact and looked away. "Thought your police associate—"

"Shut that smart mouth." She sneered. "You should've called me first. I am your mother."

"And who is Travis?"

Liz was a nanosecond away from slapping the taste off his tongue. "Don't make any assumptions about my personal life," she checked him. He stood there. His only reply was unspoken attitude. He stared over her shoulder toward the window. Liz took a moment to calm down.

"What is your problem, Malik?" The emotion spouted up in her like a mighty river. "Haven't I always been there for you and done what's best for you?"

He went on looking past her.

"You look at me," she snapped. He did. "What part of what's best for me includes you messing around with some police dude? Before him, some cat named Marvin?" His voice quivered.

"You don't question me on who I deal with," she said. He tried to look away but she moved closer. "That man Travis helped get Derrick off the street before you did something to ruin your life. That's what he had to do with it. I

342

used him to protect you and stop you from winding up dead or where your daddy is."

"He sure wasn't dressed like he was on the job." Traces of guilt surfaced in his face. "And how can he help when ain't no proof Derrick did it?"

"Jenny already told me and the police," she enlightened him.

"What?"

"Don't what me. She went to view a lineup this morning. You will too."

"You're gonna get that girl killed," he said. "I already told those people what I could. I can't pick dude out in a lineup without lying."

"You're lying now," she said. He looked away. Liz felt like crying and beating his ass. She knew he stood there and lied right to her face. It pained her all the more that he remained so secretive and withdrawn from her.

"Why are you leaving me, Malik?" she asked, feeling desperate. "What are you trying to prove?"

He didn't answer.

"Why are you trying to leave me?" Tears fell. "Did I turn you down one time in your life? Did I let go when they took your daddy? No. So why are you leaving?" she asked. "What is your problem?" The distance and alienation overwhelmed her, shook her to the core. Her son was inches from her but it felt like he was gone and she was all alone. She shook his shoulders. "Tell me!"

He broke out in tears. "I'm sorry, mama," he blurted and fell into her arms. As she embraced him, he released, "I never wanted to cause you stress or make you cry. It's been too much comin' at me. Pushin' against me. All too fast, I just lost myself in it and—" he held her tighter, unable to get the rest out.

"Talk to me then." She rubbed his back. The strength took root again as her spirit ascended. "Whether right or wrong, I'll be there, in your corner. You're my baby."

343

The tears flowed between them. They stood in the kitchen, hugging, connecting, tacitly reaffirming their love for each other. This was her child, her everything. She could feel God wrapping His hands around them. "*Faith,*" she heard the voice of the spirit say. Faith.

Outside, the rain subsided and the sun winked through the cloudy sky. The cycles. The reasons. The meaning. Everything came together for the goodness. Faith thundered when it thundered and shined when it shined. All things had their season. Liz's ups and downs were wedded to some higher purpose. She held Malik in her arms and hummed along to the music of Mary Mary coming from the next room.

CHAPTER 56

Malik couldn't stand the outrageous orange of Milwaukee County Jail jumpsuits. He was beginning to hate the color orange, period. And the darkness its brightness symbolized. That's what orange represented to Malik: darkness. Sunlessness. Captivity. Separation from loved ones. Thick glass partitions. Kevy trapped on one side and Malik on the other side. Seeing but unable to touch. Anticipation and apprehension. Tears, fears, yearning, anger, bad news and the blues. Cramped spaces. Happy as hell hellos and sad ass goodbyes. Willed smiles and depressed looks. Utterances of "I miss you," "daddy, when you comin' home?", "what's takin' so long?" and "I love you, too." Rushed conversations and limitations on communication. Dang "alreadies" and "ain't long" enoughs. Heartbreaks that inspired headaches. Leaving alone. Leaving Kevy all alone.

Now the orange represented Brian attired in one of those repulsive jumpsuits, sitting sideways in a pissy-yellow plastic chair, behind a thick glassy divider, inside a cramped visiting booth, picking up the phone receiver to limitedly communicate with Malik, who sat across from him, separated.

"That punk Derrick got moved," Brian was telling him. "I'll catch him up north though." The skin beneath his eyes was puffy with dark lines of stress.

Malik said, "Straight up?" but didn't care about Derrick's relocation. It had been over a month since he had last seen his cousin. After Brian got wind of Derrick's arrival at the county jail, he brushed up on the Sheriff Deputy working that day and asked him to see what pod "my guy is on." The deputy was cool and checked the computer and located Derrick on 5B, the pod directly across the gym from where Brian was then housed. Two days later, Brian somehow got another deputy to have him moved to pod 5B. That same night, a deputy noticed Derrick staggering out the gym with a pumpkin head. He was questioned about it and claimed he fell while balling. Two other inmates backed him up. More ass whippings ensued. Eventually a confidential snitch tipped off the authorities. Brian and three of his guys were rounded up and tossed in the hole under investigation. A month later they got released back to general population. Brian wrote Malik and let him know what all went down. Malik drove downtown to see his cousin the same day.

"You think they gone give y'all a battery charge on dude?" Malik asked. Brian seemed to have lost weight.

"I doubt it because of that deal they offered me on my case," he told Malik. "They're hopin' I help them convict dude for killin' my brother."

Malik leaned back in the plastic chair. "You gon' make a play?"

"Hell, no," he replied. " I wanna kill the nigga and all but I'm still stickin' to the G-Code. Gettin' on the stand to help these honkies convict some other nigga goes against that. A snitch jacket can't be tailored for the kid."

Malik didn't agree but did understand his thug logic. It started on the streets in a game that the twins chose to play; a game with rules that real gangstas followed and fake ones violated when it was convenient to do so. Malik wanted no parts in the blood sports of the streets. He wasn't a gangsta and no longer entertained the possibility of becoming one. He *would* honor his cousin's wish and remain uncooperative. Plus, Malik's enemies' enemy *was not* his friend. The DA's determination to convict Derrick had nothing to do with justice. It was all a hustle for the holice on the beat to the judges on the bench. The same network of jackals that had hustled Malik's father into prison over a decade ago. The same kangaroo court system. Now they sought Malik's assistance to send the next brother off to the joint? As much as Malik fought against acknowledging it, he couldn't deny the fact that Derrick was a brother, a black male. Now another statistic. He could've easily been in Derrick's shoes and Derrick in Brandon's grave. The same sequence. And the same folk eating, building their careers, feeding their families, and paying off their mortgages and cars notes off of every new case and conviction. The more people locked up, the securer their jobs, the securer the prison officials' jobs; and the communities where the majority of the captives came from are just as neglected by the tough-on-crime politicians.

Malik was starting to see exactly what his father was talking about.

"Yeah, cuz, I already know they plan to lay me down," Brian was saying. "So you and Drizzle hold me down and make it happen with the music. The sooner y'all hit millionaire status, the better chance I have of seeing some daylight again."

"How much time you think they gon' give you?" Malik asked, the hatred for orange blossoming inside his heart.

"Enough time to get tired of jailing and the streets by the time I get back home," he said. "What's goin' on with Lil Awol?"

"He's back in the studio, happy to be free and determined to blow. Him and momz had a nice long heart-to-heart after that case on Jesse got dismissed. He believes that he owes her, me, you, and Brandon. I think he feels kinda responsible for all of the recent drama."

Brian willed his signature grin. "Good. Let him think that as long as it keeps him motivated in the right direction."

Malik willed a smile. "No doubt," he nodded. "Radio stations up in Madison and Racine are spinning his songs now too."

"I'm already knowin'," Brian said. "I sub him on my cheap ass walkman every time V100 play him. Y'all take whatever loot needed from the stash to finance the vision. Time to start hittin' that highway for shows. Build up the brand and do it independent unless the majors come talkin' high seven figures or better. Anything less is a gotdamn shame." His grin became less willed, more genuine.

"I'm looking into producing," Malik said. "I've pretty much learned how to operate those beat machines y'all bought. Brianna keep tellin' me to go to school for it."

"How's ya snowbunny," Brian smirked, "Jenny?"

"Funny," he replied.

"Brianna ain't gon' do nothing but stand on ya neck like ya momz do." He thought about it and said, "Yeah, that's the type of woman you need though. Brianna's a keeper. But tell Jenny I wanna holla at her mama." This got him chuckling. Malik joined in.

"Did Maniac holla at you?" Brian changed the subject.

347

"Yeah, that nutcase came by last night. We squashed that animosity. Dude got issues and is on the verge of catchin' a case he can't come back from."

"He'll be alright," Brian said. "His love for me and Brandon is reckless at times." His eyes narrowed on Malik. "But I want you and Drizzle to forever remember something." He paused for effect. "Don't ever up a cannon on a killa unless ya gonna use it."

Malik got the point.

"Matter fact," Brian continued, "get rid of--." He lifted his hand and made a gun sign. "Toss 'em, sell 'em or whatever. This includes the one in Brandon's room."

Brianna had already taken it upon herself to toss the Desert Eagle in Lake Michigan the morning after the dog attack. She'd left and done it before Malik woke up and let him know when she returned. "I'm steps ahead of you, cuz," Malik assured Brian. Drizzle was forced to toss the other gun on the night he got arrested. He told Malik the location, but Malik didn't go looking for it. "What you want me to do with y'all rides and stuff?"

Brian sniffed. "Whatever," he said. "That material shit don't mean a damn thing to me any more. I'm on my way to the joint to do a bid. Screw those clothes, cars, jewelry, all that bullshit. I'm growing bitter towards it by the day 'cause I know it's somewhere at the root of my downfall. You decide what to do with it. You've always been the wiser one out of the family."

A deputy came and told them to wrap up their visit.

"You need anything?" Malik asked, "me to do anything?"

They stood to their feet.

"Yeah," Brian said, looking serious. "Avoid this. Stay out of trouble and out those streets. I am who I am, 'ya dig? Now you be who you be. You got a Mama who loves you, who'll kill for you to live. That's precious." Then he put on the screwface. "And if you break her heart, I'ma break ya face."

348

"No doubt, B."

"Love."

"Love," Malik hid the sadness in his goodbye.

CHAPTER 57

Liz placed the Bible on the dinette table at a tactical angle. *When he steps through the front door, it'll be right there in plain view.* She expected him at any minute. She peered inside She-She's room and found her sprawled across the bed talking on the phone and combing through Essence magazine.

"Did Wanda call?" Liz asked her.

She sat up. "Uh-uh," she said. "But Amina wanna know if she can spend the night Saturday and go to church with us on Sunday."

Liz thought back on the night she and Wanda had found the two girls hugged up, afraid, and hiding in the bathtub. "Yeah," she said, "just tell her to have her grandma call me later."

Liz left She-She to her phone conversation. She walked outside into the breezy bosom of the September wind. She inhaled the fresh air and settled down on a porch chair. Old man winter would soon make his rounds, and this past summer was one Liz wouldn't miss. Too many close calls for her. The only bright spot was that it pushed her closer to God and helped strengthen her bond with Malik in the end.

Travis cruised up in front and parked. One other dog to neuter, she thought as he got out his Ford Explorer. He strolled up her walkway, dapper in crispy denim jeans and Coogi sweater.

"Out enjoying some sun?" he greeted with a winning smile.

"Trying to," she said.

He stepped onto the porch, past one chair, and decided on the one next to hers. "I see you looking good."

"I smell you smelling good," she said, getting a whiff of his fragrance. *Damn, why did I let that slip out my mouth?* She was screwing up the script.

Travis' moist lips curled up into a contented smile. "Glad to see you're doing better. Least it seems that way."

"I'm blessed," she remembered her lines. "The Lord is enough when times get tough."

He stared out at the elements. She peeked at him on the sly. Her reference to God didn't seem to bother him.

"It is nice out," he said.

"I wonder how God does it," she said.

"Does what?"

"Nature," she said. "Its symmetry. The sky, the divinely-crafted furniture in the firmament." Next act. "Isn't God good?" she touched his shoulder.

He chuckled like he knew what she was up to. "I see you're working toward scaring me off with the religious speak." They looked at each other, she attempting to hide her guilt, he making it obvious he'd recognized her agenda.

"Why would that scare you?" she asked. "Unless your mind is on ungodly stuff."

He huffed a laugh. "Woman, you're something else."

"What?" she acted innocent.

"You're too much for me," he said. "I get it when the interest isn't mutual, so I'll stop coming at you like that."

She-She appeared in the doorway. Travis turned her way. "You must be the little sister who kept covering for Liz when she was dodging my phone calls over the last several weeks?" he accused.

She-She giggled. "Auntie, Wanda on her way over," she said. "And Kev—" she glanced at Travis. "Somebody on the phone for you."

Liz had a light bulb moment. "Wanda?" she thought out loud. Travis wasn't a bad looking brother? Actually, pretty darn handsome, she acknowledged, sizing up the prospect.

Travis rose from the chair. "I'll get on up out of here," he said.

351

"Hold up," Liz said. "I want you to meet someone." She stepped around him. "She might be too much of enough for you." He arched a wary eyebrow.

"Just have a seat, brothaman," Liz directed him back into the chair. "She'll pull up any minute. She-She, keep him company." She-She came on out and plopped down next to him, kicking up her feet to block any attempt by him to escape. "I got you," She-She said.

Travis eyed them back and forth. "What are you two up to?" he asked, then flipped the script on Liz, adding, "I know Jesus frowns on scandal."

They all laughed. "Just be cool," Liz said. "Jesus could be about to bless you."

He leaned back and relaxed. "We'll see."

Liz hurried in the house to get the phone.

"Hello."

"Hey."

"Kevy?"

"Lizzy?"

"This is a nice surprise," Liz expected some attitude from him because he hadn't called or written her in awhile.

"Well, I have a better surprise." He said.

"And what's that?" she said with child-like anticipation.

"First, who's the girl?"

"That's She-She. Now tell me, Kevy," she insisted. "Bet' not be another woman." She was not serious.

"Another woman?" He laughed, messing with her.

"Yeah," she said. This wasn't funny now.

"I went out to Oklahoma and got one of those big country farm girls, huh?"

The operator interrupted with the "This call is being monitored..." warning.

"I thought my woman was the mother of my only son," Kevy said.

"Better stay that way," she asserted. "I'll come up to Oklahoma and bring it to somebody."

Kevy smiled through the phone. "I thought you was a Christian now," he said. "What happened to turning the other cheek? What would Jesus do?"

"Don't play." Liz said. "Now what's the better surprise?"

Wanda came in. "Girl, who is bruh on the porch?" she asked. Liz covered the mouth of the phone.

"Wait, this Kevy."

"Excuse me," Wanda said. "Hey, Kevy."

"Who is that?" Kevy asked.

"Wanda," Liz said. "Hold on a sec, baby?"

Liz shoved Wanda back out of the room. "Go out there and talk to him before he gets away."

Wanda cut left to the bathroom, saying, "You coulda warned me ahead of time."

Liz closed the bedroom door.

"Hello."

"The phone is about to cut off."

"Call back," Liz said, hoping that he could and would.

"Don't you want to know the surprise?"

"Yeah, hurry up," she urged, praying it had something to do with his case.

"I'm back in Wisconsin."

The operator came on and ended their call.

Wanda barged back in. "My hair look okay?" She-She stood behind her giggling her head off.

"She-She, what did the phone say before you accepted Kevy's call?" Liz's hopes were way up in the stratosphere.

"Huh?" She seemed confused.

Wanda kept bugging them with questions about her appearance.

"Did the operator say anything about him calling from a Wisconsin prison?" Liz questioned She-She. "Like when your mom calls?"

"Forget y'all then," Wanda said, fed up with being ignored. I know I look good." She peacocked out of the room saying, "Watch me bag this brotha."

The phone rang again. It was true! Kevy was back in Wisconsin and only an hour's drive away in Waupun.

"Can I visit?" was all Liz wanted to know.

"Late visits are from six to nine. The same schedule from when I was here before," he said. "I'm on my way," Liz said. "Bye."

Liz moved with supersonic speed. Not a minute squandered. She bathed quickly, singing in the shower. What to wear? She-She suggested the outfit she'd planned to wear to church next Sunday: a brand-new peach-colored suede skirt that fell inches above her ankles and a thin, fruity-colored sweater with peach swirls stitched in it. "Forgive me, Lord," she laughed with She-She and got the outfit out the closet. "Find me some earrings."

Liz finished dressing. She-She put in the gold triple-loops and said, "Fly as can be, Auntie."

Liz spruced up her hairdo, and was out the door, smelling of Ralph Lauren.

Travis and Wanda sat on the porch with smiles on their faces, desire in their eyes, and mutual attraction in their exchange. Liz caught all this on the way past. "It's good y'all get along."

They both stopped and stared. "Where you goin' dressed to impress?" Wanda asked.

Liz waved and kept it moving. "Tell you later."

Wanda wasn't havin' it. She skipped off the porch and caught up with Liz as she opened the car door and climbed in.

"My man is back in the state," Liz boasted. "Now move."

Wanda stood her ground. "Marvin?" She subdued her excitement.

Liz started the engine. "Please," she said. "That's been over." Self-satisfied smile. "They shipped Kevy back. He's in Waupun."

Wanda lowered her head into the car. "And him?" she asked, cutting her eyes towards the man on the porch.

"Get to know him and see how it goes." Liz's patience was withering fast. "He's a cop so tell him to serve ya needs and protect ya interest. Now move."

Wanda slammed a hand on her hip and backed away. "Get on with your hot tail." She closed the door. "And tell Kevy I said hello."

Liz jetted up the highway. She hadn't taken this trip in years. Hadn't seen Kevy face-to-face in years. As she cruised down I-43, she pictured his reaction once he laid eyes on her.

She reached Waupun Correctional Institution in record time. The late visit had already started so she got right in after producing an I.D., going through the metal detectors, and placing her keys in the locker. Being in the prison brought back many memories, mostly painful ones.

Liz inserted a ten dollar bill into the change machine. She poured the coins in the little plastic bag with her locker key and found her assigned seat. And waited. Anxiously.

The visiting room looked the same; only the faces had changed. She stole glances of the inmates and their loved ones. She ignored a brother with a Prince perm hawking her with frisky eyes. The old white chick sitting across from him seemed clueless to what he was up to. The brothers in prison were getting younger and younger, Liz noticed as she checked out the scene. The beat went on. So did the racial make-up: white women with black men appeared prevalent as ever. She counted… one, two, three, four interracial couples—*that big ol' heifer right there can count for three, so that makes four O.J.'s and six Nicole Simpson's making their contributions to diversity in America.* Liz's conscience got on her about gossiping with herself. *Sorry. Bad habits.* She went back to minding her own business. Folks could date and be with whomever they wanted to. Her mind wandered off to Jenny and Malik. She wondered… No, she didn't. Wasn't her place to. Although she couldn't picture Malik… She left it alone.

Liz tensed up when a guard walked over and opened the inmate entrance door. Kevy came out looking as strikingly handsome as she remembered. More muscular than she remembered. Damn!

She got up as he approached, his rich ebony features aglow. "Hey, you," she said. They embraced. The touch felt good. He felt good. She licked her lips on the side of his ear, ready for a little sugar. He didn't make a move, nor did she. They took their seats.

"It's good you're taking good care of yourself," she complimented, admiring his muscular upgrade.

He checked her out. "I'm not the only one. Where did that extra butt come from?"

Liz almost blushed. "So what you saying?" she frowned and didn't mean it, rapping him on the hand.

"I'm saying you look stunning," he winked.

She relaxed. "I'm glad you're closer again." Warmth carried her words. "I miss you and your son needs you."

"You don't need me?" he sharpened his stare.

"You know what I mean." She tapped him on the hand, this time dragging it out. "Now we gotta get you home."

Kevy studied her, commenting, "For a minute, I had suspected that your house was no longer my home."

She maintained eye contact. "Ain't no home for us without you."

"Sure about that, Liz?" he asked. "Cause the impression I was getting—"

"Was a false one," she finished for him. "I'm here in front of you. My love still stands. Life had got a little crazy for me over the last year but my heart never stopped beating for you."

His face hinted at a smile. She waited for it to spread so she could mirror it.

"The luv better still stand," he said, then smiled.

"Always," she maintained a straight face for about ten seconds, then reflected his satisfaction.

They relaxed and fell off into their rhythm. This conversation was long overdue. They discussed just about everything and everyone. Not Marvin, though. Liz talked about the drama with Derrick, what he did to her, to She-She, to Malik. Resentment glistened in Kevy's eyes but all he said was, "He'll be up here," referring to Derrick. She spoke on old friends and family and her decision to go back to school and her future plans to start a transportation service with Wanda. She brought up the investment club she joined with some of the sisters at church and their new community group. "If we're not active in our community, we have no business griping about how bad it is," she said. He listened so intently that Liz wondered if he was really listening at all. But he was and his questions and input affirmed that. He mentioned the business plans he put together while out of state and the possibility of her being a part of it. "Send them to me so I can look at 'em," she said.

"You're pulling it off," Kevy said as time wound down.

Liz didn't get what he meant.

He elaborated. "You take pride in yourself, Liz. You stepped up to the plate when the moment demanded you to. Life threw you curve balls and you stayed on your game. Anything you've done in between time, I have no right to complain about." He stopped and stared. "Being in the joint this long, I've heard the horror stories from brothers about how their women fell off, broke bad, went bad. Some turned to drugs, dancing, hoing, or became magicians,

357

pulling disappearing acts on brothers with their kids. You did none of that. I never had to fret about losing contact with you or my son, even when the distance left our relationship strained. That's real. I'm grateful."

Liz was left speechless. The kudos pushed away the doubts that lingered. She had overcome a lot, and sometimes she stumbled, got weak, or doubted herself and some of her decisions, but Liz always forged forward through it. Most crucially, she found her way back home to God's bosom. His voice now reigned supreme in her head. She would continue to go through the motions. The struggle raged on but like she read in Isaiah 40:21 that morning:

> "But they that wait upon the Lord
>
> shall renew their strength; they
>
> shall mount up wings as eagles;
>
> they shall run, and not be weary;
>
> and they shall walk, and not faint."

Tessa had left the passage highlighted.

Liz reached out and took Kevy's hands into hers. "Thank you," she said, and she silently thanked her Lord and Savior for the purpose He placed on her life, which transcended any valley she fell into.

Liz and Kevy laughed it up, reminisced, and flirted for the rest of the visit. When it ended and they stood and hugged, he held her closer and gave a generous dose of sugar. Her heart brimmed with deep love as she walked out of the visiting room. She found consolation knowing that Malik could come see, sit down and talk with his father on a regular basis again. They needed one another—Malik needed Kevy, Kevy needed Malik. Both needed her. And she them. And they all needed God.

358

CHAPTER 58

Eryka Badu serenaded Malik through the speakers as he coasted down I-94 in Brian's Infiniti. Drizzle lay crashed out in the back seat. It had been a long Christmas vacation and longer weekend, and now they were on their way back to the Miltown after doing shows in Toledo, St. Louis, and Chicago.

Over the last couple of weeks, mostly on the weekends, Malik traveled with Drizzle, Jeff, Chill Will, and other local artists. They grinded throughout the Midwest, doing shows, selling CD's, and trying to build up a wider fan base. The experience put plenty of meat on Malik's head. It always surprised him how much more love and support they received in other cities compared to the hometown. The groupies often acted like they were already platinum artists. Some of the pornographic propositions were girls gone wild/jumpdown fiestas. Malik dug all the attention, but he and Drizzle maintained self-discipline. They accepted the girls' digits but already made a secret pact to never call. And there were plenty numbers to call, from damn near every race and ethnicity under the sun. Temptations galore. The rest of the entourage showed less restraint, especially Jeff, who Malik felt was too old to have a sexual appetite for girls so young.

Getting out of Milwaukee was also proving good for Malik's spirit and mind. All the drama over the past year had conditioned him to keep his guard up the moment he stepped out of the house. The whole atmosphere in the city tended to remind him of a lot of the things he wanted to forget about. However, during the road trips, he stayed busy, his mind occupied with better things. He got the chance to kick it in new spots, hobnob with new folks, view new sights and experience the various vibes of the different cities.

His favorite part of the trips was fast becoming the late night drives up and down the highway. Just coasting and cozy in the soft leather guts, gripping the woodgrain and contemplating. He called Brianna daily, no matter what. She usually acted indifferent, like she wasn't all that interested in what was going on with him on the road. Malik knew she was fronting and always missed him while he was away, just like he missed her.

He never needed to call home. His mother called him, morning, noon and night. She'd got him a cell phone so she could have a direct line to him 24 hours a day. Their phone calls mostly consisted of her lecturing him about everything from safe sex and the AIDS epidemic, to the signs of potential trouble and getting his "ass back to Milwaukee so you can get to school on time." Lately, she started hounding him about college since he was set to graduate at the end of the school year. Thanks to her, Malik knew about every community and technical college and university throughout Wisconsin and many beyond the state line. He had thought about taking a year off to concentrate on honing his beatmaking/producing skills. This included getting the record label off the ground. He debated it with his mother, and she wasn't trying to hear anything that didn't include him starting college in September. She had no problem summoning the Big Dawg to support her stance, either. With his momz and pops tag-teaming, Malik quickly realized that he had no wins. He was set to start college next semester for audio engineering.

Brian was never far from Malik's thoughts. The previous month, Malik had sat in a courtroom and watched as a white judge handed out prison bids like they were free government cheese. Before Brian had come out to learn his sentence, two other black males were read their fates. The first brother, only seventeen years old, was sentenced to life in prison. As the judge informed him of his parole eligibility date (in forty-five years), several people in the gallery broke out in tears. One lady cussed at the judge and was immediately escorted out of the room by two sheriff's deputies. The judge just sat there like it was all routine. Malik couldn't figure out which tears were shed for the defendant, who fought back his own tears as he was led out, and which ones were shed for his alleged victim. One thing was very clear to Malik though. The loss and pain touched both sides: one family lost a loved one to the grave, another lost one to the prison system.

Malik also saw his own mother wipe away a few tears as she sat next to him observing the proceedings.

The next brother came out shortly after and received a severe tongue-lashing and sixty-year sentence from the same judge. His crime: bank robbery. More tears shed by a different black family. This time Malik knew who they mourned for. The defendant's two preteen daughters cried their little hearts out. Malik empathized with the young girls on an intimate level; he had shed those same tears for the same reason when he was around the same age.

Malik noted something else. The judge did not show much emotion when sentencing the first brother for the homicide. But he breathed down fire from the bench on the convicted bank robber. The scene angered and saddened Malik, and by the time Brian appeared for his sentence, Malik already knew the business. The judge's animosity stormed down on Brian in the form of a scathing speech about "thugs" like him who "menace society" with "your vile, pathological, sociopathic criminality" and so on. These fiery words came after the doctor said in open court that he forgave Brian and asked the judge to show some leniency, adding, "this young man should be punished, your honor, but do take into consideration that he reacted, albeit irrationally, to the news of his twin brother's death. And I am sure you are aware of the brutal murders of his parents, which happened when he was just a kid."

Then Brian stood up and apologized to the doctor and to the courts. Next the judge had gone into his indignant diatribe and sentenced Brian to 18 years in prison, 15 years supervision, 33 in total.

Malik had imagined himself being shipped off to the penitentiary that day, and his mother being left to shed those tears.

He reflected on this as he passed the "Welcome to Milwaukee" sign posted on the side of the highway. How close he'd come to losing everything. His freedom. His mind. His life. He glanced up in the rear view mirror at Drizzle. There slept his comrade, his brother. They might not have emerged from the same womb but they were definitely cut from the same cloth and would remain joined at the hip. It ran deeper than blood, and they learned through trial, error, and observation what it meant to stand on their loyalty. The realest way to show it was by standing on each other when the situation warranted it. It wasn't only about ridin' and dyin' together, but more about livin' and thrivin' together. Encouraging one another to make the right choices. They had too much to live for. Too much to see and experience; prison and meaningless drama didn't fit into their futures. Kevy and Brian and Janice were doing enough time for the whole fam.

Malik turned off the 27th Street ramp and navigated onto the streets of Milwaukee. *Home, bittersweet home.* He flipped open his cell.

"Malik" Brianna answered on the second ring.

He appreciated how eager she sounded to hear from him. "Your king has returned to the town."

"How was your trip?"

"It was alright," he said. "You miss me?"

"Like a mug," she admitted.

"What you say?"

"I said I missed you," she said with a softness that had Malik feeling it.

"I miss you too," he said. Badu's jazzy vocals and the dim cover of the night sky added something special to the mood. Malik turned up the music a notch.

"So did you meet some fly sisters on the road?" she asked, out of the blue.

"I came across a few but none realer than you."

"I guess."

"Fo' real," he said. "I'm try'na prove myself worthy of that realness along with your love. Is it possible?"

"Rhetorical question, right?"

"So, what you saying?"

"I'll let you figure it out. When you do we'll be where we could've been some months ago."

She was spinning Malik with the vague talk. What was she saying? He hit North Avenue and slowed down. "What you doin'? You actin' strange."

"Sitting here thinking about my future and working on this business plan."

"For your salon?"

362

"Spa/salon," she corrected him. "Yeah."

"Are you going to invest your savings?"

"My uncle and his wife said that they'll invest if my business plan is A-1. I've been up for the last three days tweaking it, getting it right."

"Go get it, girl," he rooted. "I fully support ya cause. Anyway I can assist, holla at me."

"I needed to hear that," she said.

"Like you didn't already know that."

"With women, we need to hear how you feel," Brianna said. "We love to hear it through words."

"And what do brothers love?"

"What they see. That's why y'all are so crazy about customized cars, big-breasted women, and video games."

He chuckled, "That's so sexist."

"True, though," she said. "Once brothers get off that super macho stuff and get more in touch with the feminine side of their manliness, our relationships will be strong again."

Our relationships? Malik caught that, and Badu gave him an idea. He glanced in the mirror; Drizzle was still curled up hugging himself in the back seat, asleep. "Bree," he lowered his voice. His heart rate accelerated.

"I'm here," she said.

"Got something to tell you," he swallowed.

"What's that?"

He was nervous as a mug but Eryka Badu encouraged him on. "That I love you," he said, holding his breath.

Silence on the other end.

Drizzle shifted his sleeping position.

"You hear me?" Malik said. He was tempted to pull over and park somewhere.

"When did you come to that conclusion, 'Lik?" she asked.

"Awhile ago," he admitted. "It really hit me after I got shot and woke up in that hospital bed."

"What took you so long to say it?" she sounded like she had wanted to hear those three words from him for some time now.

"Probably that macho stuff," he smiled. "Seriously, I wanted to make sure I could love you the way you deserved to be loved by me."

"Can you?" she asked.

"Rhetorical question, right?" he came back.

"No."

"I have faith," he said. "All I need for you to do is believe in me. Can you?"

"I already do. I just need you to believe in you."

"What does this mean?" Malik pulled over. He was too distracted to concentrate on driving.

"What do you want it to mean?" The strength resurfaced in her voice.

"That you're my girl?" It was getting hot inside the truck. He turned down the heat. Snow fell outside, the temperature in the mid-20's.

"No," she said. Malik didn't get it and was about to trip until she said, "I'm your woman."

An explosion of joy lit up his sky. He reached behind him to wake up Drizzle and share the lovely news. But withdrew his hand and told himself to *calm down, dawg.* He cracked the window. A gush of the wind chill blew in.

"Be sure to call your little girlfriends and tell them the business," Brianna was saying. "And come get me later on around six. I want to see a movie and have dinner."

Malik was cheesing hard. "What we gon' do afterwards?"

"Is that a rhetorical question?" she teased.

"Hell, naw," he said then thought about it. "I mean, yeah. I mean—"

"Call me later when you're on your way. Horny self."

"Dawg, is you crazy?" Drizzle woke up shivering and rubbing warmth into his unclothed arms. "Raise up the window," He climbed into the front seat and blasted the heat.

Malik's cheesy smile turned to koolaid.

"What the heck you showing every tooth for?" Drizzle blinked and wiped sleep boogers out the corners of his eyes.

"It's official like a referee whistle, my nizzle," Malik said. "I got the girl!"

"Huh?" Drizzle looked confused.

"Brianna," Malik said like he should've already known. "She's wifey."

Drizzle shook his head. "Good. You waited over a year." He didn't share in the excitement.

Malik checked the time. It was 6:12 in the morning. He had to get some rest for tonight.

"Why you pulled over?" Drizzle asked. "What you on?" He was still waking up. Malik dipped out into traffic.

Drizzle listened patiently as Malik recapped the phone call. When he finished, Drizzle clowned him, saying, "Yeah, buddy, you're 'bout to get straight pussy-whipped. You fell for the oldest trick in the book, homeboy. All that time chasing her, imagining how it would feel when you got between those thighs. She got yo' ass."

"Sho' do," he assured.

"Don't trip," Drizzle admitted. "Kila got me too." They laughed.

"Beside every great man stands a great woman. We both got winners."

"No doubt," Drizzle stared out the window up Sherman Blvd. "Back in the Murda Mil," he yawned. The winter wind frosted the windows on the truck. It was freezing outside, the roads slushy and slippery. "Where Jeff 'n 'em go?"

Malik said, "I left 'em behind on the highway somewhere. Or they left me." He thought about it. "I sho' wasn't inna hurry to get back here."

"I feel ya." Drizzle picked up his cellie. "But where would we be without these Mil streets?"

"Ain't no tellin'," Malik said. "I do know where we're try'na go though."

"Where dat be?" Drizzle looked at him, knowing the answer.

"Oh, you don't know?" Malik said.

"I said, where dat be?" Drizzle said. "Where we goin', family?"

"To the top!" Malik said, knocking knuckles with him.

"Together," he added.

Malik slid Drizzle's CD into the deck and forwarded it to a track called 'Milwaukee Legends'. Drizzle had recorded it the night after Brian got sentenced. It was a song about and dedicated to the twins.

Malik subbed the sounds, leaned sideways, and drove on, appreciating all that he had and had been through, and believing deep in his heart that he and his family was gon' make it.

Author Interview
"Shed So Many Tears"
Author: Roderick 'Rudy' Bankston
Interviewed by: Vincent 'Vision' Grady

Vision: Briefly tell us about your book?
Rudy: Shed So Many Tears is a work of fiction deeply rooted in the realities of Miltown – the good, the grave, and the grimy. The story takes a serious look into the lives of the main characters Liz and Malik, a black woman and her son, and their struggles.

Vision: What inspired you to write a novel?
Rudy: A number of things but it mainly came from the determination to pull fortune out of misfortune and do my kids proud.

Vision: What was your biggest challenge in writing Shed So Many Tears?
Rudy: It's hard to distinguish any one challenge as the biggest. A major one that comes to mind is how much of a struggle it became, at times, to stay consistent in my focus and motivated. Prison is such a vegetative environment, and I often found myself distracted by the psychic pressures inherent in doing this time. Outside of that, I would have to say that my initial ignorance of what it took to write a readable story proved a huge challenge. I started off with the appetite to pen a novel but was deficient in the food for thought. I had to read books and articles on the craft, learn to study works of fiction with a critical eye and solicit constructive feedback from individuals who had it to give.

Vision: Being that you are someone who came up in the streets, why did you choose to take this path with your 'urban' fiction as opposed to the now well-traveled path of the gangsta tale?
Rudy: First let me comment on the so-called urban novel. I appreciated you putting the quote-unquote on it because I'm not really feeling that stamp. Nowadays 'urban' seems to denote generic fiction and is possibly an attempt by the mainstream to bastardize another predominantly black art form. A growing drawback in this is that some really good novels get tossed under the 'urban' banner and overlooked by potential readers. As for your question of why I went against the gangsta grain. It really wasn't a conscious effort, but more a result of where the characters took me as they came alive on the pages. Plus, my history in the streets led to too calamitous an aftermath for me to try pimping my reader. I definitely wanted to entertain. I also wanted to provoke thought, caution and hopefully encourage my target audience.

Vision: Are any of these characters based upon people you know?
Rudy: No one in particular but I'm sure there are pieces of certain people from my past and present in my characters. Pieces of myself as well. Overall, though, the characters are figments of my imagination.

367

Vision: What has been the early response to your novel?

Rudy: For the most part it's been love. Admittedly, the people who've read the manuscript are mostly those in my circle, so they might've been made partial by their pride in me writing a book. I let a couple of seasoned haters read it, too, in hopes of getting closer to the raw. Still the reviews have been really positive.

Vision: It takes a lot to bring a book from concept to production; you must've had a lot of support?

Rudy: Shout out to my first writing mentor in the joint, Jevon Jackson, who inspired me to believe and take the craft seriously. Remember that name because he's coming soon. Love also to Karen Emily out of Canada who supported the project early on. Heartfelt love to my dear friends Pat and Donna who selflessly assisted Shed So Many Tears to publication. The quality of their support has been substantial. I might've started out by myself on this project, but the harder I went at it, the more the universe responded and attracted the right people into my life. That's why I urge aspiring novelists to do what they can with what they have and the rest of what they need will eventually find them.

Vision: What advice would you have for the brother who wants to write a book, but can't find his direction?

Rudy: Pick up that pen and get in there. Write, write, and write as often as possible. Read, read, and read in the process. Study the mechanics and different styles. I would also warn him against trying to perfect the first draft; that will paralyze a person. Writing is rewriting, so first get the story out then go back and do your editing, revising, tweaking.

Vision: When can fans expect a sequel?

Rudy: I'm brainstorming on it because damn near all of the people who've read Shed So Many Tears have asked the same question or made the demand. I need to wrap up these other book projects I'm currently working on. Soon after, maybe before, I'll make it do what it do.

Vision: The lyrics in your book seem to imply that you're a bit of a closet rapper, is that true?

Rudy: (ghetto smile) I'm more a dabbler than a rapper. I'll scribble a verse every blue moon— nothing hip hop quotable. The lyrics that Drizzle spits in Shed So Many Tears were actually written by two of my fallen comrades who were assassinated together on the Northside of Milwaukee back in '02. Krisis and Dyzae Kemet. The world never got to hear how much of a problem they were on the mic, so I'm making it my business to incorporate their verses in every novel I write. Of course, I revise and add bars so they'll fit into the scenes. I'll also pen a verse if necessary, like I did for the character Al Cocoa Leaves who Drizzle battled and slaughtered in chapter six.